The

Husband
Hour

The
Husband
Hour

Jamie
Brenner

Little, Brown and Company

New York   Boston   London

Little, Brown and Company
Hachette Book Group
1290 Avenue of the Americas, New York, NY 10104
littlebrown.com

First Edition: April 2018

Little, Brown and Company is a division of Hachette Book Group, Inc. The Little, Brown name and logo are trademarks of Hachette Book Group, Inc.

The publisher is not responsible for websites (or their content) that are not owned by the publisher.

The Hachette Speakers Bureau provides a wide range of authors for speaking events. To find out more, go to hachettespeakersbureau.com or call (866) 376-6591.

ISBN 978-0-316-39490-1 (hardcover) / 978-0-316-44939-7 (Canadian)
LCCN 2017944469

10 9 8 7 6 5 4 3 2 1

LSC-C

Printed in the United States of America

This book is dedicated to all the brave men and women who serve this country and to the families who support them.

The
Husband
Hour

Chapter One

The warm winters still surprised her, every day a gift. But that particular morning, the heat was a problem. She didn't want to wear a short-sleeved dress.

It seemed the entire city of Los Angeles had turned out, like it was the Super Bowl or the Academy Awards. The Staples Center arena was filled to capacity, with hundreds more left standing outside. Lauren looked out at a sea of silver-and-black hockey jerseys, military uniforms, and American flags, all the colors blurring together like a spinning pinwheel.

She had spent dozens of days and nights in that arena cheering on her husband playing ice hockey for the LA Kings. But today, she wasn't part of the crowd. She was separate, up front and on display, sitting by the podium dressed in black and hiding behind dark glasses.

Surrounded by thousands of people, Lauren felt completely alone.

An hour into her husband's memorial service, she was dizzy with nerves and exhaustion. Grief was an odd thing. It made you numb but exquisitely sensitive at the same time. She had to admire the emotion's versatility; it now owned her completely.

She scanned the front row of the stands to find her parents. It was strange; for the first time in years she truly wanted her mother, and yet there was nothing her mother could say or do to make her feel better. She had almost told her parents not to come, and she certainly didn't want to see her sister.

"This nonsense has gone on long enough," her mother had said over the phone. "You just lost your husband. You need your family around you. Of course your sister will be there."

But she wasn't.

Now, under the glare of television lights set up for ESPN's live broadcast of the memorial service, her parents looked lost. Lauren tried to catch her mother's eye, but she was focused on the jumbotron showing the president's tribute to Rory: "Our fallen soldier, a true American hero." Her mother's expression seemed to say, *How did we get here?*

Lauren hoped she didn't have the same expression on her face. Not when the world was watching. Not when photos of her would appear everywhere. Would they see what she was thinking? That this felt like theater, a circus, a show that had nothing to do with her husband? That she was just playing her part, a role she hadn't auditioned for and didn't want?

Grieving widow. Just twenty-four years old. Such a tragedy. Such a loss.

And then the part of the show when a man she'd never met before handed her a folded American flag. She reached for it mechanically and placed it in her lap. She knew these ceremonies, the symbolism of the flag, were meant to give her comfort. But going through the motions just made her feel like a fake. It was useless; her world would never again have meaning.

Sitting there, she tried to deflect the waves of sympathy, thinking, *This is my fault. If you only knew; this is my fault.*

Just when she thought the moment couldn't get any worse, it did. She started to cry, under the scrutiny of millions of eyes on her, the flash of cameras capturing every sob. It was unbearable to have something so private—losing her husband—play out so publicly.

Just get through today, she told herself. After today, all the attention would fade. The world would move on. And she could disappear.

As a war correspondent, Matt Brio had landed in some uncomfortable and even dangerous situations all around the globe: Tsunami-ravaged Thailand. Baghdad. Syria. For a few crazy years, he had worked in unimaginable conditions. He should have been prepared for anything, and yet landing in sunny LA after flying in from freezing New York somehow still managed to throw him off his game.

Drenched in sweat outside the Staples Center, thinking he would happily trade his Canon XF100 for a bottle of water, he willed himself to focus and panned the video-camera lens across the throngs of people outside. About a yard away from him, a grown man wearing an LA Kings number 89 jersey held his young son's hand and sobbed. Matt wanted to get the man on camera and ask, "What did Rory Kincaid mean to you?" but he didn't have time. The real story was inside.

The question was, could Matt actually *get* inside? He wouldn't know until he tried flashing his long-expired press pass, a relic from his days working in journalism.

His phone buzzed in his pocket, and he ignored it. No doubt it was someone from two time zones away wondering why the hell he'd canceled the scheduled shoot for the documentary he was in the middle of directing. But if there was one thing Matt had learned, it was that it was better to beg forgiveness than ask permission, and that went for both missing the shoot today and for crashing the memorial service.

Matt made his way to security and handed his press pass to the guard. If he'd thought the whole thing through better, he might have been able to wrangle a legitimate pass from an old colleague. But nothing about this day had been thought through. The flight to LA, the decision to show up at the service, all impulses. His entire career had started with an impulse, so why stop now?

But this wasn't a career move. What drew him to the stadium on that hot and inconvenient day, the magnetic pull that he could no more ignore than he could stop breathing, was personal.

The guard waved him inside, either missing the expiration date on his pass or simply not caring. The service was half over, anyway. Matt followed a second security guy's direction to the gate and escalator that would lead to the press box.

Matt jostled for a spot in the crowded pen, nodding to a few journalists he knew and then looking up at the video of the president eulogizing the hockey star turned soldier. Beside him, a woman wearing a CNN badge began to cry at the words "American hero." *Seriously?* Matt thought. Okay, it was a tragedy. But was it more of a tragedy because Rory Kincaid had been a famous athlete? There were thousands of guys deployed overseas at that very moment.

The jumbotron screen went dark, and a three-star general stepped up to the microphone.

Matt was more interested in the woman seated just a few feet away from him, Rory Kincaid's young widow. He adjusted his camera, watching her through the lens. Her dark hair was pulled into a low ponytail, her face obscured by large black sunglasses. She was the epitome of fragile grief, and for a second Matt felt a pang. He shook it away.

Matt understood grief. He understood loss. But *his* hero had died without fanfare, just a footnote in history. One of tens of thousands; no one cared about that story.

So Matt supposed the Rory Kincaid story would have to do.

Chapter Two

Beth Adelman tried to keep up a cheerful patter of conversation during the hour-and-a-half drive from Philadelphia to the Jersey Shore. Her daughter was having none of it. A month since Lauren had lost her husband, and she was only getting more withdrawn.

Lauren slumped in the passenger seat, staring out the window. Late January; the sky was gray and the trees bare. Beth turned on the defroster and glanced over at Lauren.

It was hard not to think of all the summer Saturday mornings when she and her husband and the girls had made this same drive. She would wake her daughters at the crack of dawn, and Lauren and Stephanie would climb into the backseat wearing bathing suits under their shorts and T-shirts. Still yawning, with butter-slick bagels in their hands, the girls squabbled. In those days, arguments over foot space and other backseat boundaries began before they even pulled onto the Pennsylvania Turnpike. If a foot or stray beach-bag strap strayed over the line to someone else's side while the car was still in the driveway, yelling would ensue, and Howard, cramming their suitcases into the trunk, would call out, "I'm going to stick one of you in here!" Joyful noise.

Such a contrast to the current ride.

Beth knew she was looking at the past through rose-colored glasses, but even the eternal bickering between the girls was something she would gladly take in exchange for the current silence.

She turned off the Atlantic City Expressway, and Lauren lowered her window. Beth heard the call of seagulls, and she tried to convince herself that everything was going to be fine. That Lauren wasn't making a mistake.

Beth didn't usually think of the beach house that her parents had left her as secluded, but geographically it was out there. Absecon Island was a barrier island on the Jersey Shore of the Atlantic Ocean. Beth was afraid that it was the remoteness that attracted Lauren to the house, not just the comfort of family memories.

There was no traffic on Ventnor Avenue. In the winter, the Jersey Shore felt deserted. Beth was certain Lauren was underestimating how isolated she would feel all alone in that big house in the half-empty town under gray skies and with the chill of the wind off a cold ocean. But in the weeks since Rory had been killed in Iraq, there was just no talking to her. It was a tragedy, a god-awful tragedy. Of course it was. But her daughter had shut down, and for the life of her, Beth had no idea what to do about it.

"Lauren, look—there's Lucy!" Beth said, pointing to the six-story elephant, a tourist attraction that had fascinated Lauren as a child. "You girls used to get so excited whenever we passed her. Remember?"

Lauren glanced to her left but said nothing.

Minutes later, Beth turned off Atlantic Avenue and onto a short cul-de-sac. The house her parents had left to her was a beachfront four-bedroom Colonial Revival, gray and white but somehow stuck with the name the Green Gable. In the old days, it wasn't until hours after their arrival that the girls set foot inside. As soon as the car turned into the driveway, they pulled off their flip-flops and ran to the sand like they were "shot from a cannon," as her father said every single weekend. It was still early, and the beach was empty enough for them to make an easy beeline to the ocean, Stephanie calling out, "Last one to the water is a rotten egg!"

"It's not a race!" Lauren yelled, and yet she always dashed to keep up with her sister, her feet sinking into deep pockets of sand as she ran, stumbling but moving forward.

Beth sighed. Why couldn't life always be that simple?

Now, the Green Gable was exactly as it had always been, except the wind- and sand-battered wood sign was more faded, the moss-green words almost indistinguishable from the gray background. Beth turned off the car and closed her eyes. How she wished her own mother were still around to tell her how to deal with this. But she was gone, leaving a beautiful house that was small consolation.

Lauren just sat there, zombielike.

"Come on, Lauren. Grab one of the bags."

The house smelled musty and close. Beth cracked some windows despite the frigid wind. When she'd left in August, she hadn't expected to return until spring. She couldn't have imagined that a few months later, her handsome, vibrant son-in-law would be dead, leaving her younger daughter a widow, and that the Green Gable would beckon to Lauren with some false promise of peace.

"I'll make a run to Casel's for groceries," Beth said, heading for the kitchen to take stock of what, if anything, she had left behind.

"No, Mom. Don't worry about it. I'm fine."

Lauren lugged the heaviest suitcase up the stairs. Beth abandoned the kitchen and followed her, surprised to see her turn into her old childhood bedroom.

"Why not the master bedroom? It has the better view."

"That still feels like Gran's room."

"Don't be silly, Lauren. If you're going to be here for a few weeks, you might as well—"

"Not a few weeks, Mom. I'm staying here indefinitely."

The bedroom was white and sea-foam green with a queen-size bed framed in antique cast iron. A bone-colored French pot cupboard served as her nightstand. There was a pen on it, and a framed photo of Lauren and her older sister. Stephanie had one arm draped around Lauren's shoulders as they stood at the edge of the ocean, both of them sunburned, sandy, with long wet hair.

Beth sighed heavily. "Lauren, I love you, hon, but I'm really thinking this isn't the best idea. I understand you don't want to stay in LA but at least come home to Philly so we can be there for you. You need a support system."

Lauren turned her back to her, opened her suitcase. "I need to be alone."

Beth walked to the window, looking out at the overcast sky. "I don't know what you expect me to do. Just leave you here? Just turn around and get back on the highway?"

"Yeah. And Mom, remember, if anyone contacts you about me, you don't know where I am."

"Who's going to contact me?"

"I don't know, Mom. A reporter? Just don't say anything. Promise?"

"Of course. No reporters—got it. But you're doing the wrong thing, isolating yourself out here."

No response. Beth was overwhelmed with one of the worst feelings a mother could experience in the face of her child's pain: powerlessness.

Four Years Later

Chapter Three

Lauren's feet pounded the boardwalk in the final stretch of her morning run. With the ocean to her right, the beachfront homes of Longport to her left, she looked straight ahead. She ran without headphones so she could hear the ocean and the seagulls. Most days, they were the only sounds along her solitary twelve-mile run from Longport to Atlantic City and back.

Today felt different. It wasn't just the changing early-morning light, though that was part of it. In the winter, she did her entire run in darkness. Lately, halfway through, the sun was up. Today, by the time she passed Ventnor, at around the ten-mile mark, it was bright enough that the path was dotted with cyclists. Mothers were pushing strollers. There was no use denying it; winter had turned to spring, and summer was right around the corner. The invasion was coming.

Longport in the winter was a recluse's paradise. Some people called it a ghost town; Lauren had become quite comfortable in the company of ghosts. While most of the year-round residents gritted their teeth through the winter, waiting for beach season, Lauren felt the complete opposite.

The *summer* was her time to grin and bear it, to endure. The bright long days, the crowds, the string of patriotic holidays.

Don't think about it, she told herself. *You still have time.*

Thwap-thwap—the beat of her sneakers against the wooden boards. The steady pounding of her heart. A familiar rush of energy, almost a giddiness, carried her down the wooden steps to the cul-de-sac in front of her house.

She jogged slowly in a circle, sweat cooling against her neck, then, dizzy, she bent over, hands on her knees, her head down. She looked up at the sound of tires on gravel, a car turning onto her block. Her stomach sank.

What were her parents doing here?

Her parents were devoted summer weekenders. Starting Memorial Day weekend and going through Labor Day, they showed up Thursday afternoon and left Sunday night. It was a shock to her system after months of solitude, but she adjusted to it by the middle of the summer and sometimes felt almost sad to see them drift back into their Philadelphia routine. She never visited them in Philadelphia at the old stone house where she'd grown up. She never left the island. This was a real issue only once a year, when her sister had a birthday party for her son, Ethan. Lauren felt guilty for being an absentee aunt.

"Honey! I thought you agreed to cut down on the running. You're getting way too thin," her mother said, slamming the car door and rushing over to her.

"I'll get the bags," her father said.

"I'm fine, Mom. What are you guys doing here?"

Her mother looked at her strangely. "It's Memorial Day weekend, hon."

Was it? Lauren could have sworn that was next weekend.

She glanced at her sports watch. She had to shower and get to work. The Thursday before Memorial Day, the breakfast crowd would be lining up at the restaurant door.

"We're getting an early start," her mother said, looking tense.

"Any particular reason why?"

"Oh, just lots to do. I want to get the house ready, clean out the guest bedrooms…"

Lauren looked at her sharply. "The guest bedrooms? Why?"

"Your sister is coming."

Matt Brio climbed the three flights of stairs to the editing suite in Williamsburg, carrying doughnuts. He was unhappy to find himself out of breath by the second floor. *That's what you get for editing a film 24/7,* he told himself. And he didn't see that changing any time in the near future.

On a Thursday at noon, his suite mates were all plugged into their headsets and staring at their computer screens. Matt made a cup of coffee at the community Keurig machine and booted up his machine. Fuck coffee—he needed a drink.

He set the box of doughnuts next to his computer. He figured if he was asking someone for a six-figure check, the least he could do was provide refreshments.

"I'm going to be in Brooklyn anyway, so it's a good time to stop by," Craig Mason had said, just like that. As if Matt hadn't been asking him to look at his reel for six months.

The Rory Kincaid project had been a rough road. Matt sometimes wondered if he had bad karma due to how he'd handled things at the beginning. When it became his passion project, he dropped out of a film he had committed to directing. As a result, he ruined his relationship with Andrew Dobson, the producer who had backed his first two films. Matt's reputation took a hit, and he suspected that was why he had failed to get a solid financial investment for the Rory Kincaid story; it had nothing to do with the merit of the project. So Matt put his own money into making the movie. Four years later, the money was gone, and he needed a financial lifeline.

But it wasn't enough just to finance a movie and get it made; you had to be able to market it. Next winter would be the five-year anniversary of Rory Kincaid's death. It felt crucial to secure distribution by that milestone.

He put on his headphones and clicked open a video of seventeen-year-old Rory Kincaid scoring a hat-trick goal for his high-school team. As the puck slid into the net, Rory reacted with his signature gesture, lifting both hands into the air, then pulling his left arm sharply in, bent at the elbow, his fist tight: *score*. Next, footage of commentators on CNN: "We have breaking news that former NHL star Rory Kincaid, who walked away from a reported seven-figure contract with the LA Kings to enlist in the military, has been killed in the line of duty." Matt clicked through to footage of the memorial service. He moved forward through the frames, pausing on the widow standing against a backdrop of American flags next to a blown-up portrait of Rory in his U.S. Rangers uniform. The guy was so ruggedly handsome, he was like the person central casting sent over when you asked for "hero."

Officers in full military dress flanked the flag-draped coffin in a procession out of the Staples Center. Behind them, the grieving widow walked as if she were wading through water.

A tap on his shoulder. Startled, he turned around. Craig Mason.

Craig Mason was a former Wall Street banker now in his mid-fifties and on his second career. "Second life" was how he had put it to Matt when they'd first met for drinks six months earlier.

"Hey, man," Matt said, quickly closing the file and standing up. "Let me just find another chair."

"Didn't realize it was such tight real estate in here. Maybe we should have met at my office."

"Not a problem," Matt said, sliding a chair in front of his work space. Craig was busy looking at the two dozen index cards arranged on the corkboard above Matt's desk that mapped out all the beats of the film *American Hero: The Rory Kincaid Story*.

Craig slid into the seat next to him.

"Doughnut?" Matt offered casually. As if he weren't at the absolute end of the line.

Craig shook his head. "My new girlfriend is a Pilates instructor. The pressure is on. So, how much are we looking at?"

"Just the selects," Matt said. "Some of the interviews, to give you a sense of where I'm at since we last spoke."

"Sounds good," Craig said.

Their first meeting, Craig had told Matt that he was at a stage of life where he wanted to do something "meaningful" with his hard-earned and considerable fortune. But Matt soon realized that even people with money to burn don't want to burn it.

Still, there was glamour in feature films, and the promise of social progress with documentaries. For people like Craig Mason, that sometimes made films worth the gamble. He'd invested in two features and bought himself a ride to the award-season parties and red carpets. He'd put money into one documentary about clean water because that was his pet cause. But on that project, Craig had learned that documentaries don't make money.

One of Matt's buddies on the clean-water doc introduced Craig to Matt. But Craig was in no rush to fund a second documentary. During their initial meeting about *American Hero,* both of them drinking martinis at a gastro pub on the Upper East Side, Craig told Matt, "I'm just not feeling it on this one. I don't see the urgency."

American Hero was originally an examination of why some people answer the call to serve their country, and others don't—viewed through the lens of the life of Rory Kincaid. But the film had morphed, changed, like a breathing entity. All Matt's films felt alive to him, growing under his care and guidance. But none as much as this one.

He handed Craig headphones and they both plugged in so they wouldn't disturb the other filmmakers in the room. Matt clicked on a file. He pressed Play, and an image of the entrance to Rory's Pennsylvania high school, Lower Merion, filled the screen against the sound of the roar of a crowd. The camera closed in on the school's motto carved in stone: ENTER TO LEARN, GO FORTH TO SERVE. Then a still photo of Rory, all blazing dark eyes, looking right at the camera. Then footage of the high-school coach. "How many thousands upon thousands of kids have walked through the doors of this school over the years, and how many have actually taken that motto to heart?" And then, video of Rory as a young teenager on the ice, racing toward the net. Voice-over, a woman: "Generations of Kincaids have served. World War Two. Korea. Vietnam. My older son, Emerson, served in the First Gulf War." This from a sit-down with Rory's mother that he'd luckily gotten before she passed away. Then the film cut to her. "Rory had a gift. He could skate fast and get the puck in the net. It's as simple as that." She pulled out a photo album and flipped through pictures of Rory as a boy, several of him on the ice, a few of him running around with a Rottweiler. "He named him Polaris," she said. "What kind of name is that for a dog from a six-year-old boy? But he loved the stars."

Footage of Rory playing for the Kings. And then a press conference, Rory in a blue button-down shirt, his hair wet. "No game is perfect, no player is perfect," Rory said. "We look at our athletes as heroes." And then that wry smile, the one that always suggested that what he was saying was just the tip of the iceberg. "I have different heroes."

Next, military footage. Soldiers in the Middle East. A clip of news anchors announcing that hockey star Rory Kincaid was walking away to enlist in the military. "A remarkable move from a remarkable young man," one of them said. And then the secretary of defense, flanked by American flags, speaking at a press conference: "Corporal Kincaid sacrificed himself in the name of liberty and justice around the world."

Game footage: Rory's rookie season, the Kings against the Chicago Blackhawks. Rory takes a rough hit against the boards and goes down on the ice. Five games later, a stick against the jaw takes him down. October 2010, a fight with a Blackhawks defenseman. February 2011, a fight with Philadelphia Flyers' Chris Pronger, and he's out for weeks. Cut to his sports agent sitting behind a desk in his fancy Los Angeles office saying, "Rory's career in the NHL was over."

Craig leaned forward. "Where are you going with this?"

Matt paused the footage. "You want urgency? Fine. How about this: Rory Kincaid wasn't a perfect example of selfless heroism. He didn't walk away from the NHL—he limped away. Rory Kincaid was damaged goods. And it could have been prevented."

Chapter Four

Lauren smiled at customers waiting to get into Nora's Café as she breezed past them to start her shift. She was early for work and still the line stretched to the end of the block.

Summer had unofficially arrived and, with it, the shoobies—people who came to the shore only during the summer. They got their name from their unfortunate habit of wearing shoes to walk to the beach when any local worth his or her salt could go barefoot for blocks.

She'd barely have time to run upstairs and change into her uniform, a navy skirt and a pale yellow polo shirt. The building had a second floor with an office, a storage area, and a changing room for the staff. Most of them barely used it, but because Lauren liked to run to and from work, it felt like her personal locker room. She kept her running clothes, sneakers, and a stash of Gatorade in one of the closets.

"Morning, Nora," she called to her boss, a sixty-something redhead manning the door and putting names on the wait list. Lauren didn't bother offering to take over the task; Nora liked greeting her customers, especially the first few weekends of the summer.

Lauren signed in on the same clipboard Nora had kept by the kitchen since she'd opened her doors in 2005. Everything was done manually. Lauren took the customers' orders on an old-fashioned ticket pad, each stub three deep: one for the kitchen, one for Lauren, one for clocking out at the end of the day. It wasn't that Nora couldn't afford to upgrade to a computer system, and she was certainly savvy enough to find one that would suit the restaurant. She simply went through life with the attitude of "If it ain't broke, don't fix it."

But four and a half years ago, Nora had recognized that Lauren was broken. That first winter, Lauren would sit for hours in the café, morning after morning, nursing a coffee. Sometimes she had constructive thoughts, ideas about starting a foundation in Rory's memory. But most days, she just stared out the window.

Nora didn't pretend not to know who she was, but she also didn't watch her from a safe distance and whisper to the other employees. Both scenarios had happened endlessly in Lauren's final weeks in Los Angeles.

Nora had simply brought Lauren a plate of eggs and bacon and said, "On the house."

Lauren had looked at her suspiciously. "Why?"

"Because you've had a rough few months, and I know what that's like." Then she pointed to a painted sign above the table that read AIN'T NO PROBLEM BACON CAN'T CURE.

Lauren couldn't help but smile. Was the word *cure* a pun on cured meat, or was she giving the sign too much credit? Either way, she thanked the woman. And it took a few weeks before Nora would accept any money from her for food. It took about a month for Nora to offer her a job.

Lauren glanced at the chalkboard to get a sense of the day's specials and realized it hadn't been updated. She called out to Nora for a rundown.

"Goldenberry pancakes, a hot quinoa bowl, a kale–goat cheese omelet," she said. "I only got half the goat cheese I ordered so be prepared to eighty-six it because of this rush."

Nora prided herself on an organic menu constructed around as many "super-foods" as possible.

Lauren jotted the specials on her ticket pad, grabbed a piece of chalk and updated the board, and then started taking table orders. She loved the chaotic rhythm of the restaurant. For hours at a stretch, she didn't have time to think. She barely had time to breathe. When she was really in a groove, it was almost like running.

Lauren was in the zone during the crush of lunch when Nora summoned her to the front counter.

"You have a visitor," she said in the same moment that Lauren saw the hard-to-miss blonde in cutoffs and mirrored aviator sunglasses.

Lauren fortified herself with a deep breath and marched over to the sister she hadn't seen since Labor Day weekend, which had been Stephanie's last visit to the shore.

"Hey," she said. "What are you doing here?"

"Didn't Mom tell you I was coming?"

"Yes, but I mean *here*. At the café." She glanced around. "I'm working."

"Yeah, I know, Lauren. You're always working or running or some shit and I need to talk to you away from Mom."

Lauren sighed. "What's wrong?"

"I don't know exactly. Mom has a bug up her butt about something. Did she say anything to you?"

Concerned, Lauren thought back over the most recent phone conversations she'd had with their mother but didn't see any red flags. "No. I can't think of anything. Let's just…see how things go this weekend. Where's Ethan?"

"At the house with Mom."

"And Brett?"

Lauren barely knew Stephanie's husband of a year and a half; he and Stephanie had eloped after dating for two months.

"He's not coming."

"Okay, well. I'll see you later." She turned around and eyed her tables.

"One more thing: I need to stay here for a few weeks. Maybe a month."

Lauren turned back to her. "At the shore?"

"Yeah. At the house."

No. This could not be happening. Summer weekends, she could tolerate. But weeks at a stretch?

"Stephanie, I know it's beach season and the house is technically a beach house but it's my *home*. If I lived in Philly, you wouldn't just show up and say, 'I'm moving in for the summer.'"

"At this point, I would. I'm getting divorced, and I have nowhere else to stay."

Divorced. Lauren couldn't even begin to act surprised.

"What about Mom and Dad's?"

Stephanie shook her head. "That's a no-go."

"Why not?"

"I'm not sure. It was actually Mom's idea that I stay here this summer."

What? "I can't deal with this right now, okay? Just—go. I'll see you back at the house."

Lauren made a beeline for the kitchen. She wanted to be consumed by the heat, the clanking of dishes, the controlled chaos. She wished the lunch hour would stretch on forever.

Summer hadn't even started, and it couldn't get any worse.

Matt knew he had Craig's attention. He fast-forwarded the reel to his latest interview and paused it.

"Last week I spoke to a former assistant coach with the Flyers who's at Villanova now."

Matt hit Play, and the Hatfield Ice Arena, home ice to the Villanova men's ice hockey team, filled the screen. The coach, John Tramm, sat on a bench, the empty rink in the background.

"I can't talk specifically to Kincaid's situation because I didn't know the guy," Tramm said.

"Of course. I'm just trying to establish the overall climate in the NHL," Matt said.

"The time period you're looking at—Kincaid's two seasons—were right before things began to change."

"What changed?"

"Starting in, maybe it was spring 2011, if a guy took a hit to the head, he'd be removed from the game and evaluated by a doctor."

Matt leaned forward. "Are you saying that prior to 2011, that's not how players were treated?"

"There was no hard-and-fast protocol for players who took a hit to the head. So they'd sit on the bench and the team trainer would evaluate them. And there is the expectation for the player to just shake it off. Hockey culture demands resilience. Guys feel pressure to prove their toughness, and, frankly, they know they can be replaced. Especially the rookies."

"I understand there's a class-action lawsuit by about a hundred retired players," Matt said.

Tramm nodded. "Yes. The lawsuit is in light of the new research about CTE."

Matt knew all about CTE, chronic traumatic encephalopathy, a degenerative brain disorder. Matt still couldn't believe that he'd found a head-injury angle on the Rory Kincaid story. At first, he'd doubted himself. He thought he was projecting. He'd been obsessed with head-injury consequences for over a decade, ever since his older brother came back from Afghanistan. Everyone knew it was a problem for wounded warriors. And people knew it was a problem for pro athletes. But in Rory Kincaid, he might have found an intersection, a perfect storm that had taken down America's golden boy.

"Now researchers are looking at the brains of deceased former players," Tramm said. "One of the first to be studied was one of our guys, Larry Zeidel. He was a Flyer. Nickname was Rock. A great guy—everyone loved him. Then he retires and suffers from debilitating headaches. Starts having a bad temper, gets violent, makes crazy financial decisions. Impulsive decisions. His entire life fell apart."

His entire life fell apart.

After more than four years, Matt finally had his film.

Craig, however, seemed less sure.

"So the film is no longer about a war hero?"

"It's bigger than a story about just one war hero. It's told through that one hero to question a system that fails these athletes, just like it fails our wounded warriors. We live in a society that hails these guys as heroes, then does nothing to help them when they need it."

If Matt had known all those years ago what he knew now, maybe he could have saved his brother. Maybe, if this film got made, others would have the chance to save their own brothers, or sons, or daughters.

Craig sighed. He glanced up at the storyboard, then around the room.

"I know you had doubts about this film," Matt said. "Maybe it wasn't saying anything big enough. But I hope this new angle changes that."

"Where can we talk privately?"

"Let me check the conference room."

Mercifully, it was empty. Matt closed the door while Craig paced in the tight space.

"My doubts aren't just about the film, Matt. You really blew things up with that project you walked away from four years ago."

Matt crossed his arms, nodding. "I know. That was...unfortunate."

"Unfortunate? You cost Andrew Dobson a lot of money."

Matt should never have agreed to do the documentary about the rock star. It had been producer Andrew Dobson's idea; Matt had been between projects and he agreed. And then Rory Kincaid was killed, and Matt was reminded of why he'd gotten into the business in the first place. After a few months of trying to finish the musician project, he realized his heart wasn't in it. He had to follow his passion, his instincts. "You can find another director to get it to the finish line," he'd told his producer.

Bridge officially burned.

"I also *made* Andrew Dobson a lot of money," Matt said. "I got Andrew an Academy Award nomination for the last film we did together!"

Craig nodded, rubbing his jaw. "Okay, this is the situation: You have a theory. It's an interesting one. But there's no smoking gun."

"I'll find it."

"What does his widow have to say about all of this? His mother?"

"His mother died last year, before I was onto this. And the widow is completely off the grid."

His failure to locate Lauren Adelman Kincaid was the greatest frustration of his career. The amount of time and money he'd spent trying to track her down had almost sunk the project. The woman had no social-media footprint, no driver's license, and no real estate rental or purchase records. Her old friends either wouldn't talk to him or swore they were no longer in touch with her. Her former brother-in-law threatened him with a lawsuit. And her family in Philadelphia refused to speak with him. Well, her sister agreed to a meeting, then backed out at the last minute and never responded to his follow-up calls or e-mails. He'd hired a private investigator. He'd considered illegally obtaining her tax filings, but he hit a wall without her Social Security number.

Craig walked back to Matt's desk, stared pensively at the storyboard on the wall. After a long silence, he said, "Without interviews with the widow, someone to corroborate what you're saying, this film is too speculative. I'm sorry, Matt. I can't invest in it. But I wish you luck."

Chapter Five

Lauren locked the door to the café behind her and felt the heat of the midday sun on her back. For as long as she'd known Nora, her boss had been mumbling about starting a dinner service, but so far it hadn't happened. Every day, Nora's Café closed at three and didn't open until seven the following morning. Lauren hoped the dinner shift would actually materialize this summer. She relished the idea of working a double— or even a triple. To clock in at six in the morning and not leave until eleven or so at night? She wouldn't have a moment to think. Just the way she liked it.

She adjusted the belt pack around her waist, making sure her tips were zipped up, then bent down to tie the laces on her Sauconys for the run back to the house.

"Lauren Kincaid!" A man's voice.

Lauren stood up so quickly she felt dizzy. *You're not eating enough. You're too skinny.*

He looked vaguely familiar, but it took her a few seconds to place him. Had they gone to school together?

"Neil Hanes," he said. "From Green Valley?"

An old acquaintance from her parents' country club. She must have been in college the last time she'd seen him. The summers were like that; half of her hometown descended on the island.

"Oh, hi. Sorry, it's just been a long time."

"It really has! Probably since that party for your dad's fiftieth."

She nodded, her mind flooding with images of the live band, her cocktail dress, and the way Rory had looked in his suit. *It's like a wedding,* he'd said. *Someday we'll dance like this and you'll be my wife.*

Neil said something but she'd completely tuned out.

"I'm sorry?" she said.

"Oh, I was just saying that I see your parents sometimes in Philly. They mentioned that you live here now."

She nodded, hoping he wouldn't bring up Rory, wouldn't say he was sorry, wouldn't say he'd heard...

"Are you writing these days?" he said.

"Writing?"

"Journalism. The last time we spoke, you were really into it."

Vague recollections of a long-ago conversation. "Oh. Right. No, not anymore." She hated talking about herself. Deflect, deflect. "Weren't you into journalism too?"

He nodded. "I love reporting. But no money in it. Screenwriting— that's where it's at."

She smiled politely. "Well, nice to see you. I should get going."

"Oh, yeah, sure. But, listen, I'm here for the summer. We should hang out some time."

"I don't hang out," she said.

She knew it sounded harsh, bitchy, cold. But it was better to just be up-front about it. She didn't date, would never date. And she didn't need a new friend. It would take all of her energy just to tolerate her family.

* * *

They say a mother is only as happy as her most unhappy child.

That explained why Beth hadn't felt any real joy in years. Both of her daughters were miserable.

"I left messages for Lauren and Stephanie asking what they wanted for dinner, and neither of them have gotten back to me," she said to her husband as she poured Worcestershire sauce into a bowl to start her marinade.

"Hon, they're grown women. Why don't you and I go out to eat and they can fend for themselves?"

Was he serious?

She set the bottle down. "The point of being here is to spend time together as a family."

"Well, maybe Lauren and Stephanie don't share your enthusiasm for that. You're pushing too hard about living here for the summer."

She pressed her fingers to her temples. "I want one last summer here before we have to sell the house. Is that so much to ask?"

He sighed.

She unwrapped the flank steak.

"This isn't just for me, Howard. Ethan should be surrounded by family. He just lost the only father figure he ever had."

"That schmuck wasn't a father."

"You know what I mean. And Lauren has been out here alone long enough."

"I certainly agree with that," Howard said, looking out at the beach. "Have you told her about selling the house?"

"I haven't found the right time."

"What's the right time? It's *your* house, Beth."

"And the house in Philly was *our* house, and you just lost that! So don't lecture me."

They'd lived in the old stone house in the suburbs of Philadelphia since before Stephanie was born. Beth had been sure they would live there for the rest of their lives, that her grandchildren would run around the same yard that the girls had grown up playing in.

She still shuddered thinking about the day, only weeks ago, that he'd confessed. *I took out a second mortgage... Last-ditch attempt to save the business...*

The business.

Howard ran Adelman's Apparel, a store his grandfather had started as a hat shop in 1932. Saul Adelman had the foresight to lease a space in the shadow of the famous Wanamaker's department store, a retail behemoth that attracted visitors from all over the country. But while throngs of people went to Wanamaker's to see the world's largest fully functional pipe organ or the twenty-five-hundred-pound bronze eagle in the Grand Court, many seemed to prefer a more intimate experience for shopping. That's where Adelman's came in, with Howard's mother, Deborah, acting as a personal shopper long before there was any concept of such a thing. From the 1950s through the 1970s, it was unthinkable for a well-to-do young woman in Philadelphia to go anywhere other than Adelman's for her trousseau.

But the world changed. Retail changed. Wanamaker's closed its doors after a hundred and twenty years. The trend toward casual dressing edged Adelman's out of its comfort zone, and eventually it became impossible for the store to compete with the national chains.

Beth had known it was bad. She just hadn't known *how* bad until they'd lost their home.

Now Adelman's was closed, left half filled with merchandise Howard had failed to unload while he pumped money into the store, trying to hold on long enough to find a buyer. He was stuck with five more years on a twenty-year commercial lease.

Still, regardless of the circumstances, Beth could not stomach the idea of selling the Green Gable. Looking around the kitchen, she could envision her mother at the counter, unwrapping fresh cinnamon buns, still warm from Casel's grocery. Beth closed her eyes.

"My parents intended for the girls to have this house someday."

Howard sighed.

"You've indulged the girls too much the past few years. Now you and I need to dig ourselves out of this hole, and Lauren and Stephanie need to move on with their lives."

Was he right? Beth had known it would take time for Lauren to recover from the loss of her husband. It had taken all of them time to get over losing Rory. But it was becoming increasingly clear that her daughter was frozen.

And she was scared nothing would ever change that.

Chapter Six

Ethan asked to sit next to Lauren at dinner. She hadn't seen the kid since last summer, and yet he loved her. She wished she could still see the world through the forgiving eyes of a six-year-old.

"I saved you this seat," she said, smiling at him.

Ethan was quiet but achingly cute, with big brown eyes and the same high forehead and good cheekbones Lauren had inherited from her father. He looked more like Lauren than Stephanie, and Lauren wondered if her sister realized this, if he reminded her of when they had been young and best friends.

"I like this long chair," Ethan said, looking up at Lauren.

"Me too. It's kind of kooky. Like your great-grandmother," she said. The wall banquette was upholstered in an outrageously bold chinoiserie pattern her grandmother once had identified as Chiang Mai Dragon. The walls were cerulean blue, the modern table white marble. Her grandmother had tried as hard as she could to do a simple beach house, but with some rooms she'd caved to her truest design impulses. The living room was all distressed wood and white linen, framed starfish, and several vintage suitcases stacked next to a towering bookshelf. But if you turned a corner, you'd find a velvet-upholstered modern wingback chair under a large-scale abstract painting. Lauren's grandmother had a fondness for monogrammed trays and chinoiserie vases, and her collections of zebras—Lalique zebras, porcelain zebras, hand-carved wood zebras—were scattered everywhere.

"I don't think that's a nice thing to say," said her mother. "And Ethan, hon, it's called a banquette."

The salt and pepper shakers were little bluebirds. Ethan reached for one.

Her mother's marinated flank steak was set out on an American flag–pattern serving tray, a nod to the holiday weekend. Lauren appreciated the attempt to make things festive, but since her husband's death, she'd found the sight of the flag funereal.

"This room is pretty crazy," Stephanie declared, opening a bottle of wine. She seemed overdressed for dinner at home in her skintight jeans perfectly flared around her ankles and her strappy, high-heeled sandals. Lauren hadn't changed out of her running clothes.

"I don't think you need to drink tonight," Beth said. Stephanie poured a glass anyway.

"Listen to your mother," Howard said.

She ignored him too.

Ethan played with one of the bluebirds, tilting it so it spilled salt onto the table.

Stephanie went to the kitchen and returned with a plate of Bagel Bites. They actually looked pretty appealing. As if reading his aunt's mind, Ethan smiled at Lauren, his big brown eyes wide and adoring, and handed her one of the crusty little circles.

"Aw, thanks, hon. Looks so good, but that's yours." She tousled his hair.

"Lauren, a friend of your father's—you remember Simon Hanes—is opening a restaurant in the Borgata this summer. Seafood. Very fancy," said her mother.

So that was why Neil Hanes was in town.

"Oh, well, that's nice," Lauren said, reaching for a piece of corn on the cob.

"Tell her, Beth," her father prompted.

Her mother cleared her throat. "We were thinking, maybe once things got off the ground, you'd like to work there instead of that little place you're at now?"

Lauren shook her head. She knew her parents meant well, but their pushing and prodding was getting more invasive. They just didn't get it. Four years into her life on the island, at least her old friends had taken the hint and left her alone. At first, after Rory died, they offered to come to town for weekends or just to meet her for dinner. They sent invitations to weddings and birthday parties. For a while, she felt obligated to concoct some reasonable excuse to decline. And then, she did not.

"Why would I want to work at the Borgata?" Lauren said.

"Well, you'd be more in the swing of things. Less isolated. It might be fun. Even in the winter, you'd have steady business." Lauren could hear the subtext: *And you might meet someone.*

"Thanks, but I'm happy where I am," she said evenly. She couldn't get angry with her mother. After all, her mother never got impatient with her. Beth, on top of the long hours she had always put in at Adelman's, helped run Lauren's foundation. It was so much work, more than Lauren had imagined when she began with the simple idea of raising money to donate to various causes in Rory's memory. Her favorite organization was Warrior Camp, a place for soldiers to heal from the trauma of combat. And yet, as passionate as she felt about this work, when she was invited to fundraisers or meetings, she would not leave the island.

Her mother glanced at her father: *Well, I tried.*

Silence fell over the table. The only sound was Ethan crunching on the mini–pizza bagels. Things were always awkward when the whole family was together, but it felt especially weighted tonight, and Lauren remembered what Stephanie had said about her mother seeming upset about something—although she had put it a little more crudely, as Stephanie tended to do. She watched her mother, looking for a clue that something was wrong, and decided it was probably just Stephanie's divorce setting her mother on edge. Of course her parents had to be upset about it, though they couldn't have been any more surprised by it than Lauren was. After Stephanie had gotten pregnant by "some rando," as she put it, and decided to keep the baby, there was probably little that could surprise them.

"Speaking of Simon Hanes," her mother said suddenly, "his son Neil is here for the summer. I'm sure you two met at some point. Very good-looking young man."

"I literally just ran into him a few hours ago," Lauren said.

"You didn't! What a coincidence!" her mother said, way too delighted.

"You should spend some time with him. Very ambitious young man. He's a screenwriter now," her father added. "Moved to LA after graduating from Penn."

"Yeah, no, thanks," Lauren said.

"I'll spend some time with him," said Stephanie.

"You're not even divorced yet!" their father said.

"Oh, as if that's the issue. I could be totally single, never married, and you'd still only think of setting him up with Lauren."

Lauren glanced uneasily at Ethan. "Hon, can you get me a bottle of water from the fridge?" she asked, and he dutifully scooted away. She turned to Stephanie. "Why do you have to make everything about you?"

"Like you don't? Your whole Jackie Kennedy routine is getting old."

"Really? You're criticizing *my* life?"

In that moment, it was hard to believe they had once been close. But they had. Lauren, dark-haired, dark-eyed, quiet and watchful; Stephanie, blond and blue-eyed, outgoing and a chatterbox. A year apart, their mother called them "the twins."

Whatever shortcomings Lauren had, she knew her sister would fill the gap. And vice versa. When Stephanie was flailing in ninth-grade math— tripped up by quadratic functions in algebra—Lauren, a year younger, tutored her. Stephanie might have been the blonde, but Lauren was the golden child—well behaved, smart, caring.

Stephanie had set the course of their school years when, struggling academically, she'd fought her parents when they tried to switch her from public middle school to private school. Why didn't she want to go to private school? "Because it sucks," she told Lauren. And so when Lauren finished elementary school, she too chose public school.

"Baldwin Academy is so much calmer. More intimate. It's a better fit for you," her mother had argued. This was a time when Lauren was struggling a bit with her weight. The public-school kids could be cruel. Of course, private-school girls were no better. But when parents pay twenty grand a year, the administration has an incentive to enforce some semblance of decorum. Lauren didn't care; she was going to school with her big sister.

She was less confident that she'd made the right decision when high school loomed. By that time, Lauren had grown to her full height, five foot six. Her high cheekbones and brown eyes had won her comparisons to the lead actress on her favorite show, *Alias*. She was finally pretty. Nowhere near Stephanie's loud, flagrant beauty, but pretty enough. Still, starting high school was scary, and starting high school at a big place like Lower Merion was terrifying. So many things could go wrong. You could end up anonymous—a loser. You could end up harassed—tormented on the notorious Freshman Day, the first Friday the thirteenth of the school year. Rumor had it that some girls got their entire ponytails cut off, and some boys were stuffed into lockers.

On the first day, some of Lauren's friends' older siblings pretended they didn't know the younger ones, warned them not to even acknowledge them in the halls. But the scheduling gods had smiled on Lauren and given her the same lunch period as Stephanie. Stephanie, her long blond hair loose and lustrous, her perfect body poured into jeans and a ribbed tank top from a recent shopping spree at Urban Outfitters, had put her arm around Lauren and taken her from table to table.

"This is my baby sister," Steph had said, first to the sophomores, then to a few tables of juniors. "Don't fuck with her."

"Hey, baby sister," a few boys had said mockingly.

But no one fucked with her. Not once; not ever.

As teenagers, the sisters never had a reason to be competitive. They didn't want the same things.

At least, not until Rory.

Now, Stephanie pushed her chair away from the table.

"Where are you going?" her mother said.

"Out."

Stephanie stormed off. Lauren sighed. *Drama queen.*

"Aunt Lauren?" Ethan said, appearing in the doorway of the dining room. He had a bottle of water in one hand and the package of cinnamon buns from Casel's in the other. "Can we open these now?"

"We're still eating dinner, hon," Beth said.

Ethan looked around the table. "Where's Mom?"

Lauren and her mother exchanged a look.

"Sure," Lauren said. "We can open that now."

Matt slipped into a seat near the back of the NYU auditorium. There were a few open spots closer to the front of the room, but Matt always felt more comfortable near an exit route. Maybe this was a result of his early years working in undesirable locations, or maybe it was just a by-product of his natural impatience.

"Our thinking on head injury is evolving, and the way we research these injuries is changing."

The irony was not lost on Matt that after avoiding science as much as possible for his entire academic life (there had been one particularly miserable eight weeks of summer-school chemistry), he now spent his free time sitting in dark lecture halls learning about it. His e-mail in-box was filled with event alerts for brain-injury panels the way it had once been stuffed with announcements of Red Hot Chili Peppers tour dates.

"Today, we're challenging two core beliefs: First, that brain disease is caused by only those severe hits that result in concussions and, second, that brain injury is due to blows that cause the brain to bounce around inside the skull. That theory is incomplete."

He'd been looking forward to this talk, a public lecture given by a visiting professor of neurology at the Boston University School of Medicine, for weeks. He'd requested an interview, but no luck. And considering the way things had gone with Craig Mason last week, it was just as well. *American Hero* was on pause. Maybe permanently this time.

"We believe long-term brain damage can result from the accumulation of minor blows. And we believe the real damage happens deeper inside the brain than previously thought and that this is a result of fibers within the white matter twisting after impact. Given these two things, sports helmets as they are currently designed do not protect players from concussions and the resulting long-term brain disease."

The doctor introduced a bioengineer from the Camarillo Lab at Stanford. He'd developed a mouth guard that helped track the force of injury in football players.

"If you look at this screen, you'll see the g-forces of ten hits," the bioengineer said. Matt hated charts. He glanced down at the program he'd been handed at the entrance and flipped to the back. The Stanford study thanked a list of donors. Matt recognized many of the names, all the usual suspects in the arena of traumatic brain injury. The few he didn't recognize, he circled now with a Sharpie. He never knew where he'd find an important lead. At one name toward the bottom, his hand froze. The Polaris Foundation.

He named him Polaris. What kind of name is that for a dog from a six-year-old boy? But he loved the stars.

Could it be a coincidence?

Matt slipped from the auditorium. The sunlight outside was blinding after the half hour he'd spent in darkness. Matt rushed into a coffee shop and pulled his laptop from his messenger bag while standing in line to buy the coffee that would rent him table space.

Squeezing into the corner of a long wooden communal table, Matt gave a cursory nod to the pretty blonde who smiled at him. Then he put on his headphones to discourage conversation and did a quick search for the Polaris Foundation. He wasn't surprised to come up empty. A lot of public foundations didn't have websites. Next, he tried the foundation-center database. He hadn't used the site in a long time, not since the early days when he'd searched for any type of Rory Kincaid foundation. At the time, he'd had no doubt someone in Rory's family would start a foundation in his name, and he'd been right: his brother Emerson had started the Rory Kincaid Scholarship Foundation for student athletes. But that had proved a dead end because Emerson wouldn't speak to him and Lauren Kincaid wasn't involved.

Matt's login failed. His subscription had run out, and the credit card he originally used had been maxed out long ago. Without hesitating, he pulled out his debit card and used it for the subscription. This is how one slides into bankruptcy, he thought. But it was a fleeting concern, because within thirty seconds he had a name attached to the Polaris Foundation: Lauren Adelman.

Heart pounding, he dug deeper, searching for the Polaris Foundation's IRS form 990-PF.

The address was in Longport, New Jersey.

Chapter Seven

The boardwalk had seemed to stretch to infinity when Lauren was a kid. It was her very own yellow brick road, with the ocean on one side and beachfront homes on the other. Her grandmother, dressed in a velour sweat suit with her hair and makeup perfectly done, took her for a walk every morning. She had seemed so old to Lauren, even though now, doing the math, Lauren realized she had probably been only in her early sixties.

Lauren looked down at Ethan and wondered if she seemed very old to him. She wondered, too, if he shared her joy at the boardwalk or if he was just going along because she'd invited him and he was a polite kid.

"Your mom and I came here every weekend in the summer when we were your age. And in August we'd stay for two weeks and my dad—your grandpa—would come on the weekends when he wasn't working."

"I don't have a dad," Ethan said.

Oh, good Lord. Quick—subject change!

"Um, your mom said you're going to play soccer in the fall?"

"Yeah. I did it last fall too."

"Is this with school?"

He shook his head. "Lower Merion Soccer Club."

"What position do you play?"

He squinted up at her. "I don't know. We change around a lot."

"Okay, well, that makes sense. I guess it's a little early to lock in on something. Do you watch sports on TV? Football? Hockey?"

"Sometimes. Brett watches a lot of hockey." Oh, yes. Stepdad Brett.

"Yeah. I'm sorry Brett isn't around this summer. Are you upset about that?"

Ethan shrugged. "Not really. He wasn't around that much anyway."

Lauren, at a loss for what else to say on the matter, suggested they turn around and head back.

"Aunt Lauren?"

"Yes?"

"Are you mad at my mom?"

"What? Oh, no. Why do you ask?"

"You yelled at her at dinner."

True. She did.

"Well, sisters argue sometimes. It doesn't mean anything, really."

"Do you like my mom?" he asked. Lauren started to respond and found herself feeling choked up.

"Of course," she said. "She's my sister."

Maybe it was time they both started acting like it.

There was a bar like Robert's Place in every town. At least, in every town Matt could spend any amount of time in. In Longport, New Jersey, it took him about thirty seconds of asking passersby on the street for a "good place to drink" before he was steered to Atlantic Avenue and North Essex Street. He needed to be good and loaded to fall asleep in his car now, unlike the old days, when he could crash anywhere. That was the difference between a twenty-four-year-old news correspondent and a thirty-four-year-old filmmaker.

Inside, he was greeted by a Bruce Springsteen song playing on the juke-box, the smell of old beer, and a framed poster of the 1974 Flyers Stanley Cup championship team.

It was early enough to get a seat at the scarred wooden bar under a ceiling covered with Phillies 2008 World Series championship pennants and Budweiser posters. The walls were lined with awards and commem-orative plaques. And there, propped against the back of the bar, next to a bottle of Jack Daniel's, was a framed photo of Rory Kincaid in his U.S. Rangers uniform.

It was a good omen. He was in the right place, the right town. He was going to get this film finished.

"What are you having, doll?" The bartender had heavily bleached blond hair and a raspy voice. She might have been thirty or sixty. It was tough to tell.

"A shot of Tito's, thanks."

He glanced around the room, the filmmaker in him taking in the scene. He made a mental note to come back with a camera and get a picture of the bar with Rory's photo.

The bartender slid his shot over to him. Matt asked her name.

"Desiree," she said with a smile. Definitely closer to sixty.

"I'm Matt," he said, raising his glass.

"Nice meeting you, Matt," she said. "You here for the summer?"

"Just a week or so. Visiting."

A bearded man two seats away in a trucker hat glanced at Matt con-temptuously and raised his empty beer bottle at Desiree. She left Matt with his vodka, and by the time she drifted back, he had summoned the nerve to ask:

"Desiree, do you know a woman named Lauren Kincaid?"

"No," she said quickly. Too quickly.

Damn, he'd blown it. He'd rushed into it. *Pace yourself.*

Worst-case scenario, he could simply go to Lauren's house and knock on the door. But it would seem predatory—which was not the way he wanted to meet her. The optimal thing would be to know where she shopped, where she worked, where she drank, so he could approach her in a casual environment.

He did another shot. Pink Floyd filled the room. God, he hated Pink Floyd.

"Pink Floyd shouldn't be allowed in a bar," he muttered.

There'd been a place like this in Queens when he was growing up—many places like this. But one of them had hired a friend's older brother to bounce, and the lax door policy was his gateway to long nights of drinking against the background sound of the Steve Miller Band.

Matt pulled a few singles from his wallet, ordered a beer, then made his way to the back of the bar to the source of the offending music. He loaded two dollars into the machine and flipped through the song library.

"Don't bother," said a blonde at the end of the bar. "Everything on that thing is from, like, the Stone Age."

He barely glanced at her. The last thing he needed was a hookup.

"I guess I'm from the Stone Age," he said, programming in "Fly Like an Eagle" and "Take the Money and Run."

"Then you look pretty good for your age," she said, a comment that got him to give her a quick glance, if just for her cheekiness. He guessed she was in her late twenties. Maybe thirty. She was...

She was Stephanie Adelman.

He could barely believe it. If he'd had a few more shots, he'd think he was hallucinating. But no; he recognized her from Facebook.

The photo of Rory behind the bar *was* a sign! All he had to do was keep pushing forward. The universe was finally meeting him halfway.

"I'm Matt," he said.

"Stephanie."

"Can I buy you a drink?"

"Yes, Matt, you can."

He slid onto the stool next to her.

For sisters, Stephanie and Lauren didn't look very much alike. Then again, he hadn't seen a recent photo of Lauren. Her social media was frozen in time circa 2012, but back then, when she was the young wife of a former NHL player, she had worn her hair in a simple, shoulder-skimming bob. She had high cheekbones and exuded a gentleness and shyness that was evident even in photos. Rory was a guy who could have been banging any and every hottie in the country, and Matt thought it spoke highly of him that he had committed himself at such a young age to Lauren.

"What are you having?" he asked.

"A margarita," she said. "With salt."

He summoned Desiree with a wave. She took the order but not before asking, "You know this guy, Steph?"

"Oh, yeah. Matt and I are old pals." She turned to Matt. "Desiree and I are old pals too. She used to bust me when I snuck in here during high school. I was a wild child."

Still are, Matt thought. *Lucky for me.*

When Desiree was out of earshot, Stephanie leaned closer to him. "You here for the summer?"

"Just passing through," he said.

"How mysterious."

"Not really."

Desiree slid him his beer and handed Stephanie her cocktail. He waited until she was a safe distance down the bar and said, "What about you? Here for the summer?"

"Maybe. Things are a little up in the air at the moment. Cheers."

"Cheers. You have a house here?"

"My family does. My sister lives here year-round."

Matt's heart beat just a little faster. "Really? I can't imagine being here in the winter. What is there to do?"

Stephanie shrugged. "For normal people? Not much."

"Your sister isn't normal?"

"Depends on who you ask. My mother thinks she's perfect."

The last few syllables of that sentence were mush. Clearly, Stephanie was a few drinks in.

"And what does she think of you?"

"What do *you* think of me?" she asked, her hand on his thigh. Her eyes were glassy. Okay, he had to work fast. She was going to suggest they get out of there, he would have to say no, and that would be the end of that.

"I think," he said carefully, "I think that you're very beautiful. And I am going to tell your mother, and your sister, that I think so."

"You should," she said, slurring. "You *should* tell them! I dare you."

"Dare accepted. I am going to tell them right now."

She laughed. "You can't tell them right now."

"You're right. Okay, I will tell them tomorrow. Where can I go to tell that sister of yours that you are the one who is perfect?"

"Well, that depends," she said. "Are we having breakfast together?"

"I don't eat breakfast," he said.

"Too bad. She works at a breakfast place."

"Maybe I'll make an exception. What breakfast place?"

"Nora's." She finished her drink and set it down heavily. "Want to get out of here?"

"I wish I could, but I can't."

Her eyes narrowed. "Why can't you?"

"I'm working," he said. *And sleeping in my car.*

She stepped shakily off her stool. "Your loss."

"Agreed. Do you need a cab?"

"Fuck you," she said.

Chapter Eight

The café expanded by ten tables every summer when Nora opened the outside seating. These were the days when the waitstaff would increase by three or four college kids, and Nora might find things so busy that she herself jumped behind the griddle. Lauren always felt off-kilter during the first "outdoor day," as they called them.

She stuck to her usual section, front of the house, near the windows. Nora seated a thirty-something man, tall and good-looking enough to turn a few heads, alone at a two-top.

Lauren handed him a menu.

"Need a minute?" she asked, shaking her pen and realizing it was out of ink. She patted down her apron for another. The customer hadn't answered her question; she glanced up at him. He was looking at her in a way that once would have made her uncomfortable. When she'd first started working at the café, men would sometimes stare at her from across the room or let their gaze linger a little too long when she took their orders. She thought they recognized her from the news but soon realized that, no, that was just how men acted around a twenty-something-year-old woman.

The man smiled and turned to the menu—but not before noting the wedding band on her left ring finger. She saw him register the ring, and he knew she saw him looking.

"What would you recommend?" he said.

"You really can't go wrong with anything." She pointed at the specials board.

"That actually makes the decision harder." He smiled. Lauren wanted to put a quick end to the exchange. She didn't do banter.

"The quinoa French toast is very popular," she said.

"Sounds great."

She took his menu, relieved to be able to turn her back to him, and brushed past Nora on her way to the kitchen.

"Looks like he wanted something not on the menu," Nora said with a wink.

"You're right," Lauren said. "It's *not* on the menu."

Et tu, Nora? she thought, retrieving an order. Then she told herself to stop being cranky. But she couldn't help it; she'd been woken up in the middle of the night when Stephanie finally came home, banging around drunk in the bathroom.

She delivered the French toast to the guy at the window table.

"I'm Matt, by the way." He extended his hand.

"And I'm working," she said.

"I know. Actually, so am I." He handed her a business card. "I'm a documentary filmmaker. I directed the film *The Disappearing Sea,* about the recovery of Phang Nga after the 2004 tsunami."

"Didn't see it." She put the card down on the table.

"It was nominated for an Academy Award."

"Congratulations," she said woodenly before turning away.

"Lauren, wait." She froze. She hadn't given him her name. *Don't freak out,* she told herself. *There's probably an explanation.* Across the room, she spotted Nora chatting with a regular. She tried to catch her eye but Nora was laughing, distracted.

Her breath came fast and shallow, and she rushed to the safety of the bathroom. She closed herself inside, telling herself not to jump to conclusions, that one and one did not necessarily equal two. He might know her name because he'd heard a regular call out to her. And he was a filmmaker, but so what? That didn't mean he was interested in Rory.

That first year, she'd turned down Diane Sawyer and the *New York Times* and BuzzFeed and a *Wall Street Journal* reporter writing a book. Rory would have hated people selling a paper or a TV broadcast on his name. A book? Forget it. And why should they get to do that? Hadn't Rory given enough?

Hadn't she?

Around the same time, she got a letter from Rory's brother warning her someone was trying to make a documentary film about Rory. *Don't talk to him,* he'd written. As if she needed him to tell her that.

But after a while, it all seemed to die down. The world had moved on. Or so she thought.

She couldn't hide in the bathroom all day. She came out and found Nora by the coffee station. "Can you take table two for me?"

Nora glanced over, smiled, and was about to say something cute, but Lauren shut her down with "He's a filmmaker. He knows my name."

Nora's face fell. "I'll take the table. Why don't you just manage the front counter until he leaves."

Lauren felt safer, more in control, behind the counter. Busyness, motion, was her friend. She filled the Plexiglas display case with the muffins delivered that morning. A woman walked in to buy a mug and a baseball hat. Two regulars showed up for takeout. Falling into her usual rhythm, she tried to forget about the man in the seat by the window.

He stopped at the counter on his way out the door.

"You were right; the French toast was amazing. Those mugs for sale?" he said.

She turned her back to him.

"Lauren, I don't mean to upset you. But I am working on a film about your late husband, and I would really like the chance to talk to you about it."

She whirled around.

"Forget it. Not happening. Understand?"

"I think your husband's story is important. I think it's worth telling."

She glared at him.

He held up another business card and made a show of placing it on the countertop. "I hope you'll reconsider."

She watched him leave, then, hands shaking, tossed the card in the garbage.

Matt pulled his car onto a side street and parked. He wouldn't let the bumpy first encounter discourage him. This was what progress looked like.

He opened the browser on his phone and checked the listing for a room rental he'd found earlier that morning. When—not *if,* but when—Lauren Kincaid agreed to talk to him, he needed a work space and a small crew. With his very limited funds, he was maybe putting the cart before the horse. But the room for rent looked perfect; it was on the bay side of town and had its own entrance separate from the rest of the house. And the nightly rate was better than he had hoped to find. He didn't want to lose it.

He opened the car window and let in the smell of salt air and the squawk of seagulls. With a deep breath, he dialed Craig.

Straight to voice mail.

"Craig, it's Matt Brio. I've had a breakthrough on the Rory Kincaid film. Things are moving quickly, so please give me a call when you can."

His next call was to the number listed for the room rental. Another voice mail. And then he remembered that it was a holiday weekend and that normal people would be with their families. He had to be patient.

This is what progress looks like.

Chapter Nine

Family dinner two nights in a row was probably too much to hope for. But since it was Memorial Day weekend, Beth thought a nice barbecue wasn't a lot to ask. Apparently, she was wrong. Stephanie was out—heavens knew where. Ethan was home, of course. Lauren was holed up in her room, and Howard was on the grill with enough hot dogs and hamburgers for a dozen people.

Beth stepped onto the deck, shielding her eyes from the sun.

"Why did you get so much food?"

"I invited the Kleins and the Carters."

There was no point asking why he hadn't told her. They'd barely spoken all day. They couldn't agree on a plan for the summer. They couldn't talk about the house. They couldn't talk about money. Thirty years into their marriage, everything was suddenly a conversational landmine. And she didn't know how to fix it. There she was, in the middle of her life, and she had never felt less capable.

With company coming, she had to change out of her yoga pants. Her mother would have been appalled by the "athleisure" state of dressing these days. Even at the beach, her mother had greeted every day with full makeup and her hair done, wearing linen pants and a matching top.

And, really, it was the gradual but absolute slide into everyday casual that had been the undoing of their family business. Beth should have put up more personal resistance, but it was just so damn easy to be comfortable.

Beth stood on the bedroom deck and looked down at the pool. Today, Howard, happily grilling, seemed more like the man she loved and the father the girls adored and less like the adversary she'd been living with the past few months. She knew it had been difficult for him to lose the store, and not just because of the financial implications. It was his family business. He'd never considered another career because the store was his duty. It wasn't easy; it wasn't glamorous. But he'd shown up, day in and day out, for three decades.

If only he hadn't gone behind her back with a second mortgage on their home!

Beth headed up the stairs to warn Lauren they were having company. As expected, Lauren was less than thrilled.

"Mom, I just feel the walls closing in on me here. Stephanie wants to stay a few weeks, and I know it's not technically my house, but it is my home and I just can't deal with her twenty-four/seven."

Beth sat on the bed. This was what happened when you waited for the right time to talk: you got backed into a corner.

"Well, sweetheart, I have some good news and some bad news."

Lauren looked at her sharply. "What is it?"

"I'm going to stay here for the summer too. I can be a buffer between you and Stephanie."

"You and Dad are staying all summer?"

Beth hesitated. "Yes."

"Why? You never spend the summer here. I mean, I don't want to be a brat. It's your house. It's just..." She looked out the window hopelessly. "I'm used to being here alone. I need to be alone."

Just rip the Band-Aid off, Beth told herself. "I want to spend the summer here with you because…" She paused, probably more dramatically than she should have. But really, she needed a moment. Once she said it aloud to Lauren, it would become real. "It's our last summer with the Green Gable. We have to sell this house."

By four in the afternoon Matt still hadn't heard back from Craig. But the woman renting out the room told him he could stop by and see it before six.

"You're late for a rental this season," she said over the phone. "But lucky for you, I'm late to the game myself."

Matt parked in her driveway and noted a wooden stairway on the side of the house leading to the upper floor. He hoped the room was decent because he liked the location.

He rang the front doorbell. No response. He rang again. When there was still no answer, he wondered if the bell was broken and knocked. Still nothing.

Fighting annoyance, he walked around to the back of the house, passing the wooden stairs and a deck overlooking the bay. He could hear music playing. Nina Simone?

A woman was bent over a table painting a plank of wood with a wide brush. She seemed to be in her sixties and had cocoa-colored skin and a short salt-and-pepper Afro. She wore a blue smock and lots of beaded necklaces in reds and corals.

"Um, Ms. Boutine?"

Startled, she dropped her brush. "Can I help you?"

"I'm Matt. We just spoke on the phone about the room?"

"Oh, heavens. I lost track of time. And I have a party to get to!" She wiped her hands on the smock and held one out to shake. "Henriette Boutine. You can call me Henny. Follow me."

She took him back to the side of the house.

"Are you an artist?" he said.

"It's more of a craft," she said, leading the way up the steps to a door on the second floor. "This stairway is an add-on. When my son finished college, he ended up back here for a year, and my late husband built this entrance for his privacy—and our sanity. But my son's on the West Coast now and my husband passed, and here I've been, stuck with this eyesore staircase. But now it's coming in handy. The Lord works in mysterious ways, right?"

"True," Matt said. She opened the door to a large bedroom with a view of the bay. The space was decorated with eclectic bric-a-brac—a mason jar on the nightstand filled with shells, framed sand dollars on the wall, a smattering of wicker baskets. The sleigh bed was full-size and topped with a navy-blue comforter. Up above, a gently whirling ceiling fan. Behind the bed, a wooden sign in multiple hues of blue that read COTTAGE RULES: SAND. SUN. FUN.

He looked around for space to work and was pleased to see a small wooden desk in the corner.

"What do you think?" said Henny.

"The nightly rate is as listed?" he said.

"Yes. But I have to tell you, a couple is coming over tomorrow to see the room. So if you want it, I'm just letting you know it might not be available after tomorrow for about a week."

"I would need it for about a week too."

He glanced at his phone, willing Craig to call. If Craig came on board, his expenses would be covered. He didn't want to front the cash so early, but he also didn't want to lose the place. As was his habit, he took the gamble.

"I'd like it."

"Really? You're my first renter. I didn't think this whole thing would work. My friends think I'm crazy to be doing this."

Matt smiled politely.

"Here are the keys. The door will lock behind you automatically so be sure to take them with you. I need the first night paid as a deposit."

He handed over his debit card and she plugged an adapter into her phone to swipe it. "Isn't technology amazing?" she said.

"Okay, well, I'm just going to settle in for now. Thanks, Ms. Boutine. It's a really nice place you've got here."

"Please, call me Henny. And yes, it is a nice place. So give it a good rating or whatever it's called on the web. That's the way to build business. Or so I've read. Enjoy your stay." She closed the door behind her.

Matt unpacked his Canon C100 and set it on the desk but left his backup sound pack in his bag. Hopefully, he'd get funding to pay a local crew and he wouldn't need it.

He pulled out his laptop and booted up his Rory Kincaid folder. He opened the interview he'd done with one of Kincaid's high-school coaches, Roger McKenna.

"And that was the thing about Rory," the coach said, folding his arms behind his head and sitting back in his office chair. Above him was a framed photograph of Rory's team the year they'd won the state championship. "It wasn't just his reflexes or his speed. It was his absolute calm under pressure."

Matt nodded. He'd heard the same thing from the coach at Harvard and from members of Rory's battalion.

He fast-forwarded to the footage of the gym. Lower Merion High School had just under fourteen hundred students in any given year and every kind of team and extracurricular club you could imagine. From what he understood, LM, as it was commonly called, offered the quintessential all-American high-school experience.

Rory's retired jersey, number 89, hung framed next to a maroon-and-white banner that read RORY KINCAID. PA STATE CHAMPIONSHIP 2005. MCDONALD'S ALL-AMERICAN. GATORADE PLAYER OF THE YEAR.

While Matt's camera guy got B-roll of the gym, Coach McKenna had gotten choked up.

"I still can't believe it. What a waste," the coach said. "What a god-damn waste."

The simple statement hit Matt in the gut. It was exactly how he felt about his older brother. After 9/11, Ben had dropped out of Syracuse University to enlist. Three years later, they'd lost him.

What a goddamn waste.

Maybe, if Matt managed to pull off the film, Rory's death—and his brother's—wouldn't be a total waste.

His phone rang, startling him. He looked at the screen.

Craig Mason.

Chapter Ten

We have to sell this house.

The beat of her sneakers on asphalt steadied Lauren's nerves. Still, the run over to Nora's wasn't something Lauren had thought through very well. It was, after all, Memorial Day weekend. And sure enough, when she arrived, sweaty and anxious, on the doorstep, she found a house overflowing with guests.

Nora clapped in delight to see her. "You came after all!"

Her party. Lauren had completely forgotten.

Taking in Lauren's running clothes and less-than-festive expression, Nora said, "What's the matter? Come get a drink. Or, better yet, eat your drink. April made her famous watermelon balls." Every summer party, Nora's friend April showed up with vodka-infused fruit.

"I'm good. Thanks. I just need some quiet, so this was probably not the best place—"

"Come on upstairs."

Across the hall, her friend Henny Boutine waved at her. Lauren raised her hand in response, trying to muster some enthusiasm, then followed Nora to the second floor.

Nora's room overlooked the bay. Two of her three cats—Nadia, the Russian blue, and Benson, the tabby—had taken up residence on the bed. Both were sprawled out, reveling in the late-day sun streaming through the window. The felines were so large, she had no room to sit without encountering a paw or a sleepy cat's head.

Above the bed, a wooden sign read CATS WELCOME; PEOPLE TOLERATED.

It was one of Henny's handmade signs; she displayed them on the walls of Nora's restaurant and sold them for twenty-five dollars each. It was apparently not much of a moneymaker; she'd decided to list her house on Airbnb for the first time. Henny was nervous about it. All of her friends except Lauren were nervous about it. She figured it was a generational thing. At the book club last month, April said to Henny, "I hope you're careful. I don't know how y'all let strangers in your houses."

April, a widow, was living off the estate of her fifth and final husband. Her hair was silvery blond, her mouth never without matte red lipstick, and her cheeks always powdered. She was a throwback to a time Lauren could scarcely imagine and never would have survived.

"Some of us have to work for a living, Miss America," Henny had replied. Indeed, April had been a Miss America pageant contestant circa 1964.

Lauren looked out the window. The back deck was packed with people.

"I feel bad keeping you from the party. Go on—I'm fine."

"The *party* is fine. You still upset about that guy at the restaurant? I'll make sure he doesn't get a table ever again, I'll tell you that."

"No. I mean, yeah, I'm freaked out about that." It unnerved Lauren that he had tracked her down at Nora's. She felt her privacy had been invaded, the security of her protected island breached. As for the film itself, well, what could the guy possibly have except what the world already knew? She wouldn't speak to him. Rory's mother was gone. Who was the guy talking to? Former teammates? Someone from his battalion? She'd been going over and over it in her mind. Would probably still have been obsessing about it if it weren't for the bombshell her mom had dropped. "But that's not it. My mother's selling the house."

"The Green Gable?"

Lauren nodded, tears in her eyes. "I can't believe it. I never thought this day would come. Never. My grandparents bought that house in 1965. It's like, the one thing I have, the one thing I can count on."

"Hon, you've got your parents here. Your sister. You're surrounded by people who love you. You can count on that."

It was such a simple sentiment. And she wanted so much to believe it.

Matt told himself he hadn't lied to Craig when he'd implied that Lauren Kincaid had agreed to be interviewed. In just a day or two, Matt was sure he would be able to turn that into reality.

The important thing was that Craig was excited about the project.

When he returned Matt's call, he'd said he had just been thinking about him.

"The story stayed with me since we last spoke. I think you're onto something, but like I said, without talking to the widow, you're missing a major piece of the puzzle."

"Yes. But I found her."

"And she's willing to talk to you."

Matt, reaching for the project's lifeline, said yes. Craig asked if his budget was still the same, and again Matt said yes, this time truthfully.

"All right, I'm in," Craig said.

Now all Matt had to do was actually get Lauren to talk. For years, Matt had accepted the fact that the Adelmans had closed ranks around Lauren. But last night, in her drunken rambling, Stephanie had revealed that there was a crack in the wall of silence. Lauren was the direct route to finishing this film, and although it had been blocked, there was now a detour that just might work.

Matt grabbed his wallet and rushed out of the house, checking his phone for the time. Wondering how crowded it would be at Robert's Place on Memorial Day evening.

And then he realized he'd done exactly what Ms. Boutine had warned him not to do: he'd left his keys inside. He turned back and tried the door, though he already knew it would be locked.

"Damn it!" He paced impotently for a few minutes before calling Ms. Boutine. "Sorry to bother you," he said. It was so loud wherever she was, he could barely hear her response. "I seem to have locked myself out."

Chapter Eleven

Nora's party grew rowdier as the sun set; there was less grilling and more cocktail-shaking. That's when April, decked out in a floor-length spaghetti-strap sundress in pastel pink, tapped Lauren on the shoulder.

"Lauren, I wanted to introduce you to my stepson Connor. He's in town for a few days looking to buy a beachfront house."

April had more stepchildren than she had fingers. According to Nora, she apparently kept in touch with almost all of them.

Connor was tall and blond and could have been April's own son. He was handsome in a 1950s-movie-star kind of way. He was also at least ten years older than Lauren, and she'd gotten April's not-so-subtle hint that he wasn't exactly hurting for money.

"Nice to meet you," Lauren said, trying to find the balance between polite and discouraging. God, she hated attempted setups. Hated the fake casualness of the introduction, the way the introducer would drift away (as April did immediately) and the way the guy would look at her intently, ask a barrage of superficial questions, and then, when Lauren made her getaway excuse, say something about getting together sometime.

Connor didn't even have time to ask a question before Lauren excused herself with a quick "Just going to get some air."

Outside, seagulls squawked. A stray cat dashed across Nora's small front lawn, rustling a bush as it made its hasty retreat. The bay-side houses in Ventnor, two towns over but just ten minutes from Longport, felt secluded because of the narrow side streets buffering them from the busier throughway avenues.

Lauren settled onto Nora's front-porch rollback bench swing. She inhaled deeply, enjoying the solitude.

Headlights caught her eye as a car rounded the corner onto Nora's street. It moved slowly, clearly steered by a driver who was searching for an address. Then the car turned into Nora's short driveway. A door opened and slammed shut; she heard footsteps on gravel.

Lauren dragged one heel on the ground, stopping the swing. The visitor approached the house, but the angle of the porch light did little to bring the lawn and front walkway out of the shadows. It wasn't until he reached the front door that she could see it was a man.

"The doorbell's broken," she said, startling him. He looked at her, squinting against the overhead light, and then it was her turn to be startled. "What are you doing here?" She gasped. "Are you following me?"

The filmmaker gaped at her. Lauren jumped up from the swing.

"Are you following me?" she repeated.

"No," he said, clearly as surprised to see her as she was to see him. "I'm—the woman I'm renting a room from gave me this address. I need to pick up keys."

"What woman?"

"Ms. Boutine."

Oh my God. He was staying at Henny's?

She pressed her face into her hands, then looked up. "I can't believe this. This is a joke."

He smiled. "I'd rather look at it as the universe giving us the chance to get past the awkwardness of the last time we met."

"You corner me at my job and call that awkward? I call it *stalking*."

"Lauren, I'm not trying to upset you. I really respect Rory. I think his story is one that deserves to be told. Don't you feel that way at all?"

"What I *feel* is none of your business."

"Give me one hour to talk about your husband."

She stood, swelling with indignation and a fierce sense of pride in and protectiveness of Rory. "That is never going to happen."

Two strikes and you're out, Matt thought, heading back to his car with Henny's keys in hand. Back to plan B.

He drove to the house, retrieved his own keys, and left hers under the porch mat as she'd instructed him to. Then it was a ten-minute walk to Robert's.

The bar felt like a different place than it had been just twenty-four hours earlier; it was packed end to end, every table full. Waitresses weaved through the crowd carrying red plastic baskets of chicken wings and fries. On the jukebox, Steve Miller's "The Joker." Matt smiled. It would be okay. It had to be.

He edged his way to the bar, ordered a bottle of Sam Adams, and hung back to wait. A table opened up near the kitchen, and he nabbed it. He checked out the plaque on the wall, an award from the Philadelphia Basketball Old Timers Association. Directly above it, a framed photo of a group gathered in front of the bar. A banner hung above their heads: PO-LARIS FOUNDATION FUND-RAISER 2014. He scanned the shot, and there was Lauren in the center, wearing a black-and-white Polaris Foundation T-shirt, smiling at the camera.

An hour passed. He didn't have an appetite but felt some pressure to order wings and the fried-shrimp special to hold on to the table. And it wouldn't hurt to temper the alcohol with something.

And then he spotted Stephanie's blond ponytail, waving like a flag, in the middle of the bar crowd. Had she just walked in, or had he overlooked her? He slipped away from the table, leaving his drink to hold it. The crowd, as if sensing his approach, closed thickly around her. When he was within shouting distance, he called her name, but she didn't respond. He reached out and tugged playfully on her hair. She whirled around with a dirty look and then, recognizing him, gave a half smile.

"You again?"

"It's me. Matt from the Stone Age. I have a table in the back and I ordered too much food."

She hesitated, and in her silence he felt himself starting to fall off the tightrope. And then she said, "Perfect timing. I'm starving."

The basket of wings was waiting for them at the table. She slid into the seat against the wall.

"If there's anything else you want to order…"

She held up her half-empty cocktail, and he flagged the waitress for more drinks.

"So, you bailed on me last night and now you want to have dinner?" she said.

"I didn't bail. I just didn't leave with you. And it's because I didn't tell you the truth."

She glanced at his ring finger.

"No, I'm not married," he said.

"What, then?"

"I'm a filmmaker. I'm making a documentary about Rory Kincaid," he said.

Stephanie slumped back in her seat. "I don't get it. Did you follow me here?"

He shook his head. "No. Seeing you here was a coincidence. But I did recognize you from my research."

"Why didn't you say something last night?"

"I hadn't spoken to your sister yet, and I didn't want her to hear about this first from you."

Her eyes widened. "You talked to Lauren?"

"Barely. She doesn't want to participate in the film."

"What a shock," Stephanie said sarcastically. "I could have told you that last night and saved you the time."

"Well, I learned my lesson. And clearly, you're the one I should be talking to."

"Oh yeah? Why's that?" she said.

"Well, you knew him too. You were classmates. Then he was your brother-in-law. You have insight, and your perspective is probably more objective than Lauren's. Less emotional." He watched her closely to gauge if she was buying the ego stroking.

"Of course I knew him," she said. "Lauren acted like she owned him— owned what happened. But it affected all of us."

"I understand. It was a loss for the entire family. Would you be willing to speak on camera?"

She smiled. "Sure. Sounds like fun. What do you want to know—how Rory was such a great hero?"

"I don't want to get into specifics now. Let's save that for the shoot."

Stephanie downed her drink, leaned closer to him, and said, "I'll do your interview. But you might not like what I have to say."

Chapter Twelve

It had been a long time since Lauren had dreamed about Rory. In the beginning, it was every night. She'd wake up with a start in darkness and realize with crushing fresh awareness that he was gone. Now, thanks to that damn filmmaker, it had happened last night.

She'd been running in her dream. Running, the way she'd been when she first saw Rory. Now, in the near dawn, jogging in the salty air of reality, she couldn't remember the dream itself. But she could remember, like it was yesterday, how she'd felt that day.

It had been her sophomore year of high school, early-fall track-team practice on Arnold Field. She was losing interest in the sport. Her true passion at that point was writing—specifically, journalism. Lower Merion's student newspaper, the *Merionite,* was an elective you could take starting in tenth grade. It was a unique class, overseen by an English teacher but run day to day by seniors who had been writing for the newspaper for the past two years and were now the editors. She wanted to be one of those editors one day so badly!

She ran her warm-up mile around the track, trying not to worry about whether she'd chosen the right article to send in with her application to the *Merionite*. She'd submitted a piece that had been published in the middle-school paper about the problem of the school running late into June because of snow days. She'd also included an essay about how her interest in journalism had started after reading Katharine Graham's Pulitzer Prize–winning memoir *Personal History*.

During her second lap, she noticed the boys' ice hockey team running drills nearby. One player stood out. He was over six feet tall, with broad shoulders and dark hair.

Each turn around the track, just past the bleachers, she looked for him, scanning the group. In the final stretch, the hockey team's drill brought him to the edge of the track. He bent down to lace his sneaker just as she was rounding the bend. She looked at him, and he happened to glance up at that moment, and it was instant eye-lock. Beneath dark brows, his eyes were so brown they were nearly black and they shone with an intensity that made her lose what little breath she had.

It might never have been more than that—a shared glance, Lauren thinking about him for a few days after. Hoping to see him in the halls, feeling like the Molly Ringwald character in a John Hughes movie.

And then she got accepted to the *Merionite*.

Beth surveyed the attic, overwhelmed by five decades' worth of junk. She'd failed to sort through it after her mother died eight years earlier, and now her avoidance had boomeranged back. The idea of clearing out the space completely by the end of the summer seemed impossible.

"What is all this stuff?" Ethan asked, sitting on a box.

"Careful, hon. I don't know what's in there. Could be fragile. Here, come stand next to Gran and help me organize. Let's get all of these boxes into three sections: stuff to throw away, stuff to give away, and stuff to keep."

He jumped off the box and scurried next to her. Truly, he was adorable.

It amazed her how boy energy was so different from girl energy. After raising two daughters, she loved having a grandson.

"How do you know what to throw out?" he asked.

"That's a good question, and that's where you come in. I'm going to open all of the boxes—don't touch this, it's very sharp," she said, holding up the straight-edged razor, "and we're going to check what's inside. Then I'll figure it out."

"You're going to open all of them?" His big eyes widened.

She nodded. Fortunately, most were labeled. But it was times like these that she wished she had a sibling to share the load. Her girls were so lucky that they had each other, and they failed to appreciate that. For the life of her, she couldn't understand why or how their relationship had gone off the rails. Her husband criticized her for letting Stephanie get away with so much, but on this issue she did not give her older daughter a free pass; the problems between the girls seemed to begin with Stephanie.

Beth sighed, bending to read the faded ink on the side of a box. She was surprised to find her own handwriting. She herself had contributed to this mess? *Beth/baking/job,* she read.

So that's where they were! After turning the Philly house upside down, after literally crying because she'd thought her old baking supplies had gotten lost or thrown away. She sliced through the tape, pulling aside the wings of the box.

"Wait, Grandma, let me help," Ethan said, reaching for the tail of the severed tape. "What is this stuff?"

He pulled out a cake-decorating turntable.

"I used to bake a lot for my job. We did big, fancy parties. That's for icing a cake."

Ethan peered into the box—the pyramid-tiered cake stands, icing gun, and cutting wheel—with obvious delight.

"You made cakes with this stuff?"

She nodded and dug deeper into the box, then squealed with joy when her fingers felt the corners of a book.

"Oh, Ethan—I'll be able to show you. This is an album I kept of all the beautiful affairs I worked on. Weddings and graduations and baby showers. Wait until you see some of these desserts."

"There you are!" Stephanie called from the attic doorway. She looked too dressed up for a day at the beach in her tight white jeans and turquoise tunic.

Stephanie stepped over a box and stalked over to them. "What are you doing with him in this dusty attic? It's gorgeous outside."

Beth felt like snapping, *Well, someone has to pay attention to your son.* Instead, she replied calmly, "Ethan's helping me with a little project. Right, Ethan?"

He grinned. God, she could eat him up.

"Okay, well, Dad sent me to get you. He's ready to go."

Beth had almost forgotten they had to drive back to Philly for the afternoon. Unpleasant legal loose ends, papers needed signing. Everywhere she turned, disarray.

"Your father really could do this without me."

"No, you should go," Stephanie said urgently. Beth had a flashback to Stephanie as a teenager rushing them out the door so she could have the house free for a forbidden party. Fortunately, there was hardly any more trouble Stephanie could get into.

"Relax, I'm going," Beth said. "Hon, take him to the beach. It *is* beautiful out. Do something nice today."

"Don't worry about us, Mom," said Stephanie. "I've got it covered."

Matt pulled into the sleepy cul-de-sac just before noon, the sound of the ocean greeting him through the open car windows. He'd been surprised when Stephanie suggested they shoot at her house but didn't hesitate to say yes.

His DP and sound guy parked directly behind him.

"Not too shabby," said Paul Garrett, his soundman, a native of Cherry Hill, New Jersey, who'd been recommended to Matt by a tech on *The Disappearing Sea*.

It was a beautiful house, as nice as any of the homes Matt had visited in East Hampton over the years. He'd always had an idea that the Jersey Shore was on a lower rung of the summer-home ladder than the New York beach towns. Maybe it was less desirable geographically, but there was an undeniable charm to Absecon Island.

"Let's do it," Matt said, leading the way up the front walk. He pointed to a faded sign: THE GREEN GABLE. "Get a shot of that," he said to his camera guy, a local named Derek.

Stephanie greeted them at the front door. Matt noted her bright blue shirt, thinking it would read well on camera.

"Hey, you guys. Come on in. I thought maybe we could talk in the kitchen?"

Matt and his small crew followed her into a spacious, sun-filled room that wouldn't work for filming—too much natural light.

"Would you mind showing us around so we can choose the optimal spot?" Matt said. "We have to factor in a lot of things for shooting."

They moved on to the living room. The space had a casual elegance with a few eclectic design touches. He admired a stack of vintage suitcases.

Matt looked to Derek, who held out his phone. He had an app that let him test the light and also calculate when it would shift.

"If we close that shade and move the couch, maybe set the bookshelf behind her? This could work," said Derek.

"Do you mind if they move a few things around?" Matt asked, fully aware that "move a few things around" was a huge understatement. The next time Stephanie saw the space, half the furniture would be pushed to one side, the room would be filled with wires running everywhere, and whatever wasn't pushed out of the frame would be arranged in a completely different way.

He followed her back to the kitchen, resisting the urge to make conversation; one of the early lessons he'd learned in subject interviews was to talk as little as possible before the camera and audio were on. On his first film he'd gotten the best quote from a subject before the camera was running and then couldn't get the guy to repeat it.

Stephanie began talking about the house, how it had been her grandparents' and they'd spent summers there growing up.

"Before we get started, I need you to sign a release." He sat across from her on a chair upholstered in pale linen and passed her the single sheet of paper.

Stephanie looked at him suspiciously. "Shouldn't I have a lawyer look at this or something?"

"You can. But it's very straightforward. It grants me the irrevocable right to use whatever we film in whatever way I see fit to make and market the film you've agreed to be interviewed for."

"I have no idea what you just said." She smiled flirtatiously.

"This is the deal: You don't have to answer any questions you don't want to, and you don't have to say anything you don't want to. But once you've spoken on camera, the material becomes, essentially, property of the film company."

She looked at him, not quite with a raised eyebrow but with an expression that was certainly in the spirit of a raised eyebrow. Then, leaning forward, she tucked a lock of hair behind her ear and signed the paper. Then she glanced up at him as if she had accepted a dare.

"This will be fun," she said. "I'll get the coffee started."

He turned his phone off and shoved it in his pocket. Stephanie told him over her shoulder, "My sister would have a fit if she knew I was doing this."

Matt had already thought the same thing. It was a delicate situation. He wanted to spur Lauren into participating, not send her over the edge.

"You said she was out of the house today."

"Yeah, she's always working. Or running like a maniac."

"She runs a lot?"

"Every morning at the crack of dawn. Before dawn. All the way to the casinos and back. Totally psycho."

Stephanie's son walked into the room. Matt recognized him from her Facebook page. A good-looking kid. He clutched a soccer ball.

"Ethan! I told you to stay upstairs until I got you."

"Can I use the computer?" He dropped the ball, dribbled it for a few steps. Matt watched him. Something about the footwork triggered the idea that this kid might make for good B-roll: innocent boy, the early love of sports.

"Yes, yes," Stephanie said, exasperated. "I said that you could have computer time."

The kid fixed his dark eyes on Matt.

"Hello there," Matt said.

Ethan kicked the ball into the other room and ran after it.

"Would you mind if I filmed him for a few minutes? Later, after we're done?" he said.

Stephanie visibly stiffened. "Why would you want to interview my son?"

"No, not interview, just film him kicking the ball around. Sometimes things like a shot of scenery or a kid make good footage to juxtapose against interviews."

She shrugged. "I guess."

"Matt." His DP peeked in. "I want to get her situated in the room to check the light."

"Showtime," Matt said to Stephanie with a wink.

They followed Derek back into the living room. Stephanie gasped.

"Oh my God, you moved this whole room around. My mother will have a stroke."

"Don't worry, we'll put everything back the way it was." Derek showed her a photo he'd taken of how the room had looked before they'd made it shootable.

Placated, Stephanie followed Matt's direction to sit on the bone-colored couch next to a wood coffee table stacked with oversize, glossy books about architecture, great American gardens, and the jewelry collection of Elizabeth Taylor. A tall silver vase had been filled with fresh lavender.

Paul slipped the mic wire down the front of her shirt and hooked the sound pack to the back of her jeans. Matt sat directly across from her. Derek made a last-minute change to the camera, moving it a few inches just above Matt's left shoulder.

"You ready to get started?" Matt asked Stephanie.

"I'm ready."

"Are we rolling?" he asked.

"Rolling," Derek said.

"Action," Matt said. He faced Stephanie. "I want to thank you for participating in this film. I really believe Rory's story is worth telling. And I couldn't do it without the help of the people who knew him best."

She nodded, looking nervous for the first time.

"When I ask you a question, I need you to respond by repeating part of it. So if I say, 'What is your name?' you say, 'My name is Stephanie Adelman.' All of my questions will be edited out, so for this to make sense you need to repeat part of what I ask."

If he got a rambling answer, he would ask her to repeat the one sentence that was usable. Years of sitting in front of screens in editing suites had taught him which answers were usable and which were not. Too much padding or repetition, and no matter how important the idea being expressed, he had to cut it.

He asked Stephanie for her name, and she told him about how her name was technically Stephanie Keller now, but she was getting divorced and going back to Adelman, so should she use…

"Whatever you're comfortable with," Matt said.

"My name is Stephanie Adelman."

"And how did you know Rory?"

"High school," she said.

"Can you include my question in your answer?"

"Oh—right. Sorry. I knew Rory from high school. We were in the same year."

"Do you remember when you first met?"

"God, it was so long ago. It's like I always knew him."

"Did you meet him when he started dating your sister?"

"No! Is that what she told you? Typical. I knew Rory first. She got to Rory through me."

Matt refrained from reminding her that he hadn't interviewed Lauren. "How did she get to Rory through you?"

"Rory was in my group of friends. I mean, I don't want to brag or whatever but he and I were juniors. We were popular. Lauren was a year younger. A nobody." Matt glanced at the row of silver-framed photos on the fireplace mantel.

"Is that you up there? Were you a cheerleader?"

Stephanie smiled. "Yep. I was a cheerleader. Starting sophomore year. I was squad captain by senior year."

"Did the squad cheer at hockey games?"

She shook her head. "Just football and basketball."

"Did you go to hockey games?"

"Sometimes. Hockey wasn't the big sport at LM. It was more soccer and football."

"So Lauren met Rory through you?"

"She was writing some article for the stupid paper. The school paper. And she was like, Oh, I need to interview Rory. Can you give me his number? Like, she had zero interest in sports and suddenly she's Bob Costas."

"How well did you know Rory prior to him dating your sister?"

Stephanie paused. "I mean, we hung out. Went to the same parties. I went out with some of his friends."

"Did Rory party a lot? Drink, smoke, that sort of thing?"

She shook her head. "Didn't drink, didn't get high."

"Can you include the question in your answer?"

"Oh—sorry. Rory didn't drink or do drugs. Anyone else would have been considered totally lame, but he could get away with anything. Not only did people not give him shit for not drinking, but some of his friends didn't do drugs when he was around because they didn't want him to think less of them."

Matt decided to abruptly switch direction, a tactic he used sometimes in interviews to get a more honest, spontaneous response from a subject.

"Do you know why your sister doesn't want to talk to me?"

Stephanie hesitated for just a beat before saying, "It's not personal. She doesn't want to talk to anyone. Maybe she thinks she's protecting his memory or something."

"Protecting his memory from what?"

"I don't know. Negative stuff."

"Is there something negative to say about Rory? Because I can tell you that I've spent years talking to people about him, and no one has ever said anything negative."

A strange expression crossed her face. "I guess you're talking to the wrong people, then."

"Do you have something negative to say about Rory Kincaid?"

Stephanie lowered her gaze. He was disciplined enough not to push.

"No," she said finally. "But what do I know? Except that no one's perfect, right? I mean, Lauren always worshipped him and now the whole world does."

"Stephanie, I want to see Rory Kincaid for who he really was. I'm just trying to tell the truth."

Stephanie narrowed her eyes. "I don't know if that's going to help you where my sister is concerned."

"Why not?"

"Because not everyone wants the truth. Some people see only what they *want* to see."

Chapter Thirteen

The sun started to set. Lauren could feel the breeze off of the ocean through the open kitchen window. Outside, her parents and sister were sitting at the table by the pool. Her mother had insisted on dinner together. Lauren agreed it was a good idea. After Ethan's innocent but nonetheless provocative question—"Do you like my mom?"—she was determined to hit the reset button on her sisterly relationship.

Lauren grabbed the box of leftover muffins and doughnuts from the restaurant and brought them outside to the table littered with crumpled takeout wrappers from Sack O' Subs, her father's and sister's empty beer bottles, and stray kernels of corn from her mother's tomato and corn salad.

Her mother picked up a doughnut. "Does Nora have someone baking on the premises? These don't seem very fresh."

"She gets a delivery every day," Lauren said, slipping back into her chair. "The muffins are great. People buy them in bulk all year round."

Beth sniffed. She was a pastry snob. But Ethan's eyes lit up.

Her father stood and began clearing dishes.

"Wait. Before you go, Dad, there's something I wanted to mention to all of you." She didn't know if she should bring it up, had been debating doing so all dinner. But she couldn't shake the feeling that the filmmaker showing up at Nora's house hadn't been a coincidence. And even if it had, he was getting too close for comfort. All day she had braced herself for him to appear at the restaurant. He didn't.

Still, not wanting a false sense of security, she texted Henny and asked if her renter had left yet. He's here for the week, she wrote back. Why? Do you know someone else who wants the room? Give them my number.

If Lauren wasn't talking to him, what was he doing in town all week?

"So, um, this annoying thing happened at work the other day and I just wanted to tell you guys so we're all on the same page." Her mother and sister looked at her expectantly. "It's not that big of a deal but this guy tracked me down at work and said he's doing a documentary. About Rory. Obviously, I told him to leave me alone, and hopefully that's the end of that. I doubt he'd approach any of you but if he does, I just want you to be prepared."

Her mother looked horrified. "Oh, Lauren. How intrusive!"

"Everyone's out to make a buck," said her father.

"Prepared for what?" Stephanie said.

Lauren looked at her. "To tell him to leave you alone—that you're not talking to him."

"Why is it your business if I talk to him?"

"Why would you *want* to talk to him?"

"I just wonder why you think you get to dictate who we talk to. We knew Rory too, you know."

Lauren's heart began to pound. "This has nothing to do with you, Stephanie, and you know it. So just stay out of it."

"If someone wants to talk to me, then clearly they think it does have to do with me. You don't *own* what happened, Lauren."

"Fine, you knew Rory too. So you know the last thing he would want is some exploitative film about him."

"Girls, please," Beth said. "This is not worth arguing over. Lauren, of course you're right. The last thing you need is someone dredging all of that up again. Stephanie, you have to respect your sister's wishes on this."

"Well, it's too late for that," Stephanie said, looking pleased with herself. "I already spoke to him."

Lauren stared at her, dumbfounded. "No, you didn't."

"Yeah. I did."

"You better not be serious, Stephanie."

"Ethan, buddy, come with me to see if there's any ice cream in the freezer," Howard said.

"I am serious."

"You've really crossed a line this time!" Lauren turned to her mother. "I'm sorry, but she has to go. I can't live with her all summer."

She pushed herself up from her chair so hard it toppled to the ground.

Howard made it so damn hard for her to admit when she was wrong.

He didn't say anything while they put away the dinner plates, but his silence spoke loud and clear to Beth. *This was a big mistake.*

Fine. Maybe she was naive to think a summer under the same roof would magically make the girls best friends again. Maybe she shouldn't have insisted Stephanie move into the Green Gable and then insist to Howard that they do the same. But the reality was that they wouldn't have had to move at all if Howard hadn't lost their home. She'd spent decades working beside him in that store, the last few years strategizing with him on how to keep things afloat. And yet he never thought to mention he'd taken out a second mortgage.

That was the thanks she got for giving up her dream of having her own catering company to join him in his family business. To stand by his side like a good wife.

"I bought tickets to Florida for next week," he said suddenly.

"What? Why on earth would you do that?" Beth, stacking dishes in the cabinet, stopped mid-reach. She set the plates down on the counter.

"Bill and Lorraine invited us. They're having a retirement party. Bill just bought a boat." Bill and Lorraine were friends from the country club they used to belong to. Howard and Beth had dropped out of the club a few years earlier. Money had become tighter, and Beth stopped enjoying the annual cycle of social events after losing Rory. She had suddenly become high profile, exposed. It was a fraction of what her daughter experienced but enough to take away her pleasure in large gatherings. Bill and Lorraine had also left the club, trading their house in Villanova for a home on a golf course in Frenchman's Creek, Florida.

"Why didn't you talk to me about it first?" There was no way she was flying off to Florida. She didn't want to travel, and she certainly didn't want to go put on a happy face when everything was falling apart. "This isn't a good time. We have so much to figure out."

"I know. But now I'm thinking Florida might be worth looking into."

"Looking into? In what sense?"

"We'd get more for our money out there. And there's no income tax."

"Well, we have no income. So that's not a huge plus."

"Can you try to be positive for once?"

"Howard, no. I'm not moving to Florida."

"You can't even be open to the idea? Give me one good reason why not."

"For one thing, I have work. The foundation—"

"Let Lauren get more involved! She needs to get off this damn island. If you stop enabling her, maybe she will."

She shook her head. "You just get to make all the decisions, don't you?"

"Do you have a better idea?"

"Maybe I would have if you'd leveled with me sooner! And what about Ethan?"

"What about him?" Howard said blankly.

"Don't you want to spend time with your grandson?"

"Of course I do. But Beth, you and I have to rebuild. And Stephanie's going to have to step up. And you know what? Lauren has to get on with her life. Even if we weren't selling the house, she should be looking for an apartment. It's outrageous to heat this place all winter for one person."

"You're so hard on them," she said, feeling heartbroken. "You're not perfect either, you know."

"Never said I was. But I did say, from day one, that Lauren was too young to get serious with that boy. Didn't I? She was so bright, had so much going for her. Now look at her."

"She's going to be fine," Beth said, a whisper.

Howard shut the dishwasher, pressed the buttons so the room filled with the hum of the machine.

"I'm leaving next Thursday. Flight's at noon out of Philly," he said, tossing the sponge behind the sink. "I hope you'll be with me. But I'm going either way."

Matt didn't feel like he had a ton of reasons to pat himself on the back lately, but getting the footage of that kid was a stroke of genius.

He barely noticed that the room had fallen dark as the sun set, the only light coming from his screen. Again, he played the clip of Ethan kicking the soccer ball around the beach, the sun-dappled ocean behind him, seagulls fluttering nearby like birds in a goddamn Disney film. Of course, it would have been a thousand times better if he'd been able to get footage of Rory playing ball as a kid, but he'd lost that opportunity when Mrs. Kincaid died shortly after he interviewed her. She'd kept promising to send him some childhood photos and video clips, but it never happened. At least now he could use this kid as juxtaposition. It wasn't perfect, but it was a good enough work-around.

He jumped to footage of Rory's high-school athletic field: General

H. H. Arnold Field, named after aviation pioneer Henry Harley "Hap" Arnold, the only officer to hold a five-star rank in two different U.S. military services.

Matt couldn't have scripted it better.

ENTER TO LEARN, GO FORTH TO SERVE. Matt had filmed the words carved into the entrance to Lower Merion High School the day he interviewed Rory's coach and he'd looked at the footage again and again since then, the coach's haunting question now his own: *How many thousands upon thousands of kids have walked through the doors of this school over the years, and how many have actually taken that motto to heart?*

He switched back to the clip of Ethan. A pounding on the door startled him. He blinked in the darkness.

"Matt, open up. Henny told me you're in there."

He stood from his desk chair and walked slowly to the door. The external door, an add-on to the original house, didn't have a peephole.

Knock, knock, knock.

"Okay, calm down." He swung open the door to find a sweaty and disheveled Lauren Kincaid. She wore a Nora's Café T-shirt, running shorts, and sneakers. Her hair was loose, damp tendrils clinging to the side of her face. Her cheeks were flushed.

She marched into the room and closed the door behind her.

"Can you turn a light on?" she said.

He was already reaching for the switch. When he turned back, he found her standing with her arms crossed peering at his computer screen.

"Can I help you with something?" he asked. The screen was paused on a shot of the beach. Ethan wasn't in the frame.

"You have some nerve. I tell you I don't want to do your movie and so you start harassing my family?"

"In my defense, I didn't harass your sister. I ran into her by chance at a bar and when I told her what I was doing in town, she was game for an interview."

Lauren leaned back against the desk, facing him. "I don't know how people like you sleep at night."

"I'm not doing anything wrong, that's how. Honestly, Lauren, I've gone into this project with the best of intentions. I admired your late husband. I want to pay tribute to him."

"Mm-hmm. And who does that benefit? Not Rory. You. It benefits you."

"This film will benefit a hell of a lot more people than it will me."

"I highly doubt that."

"Of course you do. Because that justifies you stonewalling me."

Her mouth dropped open. "And, what, you think my sister has some pearls of wisdom for the greater social good?"

"Hey, she wasn't my first choice. But you said no. I'm doing the best I can here."

Lauren seemed to consider this. He waited for her to take the bait. It was difficult not to smile when she finally asked, "What did Stephanie say?"

Chapter Fourteen

Lauren instantly hated herself for asking the question. She wanted to know what her sister had said on camera, and at the same time, she didn't.

She hugged herself, watching over Matt's shoulder as he clicked through still images just slightly larger than thumbnail size, all of them numbered.

Wait, was that her living room?

"You were in my house?" she said.

Stephanie filled the screen. She wore white jeans and a turquoise tunic; her hair was loose and gold under the light, her deep blue eyes arresting and steady as she gazed at someone off camera. Then, Matt's prompt: "So Lauren met Rory through you?"

"She was writing some article for the stupid paper," Stephanie said. "The school paper. And she was like, Oh, I need to interview Rory. Can you give me his number? Like, she had zero interest in sports and suddenly she's Bob Costas."

Lauren tensed, waiting for Stephanie to make it all about herself, as she always did. As she certainly could have when Matt asked, "How well did you know Rory prior to him dating your sister?"

Lauren felt Matt watching her, and she struggled to maintain a poker face. Had he noticed Stephanie's split second of hesitation before answering the question? Because Lauren saw it. She followed it with a sharp intake of her own breath, not exhaling until Stephanie spoke. "I mean, we hung out. Went to the same parties. I went out with some of his friends."

So she did have some sense of decency. It wasn't that Lauren wanted Stephanie to lie, but why make something insignificant into a tawdry sound bite? For once, her sister had showed some class and restraint.

Really, it wasn't a big deal. Lauren hadn't thought about the night of the party for years now.

It had been early fall in her sophomore year of high school, a few weeks after Lauren first spotted Rory at practice. After the day at track, she'd seen him only one more time. Her second sighting happened during sixth period, when the halls were empty. She'd left the newspaper classroom to pick up a USB drive from the science room and passed him. They were the only two people in the hallway, and it was as if there were a magnetic field around him. Her heart pounded so hard she was afraid she would faint. Again, they made intense eye contact. But neither said a word.

She felt a high that lasted for hours.

Two weeks before Thanksgiving break, her parents went to New York for a wedding. They warned Stephanie: "No parties."

"I know!" Stephanie said.

By seven that night, a Friday, their house was wall-to-wall people. It was surreal for Lauren to see upperclassmen she recognized from the hallways suddenly in her living room, sitting paired off on the stairs, drinking from a keg in her dining room. She drifted among the crowd, practically invisible, a stranger in her own house.

When she got tired of trying to find someone to talk to, when she lost track even of Stephanie, she retreated upstairs. At the second-floor landing, she heard Stephanie's bedroom door click open.

"Steph?" she called out. But it wasn't Stephanie.

It was the hockey player.

Seeing those dark eyes flash at her just feet from her own bedroom was the shock of her life. The only thing saving her from a complete freak-out was the realization that he was surprised to see her too.

"I'm looking for my sister," she said.

"Stephanie?"

Lauren nodded.

"She's in there."

With that, he brushed past her, went down the stairs. It took a minute for her to breathe normally again. It also took that time to process the fact that the boy she had been obsessing over for a month had just walked out of her sister's bedroom. *Maybe they're just friends,* she told herself, inching toward Steph's room.

She knocked softly on the door.

"Party's downstairs," Stephanie called out.

"It's me."

Silence. The door opened a crack. Stephanie was wearing cutoff jean shorts and a tank top. She was braless, her breasts barely concealed by the thin fabric. Barefoot, she smoked a cigarette.

"What's going on?" Stephanie asked. Her eyeliner was smudged.

"I'm going to bed," Lauren said.

"With who?" A wicked little smile.

"Ha-ha. Very funny," Lauren said.

"Yeah. Okay, whatever. See you in the morning."

"Wait—Steph?"

"Yeah?"

"Who was that guy I just saw leaving here?"

"Oh. That's Rory Kincaid. Hottie, right?"

Lauren nodded. "Are you... dating him?"

"Dating him? It's not 1985. Go to sleep, Laur."

The next time Lauren spotted Rory Kincaid in the hallway, she averted her eyes. Stephanie didn't mention him again the rest of the year. But then came the article.

Every week, the fledgling reporters for the school paper submitted their pieces. Some were assigned, some were spec. Senior editors put the paper together on Thursday evenings, and the writers didn't know until Friday if their articles made the final cut. But the kids who'd been around long enough knew that their chances for getting published were higher if they wrote something for the favored pages.

The editor in chief of the *Merionite* was a lanky, pale-faced guy named Aaron Rettger. His personal pet was the op-ed page, and he also paid close attention to the front page, the news section. The bastard stepchild of the paper was the sports section. According to Aaron, it was a waste of ink: "Anyone who gives a shit about sports goes to the games. They don't even read the *Merionite*." Lauren suspected his stance on the sports articles was based less on his instincts about their readership and more on his own bitterness over never having made a sports team in his life. In issues when they were tight on space, the sports articles were the first to be cut.

This made Lauren's assignment to profile the LM hockey team, currently first in the division and headed to the state finals, a challenge. The dreaded sports assignment had little chance of being published. Still, Lauren was determined.

She strategized the piece; hopefully, there would be a game that week that she could go to. And she would schedule interviews with the coach and a few key players. She started with the facts: The Lower Merion Aces were in the western division of the Inter County Scholastic Hockey League, the ICSHL. That year, the highest scorer in the entire ICSHL was Lower Merion's team captain, Rory Kincaid.

The first challenge of her journalism education would be getting up the nerve to talk to him. And then she remembered the Katharine Graham memoir and some advice Graham's mother had given her: "Be a newspaperwoman, Kay, if only for the excuse it gives you to seek out at once the object of any sudden passion."

In Matt's room, Lauren refocused on the computer screen. His interview with Stephanie concluded with a few innocuous questions.

"What do you think?" he said to Lauren.

"I think that you're wasting your time here. I mean, aside from Stephanie's stunning revelations about the social strata of Lower Merion High School."

He smiled. "Maybe you'd have something to say about other interviews. You could look at them and correct any misinformation. I'm interested in your perspective on what other people have said. Despite your cynicism, I do want to get this right."

"You think this is about me being cynical? This was my *life,* Matt! I've worked really hard to find some sort of peace."

"I get that. And if it's any consolation, I'm hearing only good things about Rory. It's all positive. Even the stuff about him hiding his concussions is totally understandable—"

Lauren froze. "He never had concussions. Okay, he had *one* and he sat out a month. Everyone knows about that."

"That's not how his former teammate Dean Wade remembers it."

Lauren's hands clenched, her fingernails digging into her palm. "Well, it seems you've got some unreliable sources." How could Dean Wade have talked to him? And how could Dean's wife, Ashley, not have told her about it? Ashley was her friend; she was on the board of directors for the Polaris Foundation!

"So help me get it right," Matt said.

"Why should I do that?"

"You were a journalist. You must believe in the truth. At least, you must have at one time in your life."

Lauren couldn't think of a damn thing to say to that. All she could do was leave.

Beth lifted a box and felt a twinge in her lower back. She dropped the box and heard glass break.

"Darn it!" She stretched for a few seconds, making sure she hadn't done any real damage, then cut through the tape. Inside, she found shattered dishes. At least it wasn't good china.

"You okay up there?" Howard called from the bottom of the stairs.

"Fine," she said.

She heard the clop of his footsteps climbing up. The last thing she needed was him bothering her.

"Did you break something?" he asked from the top of the stairs.

"No," she said.

"Beth, don't make yourself crazy going through all of this junk. Just hire someone to take it to Goodwill. If no one's missed it in all these years, no one's ever going to miss it."

She looked at him incredulously. "I can't just toss this stuff away sight unseen. What if there's something important in here?"

He threw up his hands in irritation, and she realized the conversation over the boxes was similar to the one they were having about the girls. Whatever was inside the boxes hadn't been worth her attention in years and therefore never would be. Likewise, whatever was broken between the girls—between all of them as a family—had been broken for years and would stay broken. But Beth didn't agree on either count.

"Howard, it's fine. It gives me something constructive to do."

The argument between the girls at dinner was terribly upsetting. And where had Lauren run off to?

Howard sighed with disapproval and trekked back down the stairs.

She was so relieved to see him go, felt such a remarkable lifting of stress in his absence, that she realized it was a good thing he was taking a trip to

Florida. He would go, and she would stay, and the time apart would do them both good. She could deal with the girls without his judgment, and he could figure out their next move without the weight of her resentment about losing the house. Both houses.

Reenergized, she turned back to the rows of bags and boxes, the front half of them loosely organized into three sections: boxes that were clearly hers, boxes and knickknacks that had belonged to her parents, and unmarked boxes or random things she couldn't place. She stepped over a stack of full garment bags and made her way deeper into the room. In the space between boxes, she noticed a trail of tiny pellets. She groaned. Mice.

She moved on to another section, packing boxes labeled in Lauren's handwriting. Oh, good Lord. She kept things from her LA house up there? When Beth told her to put them in storage, this wasn't what she'd meant. She bent down, reading the Sharpie scrawl: *Rory/LM* and *Rory/ LA/Press Clips.*

Beth would have to take care of these boxes. She didn't even want to remind Lauren they were there. No need to reopen the wounds, although they already had been by that filmmaker hounding her. How dare he? What were people *thinking?* And Stephanie, going behind Lauren's back to talk to him. Nothing Stephanie did should have surprised Beth at that point, but she still had hope that Stephanie would turn things around—for herself, and for the rest of the family.

"Mom? What are you doing up here?"

Lauren! Why did she feel like a kid caught with her hand in the cookie jar? "Oh, honey. I'm glad you're home. Where did you go?"

Lauren, her face red and her hairline wet with perspiration, walked closer to her. Why hadn't she just taken the car? This obsessive running everywhere had to stop.

"Why are you going through these boxes?" Lauren said.

"Because I have to clear out the house, hon."

Lauren looked panicked. "There must be some other way—"

Beth hated to cause her any more distress. It had been difficult to let her hide out at the beach for the past four years. But it was what Lauren wanted, and if Beth couldn't change what had been lost, at least she could give her the sanctuary of the Green Gable. And now she had to take that away too. She felt a fresh wave of fury toward Howard. Why hadn't her husband talked to her? How could he have gambled with the house behind her back? It was a betrayal—almost as much a betrayal as a sexual infidelity.

"I'm sorry, hon. There's nothing I can do."

"I have personal things up here," Lauren said, her face reddening even more with emotion. She wasn't going to cry—Lauren rarely cried. But she was close.

Beth nodded. "I just saw the boxes. If you want, I can put them in—"

"No!" Lauren said. "Don't touch them. I'll deal with it."

Beth sighed as her daughter retreated back down the stairs.

Chapter Fifteen

Matt unpacked his new running sneakers. At a quarter to five in the morning, it was still dark outside.

Desperate times call for desperate measures, he thought grimly. And then: *This is going to hurt.* He got winded walking up the stairs to the editing suite back in Brooklyn. He hadn't slept last night. How was he going to jog miles on the boardwalk in hopes of "casually" bumping into Lauren?

It was a far cry from the days when he was running around tsunami-ravaged Southeast Asia, armed with only a camera. Back then, he didn't need sleep, didn't need food. Those weeks and months following his brother's death, he was fueled by pure adrenaline and a youthful, reckless fury.

The tsunami hit the day after his brother's death. Matt, reeling from his grief, felt the pull of something larger than his personal tragedy. He had to do something. So he got on a plane to Sri Lanka.

Thailand had been a landscape of utter devastation. His photos captured as much as the camera could capture, and ultimately that was never enough. Across the region, two hundred thousand people had been killed. So many dead—almost enough to make him forget his own loss. Almost.

Those photos started his career in journalism.

Surely he could run a few miles to convince a widow to talk to him. Her reticence was nothing compared to his resolve.

Sunrise caught Lauren by surprise; her precious darkness was slipping away faster day by day. She would have to start getting up earlier. Today, she dragged herself through the run, first sluggish, now fighting light-headedness.

Ride it like a wave, she told herself. If it got really bad, she had a protein bar in her pocket. But it always felt like a defeat to stop. No, she wouldn't be sidelined by her body's weakness. It was bad enough that she constantly had to fight her mind.

In her dreams last night, it was that sophomore-year party all over again. Except instead of looking upstairs for Stephanie, she was searching room to room for Rory, her panic mounting with each closed door. She woke up, heart pounding, at three in the morning and never fell back asleep.

Push through! She moved faster, her chest heavy with each intake of oxygen. A low-flying seagull swooshed past her. She loved the birds, envied the birds. Her legs were slow, but her thoughts raced with the questions from Matt's interview with Stephanie.

Lauren remembered the days when she had been the one asking questions. God, she hadn't thought about that *Merionite* article in so long. She'd spent so much time trying to forget the ending that she never let herself remember the beginning.

She'd enlisted Stephanie's help.

"I don't get it. You're writing an article about him?" Stephanie, sitting cross-legged on her bed, barely glanced up from her phone. Just a few months earlier, Lauren had met Rory in the dark hallway outside that very bedroom. She shook the thought away.

"No! Not about him. It's about the hockey team. But he's the highest scorer. I have to get a quote from him."

Stephanie sighed dramatically and tapped her phone before handing it over.

"That's his number. But don't expect too much. He's kind of an arrogant asshole."

Maybe so. But as she sat in the school library waiting for him to show up for the interview, her body hummed with anticipation. She had typed up her questions and printed them out, and now she unfolded the paper on the library table. She reread the list for the umpteenth time.

"Preparation. I like that," a voice said behind her. She jumped and covered the questions with her hand, feeling kind of busted, though in what sense, she wasn't exactly sure.

"Hi. I'm Lauren," she said, standing and almost knocking over the chair.

"I know," he said.

He pulled out a chair, sat next to her. She felt dwarfed by his size. She pulled the questions onto her lap.

"Okay, so like I said, I was assigned to write an article about the hockey team."

"You like hockey?"

She nodded.

"Have you ever been to see one of the games?"

"Um, no."

"I thought you just said you like hockey."

"I do. I watch the Flyers. Do you mind if I tape this?" She positioned her mini–cassette recorder between them.

"Very professional."

Was he teasing her? No. His expression was serious.

"So who's your favorite player?" he asked.

"On your team?"

"No. The Flyers."

She thought quickly. "Éric Desjardins."

He narrowed his eyes. "Not a bad choice, though I'd have to go with Primeau."

Lauren nodded. She needed to get control of this conversation. "Okay, well—we should get started because I know you don't have much time."

"What do you think their playoff chances are this year?"

She looked at him, his dark eyes and square jaw. Something deep inside of her twitched.

"They'll make the playoffs," she said. "I just don't know if they can go all the way."

He smiled. "I'm with you on that."

She felt her heart might stop.

Focus.

"So what do you think is making your team successful this year?"

"Well, we haven't succeeded yet."

The comment threw her for a second. She recovered with "But you're leading the division."

"We are. Today. But success is winning the league championship, and real success is states."

"Okay. So I'll ask you what you asked me about the Flyers: What do you think of your chances?"

"Cutler's been strong in net. Everyone's working really hard. I think if we're focused, we can do it."

She checked the recorder, praying it was working. She glanced at her notes and said, "You have the most goals and most assists in the western division. You have to see that as some kind of success."

"Doing your job isn't success. It's doing your job. Right? I mean, you're going to write this article and it will run in the paper, but is that success?"

"It feels like success to me," she said.

"All right, well. Maybe it's different for writers." He looked at her hard. "You sure you're Stephanie's sister?"

"What's that supposed to mean?"

"You just seem so much more serious."

"I'm not that serious," she said defensively.

"Don't get me wrong," he said. "I'm all for serious. If you're not going to do something with intensity—with intent—why do it at all?"

His eyes met hers. She forgot her next question.

"We're playing Radnor Friday night. You should come," he said.

She nodded. "Yeah, I was planning to go to a game before I finished the article."

"This will be a good one. We're going to win."

"That's confident of you."

He smiled. "I think when you want something badly enough, you make it happen."

They won the game. Rory had a hat trick that night. Back then, Lauren had believed what he said, that personal will was strong enough to make something happen, to direct fate.

She wondered how long he himself had continued to believe it.

Chapter Sixteen

Matt's strategy was to run in circles on the boardwalk within the boundaries of Margate. He knew Lauren had to cross through Margate to get back to Longport, so unless he'd already missed her, it was inevitable they would cross paths. Stephanie told him Lauren usually got home around six in the morning, and if it was an hour-and-a-half round-trip run, she should be hitting Margate by a quarter of six.

Pathetically winded, he had slowed to a trot by the time he spotted her in the distance, her brown ponytail waving. He had the luxury of watching her for a few seconds, noting she had, truly, an incredible quiet beauty. She would look great on camera. And then she was in shouting distance.

"Lauren, hey—wait up," he called, picking up speed to keep up with her. Praying he could summon some unknown reserve of stamina.

She did a double take, then ignored him. Undaunted by her lack of welcome, he ran up beside her.

"What a surprise," he said.

"Give me a break."

"What? I've been totally out of my running routine since coming here. And I usually run with a partner, so this is great luck."

She glanced at his feet. "Your sneakers look like they've never seen the light of day."

Busted! He glanced at hers, and the thing was, they seemed pretty new. "So do yours."

This seemed to take her aback. "I have to replace mine every few weeks. I run twelve miles a day," she said.

"Me too! Gets expensive, right?"

"Go away, Matt. I want to be alone."

He matched her pace, breathing too heavy to talk. She glanced at him and increased her speed. By the time they reached Longport, his heart was pounding so hard, he was certain it was going to give out. He dropped to the ground and looked up at the sky. The light suddenly dimmed, and he thought, *This is it. Going out in a blaze of physical and professional failure.*

"Are you messing around or are you having a heart attack? You better tell me now before I call an ambulance."

Lauren loomed over him, blocking the sun.

"I am not messing around, but ... I'm not having a heart attack. Just an acute case of humiliation."

"Are you dizzy?"

"I'm not sure. Is the sky full of dots, or is it just me?"

She knelt next to him. "You just overexerted yourself. You should be more careful. That's how men your age drop dead."

Men his age? How old did she think he was? "I'm thirty-four."

"Exactly."

Okay, this was more than his already bruised ego could take. He sat up—too fast. He sank back down. People walking by turned to look at him.

She crossed her arms. "I have things to do, but I feel like if I leave you and something happens, I'm being negligent or something."

"True. I still could have a heart attack. That might be manslaughter."

"You think this is funny?"

"Lauren, if you think I am amused by this, then you know absolutely nothing about male pride."

That silenced her. He felt his heart rate begin to normalize and he sat up. She shifted impatiently.

"Can I go now?" she said.

"I just want to say one more thing."

She sighed and looked around.

"Lauren, before I was a documentarian, I was a war photographer. I'm not a carpetbagger trying to make a buck off your tragedy. I've been over there, okay? I worked as an overseas correspondent. I know what those guys went through."

"You've been where?"

"Iraq."

"Can you eat the butterflies?" Ethan flipped back a page in the photo album, awed by a three-tiered wedding cake decorated with wafer-paper butterflies.

"Yes, the butterflies were edible," Beth said. "I remember that cake. No one wanted to cut into it because it was so beautiful."

"Did you really make that?"

"I did," Beth said. "A long time ago."

She glanced out the kitchen window at Stephanie, sunning herself on the deck. As much as she enjoyed showing her grandson the photos of her work, she thought that surely there were better things for a six-year-old boy to be doing on a beautiful day on the beach. What was her daughter thinking? Clearly, only about herself.

"Can you make one now?" he asked.

"What?" she asked, distracted.

"One of these cakes. Can you make it again?"

"Oh, honey, it's a lot of work. And I'm out of practice. I can bake something fun, but probably not that elaborate. Let me think about it." She patted him on the head. "I'm going to talk to your mother for a minute."

She opened the sliding-glass door to a wave of humidity. Sunglasses covered Stephanie's eyes, and Beth wondered if she was even awake. Standing at the foot of the chaise longue, Beth crossed her arms.

"Stephanie, I need to speak with you."

"What's up?" Stephanie barely stirred.

"Can you take off those sunglasses, please," Beth said. Stephanie sighed, removed them for a second, squinted against the glare, then put them back on her face.

"It's okay, Mom. I listen with my ears."

"I want to know what your plan is for Ethan this summer. He can't just sit around all day. The poor kid is so bored, he's looking through my old catering photographs."

"Oh, please. You're the one who dragged him into the mess of boxes upstairs. If he's looking at your old crap it's because you're forcing him to. Don't blame me."

Beth had the urge to grab those mirrored lenses off her face and toss them into the pool. *You've always indulged them, and now…*

She pushed Stephanie's outstretched legs aside and perched on the edge of the chair. "I'm not kidding. This isn't a vacation for you. You're still a mother. I don't care what turmoil you have going on in your personal life. You have responsibilities."

"Mom, relax. Okay, he has two weeks left of school after this break. When I get back here in the middle of the month, I'll figure something out. In the meantime, he doesn't have to be entertained every second. Just chill."

Shaking her head, Beth retreated to the kitchen.

Chapter Seventeen

Lauren locked the café door behind her and bent to lace up her sneakers. After a full day of work and the pent-up agitation from her morning encounter with Matt, she couldn't wait to burn off her frustration.

He had some nerve. Okay, so he'd been to Iraq—as a journalist. Did that give him the right to get into her business? Rory's business? And to hound her during her morning run! What was next—showing up in her bedroom?

With the wind at her back, she thought of a morning a decade and a half ago when another man had interrupted her run. Well, a boy.

It had been a Saturday, the morning after watching her first LM hockey game. She was running around the track at Narberth Park, close to her friend's house, where she'd spent the night. Halfway through her second lap, just as she was starting to break a sweat, someone called out her name.

She turned, jogging in place.

It had been barely twelve hours since she had watched Rory Kincaid win the game against Radnor, and now he was in front of her.

He was dressed in an Aces sweatshirt and white Champion running shorts, and he had an iPod strapped to one arm, the earbuds in his ears. His cheeks were ruddy, his dark eyes flashing. She, unfortunately, was wearing baggy sweats and a Britney Spears Baby One More Time concert tour T-shirt that she'd slept in.

"Oh. Hey." She was amazed at how casual it came out.

"What are you doing around here? I know this isn't exactly your neighborhood."

The way he said it made her feel embarrassed. Not exactly her neighborhood; no, that was true. In her neighborhood, the houses were about three times the size, spaced some distance apart, with wide backyards and manicured hedgerows. She ran on private, winding back roads that invited very little vehicular traffic because most of them ended in cul-de-sacs.

"I slept at my friend's house last night. You live around here?"

He nodded over his shoulder. "Yeah. On Conway."

Silence.

"Good game last night," she said. They had beaten Radnor, 3 to 0. Rory had scored every goal.

"You finished your article?"

She nodded. Almost finished. It took a lot of effort to craft the article so it was more about the team and not a profile of Rory Kincaid. And the truth was, it probably wasn't going to make the cut anyway.

"Look, I have to tell you—it might not even get published."

"Why wouldn't it get published?" He seemed genuinely outraged.

Great. Now it looked like she'd wasted his time.

"I mean, that's just how it is at the *Merionite*. A lot of articles get submitted and the editors decide which ones make it into the paper. And I'm just a sophomore. Most sophomores don't even get to submit."

"So you're special."

She turned red. "No, I'm just saying, there's a good chance that it won't—"

"How much do you have left of your run?"

"My run? Oh, a few more laps."

"Good deal. Let's go—if you can keep up with me." Typical alpha-male competitive bullshit. Of course she could keep up with him. But running laps was not the world's most attractive pastime. Was it too late to say that, actually, she was finished running?

They started out at a moderate pace, passing the basketball court. He picked up speed and she matched his stride. Two, three, four...seven laps around, and he showed no signs of stopping. Lauren wasn't going to be the one to quit.

She'd lost count of their mileage when he looked over at her and said, "You've got some stamina."

"I run track," she said.

He laughed, then stopped running, leaned over, and braced himself with his hands on his thighs. "I actually knew that. I knew it, and I forgot." He straightened, and she looked up at him. It was like staring at the sun.

Lauren reached the Green Gable, hoping no one was home. When she got upstairs, she called out, "Mom? Steph?"

With the coast clear, she headed up to the attic with a pair of scissors.

Lauren found her boxes sequestered in their own corner.

After Rory's death, her mother had offered to shut them up in storage. But ultimately, it didn't sit right with her; locking away the remnants of her life with Rory felt disloyal. Now the best thing for her to do was to move the boxes into her bedroom until the house was sold. She still couldn't quite believe that was happening.

The first box, marked *House/Stuff*, was secured with so many layers of packing tape, it would be a project just to get it open. The smallest box, the one that would be easiest to move, was marked with her name and the years 2002 to 2006. All of her high-school things were packed inside, but it was difficult to remember exactly what she'd saved. She wondered if she still had that issue of the *Merionite*. Should she...

Before she could second-guess herself, she found an X-Acto knife and sliced through the taped center of the box.

The pile of old newspapers was on top. She hadn't packed them in plastic or anything to keep them preserved, so the edges were yellowed. She had, however, been careful enough to store them in reverse chronological order, so the top edition of the *Merionite* was the final issue she edited her senior year, and the bottom of the stack was the issue with her first article: "LM Hockey Skates to the Finish Line—State Title Is Within Reach."

She pulled it out gingerly. Sometimes, it seemed like she had imagined a lot of the things that had led up to her falling in love with Rory. It had taken on a fairy-tale quality in her mind. But touching the faded newsprint in her lap, she thought, *It was real, it was real, it was real...*

She remembered how proud she'd felt seeing her byline for the first time. It was the lead article in the sports section. And just when she thought she couldn't be any happier, a text came from Rory: Congrats.

She hadn't responded right away. She wasn't trying to be coy; she really just couldn't think of an adequate reply. *Thanks* seemed too curt. *I hope you liked it,* too needy. *Great quote from you,* kissing ass. Maybe it was her silence or maybe he would have suggested it anyway, but an hour later a second text vibrated in her book bag. We should hang sometime.

Lauren, stunned, stared at her phone, completely at a loss as to how she should respond. She was distracted by hearing her name shouted from across the hallway in the confident bellow of a born cheerleader.

"My sister is famous! She's the next J. K. Rowling!" Stephanie swung her arm around her.

"J. K. Rowling is a fiction writer," Lauren said.

"I just have one critique," Stephanie said. "You gave too much ink to that asshole Rory Kincaid." That settled it. Lauren would not respond to the text.

The sound of footsteps brought her back to the present day, to the attic, the boxes.

"What are you doing up here?" her mother asked from the top of the stairs.

"You startled me. I didn't think you were home."

Her mother's face was red; she had a streak of white zinc oxide on her nose.

"I just got back from the beach with Ethan," she said.

"I thought Stephanie was taking Ethan back to Philly." He still had two weeks left of the school year.

"Tomorrow, apparently." Her mother crossed her arms, her face tight with consternation. "I feel so bad. She does nothing with him."

"Well, he's a great kid. Maybe she's doing something right."

Her mother looked unconvinced. "I know it's a lot to ask, but could you take him for ice cream? I have to make some progress up here, and Stephanie is too busy working on her tan."

"Sure," Lauren said, closing the box. "Mom, just do me a favor? Don't touch any of this stuff. I'll take care of it."

"I don't know why you always refuse my help," Beth said, eyeing the ribbon of torn tape. "Going through all of that is probably not the best thing for you. I don't want you getting mired in the past. Sweetheart, you need to move forward." She teared up.

Lauren shook her head, knowing her mother meant well but also knowing her mother could never understand. "I've moved forward as far as I want to, Mom."

Chapter Eighteen

Two Cents Plain, an ice cream parlor on Ventnor Avenue, was forty years old and hadn't changed since Lauren and Stephanie used to go when they were around Ethan's age. The black and white tiles on the floors and illustrated walls gave her a rush of happiness, and the simple joy Ethan got from his waffle cone with mint chocolate chip ice cream reminded her so much of how she used to feel at the shore all those summers ago.

On the walk back, she held his sticky hand but he ran ahead when the Green Gable came into view. Stephanie was on the back deck sunning herself, and he raced toward his mother, calling out to her. Stephanie sat up in the chaise with a wave. Lauren fought the impulse to slink off to her room. Instead, she followed Ethan up through the gate to the pool.

"Hey, big guy. I didn't know where you went until Gran filled me in." Stephanie eyed Lauren accusingly.

"Sorry," Lauren said. "We just got ice cream. Two Cents Plain. The place looks exactly the same."

Stephanie's expression softened. "Did you have a good walk?" she asked Ethan.

"Yeah. But I want to ride my bike next time."

"We can do that. Aunt Lauren and I used to bike to the place where we had cheesesteaks yesterday. Right, Laur?"

Laur. She was startled by the casual shorthand, the way her sister used to speak to her.

"Yeah," Lauren said, searching for a way to continue the positive thread and coming up empty.

"That's far!" said Ethan.

"We were a little older." Steph pushed up her sunglasses and squinted at his face. "You're getting red. Go to my bathroom and put on more sunblock."

Ethan scooted off, leaving Lauren and Stephanie in awkward silence.

"He's a great kid," Lauren said.

"Thanks."

"Look," Lauren said. "I'm sorry I freaked on you the other night. I was just really upset about the idea of a film being made."

"Apology accepted. I'm sorry too. I didn't mean to upset you. Besides, we really should be coming together to deal with Mom and Dad. Not fighting each other."

For once, Stephanie was making a lot of sense.

"You mean, the whole selling-the-house thing?"

"Yes! Are they out of their minds?"

"Um, clearly they are out of money."

"God, why does everything have to go to shit? Why can't it be the way it was when we were kids? So simple. You know, I was at the Wawa this morning and these teenage girls were there. One was wearing an LM sweatshirt, and I realized it was prom weekend. I felt so old."

"You're not old," Lauren said.

"Remember when I had the after-prom party here and the house got trashed?"

Lauren smiled. Of course she remembered, though it was just one of many memories that had been hidden away in her mental vault for so long. Stephanie remembered it as the weekend she almost got banned from the Green Gable. Lauren remembered it for another reason.

It was a long-standing Lower Merion High School tradition that everyone went to the shore following the senior prom. Once an informal, haphazard migration headed by whoever was willing to stay sober enough to drive on prom night—or who had parents willing to chauffeur—it became a school-sanctioned trip complete with buses leaving straight from the prom and making drop-offs at various Longport and Margate houses.

Typically, this epic party night was the exclusive domain of seniors and their dates. But every year, juniors with enough social clout and access to beach houses were included in the after-prom weekend. In the spring of Lauren's sophomore year, Stephanie was one of those chosen few.

"And Mom's okay with this?" Lauren had asked, perched on the edge of Stephanie's bed, watching her paint her toenails deep burgundy.

"Yeah. Totally."

"I just can't believe Gran and Pops trust you with the house for a weekend."

"What's that supposed to mean?"

"Come on, Stephanie. You won't even know half the kids that show up. It's going to be like *American Pie*."

"It's not going to be like *American Pie*," Stephanie said. "It's going to be way more epic. And you have to come."

Saturday night of the prom, just after midnight, the Green Gable filled up with drunken revelers. Lauren was pretty sure there were kids in the living room who didn't even go to their school. Two girls in the pool were topless. There was a keg in the dining room and in the living room, and the kitchen counter was littered with bottles of Stoli, Ketel One, orange juice, and tequila. The soccer team did Jäger shots. Stephanie disappeared with her boyfriend du jour.

Something broke in the living room. Lauren heard it over the music only because it happened right behind her. Someone yelled, "Party foul!"

One of her grandmother's glass zebras from the mantel.

"Oh my God, be careful!" Lauren said, shooing people away, bending down to see if the piece could be salvaged. It was shattered.

She realized she should lock her grandparents' bedroom. There were more breakable things in there, and who knew how many people were milling around on the second floor. Why hadn't she thought of this sooner? She rushed up the stairs, taking them two at a time. The problem was that the only way to lock the door was from the inside, so she locked herself in and then walked outside to the deck so she could take the stairs back down.

Someone was on the deck. How could anyone be rude enough to go through the bedroom? Then she realized it was more likely the person had simply walked up the external stairs from the pool. That hardly made it better.

"Hey—this is off-limits," she said in the darkness to someone's back. The guy ignored her, looking up at the sky. "Do you hear me?"

Fine, so she was going to be that girl. Whatever. No one would remember in the morning except her.

He turned around. "Oh. Sorry."

She gasped. Rory.

"I didn't know it was you," she said.

"Lauren?" He moved closer.

"Yeah."

"What are you doing here?"

"What am I doing here? It's my grandparents' house."

The sky was clear, bright with stars and a three-quarter moon. He was beautiful in the shadows but, unlike most people, no more so than he was in broad daylight. She felt the night start to shift.

"I mean here now—on prom weekend," he said.

"Oh. That's a good question. I don't know, actually. Did you go? To prom, I mean?"

He nodded. "I went with my friend Heidi."

"Heidi McClusky?" She was captain of the girls' lacrosse team. She'd be playing for Duke next year.

"Yeah. She was going to skip it but I convinced her she should go, that we could have a good time."

"Did you?"

"You know, it wasn't bad. But we should have quit while we were ahead. Your house is getting trashed, you know."

"Oh God. Yeah, I do know. I came up here to lock the bedroom door."

"And barricade yourself in?"

She laughed. "It's tempting."

He looked up again. "It's pretty nice up here, though. You can see every constellation. Want to take a walk on the beach?"

She looked out at the ocean. "Now? We can't. The beach is closed until six a.m."

He leaned over the ledge, following her gaze. "Some rules are worth breaking. What do you say?"

Across the street from her house, stairs led to the beach. But Rory didn't bother with the stairs; he jumped over the low wooden balustrade dividing the end of the drive and the beach. He held out his hand and helped her down. It was only three feet high on the street side, but the sand had receded, so she misjudged her landing on the sand and he had to steady her.

The physical contact was more shocking than her near fall. But he released his hold as soon as her footing was solid. She'd barely had time to process the fact that he'd put his arm around her waist, never mind enjoy it.

It was darker than she'd anticipated. She felt like she was on completely foreign terrain, not the beach she'd walked on her entire life. Maybe it was because she knew they weren't allowed to be out there. It felt risky, dangerous.

They took off their shoes, and she followed Rory close to the water. The sand was wet and cold. In the dark, the roar of the waves sounded so much louder than it did during the day. She sensed the power of the ocean and, under the bright stars, felt her own insignificance.

"Look that way—east." Rory pointed out three particularly bright stars. "That's Vega, Deneb, and Altair. The Summer Triangle. Do you see?"

"Yes, I do," she said. "So, you're really into constellations."

"It's not a constellation. It's a star pattern called an asterism. But, yeah, I'm into astronomy. Do you ever go to the Franklin Institute?" he asked.

The Franklin Institute was a science museum in Center City, Philadelphia. The last time she had been there was for an elementary-school field trip, and she told him that. "You should check out the planetarium. It's fun when you're a kid but I think now you can really appreciate how incredible it is."

"Oh, I remember that! Maybe I will."

"Maybe I'll go with you," he said. She was still looking at the stars but felt his eyes on her. Heart pounding, she turned to him.

"I don't know if I should hang out with you," she said.

"Really? Why not?" He was clearly surprised. It probably was a rare event for a girl to turn him down.

"Don't you remember the first time you saw me? It was upstairs at my house. You were just leaving my sister's room."

"That wasn't the first time I saw you," he said. "I'd noticed you. And I've thought about you."

"Why?" she asked, barely breathing.

"Not sure," he said. "But I want to figure it out."

She knew she shouldn't say the thing that was on her mind, the one thing that would ruin the moment, but she couldn't stop herself.

"You hooked up with my sister."

"Lauren," he said, looking up at the sky and then back at her. "I don't want you to take this the wrong way. But if you rule out any guy who's ever hooked up with Stephanie, you're going to have a very limited playing field. You might have to transfer to Wissahickon School District."

Her first instinct was to defend Stephanie, to say that was insulting and outrageous. But the truth of the matter was, she knew he was right. It was one of the things about Stephanie that was really starting to bother her. That, and the fact that her mother was somehow oblivious to all the nights when Stephanie sneaked out.

Before she could figure out what to say, he took her hand. Startled, she looked up at him and he bent down and kissed her. After the initial shock, she leaned into him, worried if she was doing it right. He pulled her closer, and the smell of him, the feel of his mouth opening to hers, his arms around her, silenced the endless barrage of questions and doubt that played like a constant loop in her mind. There was only that moment, and it was a moment that divided her life into before and after.

Chapter Nineteen

Some people only see what they want to see."

Matt paused the video, then replayed Stephanie's words from the audio file alone. He closed his eyes in the dark room. What was he missing?

Frustrated, he stood up and paced away from the desk. He knew this was part of the process; every film was a puzzle that had to be painstakingly assembled.

He opened the closet and felt around in the dark for the backpack on the floor. He pulled out a stack of blank index cards and a Sharpie. His stomach rumbled; he couldn't remember if he'd had lunch and it would be a long time before he gave any thought to dinner. He turned on his bedside lamp and spread the index cards out on the floor. He scrolled through a few photos on his phone until he found the shot of his storyboard from the office. He'd taken it before he left New York just for reference, thinking it would be enough to get him through a week in Longport. Now, feeling the film slipping away from him, he wrote on an index card, *Opening Image: Rory soaring toward the net, Kings vs. Flyers.* On the second card, *Entrance to LM, motto, coach VO.*

When he finished writing his notes on the fifty or so index cards, the board was re-created on the floor next to the bed. He'd make a quick trip to the convenience store, the one called Wawa, for Scotch tape to get them all up on the wall. And while he was out, he might as well stop into Robert's for a liquid dinner.

And if he ran into Stephanie Adelman? Well, that would just be a bonus.

Lauren waited until her parents had gone into their bedroom for the night before climbing the stairs to the attic.

She had tried telling herself to just go to sleep, not to give in to the pull of the memories. But there was no putting the genie back in the bottle. She had been so disciplined the past four years, never thinking about the boxes, never even tempted to look inside. Her mother accused her of not moving forward with her life, but truly, she had. Never looking back was her progress. At first, she felt like an alcoholic struggling not to take a drink; every day the effort not to wallow in her grief and her memories was as fresh and agonizing as if it were the first. But gradually, her tunnel vision, her focus on only the day in front of her, became easier, and eventually it was second nature.

But the time for tunnel vision was over. With Matt poking around in the past, it was impossible not to think about the truth. About the story buried in these boxes.

Lauren wrestled with the packing tape and heard something solid sliding along the bottom of the box, something small but weighty. Emboldened by the silence of the house, and by having come this far dipping a toe into the past, she reached inside and pulled out the first thing she touched. It was a paper napkin; Lauren handled it as carefully as if she were capturing a butterfly. Holding her breath, she smoothed it out on the floor. And Rory's words, in stark black ink, a note intended for his older brother, Emerson, greeted her like a kiss: *She's my girlfriend. She stays.*

How could a simple note last longer than their marriage? Longer than Rory himself?

In the beginning, after the night on the beach, things had grown slowly between them. She'd never planned for their relationship to be a big secret. But with everyone away for the summer—or, at the very least, not congregating every day at school—it was easy to fly under the radar.

Lauren and Rory had a routine. They went to a movie or ate lunch at Boston Style Pizza. They talked about everything—her family, his family. Rory had been a surprise, born when Kay Kincaid turned forty. His father, a Vietnam veteran and a police officer, died of a heart attack when Rory was four. His older brother, Emerson, fifteen years his senior, was an instructor at West Point. Rory said, more than once, that Emerson was the closest thing to a father that he had, aside from his coaches. It was Emerson who had drilled into his mind the imperative to excel. Rory told her, "I don't think I'd be happy if I wasn't good at something. Great at something."

The week Emerson visited that summer, she didn't get to see Rory at all. It hurt her feelings that he didn't want to introduce her, but Rory told her it was for her own good. "He can be tough," Rory said. "He wouldn't approve of me being serious about a girl. I should be focusing on school and hockey right now."

All she'd heard was *serious about a girl...*

And besides, she wasn't exactly rushing to make things public in her own household. It shouldn't matter about Stephanie—it couldn't. That was so long ago. And it had been nothing, really. Still, she kept quiet. She snuck around. And with her parents working at the store long hours every day and Stephanie at their grandparents' beach house for the summer, it was easy to be invisible.

But then school started.

The first hockey game of the new school year fell on a Thursday in late October. It was home ice, and Lauren, with her newly earned driver's license, drove herself and a few friends to the game. Rory's mother and Emerson in the stands, and being invisible to them felt terrible.

The Skatium was unusually crowded that night. The hockey team had gotten so close to states the previous year that there was a surge in community interest in them. And it didn't hurt that a month or so ago, the *Philadelphia Inquirer* had published an article about the best local high-school athletes. They ran a photo of Rory from the final game of last year. He was crouched in position for a face-off, his expression intensely focused. It was a gorgeous picture, even in the grainy black-and-white of newsprint. She bought three copies of the paper and put them on a shelf in the back of her closet.

Lauren had watched him practice a few times over the summer, but this was the first game she'd been to since they'd become a couple. When he skated out onto the ice in the first moments of play, she felt a swell of pride that made her chest almost physically ache. It was strange to be surrounded by all those people watching him, hundreds of eyes on the boy she'd come to know so well.

The crowd jumped to its feet. One minute and fifty seconds of play, and Rory had scored his first goal of the season. He made his signature gesture—lifted both hands into the air, then pulled his left arm in sharply at the elbow, his hand a fist. Score!

She settled back in her seat and someone yanked on her ponytail. Hard.

She whirled around to confront the offender and was surprised to see Stephanie.

"Oh, hey! I didn't know you were coming," she said, naively interpreting the hair-tug as a playful greeting. Stephanie was all decked out in Seven jeans and a top that made her look like she'd stepped out of a scene from *The OC* (her favorite show). Her hair was loose and as golden as the oversize hoops in her ears.

"Are you fucking kidding me?" she snapped.

With a sinking feeling in her stomach, Lauren looked around nervously.

"About what?" She noticed Mindy Levy standing next to Stephanie, arms crossed.

"Rory Kincaid," Stephanie said.

She looked electrically beautiful in her rage, and it was hard in that moment for Lauren to believe that anyone would choose her over Stephanie. But it was clear that Stephanie realized that someone had.

"Let's go outside," Lauren said.

"Do you want me to come?" Mindy asked Stephanie.

Stephanie ignored her—seemed to be ignoring both of them—and stalked out of the rink. Lauren didn't know if she was simply leaving or if she was agreeing to continue the conversation outside. Reluctantly, she followed her, just steps behind. Stephanie didn't turn around, and the heavy doors to the rink almost slammed on Lauren before she caught them. Behind her, she heard the roar of the crowd, and she wondered if she'd missed one of Rory's plays.

The hallway was ten degrees warmer than inside the rink, and perspiration immediately made her layers of clothes feel suffocating. Stephanie kept walking, still not glancing back, until she was gone from the Skatium. Lauren followed her outside.

"Stephanie, stop!" Lauren yelled. Her sister whirled around, and even in the darkness, Lauren could see the glisten of tears in her eyes.

"I can't believe you," Stephanie said. "How could you lie to me like this?"

"I didn't l-lie to you," Lauren stammered. "I just didn't want to talk about it."

"Oh, now you didn't want to talk? We talk about everything else. And I felt bad for you. I invited you to everything because I didn't want you to be a loser, and this is how you pay me back?"

"Stephanie, I don't really get why you're upset. You never, ever mentioned him to me."

"You know we hooked up!"

Lauren couldn't believe it. "Yeah, and I asked if you were dating and you said this wasn't 1985 or something like that. As if it were the dumbest question in the world. And then you never mentioned him again, and the next time I brought him up, you said he was an asshole. So what do you care if I'm...hanging out with him?"

"Hanging out with him? You mean fucking him."

Lauren felt herself turn white. Was that what she'd heard? "I'm not...fucking him," she said, the words catching in her throat.

"Well, then I guess this whole thing should be over soon."

"What's that supposed to mean?"

Stephanie smiled an odd smile. "Don't say I didn't warn you when he realizes he's wasting his time with you. You're on your own."

She turned and walked briskly to the parking lot. Lauren trotted behind her.

"Fine, I should have told you. I'm sorry. It was wrong for me to let you hear it from someone else." She resisted the urge to ask who had told her. "But why do you care about some guy you hung out with last year?"

"Some guy I hung out with? What do you think we were doing in my room that night, Lauren? Playing Monopoly? Maybe that's what you do, but we fucked. And it's the girl code—no, forget that, the sister code— not to sleep with guys your sister already slept with!"

Lauren reeled back as if she had been slapped. That's what it felt like, a physical blow. In all the months she'd been with Rory, she had not thought about—had not allowed herself to think about—the extent to which he had hooked up with Stephanie.

She realized, standing alone in the dark, long after her sister had peeled off in her car, that she had been living in denial. And fine, maybe Stephanie had sex with a lot of people. And she acted like it never meant anything, and maybe it didn't. But that didn't change the fact that what was going on between herself and Rory merited a conversation with her sister. Deep down, on a level Lauren didn't want to acknowledge, she had known this all along.

I'm going to fix this, she told herself, hugging her arms tight around her torso. *I'm going to make things right with Stephanie. Even if it means ending things with Rory.*

Lauren walked slowly back to her seat, feeling sick.

Watching the game was now the exact opposite experience she'd had before the argument with Stephanie. Whereas then she couldn't keep her eyes off Rory, now she couldn't stand to look at him.

That's why she missed the freak accident.

Later, she would read all about it—how Rory was in LM's defensive zone because there was some slack in that area. Penncrest's Jake Stall passed the puck to teammate Eric Layton, who let it rip with a slapshot. Rory turned to block the shot and it smashed into the lower half of his face.

But in the moment, all she knew was the crowd gave a collective gasp, and all of them were suddenly on their feet. It's human instinct to follow the energy of the crowd, and so even though she was lost in her own world, Lauren found herself standing, looking at the ice, where she saw the player down. She knew instantly it was Rory. And was that...blood?

She didn't remember running down the stairs, but there she was on the ice, the assistant coach Jim Reilly shooing her away. Mrs. Kincaid was bent over Rory, along with Coach McKenna and a few others.

"What happened?" Lauren asked, turning to a stranger in the first row. Paramedics raced down the stairs. Rory was sitting up now, a towel against his face, blood seeping through it.

No one spoke to her. A flurry of activity, and then he was gone from the ice.

Bryn Mawr Hospital was a ten-minute drive down Lancaster Avenue, maybe even less. Lauren had been born there, and that had been the last time she was at that hospital—or any hospital. Lauren parked in the visitor lot and hurried to the information desk. Breathless, she asked where she could find Rory Kincaid. "He's my brother," she added quickly, figuring they'd only let family see him.

The weary-looking woman behind the desk consulted a computer and directed her to the fourth floor.

The wide, oversize elevator, the antiseptic smell, the people in wheelchairs, all made her feel like an interloper in some adult world where she didn't belong. The elevator pinged open, and she felt sheer terror. What if Rory was terribly injured? What if he didn't want her there? Suddenly, showing up like that seemed like a very bad idea.

Lauren stepped out of the elevator and into a jarringly bright corridor. She went down the hall and into a glass-enclosed waiting area, not sure what to do next. Inside, a TV played CNN. Only two other people were in the room, an elderly man and woman drinking coffee out of Styrofoam cups. Through the glass, she spotted Mr. Reilly, the assistant coach, heading in the direction she had just come from. Why not Coach McKenna? For the first time, it dawned on her that the game had continued. The rest of the team was still on the ice, and Rory was here, injured.

She poked her head out of the room. "Mr. Reilly!" she called.

He was surprised to see her.

"Is Rory okay? Can I see him?" she said.

He said she should follow him.

It was the world's most awkward minute of walking. They passed the nurses' station and finally reached Rory's room. The door was open, and Mr. Reilly knocked on the frame. Peering inside, Lauren spotted Mrs. Kincaid. The edge of a hospital bed was in view, but little else.

"Mr. Reilly, come in," said Mrs. Kincaid. "My older son just went to find you to tell you the good news—it's not a break. We'll have him back on the ice in no time."

That's when she spotted Lauren, and her face crinkled with confusion.

Lauren, anxious to see Rory, didn't feel the polite hesitation that might have held her back in other circumstances. Instead, she edged past Mr. Reilly into the room.

Rory was sitting in a chair, a bandage around his head and wrapped under his chin. His mouth didn't move when he saw her, but his eyes smiled.

"Oh my God, are you okay?" She moved to hug him and felt a clawlike grip on her arm.

"Young lady, excuse me. Who are you?" Kay Kincaid said.

Rory reached for Lauren's hand. Clearly, he couldn't speak. Lauren didn't know what to do—she didn't want to leave him, but she wasn't a big fan of pissing off adults. Especially not adults who were related to Rory.

The energy in the room shifted as Emerson walked in; he was as big as Rory, and his presence took up a lot of space. He immediately began talking with Mr. Reilly. Rory squeezed her hand.

"Rory, this isn't the time or place," Emerson said. "Your friend is going to have to leave." Rory grabbed the pen attached to the clipboard by his bed, then reached for a paper napkin. He scribbled something, then passed it to Emerson, who frowned and then passed it to his mother. And that was the end of anyone telling her to go.

Later, Lauren saw the napkin crumpled up on the edge of the bed. While everyone was getting ready to leave, she managed to slip it into her bag unnoticed.

Alone in her car in the dark parking lot, she turned on the overhead light and read it: *She's my girlfriend. She stays.*

Any thought of breaking up with him to appease Stephanie was gone.

Chapter Twenty

It's not too late for you to change your mind," Howard said, packing his suitcase.

Beth, reading in bed, ignored the comment. Then, to fill the silence: "I want to be here. In this house. With the girls. I told you the one thing I wanted this summer. Why can't you give me that?"

Howard shook his head, as in *Here we go again*. Then he straightened up, holding a pair of swimming trunks, and looked at her. "You know what? If you're not using the ticket, I'll take Lauren."

"What?"

"Yes. It will do her some good to get away. Change of scenery."

"She'll never agree."

"Well, I'm going to ask her."

"*I'll* ask her. I don't want you browbeating her over it."

"You asking her is as good as not asking at all. She'll say no, and you'll say, Okay, fine, and that will be the end of it. At some point, Beth, she has to be pushed out of her comfort zone."

Says you, Beth thought, closing her book and climbing out of bed.

"Where are you going?" Howard called after her.

"To talk to Lauren."

Really, she just wanted to get out of the bedroom. It was suffocating, his arrogant certainty that he alone knew best for their daughters. He couldn't fix the sinking store, so now he was going to fix Lauren. That wasn't the reason she wanted them all at the shore together. Although she suspected that her own motive—her longing to recapture a time when they had been a happy family—was just as misguided.

When she didn't find Lauren in her room or on the back deck, she climbed the stairs to the attic. Sure enough, she was sitting next to an open box, reading through a pile of old newspapers. Oh, how Lauren had loved writing for the school paper. And then, her junior year in high school, she'd entered one of her pieces in a writing competition and won a trip to Washington, DC. Lauren took the Amtrak there and met up with the other contest winners from schools around the country. For three days, she toured DC. She visited the offices of the *New Republic,* the *Washington Post,* and the *National Journal.* She showed Beth photos of a picnic lunch on the National Mall with the Lincoln Memorial behind her and the Washington Monument in the distance, the Reflecting Pool in between. Lauren was clearly in love with DC, and Beth suggested she apply to college there. But Lauren's response to that was lukewarm, and Beth knew what she was thinking: Rory was already set to go to school in Boston the following year, and Lauren would no doubt apply to colleges based on their proximity to him. The thought of her limiting herself like that bothered Beth, and it infuriated Howard. In the end, that conflict, at least, had worked itself out. Back then, Beth believed that things usually did. Now? She wasn't so sure.

She would not try to force Lauren to take the trip to Florida. But she would at least ask, and she felt that was enough of a compromise with Howard.

"Hon? How's it going?" Beth asked, stepping over her own corner full of boxes. She was making very slow progress.

"Oh! I thought you guys went to sleep."

Beth started to answer but then noticed the glint of silver around Lauren's neck. Oh, good Lord.

She was wearing the heart necklace.

Beth swallowed hard. "No, we were just talking. Hon, you know Dad is going to Florida for a few days, and we thought it would be nice if you went with him. A change of scenery, keep Dad company. What do you say?"

As expected, Lauren looked at her like she was out of her mind. "Mom, I'm not going to Florida."

Beth tried not to stare at the necklace. "Why not?"

"For one thing, I have a job. It's the start of the busy season. I can't just take off."

"Have you ever taken a day off in the four years you've worked there? I'm sure Nora would understand."

"Okay, I don't *want* to take time off. I don't want to go to Florida, Mom."

Beth moved closer to her, biting her lip to keep from crying. "Lauren, hon, why are you wearing that necklace again?"

Lauren's hand fluttered to her throat as if she had forgotten about the Tiffany heart necklace, though she could only have put it on in the past hour or so. She certainly hadn't been wearing it at dinner.

"I just found it. In this box."

Damn it, Beth knew she should have just taken it upon herself to get the boxes in storage.

"Let me take care of this stuff for you," Beth said, reaching for one of the boxes.

"No!" Lauren said, jumping up and lunging at the unopened box. "I've got it." She tried to pick up the box but struggled with the weight.

Changing tactics, she stood behind the box and pushed it like a cart on wheels until she reached the stairs.

"Lauren, come back," Beth said. But Lauren was already dragging the box down to her room.

"Unbelievable," Lauren muttered, shoving the box into her closet. There was plenty of room on the floor considering that her only footwear was a pair of flip-flops and three pairs of running sneakers. Later, when everyone was asleep, she would go up to the attic and move the rest of the boxes into her bedroom.

What did her mother care if she wanted to wear an old necklace? And the whole Florida suggestion? Lunacy.

"Aunt Lauren?"

She turned to find Ethan standing in the doorway. He wore Batman footie pajamas, his dark hair wet from the bath. She smiled.

"Hey there. What's going on?"

"I'm saying good night."

"Oh, good night."

He walked over to her and she put her arms around him. He smelled like baby shampoo, though he was far from a baby. She'd missed so much of his young life, and she felt a pang. She'd try to make up for it this summer.

"So, you're going back to Philly tomorrow?"

He nodded.

"Are you excited for the end of school?" she asked.

"I want to stay here," he said. He looked so forlorn, she gave him another hug.

"Oh—well, we'll be here waiting for you to come back. The house isn't going anywhere." *Not yet, anyway.*

She heard Stephanie calling for him from the hallway.

"In here, Steph," Lauren yelled.

Stephanie poked her head in. "Hey. Bedtime, mister."

Ethan gave Lauren a little wave, then dutifully marched off to his room.

"See you later," Stephanie said to her.

"Wait—come in for a second," Lauren said.

Stephanie walked into the room. "What's up?"

"Look, I don't know who you still hang out with back home," Lauren said. "But if you hear about anyone talking to Matt, will you let me know?"

"Are you still worried about the stupid film? Just forget about it."

"I can't, okay? Not as long as he's still here trying to dig into my life." She instinctively touched her necklace.

"Fine, I'll keep an ear out. But aside from old coaches or a few guys from high school, who would he talk to? Although, you know Emerson is back in town."

"What?" She froze.

"Yeah. He's teaching at Villanova. One of my friends takes his wife's yoga class."

Lauren pressed her fingers to her temples. "Ugh. I don't want to think about Emerson."

"So don't. Forget about it. And forget about the film. We've got bigger things to worry about." She nodded her head in the direction of their parents' bedroom.

Stephanie left and Lauren closed the door behind her. Would Emerson talk to Matt? No, there was no way. Emerson, the control freak, had already warned her off a film project years earlier. Could it be this same film?

But then, Emerson was never one to sit by and let things just happen. What if he talked to Matt specifically to control the direction of the film? If he had, he certainly wouldn't be neutral on the subject of her marriage.

She'd never told Rory what his brother had said to her on their wedding day. She'd meant to, but there was so much going on that she never got around to it. She'd never told anyone, and it bothered her still.

Emerson had pulled her aside an hour before she walked down the aisle. Lauren was already in her dress, having just taken photos with the bridal party on the roof deck and in front of the famous twenty-foot statue of Benjamin Franklin in the rotunda of Philadelphia's Franklin Institute.

"Lauren, can I talk to you for a minute?"

Lauren smiled and happily followed him to a quiet corner in the massive room, a domed space with an eighty-two-foot-high ceiling and so many pillars it was like the Roman Pantheon.

Emerson put a hand on her back and led her to the museum lobby. Lauren still felt nervous around Emerson. Rory revered his brother so much; Lauren was desperate for his approval. Now that they were about to become family, she thought she might finally get it.

"My parents were married for twenty-two years," Emerson said. "Till death did they part, as promised in their vows."

Lauren nodded, not sure where this was going.

"Now is the time to ask yourself if you are really prepared to make the same commitment," he said.

"What? Of course."

"Lauren, let's be honest. You can barely handle being a hockey girlfriend. How will you be able to endure being a military wife?"

Lauren, floored, couldn't think of a thing to say. At that point, Emerson was the only person other than Lauren and Rory who knew that Rory was planning to enlist. Lauren had made Rory promise not to tell anyone else until after their wedding. She didn't want to worry her parents, didn't want the specter of it hanging over the day. Lauren hated herself for her weakness, but a part of her wished Rory had also spared her the news until after the wedding. But that didn't make her a bad person or a bad wife-to-be.

"I know you see yourself as some sort of surrogate father to Rory," Lauren said, shaking. "But you're not his father. And I'm going to be his wife. So don't ever talk to me like that again."

Emerson shook his head. "Fine. Have it your way. But next time there's a problem—and we both know there will be—don't come crying to me."

Oh, how the damning judgment of Rory's revered older brother had stung. Maybe on some level, she had taken it to heart. Maybe she hadn't told Rory about the conversation because she'd been afraid Emerson was right.

Lauren shoved the box deeper in her closet and closed the door. He wasn't right. Was he? It was so jumbled in her mind, what had happened versus her feelings about what had happened. All these years later, she still couldn't make sense of it.

Matt Brio wanted the truth about Rory's life and death. If Lauren was being honest with herself, so did she.

Had he spoken to Emerson? If so, what had her former brother-in-law said?

She paced back and forth, then finally reached for her phone and left Nora a message that she'd be late to work tomorrow.

Chapter Twenty-One

Matt woke to a loud mechanical grinding sound.

He groaned, regretting the last two—make it three—shots at Robert's. And he hadn't even managed to see Stephanie. All of the hangover, none of the payoff.

What the hell was that racket? He stumbled out of bed and looked outside. Henny was on the back deck, cutting wood planks with an electric saw. Not an ideal wake-up call, but he was overdue to talk to her anyway. She probably thought he was packing to leave or already gone.

Sure enough, when he unlatched the gate and walked out onto the deck, she was surprised.

"Oh! I thought you'd checked out. I didn't see your car..."

"A hazard of a night out at Robert's Place," he said. "I probably have a hell of a ticket on my car over on Atlantic Avenue."

"Oh, honey," she said. "You'd best be getting yourself over there. Do you need a ride?"

"Thanks but I'll walk over. I could use the exercise." As his disastrous run yesterday morning had made more than clear. "Oh—I wanted to ask if I could extend my stay if I need to."

She smiled. "I'd be happy to have you stay longer. It saves me from having to go back on that website. I do hate dealing with the Internet. Facebook? I just don't get the appeal. Why would I talk to Nora on a website when I can just hop on over to her place?"

"I hear you," Matt said, looking around at Henny's work space. She had a professional-looking sander, a table covered with half a dozen paint containers, stencils, and sponges, and a smaller table holding piles of uniformly sized, smooth wooden planks. "So, do you sell these or what?"

"I do," Henny said, smiling. "Have you been to Nora's Café? I sell them there. You can buy 'em right off the wall."

He nodded. "I liked the one about bacon."

She laughed. "That was just something I said to myself in the kitchen one day. Ain't no problem bacon can't cure. That was before I started making the signs. After my husband passed, I was really feeling down. The only time I felt okay was when I went to church and the pastor would say something positive and I'd try to hold on to it. But a day or two later, I was back in a funk. So I started thinking of my own positive messages for myself. I'd write them on Post-its and leave them around the house. And it helped. So I wanted the messages to be more permanent and decorative. That's when I started making these."

"Well, they're great. I might just have to buy one before I leave."

"Sounds good to me! But don't rush to go. Like I said, makes my life easier not having to fill the room again."

Well, at least one person was happy to have him around.

"Oh, we have a visitor," Henny said, waving to someone. He turned to see Lauren opening the gate.

A surge of hope broke through his hangover. Had something he said yesterday actually gotten through to her?

"I tried calling but you didn't answer," Lauren said to Henny. "Sorry to just show up like this. I was hoping to catch Matt before he left."

"You two know each other?" Henny said, turning to him.

"Sort of," he said. "It's a long story."

"Did you drive over?" Henny said to Lauren. "He needs a ride to pick up his car."

Lauren looked at him quizzically, but he waved off the comment, saying, "It's all good, Henny. I'll take care of it later. And thanks again."

Lauren didn't say a word until they walked to the side of the house, out of Henny's earshot. Standing at the base of the stairs, he said, "This is a surprise."

"You said I could look at your interviews and correct any misinformation."

He tried to appear casual, as if she hadn't just given him the first shred of hope in the past twenty-four hours.

"I did."

"Okay, let's do it," she said.

Now? He thought of the disarray in his room, the aftermath of manic hours of working followed by a sleepless post-binge-drinking night. Mostly, he thought of the notecards all over the floor spelling out the trajectory of her husband's doomed life.

"I'm all for it, but I need a few minutes to charge my computer and get things together," he said.

She looked impatient.

"Five minutes," Matt said. He'd throw a sheet over the notecards. And do them both a favor by taking a quick shower.

"I hate being late for work," Lauren said, mostly to herself. "This is crazy."

Henny looked up from the can of paint she was opening and smiled.

"You know what they say about all work and no play," she said. "Sometimes you need a day off. And he really is a handsome fella."

Lauren's jaw dropped. "Henny, no. That is *not* what this is."

"I'm ready when you are," Matt called from the gate. He had changed clothes, wearing jeans and an NYC T-shirt. His hair was wet. Had he *showered?*

"Well," Henny said, looking at him. "From one widow to another, may I just say, that is a mighty shame."

Matt pulled a bench in front of his desk. Lauren sat on the end of it, as far away from him as possible. Clicking his keyboard, eyes on the screen, he said, "I don't bite, you know."

She said nothing. The screen filled with an image of Rory, young Rory, wearing his LM hockey uniform. She recognized the Havertown Skatium. He raced down the ice, and she could imagine the intense look of concentration on his face even though the camera didn't capture that view. He raised his stick and launched the puck in the air; it landed just beyond the goal line. Rory pulled his left arm sharply in, bent at the elbow, his fist tight. The familiar gesture brought tears to her eyes.

"I could show you the Dean Wade interview," Matt said.

"Actually," she said, feeling nervous, wondering if now that *she* wanted something from *him,* he might turn her down, "I was wondering if you interviewed Emerson Kincaid."

Just saying his name felt taboo, as if, like in the film *Beetlejuice,* the mere act of uttering it would conjure him.

"The older brother?" Matt said casually, as if he were, in fact, a movie character, not someone real, not Lauren's former brother-in-law, not someone who had the power to cut her down or even change her world with a few choice words.

"Yes. Did you talk to him?"

Matt shook his head. "I tried to. The only response I got was a legal letter threatening to sue me if the film exploited or misrepresented Rory, the Kincaid family, or the U.S. military. If I remember correctly." He smiled wryly.

Yeah, that sounded like Emerson.

"Oh," she said. She didn't know if she was relieved or disappointed.

Matt clicked around his keyboard, and a still frame of Dean Wade, Rory's former NHL teammate, filled the screen. Dean had the all-American good looks of a Midwestern farm boy, though he was actually from Vancouver. The sight of his face brought Lauren back to a different life. She could imagine sitting across the table from him and his wife, Ashley, at their favorite Mexican place in West Hollywood. She could hear Dean calling her "the missus," something he did even before she was married to Rory.

Everywhere they went, she could feel the eyes of envious women. Lauren would talk about it with Ashley, how it felt to be the recipient of glares like daggers. They were the lucky ones, the chosen, and she could hear the unspoken words: *Why her?*

Matt played the video. He asked Dean questions off camera, general stuff about the team, when he'd started, how the other guys felt about Rory joining the Kings. How he felt about Rory personally.

The last time she'd seen Dean in person had been the day of Rory's memorial service, and it was jarring now to hear his voice. She tuned in and out, half listening to Dean talk about Rory's first season with the Kings, half fighting off a flood of memories.

"So that hit he took in December, the game against the Blackhawks. That seemed pretty bad but they said it wasn't a concussion, am I getting that right?" Matt asked him.

Lauren focused intently on his answer.

Dean nodded. "You're right—that was the party line. But I'll tell you, he got his bell rung that time. I know what the doc said, but I was with Rory that whole night. He was out of it. I mean, he was a tough guy, but none of us can shake off a hit like that."

Matt asked him another question, about how Rory had played the next game. Lauren interrupted the video.

"He's wrong," Lauren said. "I flew to LA that night and Rory was fine. The doctors said he was fine."

Actually, he hadn't been fine. But Rory didn't want to admit he was injured. And now Lauren felt obligated to portray the incident as he would have wanted.

"Did you go to a lot of games his first season?" Matt asked.

"I saw him play whenever he was in DC or Philly, and I flew to LA for a few home games."

Watching him play at the Staples Center, surrounded by eighteen thousand rabid fans, was surreal and thrilling. When he skated onto the ice just before the national anthem, his signature number 89 on his back, it brought tears to her eyes.

The Kings had retired his number three years ago. She'd declined to attend the ceremony.

The truth was that the NHL had been an adjustment for him. For as long as she'd watched him play, he'd always been one of the top players on the ice at any given moment. But things were different in the NHL; he was competing with guys who had all been the best where they came from. Sometimes Rory rode the bench, and this bothered him deeply. But Rory was Rory, and he figured out how to get more ice time by simply throwing his size around.

Lauren read every article written about the games, had every mention of him memorized. He gained a reputation as a double threat, a player who could score but could also fight. Still, it was never easy seeing him get into fights. Or, like that night in 2009, seeing him on the receiving end of a bad hit. It was all part of the game, and certainly part of the game at the pro level. Still, whenever anyone touched him, she felt a burst of indignant fury, even though he was always okay. That night, in the seconds between his contact with the boards and him hitting the ice, she told herself it was okay—it always was. But that time was different because he didn't get up.

"Like I said," she told Matt, "I flew out there the night he took that hit from the Blackhawks. And he was fine."

Watching from her Georgetown apartment, she'd panicked when he didn't stand up from the ice. The TV broadcast cut to commercial. Frantic, Lauren called Ashley Wade. Ashley was from Canada and, like Lauren, had been with her husband since high school. Except Rory wasn't even Lauren's husband at that point. Which was why she knew she wouldn't get a call, would be in a complete information blackout.

When Ashley's phone went straight to voice mail, Lauren called the airline and booked the next flight out of Dulles.

Landing in LA, she found out that Dean had stayed the night at Rory's. The team doctor didn't think it was a concussion, but Dean wanted to be on the safe side.

"I'm fine," Rory assured her in his bedroom with the shades pulled down, not watching TV or anything, just sitting there. "But I'm happy you're here."

He didn't seem fine. He was cranky, wouldn't let her put on any lights, and asked her to check his phone when it buzzed with messages because the glare of the screen bothered him.

"Are you sure you don't have a concussion?" she asked.

"Jesus, Lauren. Now you're a doctor?" he snapped.

She wasn't a doctor, but it didn't take a doctor to know that something was seriously wrong. But the team clearly didn't want to sideline him, and Rory didn't want to be sidelined.

Now, she knew Rory wouldn't want to be remembered as someone who had been weakened or diminished in any way.

"He was okay," she insisted.

"You and Dean Wade see things differently."

"I think I knew Rory better than Dean Wade," she snapped.

"Of course you did. But Wade's in the film and you're not."

She shook her head. "I don't want to be in this film. I'm just telling you that you're getting it wrong." Her instinct to stay on the surface of everything that had happened, not to dig too deep, was as much for her own sanity as it was to protect Rory's reputation.

"I don't think I am," he said calmly. Confidently. "But I'm offering you the chance to tell your view of events."

Her view of events? As if the past were purely open to individual interpretation.

"It's not my *view* of events. I know what happened."

"There's no doubt in my mind that you do," he said, locking eyes with her.

"I'm late for work," she said.

Chapter Twenty-Two

Beth wiped her hands on her apron. It was new, a gift to herself. A token to remind herself that she had been good at something once.

The kitchen counter was covered with packages and jars and containers: confectioners' sugar, vanilla extract, milk, eggs, salt, vegetable oil, and shortening. The kitchen island held two other gifts to herself: a brand-new deep fryer and a stand mixer. For the first time in years—certainly since the girls had grown up and left the house—she was making doughnuts.

She didn't know how to do leisure. After thirty years of spending nearly every day at the clothing store, the sudden stretch of endless free time was more than unwelcome. It felt hostile, as if the universe were telling her in no uncertain terms that she was obsolete. Even work for the Polaris Foundation quieted during the month of August.

The past week, with Howard in Florida, Stephanie and Ethan back in Philly, and Lauren at the café every day, she had no idea what to do with herself. She could spend only so many hours clearing out the attic before becoming overwhelmed with a crushing sense of failure. The end of Adelman's, losing the house the girls had grown up in, and now facing the sale of her parents' house.

And Howard was clearly running away from it all.

The doorbell rang. Beth had forgotten the sound of the Green Gable doorbell, the gentle melodic pinging of a chime that her mother had custom-ordered. She couldn't remember the last time someone had used it.

"Damn it," she muttered, the sugary glaze not budging from her hands as she rubbed them against the apron. She ran them under the faucet.

The doorbell pinged again.

Well, the yeast, milk, and flour paste had to rest for a half an hour anyway. She covered the bowl with plastic wrap, walked to the front door, and peeked out the window, fortifying herself to make excuses to get rid of the real estate agent. She found herself smiling instead.

"Neil! How are you? Come on in."

He was a good-looking young man. Not devastatingly handsome like her son-in-law had been, but Rory's type of charisma was always a double-edged sword. Neil Hanes was the kind of man she had imagined one of her daughters ending up with, ambitious but grounded, from a good family. And, well, yes, Jewish. Not that she minded that Rory had been Catholic. The truth was, she had adored Rory. They had all fallen in love with him.

"This really is a nice surprise," Beth said, steering Neil into the living room. They sat on the couch and he eyed her mother's vintage suitcases with obvious appreciation.

"I'm sorry to come by without calling but I was just a few doors away, at the Kleins. They built where the red-brick house used to be up the block?"

"Yes, yes—it's amazing, what they've done. I mean, that modern architecture isn't for me but I can understand the appeal."

"Well, this place is a classic. They don't make them like this anymore."

Beth looked around with a sigh. "It was my parents' house, you know. I grew up coming here for the summers."

"My father mentioned that you're selling," Neil said.

Beth looked at him, surprised. Well, she supposed people did talk. "Yes."

"Are you waiting until after the summer?" he asked.

"I'm not sure. It's a fairly recent decision."

"Well, I'd be interested."

"You want to buy this house? You're *able* to buy this house? How old are you, Neil? Thirty?"

He laughed. "Sad to say, I'm turning thirty-one in the fall. But I'm about to sell a big script, and aside from that, my father would always float me."

"Well, let's put this conversation on hold for the moment. I'm not in a rush, though my husband feels differently on the matter. He's in Florida right now."

"My parents love it there. They haven't seen an East Coast winter in ten years."

Neil walked to the mantel and looked at photos of Lauren and Stephanie.

"These are great," he said, turning to her. "Is Lauren around?"

Beth smiled. "She's at work. But why don't you come by later? Have dinner with us. I'm sure she'd love to see you."

"I feel ambushed," Lauren whispered to her mother, though Neil Hanes couldn't possibly overhear their conversation. They were in the kitchen and he sat outside at the table set for the dinner.

"That's a bit dramatic," Beth said, opening the bottle of wine. "And there's plenty of time before the food is ready. Maybe go change out of your shorts and sneakers?"

Lauren glanced uneasily at the deck. What could she do? Flee and hide from visitors in her own home? She was exhausted after a nonstop day at the restaurant.

The front door opened and closed.

"Who else did you invite?" Lauren said. "Is this dinner going to be like an episode of *The Bachelorette*?"

Beth looked in the direction of the hallway. "I didn't invite anyone else."

Stephanie, with Ethan in tow, walked into the kitchen dragging a large suitcase.

"What are you doing back?" Beth said. "I thought you were in Philly until the middle of next week."

"Yeah, well, plans changed," Stephanie said. Ethan ran over to Beth and hugged her, then made his way to Lauren.

"Hey, cutie," she said.

"E., run upstairs and put your stuff in your room. I need to talk to Gran for a sec." Ethan dutifully scooted off. Stephanie pulled a bottle of wine from the refrigerator.

"Doesn't he still have school?" Beth said.

"So he'll miss the last few days. He's six. I think Harvard will overlook it."

"I don't appreciate the sarcasm," Beth said.

"Brett reneged on letting me stay at the house for the rest of the month, okay? I just had to get out of there."

"Nice guy," Lauren muttered.

"This is just so unfair to Ethan," said Beth.

"He'll be fine. Kids are resilient," Stephanie said. She peeked into the pot on the stove. "Smells good, Mom."

Beth glanced nervously outside. Stephanie, following her gaze, realized they had company.

"Who's here?"

"No one," said Beth.

"Neil Hanes," said Lauren.

"Oh, shit. Did I just walk in on a date?" Stephanie laughed.

"Don't be an ass," Lauren said. "In fact, I'm leaving."

She brushed past Stephanie, ignoring her mother's protests.

Outside, the sun was not close to setting. Lauren wished for a blanket of darkness for her run to the boardwalk. She didn't know what was worse: her mother's not-so-subtle attempt to fix her up or the fact that it was understandable. She was twenty-nine years old, a widow for four years. She was the one who was abnormal, not the people who expected her to someday have a life again.

The problem was, from the time she was fifteen, she'd known she was meant to be with Rory, and only Rory. Even while they were broken up, she knew it. During their first split, when he was a freshman at Harvard and she still had a year left in high school, everyone told her to hook up with other guys, that it was the only way to get over him. But Lauren knew better; she knew that to spend time with any other boy would make the loss of Rory Kincaid only that much more unbearable. No one could compare.

The boardwalk was too crowded for a good run. She stopped and rested on the rail facing the beach. She leaned over, and the heart pendant of her necklace clanged against the metal. Lauren wrapped it in her hand, closing her eyes.

She could see the Kincaid family living room, the house on Conway crowded with guests, a towering Christmas tree in the center of it all.

"Come with me for a sec," Rory said, taking her by the hand.

"Where are we going?" she asked after he pulled their coats from the closet.

"I want to give you your gift in private," he said.

"Oh. Well, should I get yours? It's under the tree." She tried not to think about the card. She'd agonized about how to sign it. *Love, Lauren* seemed to say too much. But she felt that and more and so she wrote it.

"You can give it to me after," he said, leading her to the garage.

"Did you get me a car?" she joked.

"This is the only place without a million people. I didn't want my family to see us going upstairs. They'd get the wrong idea."

The cold garage smelled of rubber and gasoline. She stumbled over a rake, and he caught her. "Careful," he said. "Here—sit on this." He opened two lawn chairs and brushed off the dried leaves. They sat hidden behind his mother's Buick, the single lightbulb in the ceiling bathing everything in yellow.

Rory pulled a small box out of his coat pocket. It was robin's-egg blue and tied with a white ribbon.

"Oh my God," she said. "What did you do?" He handed it to her with the shyest smile she'd ever seen on his face. Hands shaking, she untied the ribbon and lifted the lid to find the iconic silver Tiffany Open Heart necklace.

She'd signed her card exactly right after all.

Now, as much as Lauren longed for the pure happiness she'd had as a teenager, she also felt sorry for that clueless fifteen-year-old self. It was human nature to open yourself up to love, to seek it and give it. But losing it was so painful. She'd read once that the opposite of love wasn't hate, it was indifference. She'd told that to Rory, and he'd said that love, like energy, "can neither be created nor destroyed." It was a conversation under the stars, sitting on a metal bench in Narberth Park.

Another lesson about love happened in that park, a lesson about its flip side.

It was August, the summer before her senior year. He would be leaving soon for Boston. Every minute felt delicate and precious. They planned to drive to the shore for a night at the Green Gable. She picked him up that morning, car windows down, sunroof open, "Hollaback Girl" playing on the radio.

It was only after she parked the car that she noticed his text. Today's not going to work.

She hurried up the sidewalk to his house. Rory was standing out front watering the lawn with Emerson, who was visiting for two weeks.

"Oh—hey," he said when he spotted her. "Didn't you get my text?"

She looked at her phone. "Yeah. Like, two seconds ago. Hi, Emerson." Emerson gave her a distracted wave.

"What's going on?" she said.

Rory seemed stressed. She touched his arm. "Is everything okay?"

"Yes," he said, annoyed.

"What is it, then?"

He glanced back at the house. "Let's go for a walk."

Her stomach knotted, but she followed him to the park. They found a shady spot on the bleachers near the basketball court. Even under the trees, the metal was hot, and she slid forward so her bare legs weren't touching it. Rory stared into the distance, leaning forward, his elbows on his knees.

"Rory, you're scaring me," she said.

He looked at her as if he'd forgotten she was there. "Sorry. I don't mean to upset you. But I've been doing a lot of thinking. I'm leaving in a week, and you know I won't be back until Thanksgiving."

Lauren clutched the edge of the bench. "I know. But I'll come see you. We've talked through all of this."

Rory shook his head. "I feel like we're not being realistic about this whole thing."

What? "Is this coming from you? Or from Emerson?"

He finally turned to her. "Come on, Lauren. I mean, yes, Emerson went to West Point. He knows what it's like to be in an environment where you're challenged every day, where you have to keep your self-motivation sharp. I can't have distractions right now. Between hockey and academics, I won't have time for a long-distance relationship."

She felt like she'd been slapped. "Wow. How convenient. I bet you'll find time for a short-distance relationship, though, won't you."

"That's not what this is about."

He reached for her hand, but she snatched it away. "Don't touch me." She stood up, the sunlight blindingly bright against the metal as she climbed down the bleachers. She broke into a run as she headed back to her car, and it wasn't lost on her that their relationship had begun with her running through that very park.

At the time, Lauren had thought that it was the worst pain she would ever feel. Her young self could never have imagined that one day she would be standing alone at the beach, alone in the world, looking back on that argument with nostalgia.

Her mother assumed that the key to her happiness would be finding love again.

Lauren never wanted to feel that way again. Alone, she was safe. Alone, she was in control.

She wouldn't let anything get in the way of that.

Chapter Twenty-Three

Matt plugged in his headphones. Outside, the sun began to set on another perfect June beach day. For all Matt cared, it might as well have been snowing.

Downstairs, Henny hosted her friends for dinner and a book club. She'd warned him earlier in the day. "Hope we don't disturb you! Come down and say hi. I'm sure the ladies would love to meet you."

He unpaused the section of the video he'd been watching.

"We really started talking about CTE vis-à-vis sports in 2002," said Dr. William Massey. He'd let Matt film him in his office at Mount Sinai Hospital.

"And can you tell me again what exactly CTE is?"

"Chronic traumatic encephalopathy. In 2002, we saw it in the brain of football player Mike Webster. Since then, dozens and dozens of cases have been identified."

"All in older players?"

"Not at all. Some of the guys are as young as seventeen."

"And can you explain exactly what CTE does to the brain?"

"In CTE, a protein called tau builds up around the blood vessels of the brain, interrupting normal function and eventually killing nerve cells. The disease evolves in stages. In stage one, tau is present near the frontal lobe but there are no symptoms. In stage two, as the protein becomes more widespread, you start to see the patient exhibit rage, impulsivity. He most likely will suffer depression."

The doctor pulled up a slide showing a normal brain next to a brain afflicted with stage 2 CTE, images from an autopsy. "See those darkened spots? Okay, then here in stage three—" He pulled up new slides. "We see progression to the temporal section of the brain. By now, the patient suffers confusion and memory loss. Then we get to stage four."

Matt's camera guy zoomed in on the slide of a healthy brain next to one with stage 4 CTE.

"That's significantly smaller than the healthy brain," Matt said.

"Half the size," said Dr. Massey. "The brain is now deformed, brittle. The cognitive function of the patient is severely limited."

Matt's phone rang. Craig.

"Hey, man," he said, pausing the video. Painfully aware of the footage he did *not* have a week after telling Craig that Lauren had agreed to an interview.

"Just checking in," said Craig. "How's it going?"

"Good, good. Making progress."

"When you have a minute, send me your interviews with Lauren Kincaid. I know you haven't had time to edit. I just want to get a sense of where we're at."

Matt closed his eyes. "Craig, I'm really close."

"Close to what?"

"To interviewing her."

"Last week you said she agreed to talk to you. Did she change her mind?"

"No. It's just…a process."

"So you lied to me."

"It's a process," Matt repeated. "I really am making progress. This is delicate work, Craig. You gotta trust me. I just need a little more time."

In the silence that followed, Matt wanted to say something but kept quiet. The project spoke for itself. It was important. Craig knew it—Matt was certain of that.

"It's not the fact that you don't have the interview yet," Craig said. "It's that you lied to me. Andrew Dobson warned me that you were unreliable, and now I have to believe him. I'm sorry, Matt. I'm out."

Lauren couldn't tell if her mother and sister were still entertaining Neil Hanes on the back deck, but she wasn't taking any chances. She slipped in quietly through the front door and carried her takeout from Sack O' Subs upstairs.

The upstairs hallway was dark, but behind the door of the guest room, Ethan's light was on. All she wanted to do was close herself in the privacy of her room, but she felt bad for the kid.

She knocked once lightly on the door and opened it. Ethan, wearing short-sleeved Spider-Man pajamas, sat on his bed playing with some sort of robot action figure.

"Hey there," she said from the doorway. "How's it going?"

"Okay," he said, looking up. "Aunt Lauren, did you read the Harry Potter books?"

"Absolutely."

"When you were my age?"

She shook her head, moving into the room. "I was a little older than you. The first book didn't come out until I was in fifth grade."

He looked at her in amazement. She was older than the Harry Potter books. *Great. Because I don't feel ancient enough already.*

"I got a copy for my birthday and my mom said she'd read it to me but she hasn't yet."

"Oh," Lauren said. How ironic that Stephanie had a kid who loved books. Stephanie once told Lauren that the act of reading was like trying to eat through a straw shoved up her nose "except more painful."

"Do you want to see it?" he asked, already scrambling off the bed. Before she could answer, he'd unearthed the thick paperback from a pile of books next to his unpacked suitcase.

"Very cool," she said when he handed it to her. And then, ignoring the call of her cheesesteak growing cold in the plastic bag, she said, "I could start reading it to you. If you're not too tired."

"I'm not tired," he said, stifling a yawn.

"Okay." She laughed. "So...I'm ready when you are."

She sat on the edge of his bed, feeling awkward. She wasn't used to being around children. Clearly, they had a very different sense of personal space than adults, because he wriggled right up next to her.

"Is the author a boy or girl?" he asked.

"She's a girl. A woman."

Ethan looked disappointed.

"But there are lots of great men writers," she added.

"Like the man who wrote *Star Wars*?"

"Yeah, well, *Star Wars* is a movie, not a book."

"*Harry Potter* is a movie."

"True. But it was a book first."

"What's harder, writing a book or writing a movie?"

"Um, I don't know. Probably writing a book. Why?"

He shrugged. "My mom said you were a writer."

"She did?" It was strange to imagine Stephanie talking about her or even thinking about her at all. "Well, I wanted to be a writer. But articles in the newspaper, not books."

"And you don't want to be one anymore?"

Oh God. "Well, I got really sad for a while and it's been hard to think about writing or a lot of the things I used to do."

"Why were you sad?"

She hesitated, but then, why not? It was the truth.

"My husband died. You don't remember him but, well, that's why I've been sad."

"My mom says when I'm sad I need to think about things that make me happy and then I won't be sad anymore."

Lauren nodded. "That's good advice. I guess I should try that sometime."

"I'm ready," he said, touching the book with reverence.

She opened to the first page. " 'Mr. and Mrs. Dursley, of number four, Privet Drive, were proud to say that they were perfectly normal, thank you very much' . . ."

Ethan's eyes locked on the page, and he read along as best he could. She put her arm around him, falling into the rhythm of the words, feeling a strange sensation. If she had to pinpoint what it was, she would have to say she was almost . . . content.

Matt elbowed his way to the bar and flagged Desiree for a beer and a shot of Tito's. The guy next to him nodded at Matt in recognition. Matt wondered how many more nights of complete obliteration would be necessary before he counted as a regular.

Game six of the Stanley Cup finals played out on the two screens on opposite ends of the bar. He watched one of the centers fly down the ice and imagined how it would feel to be knocked into the boards at that speed.

"Hey," someone said, tugging on his T-shirt, barely audible over the music and the crowd. He turned around. Stephanie, holding a beer, smiling drunkenly.

"It's your unlucky night," she said.

"I don't need you to tell me that."

"I'm here with someone," she said conspiratorially.

He looked around. "Well, good for you."

"He's in the bathroom."

"More information than I need, but okay." He turned back to the game.

"Who are you rooting for?" she asked, squeezing in next to him.

"Myself," he said, downing the shot. "Hey, let me ask you something. Do you think Rory changed over time? Did he become...angrier? More difficult?"

"Hmm," she said. "Was Rory Kincaid born an asshole or did he become an asshole? That's a tough one."

"I still don't know why you keep insisting he was such a bad guy."

Matt barely got the question out before a man appeared, put his hand on Stephanie's shoulder. He had reddish hair and wore an expensive watch. If Matt had to bet, he'd say he wasn't local. He was a New Yorker. Maybe LA.

"See ya," Stephanie said, slipping off with the man into the crowd. He watched her until she was out the door, his unanswered question hanging like a rope around his neck.

Chapter Twenty-Four

W hat's up with these?" Lauren signed in at the counter, stepping around a stack of framed photos. "Redecorating?"

"A little business venture," Nora said. "What do you think of them?"

Lauren bent down, looking at the first in the pile. It was a black-and-white shot of an empty beach and the ocean, mounted on white in a simple black frame. She flipped through, looking at the rest. All were in black-and-white, all various nature scenes around town.

"Simple. Nice. What's the business angle?"

"The photographer offered me a commission if I hang them on the walls here for sale. They go for a couple hundred apiece so it could be a nice chunk of change for me."

"Do you even have space on the walls?"

Nora handed her a scribbled list of the day's specials. "Can you please get these on the board for me? I have to check on the pastry delivery. They were stale yesterday. Did you have complaints?"

"No, not from my tables." Lauren walked to the chalkboard and realized all of Henny's signs were gone from the main dining room. "Nora, what happened to Henny's signs?"

"Yeah, that's the catch in the photography deal. I need to take those down."

"Oh no! Henny is going to be devastated."

"She'll be fine. She doesn't make more than twenty bucks or so a sign. It's a hobby, but this place is a business. If I can generate some income off the wall space, I gotta go for it."

Lauren knew it was tough to run a business year after year. Just look at what her parents went through with the store. Still, she felt bad for Henny. She would try to remember to buy a few of the signs before the end of the day. It was difficult, though, to think of anything once the breakfast rush started. When she was in the zone, her life and thoughts outside of the rhythm of taking orders, filling drinks, and delivering plates to the tables didn't exist.

That's why she was oblivious when her past walked through the door.

She rounded the counter, holding two full pitchers of iced tea, freshly sliced lemons floating on top. She didn't notice Emerson Kincaid until she nearly collided with him, at which time she promptly dropped both pitchers, soaking herself and the floor. Lauren was vaguely aware of busboys and Nora scurrying around her, containing the mess. All she could do was back away, useless.

She was never more thankful than she was in that moment that he and Rory didn't look very much alike. It was not like seeing a version of Rory walk in the door. But it was very much the physical incarnation of a different life, of a time that had begun to feel more and more like it existed only in her memory. The idea that players from that particular drama still roamed freely, still had lives beyond the brief moment when their worlds intersected with hers, was almost too much to think about.

"What are you doing here?" she said.

She hadn't seen or heard from him since the day of the memorial. A conversation that haunted her.

"I need to talk to you," Emerson said.

"Why?"

He looked older than she remembered. He was completely gray with deep lines under his eyes like his mother had. Lauren did the math; he was in his mid-forties. But he was still clearly in good shape, his shoulders broad and arms muscular under his T-shirt.

"You still wear your wedding band," he said.

"I have nothing to say to you, Emerson."

"This will take five minutes. Where can we talk?"

Lauren, feeling trapped, glanced around the packed restaurant.

"Sir, would you like a seat or are you looking for takeout?" Nora asked, holding menus. Nora obviously knew he was not there for food, that this was personal. Lauren thought of the first time Matt had shown up here and cornered her. That was a cakewalk compared to this.

"I'm so sorry, Nora. He's a...family friend. Can I take five? Aside from the iced tea, everything else is in order. Just waiting on tickets."

Nora gave her an *Are you sure?* look and Lauren nodded.

Lauren felt guilty that her personal drama kept showing up on Nora's doorstep. But, well, for the past four years, Nora had been telling her she needed to have a life. And this was what Lauren had been afraid of; this was what her life looked like.

Emerson followed her outside and half a block down the street, safely out of earshot of the sidewalk tables.

"What do you want?" she asked.

"Remember a few years ago I warned you that someone was trying to make a documentary about Rory? Well, he's still at it. I just found out he interviewed the Villanova coach last month. I want to make sure you're not talking to him."

"Your own mother spoke to him."

He looked at her in disgust. "I can't believe it. You *are* talking to him."

"I didn't say that. What I said was that *your mother* spoke to him."

"My mother was extremely upset at the idea of some New York film guy exploiting Rory's legacy. But since we had no legal recourse to stop him, she at least wanted to do her part to represent him in the way we want him represented."

"You just have an answer for everything. As always."

Emerson narrowed his eyes. Rarely, in all the years she'd known him, had she been anything less than respectful to the great and powerful Emerson, the man who could change her life with a single conversation. *Had* changed her life with a single conversation. Yes, there had been a time when she had seen him as a confidant, when she had sought his counsel. When she had bought into Rory's reverence for him. Her mistake. A tragic, costly mistake.

"Lauren, I want your word that you won't participate in this film."

"That's none of your business."

"Are you trying to say my brother's legacy isn't my business? It isn't *your* business. You were barely married by the end."

She felt herself begin to shake. "We *were* married. And if I want to talk about my late husband, that's my right." The rage was more about a conversation that had taken place behind her back half a decade ago than about the one taking place in that moment.

"If you say one word against my brother, we're going to have a big problem."

"Are you threatening me, Emerson? Don't bother. Rory's gone. There's nothing more you can take from me."

"Take from you? That's a joke. You ran away so fast, you left skid marks. The going got tough, and you sure as hell got going."

"Fuck you, Emerson." She walked toward the restaurant, but then turned back for a moment. "Oh, and if you want to know if I said anything on camera, you'll have to buy a ticket to the movie."

Beth spread out all her tools: doughnut cutter, rolling pin, doughnut pan, piping bag, and parchment paper. Ethan seemed most fascinated with the electric mixer.

"How long will it be before we can eat them?" he asked.

"Well, it takes about a half hour to do all the baking, but there are periods where we have to let the dough rest, so it will be about two hours."

"Two *hours?*"

She laughed. "It goes by quickly. And it's worth the wait. All good things are. Besides, it's only nine in the morning. We can't eat doughnuts before lunch."

He seemed to contemplate this reasoning.

"What kind are we making?"

"I thought we'd start simple for our first try. Just regular glazed. But if you like helping out, we can really make any kind of doughnut."

"Chocolate?"

"Sure. Chocolate, coconut. I made an apple-pie doughnut once that was delicious. If you could make any doughnut in the world, what would you make?"

He thought a minute. "Peanut butter and jelly."

"We could do that," she said, already thinking about what kind of peanut butter would work best as filling. "But for now, we start with the basics. In the kitchen, you have to be organized. So we have all of our ingredients there, and we have our equipment here."

She pulled a bowl in front of them and combined the yeast, milk, and flour, explaining to him that baking was like science. "You have to measure and be very precise. Now we're going to stir this into a paste, and then it has to sit for a half hour."

"That's it?" he asked, disappointed.

"No, it's just the beginning! When it's ready, we're going to combine it with other ingredients in the mixing machine, and then the fun part: we get to roll out the dough."

The deck door slid open. Stephanie appeared, wearing the same clothes she'd worn at dinner the night before. Beth swallowed her rage as Ethan ran to his mother.

"Mommy! Where'd you go?"

"Hi, hon. I went for an early walk," Stephanie said, eyeing Beth. "Are you baking with Gran?"

"We're making doughnuts," he said. "Today just plain but Gran said we can make any kind. Even peanut butter and jelly."

"Well, your gran is an amazing baker, so if she says so, it's true."

"Stephanie, can I talk to you for a minute? Ethan, hon, like I said, that mixture in the bowl has to rest. I'll be back in a few minutes and we'll do the next step."

She took her daughter by the elbow and practically dragged her up to the second floor.

"Where the hell have you been?" Beth whispered.

"Mother, I'm a grown woman. Last I checked, I don't have a curfew."

"No, but you have a child. You can't just run around all night. This is unacceptable, Stephanie. It's time for you to grow up!"

Stephanie brushed past her and headed upstairs. Beth's eyes filled with tears.

Howard had been right. This summer was a disaster.

Chapter Twenty-Five

Matt packed up his camera. His laptop and clothes were already in the suitcase, and his key was on the desk. The only thing left were the index cards organized and spread out on the floor. He bent down, looked at the timeline of Rory's story, the painstakingly constructed puzzle, and then scooped them up and tossed them into the trash.

All that was left to do was say good-bye to Henny. Technically, he could just walk out, let the door lock behind him, and be done with it. Maybe he was procrastinating; when he got into his car and drove onto the highway, it would really be over.

He walked to the back deck, where he could usually find Henny sanding or painting first thing in the morning, but the tables were empty and she wasn't outside. Her car was in the driveway, so he walked to the front porch and rang the doorbell.

"What are you doing out here? You lock yourself out again?" she asked when she finally opened the door. It took her so long to respond to the bell he thought maybe she wasn't home after all.

"No. I'm checking out. I left my key on the desk. I just wanted to say good-bye."

"So you're not extending your stay?"

He shook his head. "Unfortunately, I have to get back to New York."

Henny burst into tears. Okay, this was a bit more of a good-bye than he had bargained for. His phone rang, but he ignored it. Dropping his bag, he asked, "Is something wrong?"

"No, I'm fine." She sniffed. "I'm sorry. This is very unprofessional. You were a model tenant. It was great to meet you. If you can rate me on the website, that would be helpful."

"Sure. Not a problem. But maybe…can I come in for a second?"

Matt hadn't spent any time on the first floor of the house. The living room was just as quaint and comfortable as his bedroom, with cozy reading chairs upholstered in pale blue and yellow, a white wicker couch decorated with starfish throw pillows, a white wooden coffee table, and, of course, painted signs everywhere.

"Oh, you know, I want to buy one of your signs before I go," he said, an attempt to cheer her up so he could leave without feeling like he'd walked out on her. "Something to remember this trip by." Though he wouldn't soon forget it. The place where his film died.

The comment brought a fresh wave of tears. "You'll be the last person to buy one."

"Why's that?"

"Nora took them down from the restaurant walls. She needs room to sell fancy, expensive photos!" She blew her nose loudly into a handkerchief. "My signs have been on the walls of the café since the day it opened."

This is what he got for procrastinating.

"Well, um, maybe another place in town will sell them."

"I've been looking around but any other place wants too much of a percentage of the sale. I won't make any money. And I don't want to raise the price."

"Maybe you should sell these online. Then you keep most of the money and you have your own virtual store. I know you said you don't like doing things on the Internet, but that's really where things are at now. You can sell to people all over the country. All over the world."

She sighed. "I don't know. Maybe when my son comes to visit for Thanksgiving he can set it up for me."

"It's not complicated. I can get you up on Etsy in no time."

She brightened. "Really? If you can do that for me, I'm happy to give you a few nights here free of charge."

"Thanks, but—"

"I insist!"

"I appreciate it, but I was here for work and now things have fallen through. I don't have any reason to stay."

The doorbell rang.

"Now, who in heaven can that be? And I'm a mess." She dabbed at her eyes.

"Do you want me to get it for you?"

She nodded. Matt walked to the door, recalculating his timeline. He could set her up on Etsy, then grab lunch, then hit the road. He'd be back in New York by four.

Matt opened the front door.

"I changed my mind," Lauren said. "I'll do the interview."

He stared at her.

The irony of timing was too much for him. He didn't even have money to pay the sound guy and his DP.

"What changed your mind?" he asked, really just curious about the extent to which the universe was fucking with him.

"You were right about one thing. I do care about the truth."

He looked at his packed bag just inches away from her. He thought of the two dozen index cards in the garbage upstairs.

He thought of Rory, chasing the puck in the crease, forty seconds left on the clock, game six of the Stanley Cup semifinals. *He shoots, he scores...*

"Come back in twenty minutes," he said.

* * *

Lauren's decision to talk to Matt had been a knee-jerk reaction to Emerson's warning, and now that the moment had arrived, she was scared.

She stood outside Henny's front door, her heart beating so hard and fast she felt she could barely breathe. *I can just leave.*

But no. She'd been going over and over it in her mind, and talking to Matt was the right thing to do. Yes, when he'd first shown up, when she'd learned about the film, she saw it as Matt asking something of her, taking something from her. And then when Emerson told her not to talk to Matt, she realized that Matt was actually *offering* her something. The chance to tell her story. Maybe it could serve a purpose. The truth might matter.

"Hey. Come on in. Almost ready for you," Matt said.

"Wow. Is Henny okay with all of this?" Lauren asked.

All the framed photos and Henny's signs were gone from the walls, and most of the chairs and the sofa had been pushed to one side of the room.

"Yes, she's fine with it. Don't worry. We'll have this room back in shape by the time she gets home tonight. Can you have a seat in that chair?" He directed her to a dove-gray armchair that had been angled in front of the window.

"We're going to…like, get right into it?" she said nervously.

"Let me check the setup here," he said, twisting the legs of a tripod to stabilize it. She perched on the edge of the chair.

"And you said this would just take an hour?"

"Lauren, if you can just slide back an inch," he said.

Lauren fidgeted nervously in her seat. Matt moved from behind the camera and sat across from her. He grabbed some papers from a nearby end table and handed them to her.

"Before we start shooting, I need for you to sign this release."

"What? I never agreed to sign anything."

"It's standard operating procedure, Lauren. You don't have to sign it, but if you don't, I can't film you."

She glanced down at the pages in her hands.

"You don't have to answer any question you don't want to, and you certainly don't have to say anything you don't want to."

"But everything I say on camera you can use or edit?"

"Yes. Once you've spoken on camera, the material becomes, essentially, property of the film company."

She scanned the paperwork, then looked up at him.

"I need to know why you're doing this film," she said. "Why this? Why Rory?"

He met her gaze, and the intensity was unnervingly familiar to Lauren. There had been only one other person she'd known who could convey all his passion and focus in a quiet glance.

"My older brother, Ben, was a Marine," Matt said. "He enlisted right after 9/11. Fought in Operation Enduring Freedom. And we lost him in 2004. There was no fanfare. He wasn't on the front page of the *New York Times*. There was no memorial in an arena televised for the world to see. No one except for the people who loved Ben cared that he was gone. He was just another statistic. But when your husband died, he became America's hero. I couldn't tell my brother's story, but I knew I could at least tell Rory's."

She nodded slowly. And signed the release.

"I have to mic you up," Matt said. "Normally I have a sound guy, but you threw me a curveball today." He knelt in front of her chair, leaning close to feed a wire down the front of her shirt. Her pulse raced from his nearness. "Sorry—almost done," he said. He reached around her to clip a sound pack to the back of her jeans.

She felt relief when he stepped away and looked at her from behind the camera.

"One more thing. I just need to fix this so it's not visible." Matt moved back to her and reached around her waist to adjust the sound pack. Then he checked her mic before returning to the chair opposite her, picking up a laptop, and resting it on his knees.

She exhaled.

"You ready to get started?" Matt said.

"Um, yeah." She was still unnerved by his nearness, the way it had felt to have him invade her personal space.

"Okay, so just look at me. As if we're having a conversation. Yeah, like that. I know it's strange, but try to forget about the cameras."

"I'll try," she said.

"When I ask you a question, I need you to respond by repeating part of it. So if I say, 'What is your name?' you say, 'My name is Lauren Kincaid.' All of my questions will be edited out, so for this to make sense, you need to repeat the question."

Lauren swallowed hard. Behind the cameras, a tall square light beamed down on her.

"So, just to get the ball rolling: Tell me your name and your relationship to Rory Kincaid."

"My name is Lauren Kincaid. Rory Kincaid is my husband."

"Lauren, I'm sorry—can you repeat that but using past tense."

It took her a few seconds to register what he was saying. When she got it, she took a short breath before saying, "My name is Lauren Kincaid. Rory Kincaid was my husband."

"How did you two meet?"

"We met in high school. I was writing an article for the school paper about the hockey team, and I interviewed him."

"What was your first impression of Rory?"

"When I met him, I guess you could say the school had put him a little bit on a pedestal. The hockey team was doing great, he was the captain even though he was only a junior, and he was the lead scorer. He was the lead scorer in the entire division."

"So he was a big deal."

She nodded. "I interviewed him for the school paper, but the *Philadelphia Inquirer* wrote about him too."

"What did the *Inquirer* article say?"

"It was about Philadelphia-area high-school athletes who had the attention of college scouts all over the country. The only one mentioned from Lower Merion School District was Rory. They even ran a photo of him."

"Do you have a copy of that?"

"Somewhere. I can look for it."

"That would be great. Okay, so, when did you first go to one of his hockey games?"

"After I interviewed him for the article, I went to his game that Friday night. They played against Radnor and won in a shutout."

As much as she'd tried to be a neutral observer of the game, reporter-like in her attitude, she couldn't take her eyes off Rory during the three twenty-minute periods. Even when he was on the bench, she watched him drink from his Gatorade bottle or wipe his brow with one of the white towels the team assistant handed around. He scored a hat trick. After his third goal, the crowd tossed their LM baseball hats and ski hats onto the ice. The energy in the rink was electrifying, and Lauren was hooked—on hockey, and on Rory. "Rory scored all three goals."

Matt asked if Rory was thinking at that time about a career in the NHL, and she told him that he liked hockey but he was also interested in astronomy.

"Astronomy," Matt repeated.

"Yes. In high school, he was always reading astronomy books. And he was really gifted in math, so he knew astronomy was something he could get into someday."

When she'd met him, he had a Rottweiler named Polaris. *The North Star,* he'd explained to her. *The brightest star in the constellation Ursa Minor.*

Matt nodded, consulting his laptop. "Were you at the game the night the puck hit him in the jaw?"

"Yes. I didn't see it happen because I was…talking to someone. But I went to the hospital immediately after."

"Was there any talk at that time that he might have sustained a concussion in addition to injuring his jaw?"

"No. Not that I know of."

Matt asked more about how Rory had homed in on a hockey career, and she told him about the agents showing up at Harvard by his junior year.

"They threw around such crazy numbers in terms of money," she said. "Rory's mom was a widow, and he worried about taking care of her. Once the money became a reality, there was no question he would go into the NHL."

"And yet he opted to play for only two seasons," Matt said.

Lauren swallowed hard. "That's right."

Matt asked about Rory's injury in December of 2009, and she repeated what she'd told him off camera: Dean Wade was wrong. Rory hadn't gotten a concussion. "He was back on the ice the next game."

"But a few months later—the fight with the Flyers' Chris Pronger. That was unquestionably a concussion," he said.

"Yes," she conceded. "It was. And a fight with the team we'd grown up watching. Talk about insult to injury."

Rory would be out of play for a few weeks at least. The timing couldn't have been worse: Rory had been scheduled to represent the United States in the Winter Olympics alongside an LA Kings teammate, goalie Jonathan Quick.

Lauren didn't rush to buy a plane ticket after that injury, but then his mother called to say she was spending a week with Rory and maybe Lauren could find time to come the following week. With a lump of alarm in her throat, she'd said of course.

She had one day of overlap with Kay. Looking back on it, that was a mistake in planning. Rory's mother busily cooked for him and fussed around the apartment, making Lauren feel extraneous. Kay talked endlessly about Emerson, who had just announced he was going back to West Point as an instructor.

"Your father would be so proud," Kay said with a sniff over lasagna that night.

After dinner, Rory retreated to the bedroom. He watched CNN, as he apparently had been doing all day long for the past seven days. He was obsessed with the November shooting at Fort Hood.

"Try to get him out and about," Kay said on her way to the airport in the morning. "I know you're not much on cooking, so maybe a restaurant here or there will do him some good."

Lauren convinced him to walk the few blocks to Hugo's for dinner that night, but he was sullen and quiet. She'd been told that depression was a side effect of the concussion and tried to reassure herself—and him—that it was temporary.

"What am I doing with my life?" he said, slumped back in his seat at the restaurant, looking out at Santa Monica Boulevard.

"Come on, Rory. This is irrational. You'll be back on the ice in a few weeks. This happens. It's part of the deal when you play at this level—you know that."

"What do you know about it?" he snapped.

"I'm just trying to help!"

"Well, don't."

She wanted to say fine, he could wallow in his self-pity by himself. She had exams to take. Instead, Lauren tried turning the conversation to more positive things, like their plans to spend July at the shore house. Her grandmother had died earlier in the year. She'd left the Green Gable to Beth, who told Lauren and Stephanie they could have the house for the summer—it was too soon for her to be there without her mother.

A quick negotiation determined that Stephanie would have the house in June, Lauren would take it in July, and they'd split August depending on their schedules.

"It will be good to have some time for just the two of us," Lauren told Rory. "In the place where it all started. Prom weekend, remember?"

He grumbled a response.

Later, when he was in the shower, she went outside and, standing among the exotic plants outside the apartment building, called Ashley Wade.

"Don't take it personally," Ashley said. "They all get nasty when they hit their heads. Trust me, in two months you'll tell him, 'You were a real jerk back then, you said such and such,' and he'll laugh and say he doesn't remember."

But she would remember. And for the first time in a very long time, her future with him seemed uncertain. He wasn't the Rory she knew, and this made her nervous.

She called Emerson—a mistake.

"You can't freak out over every little injury," he said. "You're dating a professional athlete."

Lauren didn't say any of this aloud to Matt.

And then Matt leaned slightly forward, not glancing at his computer but looking straight at her. He said, "His style of play changed after that. Everything changed after that, didn't it?"

Lauren stared at him. She began to speak, then stopped. It would be a betrayal of Rory to reveal his weakness to the world; it was the last thing he would have wanted. "I don't know what you mean by that." Her hands fluttered to the mic clipped to her shirt. "Your hour is up."

Chapter Twenty-Six

Beth heard a car pull up in front of the house. She was neck-deep in the pool, her hair piled carefully in a clip on top of her head.

Was it that late in the afternoon already? She wasn't expecting Howard back from Florida until close to dinner. She climbed out of the pool and wrapped herself in a towel, wishing she had time to get herself dried off and pulled together. Yes, she still cared about how she looked when she greeted her husband. It was old-fashioned, she knew. It went back to advice her mother had given her when she was just a teenager: "Always make sure when your husband comes home that the house is in order and you're dressed and made up. If a man doesn't like coming home, the day will arrive when he doesn't." It was outrageous, of course. Something straight out of a Helen Gurley Brown advice manual. But her mother had seemed to manage her own marriage nearly effortlessly, so what did Beth know? Nothing, she'd come to realize. She certainly never had such easy pearls of wisdom for her own daughters when it came to marriage—or, in Stephanie's case, to divorce.

Beth's mother seemed to be in the last of the generations that saw divorce as a disgrace, or, as her mother would mutter in Yiddish, a *shonda*. Beth couldn't remember a single one of her parents' friends getting divorced. Of course, by the time Beth was a teenager, in the seventies, at least half of her own friends were from "broken" homes. Still, divorce was never something she viewed as a viable option, and certainly not, as many of her peers saw it, a likely outcome. No matter how tough the time with Howard, she'd never doubted that they would stick it out.

Not until now.

Lately, things felt different. Was this what marriage came down to? You spend decades doing the best you can, and then in midlife, you tally up the blame?

"Howard?" she called, walking through the kitchen.

"Upstairs," he said.

His suitcase was open on the bed. He wore a golf shirt and navy pin-striped shorts and was deeply tanned.

"Hi," she said, trying to remember how their last phone call had ended. When had they last spoken? Two days ago? "How was the flight back?"

"Uneventful. What's going on around here?" he asked. "Did Cynthia come by?"

"Who's Cynthia?"

"The real estate agent. She was supposed to take photos."

She had, in fact, stopped by. Beth had ignored the ringing doorbell until the woman retreated back to her car.

"Nope. Not yet."

Howard huffed his irritation.

"So how was Florida?"

"Incredible," he said. "Bill and Lorraine's place is right on the golf course."

"Well, I don't play golf, so that's not a huge selling point."

"It's a nonstarter, anyway. Their place is beyond what we'll be able to afford even if we sell this place at our full asking price."

Beth tried not to panic. "It's not just about money. I can't ride off into the Florida sunset with you while things are so unsettled. And you're wrong about this summer not helping things; Neil Hanes was here for dinner last night. I think he's interested in Lauren. He keeps asking about her." She conveniently omitted the part about him leaving with Stephanie. And that he was potentially interested in buying the house.

"Okay, but you don't need to be here micromanaging. Has Lauren started looking at apartments yet?"

No, of course not. Lauren was more in denial about the house sale than Beth.

"I'm not sure." She felt a flash of irritation. Why did he act like she had to answer to him? He was the one who'd put them in this predicament.

"Hi, Grandpa!" Ethan ran into the room and hugged Howard before turning to Beth and asking if he could have another doughnut.

"Sure. Just make sure to put the plastic wrap back on tight. We want to keep them fresh."

"We baked," Ethan told Howard with a grin.

Howard shot Beth a look. "Sounds good, buddy," he said.

When Ethan was out of the room, Howard said, "You've got him baking?"

"It was a nice activity for us to do together."

"I mean, it's bad enough the kid doesn't have a father..."

"Oh, Howard, don't be ridiculous. Why don't *you* do something with him instead of criticizing me?"

"I will," Howard said, turning back to his suitcase. "I'll take him to the beach. Just as soon as I unpack and make a few phone calls."

"Great," she said, feeling oddly like she'd lost the round. With a deep exhale, she said, "Howard, let's just slow this thing down. Give some time here a chance."

He shook his head wistfully, as if she were missing something obvious.

"Time won't help, Beth. I feel stuck. And I'm trying to find my way out of it. I can't spend one more goddamn day mired in negativity. Problems with the girls, problems with the business. It's been going on so long, it's a habit. Life doesn't have to be like this."

"Of course it does! That's why it's called life."

"No, that's *our* life. Yours and mine together. You know, Lauren's husband died four years ago—but yours didn't."

"What's that supposed to mean?"

Howard looked around the room like a trapped animal. "Beth, we need to either reset, or separate. But I'm not spending one more year like I've spent the past few."

She knew she should have felt scared or upset that her husband was talking about leaving, but all she felt was a wave of anger. Then a thought exploded, a thought that maybe had been glimmering, a tiny spark, for weeks now.

"Did you lose our house on purpose?"

"Why would I do that?"

"I don't know. To give yourself an excuse to leave."

Howard put down the sports jacket he was holding and moved closer to Beth. He took one of her hands and squeezed it.

"I don't want an excuse to leave. I want an excuse to stay."

"Your children need you here this summer. Your grandson—"

"Let me rephrase that: I want an excuse to stay in this *marriage*."

Beth pulled her hand away. She felt like she'd been slapped. What was he referring to? Their sex life? Okay, things had dwindled the past year or so. But they weren't teenagers anymore. And the money problems didn't help. Nor did their tension over the girls. Howard had never agreed with Beth about letting Lauren isolate herself at the shore, and he had also taken Stephanie's wayward personal life very hard. But none of this was Beth's fault!

"Well, maybe I don't have one for you."

Howard nodded. "Then I'm going back to Florida next week to stay with Bill and Lorraine."

Was this how it ended? Thirty years, dismissed with a few words and a half-packed suitcase?

"That's fine with me, Howard."

But it wasn't fine. None of this was fine. Lauren widowed; Stephanie a single mother. Her own marriage disintegrating at middle age. And yet she had no idea how to fix any of it.

The sign, aqua blue with white lettering, read YOU CAN SHAKE THE SAND FROM YOUR SHOES BUT IT NEVER LEAVES YOUR HEART. Matt staged it against a white wall, propped on a table that he kept under the sightline of the camera lens. Then he took another shot of the sign hanging on the wall.

"Which one do you like better?" he asked Henny, showing her the options on the digital screen of his camera.

"I think the hanging version," she said. "This Etsy thing is complicated!"

"Getting the photos right is the most labor-intensive part," he said. "Once we have them uploaded, the rest is easy. Did you decide on a name for the store?"

She had told him a few she was thinking of, including Hung by Henny. He had to gently point out the potential sexual connotations with that one; she didn't believe him until she Googled the old HBO show *Hung*.

"What do you think of Hen House Designs?" she said.

"I like it."

"I really appreciate your help with this. I hope you'll take me up on the offer to stay here a few nights free of charge."

"Henny, I think I will."

Ethan turned the page impatiently.

"Do we need to refresh where we were?" Lauren asked.

"No. I remember," he said, yawning.

"Uh-oh. Are you going to make it through a whole chapter?"

"Two chapters," he said.

She laughed. "That might be a little ambitious. I don't know if *I* can stay awake through two chapters."

"But it's a good book!" he said, outraged.

"True." She smiled, realizing she enjoyed reading the book aloud to him more than she'd enjoyed reading it herself. Ethan, nestled against her on his bed, radiated heat.

She read slowly, trying to do a decent job with the voices to make it lively. Feeling herself perspire, she turned the page and reached for his bedside fan. "Hey, are you hot?" she asked. No response. Slowly, making as little movement as possible, she closed the book, easing Ethan's back against his pillow. He barely stirred. She kissed him on the top of the head and pulled his light summer quilt up to his shoulders, careful not to upset the meticulous arrangement of stuffed animals on the far side of the bed.

Ethan was neat for a six-year-old, maybe with a touch of OCD. She had been that way as a kid too, always needing to line up her dolls in a certain way before she could fall asleep.

She crossed the room to the bookshelf, where Ethan liked her to put *Harry Potter* back between *Shark vs. Train* and *Dinotrux*. Stephanie had brought a lot of books for the summer. Lauren hadn't looked through them all but thinking about her old doll collection made her nostalgic. She wondered if Ethan's book collection included any of her old favorites, like *Where the Sidewalk Ends* or *Where the Wild Things Are*. She scanned the spines, and a familiar title jumped out at her: *Lights in the Dark: A Practical Guide to Viewing the Universe*.

Hands trembling, Lauren pulled it off the shelf. It was clearly a new book, but the cover was the same as the one she'd given another boy to put on his bookshelf.

How strange. Just that morning she'd been telling Matt about Rory's interest in astronomy. It had felt good to talk about the high-school stuff, to say things aloud that had begun to feel like they'd happened in another lifetime. Sometimes she felt oddly burdened, as if Rory lived on only in her memory—the real Rory, not the icon the press and the public made him into. For the one hour she spent talking to Matt, that burden had lifted.

She opened the book, her mind many miles and many years away.

Senior year, the only upside to the breakup with Rory was that she didn't have to worry about getting into a school in Boston to be closer to him. She was free to make Georgetown her top choice, as it had been since the beginning of junior year when she'd won a journalism competition and a trip to DC.

Accepted to Georgetown, she replaced Rory's old Lower Merion ice hockey T-shirt that she'd slept in for almost a year with a new gray and blue Hoyas shirt.

Still, she wasn't happy. Not truly happy, not the way she'd felt when they were together. Once you'd known the complete, deep-seated joy of being in love, nothing else compared. Not even personal accomplishment. She tried not to think about him, but every corner of the school, of her house, of the neighborhood streets triggered memories of their relationship. How cruel, how unfair that he should be the one to end it and also be the one to start in a new place free and clear. It was this sense of injustice that had helped turn her heartbreak to anger, and it was this anger, festering for five months, that had steeled her to ignore his texts when they finally appeared.

He was in town for Christmas break. He missed her; they needed to talk. He was sorry. He'd meet her anywhere. Didn't they owe it to their time together to at least talk?

Delete, delete, delete.

And then, the Thursday before Christmas break. In the *Merionite* classroom, a makeshift holiday party of Dunkin' Donuts and Wawa coffee.

"You have a visitor," the sports editor said.

Rory, standing in the doorway.

The past few months, she had of course imagined seeing him again. In all the scenarios she'd come up with, she hadn't anticipated that he would be even more beautiful, his chiseled good looks sharpening and deepening, the last vestiges of boyhood gone. For the first time, she saw a preview of Rory the man, and maybe it was best that they had broken up. His perfection was maybe more than she had bargained for.

He invited her to his house for Christmas Eve. *It's over,* she'd told him.

And yet, seventy-two hours later, she stood on the sidewalk outside of his house.

The ground was a sheet of ice. She took slow steps, glancing at the front yard, remembering the last time she'd seen it—late summer, verdant. Before everything changed.

She stepped carefully up his driveway, holding an apple pie from the Bakery House on Lancaster Avenue for Mrs. Kincaid and a book for Rory. He had told her she didn't need to bring anything, but she remembered the bounty of last year, and so of course she could not show up empty-handed.

Her gift was simple, something a friend would give another friend. But it was tied to a memory she had, an afternoon of studying side by side with him in the Ludington Library. She'd barely been able to focus on her work with their feet touching under the wooden table, the occasional shared glance. When it was time to leave, he'd borrowed a big hardcover book on astronomy, *Lights in the Dark: A Practical Guide to Viewing the Universe.*

Two nights earlier, she'd ordered a copy of the book online. She wrapped it in green and red paper and taped a card—a painting of a snow-covered pine tree—to the top. This time, there had been no agonizing about whether or not to write *Love, Lauren.*

Dear Rory:

I know things are different now. You've moved on to Harvard and I'm leaving for DC in a few months. But I want you to know our time together meant a lot to me. I wish you the best in everything you do.

Your friend always, Lauren

He greeted her on the front patio, dressed in a Harvard windbreaker and his good pants. The sight of him made her chest feel fluttery. After so many months of trying to forget him, there she was, walking toward him.

"I want to talk to you in private," he said, steering her to the garage. They walked in silence, their breath visible.

She thought about this time last year, how hopeful she'd been, certain it was just the first of many Christmases together. Reflexively, she touched her neck. It had been so hard to take off the necklace, to put it in its box and shove it to the back of the highest shelf of her closet. For a long time she'd felt it burning in her room, something aglow, toxic.

"It's freezing," she said.

"Just a minute, then we'll go in the house," he said, pulling the heavy door down behind them.

"You're not going to give me another piece of heart jewelry, are you? Because I'm really not in the mood for more empty symbolism."

"Ouch. You've gotten hard in our time apart."

She wanted to make a joke—something about how she hoped he hadn't gotten hard in their time apart. But there was nothing funny about their situation. She'd thought she was showing up for closure, but it was like the wound was ripped right open again.

Then he said suddenly, jarringly, "I love you. I've missed you. I'm not going to say it was a mistake to break up, because I needed a few months of focus. And I needed some distance to know if this thing was real."

Tears sprang to her eyes. "Well, it's not just about what you need," she said. "It isn't just about you all the time. Did you ever think of that?"

"Of course. And I took a big chance. I'm sorry to have hurt you. I really am. But I think if you can just forgive me, we'll be stronger for the time apart."

"I don't know," she said. Of course she knew! She was in love. "Maybe we should just be friends."

"I don't want to be friends. I love you. I never stopped thinking about you. I don't have anything going on with any women in Boston. I just worked my ass off. And I'm going to continue to work my ass off because I want a lot out of life. And one of those things is you—by my side. As much as possible."

She stepped into his arms. He kissed her face, not seeming to mind that she sobbed like a child. When she calmed down, he pulled back, tilted her face up to his with his thumb under her chin.

"Lauren," he whispered. "I'll never let you down again."

I'll never let you down again.

She reshelved the astronomy book, slipped quietly out of Ethan's room, and closed the door behind her.

Chapter Twenty-Seven

Matt paused the frame.

Lauren looked beautiful on camera, her dark eyes big and luminous. She had the type of bone structure that was slightly angular in person but flawless on film. She'd worn her hair back in a ponytail that afternoon and dressed in a plain black T-shirt and jeans. There was something steely and fragile about her at the same time. From a filmmaking perspective, he couldn't have cast anyone better.

"Rory's mom was a widow," she said, a lock of hair falling free from her ponytail. She tucked it back behind her ear. "And he worried about taking care of her. Once the money became a reality, there was no question he would go into the NHL."

Matt forwarded through his reel, moving to an interview with Rory's former sports agent. Jason Cavendish, a slickly handsome LA native, looked barely older than his athlete clients. It had been an expensive shoot, flying to Hollywood and staying at the Standard. They couldn't film at Jason's high-profile office building, so Matt needed a sharp-looking hotel suite. The day of the scheduled shoot, Jason had an emergency meeting, and it was postponed to the tune of another six-hundred-dollar night. But it was worth it for this bombshell:

"The Kings didn't make an offer once he was a free agent," Jason said. "I don't know where the press got that seven-figure rumor. But I sure as hell wasn't about to correct them."

Matt's phone rang. He glanced at the screen, was surprised to find Craig Mason.

He'd been wrestling with when and how to reach out to Craig, to send him the footage of Lauren. He'd decided to wait until he had more, but this call was an encouraging turn of events.

"Great to hear from you," Matt said. "I'd been thinking of calling you myself. I interviewed Lauren Kincaid."

That's how these projects went sometimes. How many film-festival panels had he listened to where people talked about things falling apart, the film looking like it would never get made, and then all the pieces clicked into place. He could see the two of them sitting side by side at Sundance...

"Good for you," Craig said. "But I just called to share some news."

"News?"

"I heard something through the grapevine, and since I am rooting for you—you know that, right? Anyway, I want you to know there's a feature film about Rory in the works."

Matt felt a rushing whoosh as he lost his breath.

"Who's making it? When's it coming out?"

"I don't know anything more about it."

"Okay," Matt said. "Well, I think this just shows I have a hot topic. It's not a concern."

"I'm glad you feel that way."

"Yeah. Thanks for the heads-up. I'll keep an eye out for that. But in the meantime I'll send you the Lauren Kincaid footage—"

"I'm afraid I have to pass," said Craig. "Good luck."

"Thanks, man," Matt said calmly. He hung up.

And then he threw his phone against the wall.

Lauren pulled a photograph down from the wall of the restaurant and carried it to the front counter.

"Table three wants to buy this one," she told Nora, glancing at the price sticker: $250. It was just a shot of a narrow house on the bay. Lauren knew the house; it was painted a pretty moss green but the photo was in black-and-white so it didn't even have that going for it. She supposed summer visitors wanted to take any piece of Longport home with them.

"Great. I'll wrap it up," Nora said. "Hey, I wanted to ask you a few things. First, you're coming to my Fourth of July party, right?"

"Of course." Every Fourth, Nora hosted a huge barbecue at her own house on the bay. It usually started midafternoon and lasted until the sun began to set, at which time the guests would make their way over to the boardwalk to view the fireworks.

"Great. Bring your parents and your sister; the more the merrier. Also, would you be able to work nights in August?"

Lauren smiled. "You're finally making the leap to dinner service?"

"I'm working on it. I realize I've been playing it too safe. The way these photographs are flying out of here—I should have thought of selling something higher ticket on the walls years ago. Makes me think I've been doing things the same way for too long. I just have to worry about staffing up midway through the season. Not the easiest task."

"Well, I'm ready to take more shifts, so just let me know what you need."

Nora, distracted, eyed the door. "Your friend is back."

Lauren followed her gaze and turned to see Matt in the front of the crowded room, not standing in line but next to it.

"Henny told April that he interviewed you at her place yesterday."

"Henny told April? What is this, whisper down the lane?" Lauren said.

"Well, Henny's not speaking to me at the moment, so yes, I'm relying on secondhand information."

"Oh no. Because of her signs?"

Nora nodded. "Yeah. A casualty of progress. I really didn't think she'd take it so hard. It was barely any money in her pocket."

"It's probably not about the money. Have you tried talking to her? Do you want me to talk to her?"

Nora shook her head. "Go see what your visitor wants."

Lauren threaded her way through a party of six leaving the restaurant. Matt spotted her and waved her over.

Yeah, I see you.

"I hope you're only here to eat," she said, "because I don't have time to talk."

"I'd love to eat," he said, smiling. "But *I* don't have time for that line. Can you bump me ahead of the crowd?"

"This isn't Studio Fifty-Four. Seriously, I gotta work, Matt."

He looked at the photographs on the wall. "She replaced Henny's hand-painted signs with this crap?"

"You know about that?"

"Yeah. But I set her up on Etsy so she's back in biz."

Lauren looked at him in surprise. "That was nice of you."

A woman stepped in front of Matt. "Miss, can you tell us how much longer? It's been forty minutes. We're on the list. Last name is Feld."

Lauren looked around for the hostess, a college kid. She directed the woman to the side. "Please check with the hostess." Turning back to Matt, she said. "I'm really busy."

"Someone is making a feature film about Rory," he said.

"I know. *You* are."

"No, I'm making a documentary. The other project is a scripted movie. Someone is writing their version of the story."

She felt the room tilt. "Who? Can they do that?"

"I don't know who. It's not listed on IMDb. A friend told me. And yes, they can do that. But Lauren, you know the *real* story. The truth. And I can help you get it out there. Don't you want that?"

"I already did an interview. I gave you your hour! What do you want from me?"

"More," he said.

The room, overcrowded, felt suddenly like it was closing in on her.

Beth hesitated outside of Stephanie's bedroom door. She looked again at her watch, stalling. Eleven in the morning. Goddamn it, she hated being put in this position, having to treat her grown daughter—a mother herself—like a recalcitrant teenager.

She pushed open the door after one brisk knock.

"Rise and shine," she said, walking in and drawing back the curtains. Stephanie groaned.

"What are you doing?"

"Your son is in the kitchen, waiting to go to the beach. And you're going to take him."

Stephanie buried her head deeper in her pile of pillows. Beth could smell the alcohol seeping from her pores. Furious, she grabbed the comforter and pulled it off the bed.

"Mom! Jesus, what's wrong with you?"

"Nothing is wrong with me. But there is plenty wrong with you, and we're going to deal with it, starting today. Right now. You're drinking too much. You're not spending enough time with your son. And you did a lousy thing to your sister the other night."

Stephanie sat up. Beth had known that would get her attention.

"Oh, now I see what this is about. Once again, Lauren the angel has been wronged."

"I invited Neil Hanes over to spend time with her. He was asking about her. And then you..."

"I what? She's the one who freaked out and left."

"And you didn't waste any time moving in," Beth said.

"Oh, please. As if it were ever going to happen with Lauren. She hasn't dated in all of this time—that's on her, not me. But you know what? If Neil Hanes is going to be the one, she can go for it."

"I don't think that's a good idea now that you've slept with him."

"I didn't 'sleep with him,' Mother. We just hung out. The guy's a talker. Frankly, he's exhausting."

Beth brightened. Was it true? Neil and Stephanie had just talked? She felt the universe was rewarding her for trying—and for pressing the issue with Stephanie. Emboldened, she said:

"I want you to take Ethan to dinner and a movie tonight. The only one you should be running around with is that little boy. I'll give you the money for a night out, and I expect you to make yourself scarce." She walked out of the room but turned around just long enough to add, "And get yourself dressed."

Beth was already dialing Neil's cell before she reached her own bedroom.

Chapter Twenty-Eight

Running home after work, the sidewalk damp from an afternoon sun shower, Lauren nearly stepped on a slug but was able to jump over it at the last second.

She used to think slugs were snails that had left their shells, and then she learned that a slug had never had a shell to begin with. Looking at that soft, vulnerable creature, she felt a kinship; just when she'd been thinking the situation with the documentary was under control, she'd heard the news that another film project was out there. Would it never end?

The worst part was the realization that the past four years of pretending the outside world did not exist had given her a false sense of control. She was not a snail who had suddenly lost her shell; like that slug, she'd never had one. So now what?

There had been a time when she felt passionate about journalism. She had believed in discovering facts, in finding and telling a story. *But Lauren, you know the* real *story. The truth.*

Yes, she did. And she couldn't imagine sharing it. Not for any reason. Not for anyone.

"You're home!" her mother said, smiling as Lauren walked into the kitchen. "I tried calling but you didn't answer your phone."

"Busy day," Lauren said, checking the time. Maybe she should talk to Matt now, before she lost her nerve. Before she changed her mind and had the urge to run away again.

"Well, I'm glad you're here. Why don't you take a quick shower? We're having company for dinner. Neil Hanes."

"Oh, Mom, I'm not up for that tonight."

Her mother's face fell. "I'd really like for you to be here."

Lauren shook her head. When would her mother stop pushing?

"Sorry, but it's going to have to be just you and Stephanie and Dad."

"Stephanie is taking Ethan to a movie."

"But Dad's going to be here, right?"

Her mother hesitated. "I'm not sure."

Lauren felt a pang of alarm. "What's going on with you two?"

"Oh, just a little difference of opinion."

"About what?"

"The past. The present. The future." Beth gave an awkward laugh.

Lauren leaned on the counter. "That doesn't sound good."

"Sometimes people just need time apart."

Time apart? Before this summer, Lauren couldn't remember her parents spending so much as a night apart in three decades. Was their marriage in jeopardy? When had the problems started? If there were signs of trouble, she had been too caught up in her own life, too removed, to notice.

"Is this about the money issues?"

"Hon, this isn't for you to worry about. Your father and I will figure it out."

But she *was* worried. She realized, now that she was paying attention, how tired her mother looked. She had aged in the past year. Of course, she was pushing sixty, although in Lauren's mind's eye, her mother was still a young woman. But that wasn't it; there was a weariness in her eyes, a tension to the set of her mouth.

"Okay, I'll stay for dinner."

Howard walked into the house sandy and wearing his bathing trunks at a quarter to six, fifteen minutes before Neil was supposed to arrive.

"Where've you been all day?" Beth asked, sounding more confrontational than she'd intended.

"I told you I was going to the Kleins'. Jack and I hit the beach for a few hours."

"No, actually, you didn't mention it. Can you shower? Neil Hanes is coming for dinner."

Howard raised an eyebrow. "Second dinner here in as many weeks. Is he showing up for our daughter or the free meals?"

Beth took the marinated chicken out of the refrigerator. "Can you, for one night, put your cynicism on hold?"

The doorbell rang.

"I'll get it," Lauren called from somewhere in the house.

Beth smiled. There was nothing Howard could say to upset her tonight. She was doing the right thing. She could feel it.

"I wonder if Neil is as interested in real estate as his father is," Howard said, heading up the stairs. "I'll have to ask him at dinner."

Her smile disappeared.

It had been a long time since Lauren had cooked dinner and even longer since she'd actually enjoyed it. Most days after working at Nora's, she didn't have the energy for more than takeout. But tonight her mother had bought the ingredients for an heirloom tomato and feta salad, probably from one of Ina Garten's recipes, and Lauren had stood by her mother's side in the kitchen dicing the feta and mixing the olive oil, white wine vinegar, and kosher salt.

Her mother barbecued chicken and served it with corn on the cob.

"Beth, this is just outrageously delicious," Neil said.

"Oh, please. It's so simple!" Beth beamed.

The sun set. Beth lit the citronella candles, and in quiet moments, the only sound was the ocean. Lauren tried not to think about Matt or the movie that someone else was trying to make.

"The Lascoffs consider their place a teardown," Neil said. Lauren's father nodded in vigorous agreement. It seemed all Neil wanted to talk about was real estate. Maybe her fear that her mother was colluding with Neil for a setup was just paranoia.

"Absolutely. With what it would cost to renovate? I remember when the place went up. Mid-eighties. It seemed so modern at the time."

"But this place? Now, *this* is timeless," Neil said. "I told Beth I'm thinking of buying out here."

Lauren and her mother locked eyes.

Howard turned to Beth, then back to Neil. "Oh? She didn't mention it."

"Yeah, I mean, I'm mostly West Coast at this point. But I love the summers here. You know my parents might sell their house in Philly and move to Malibu? So I definitely want a house on the East Coast somewhere."

"Malibu is fantastic. Can't beat the weather. Personally, I prefer Florida," Howard said. "So, who knows? Maybe we can work something out so everyone's happy."

Neil raised his glass to Howard's.

Chapter Twenty-Nine

I'll clear," Lauren said abruptly, standing and reaching for the salad bowl that held nothing but a lone chunk of feta floating in a small pool of dressing. Inside the kitchen, she closed the sliding-glass door behind her, not wanting to hear the ongoing conversation about the Green Gable.

The doughnuts her mother had baked were covered in plastic wrap on the counter. Lauren set the salad bowl in the sink, filled it with warm soapy water, and then investigated the doughnuts. They were golden brown and topped with a light glaze. She opened the edge of the plastic and bent close to see if the aroma would clue her in on the flavor. She inhaled and it was the sweet, rich smell of apple pie. Apple-pie doughnuts! How many years had it been since her mother had made them? Lauren must have been in grammar school.

"Busted!"

She turned around to see Neil smiling in the doorway.

"Oh, yeah. Caught with my hand in the cookie jar. But it's doughnuts."

"Your mom sent me in here to let you know that she'll clean up. She said we should go for a walk."

Ugh, Mom! Making it really difficult for me to be a team player here.

"You sure you and my father don't need to talk some more about real estate domination? Plans to kick me out of my home?"

"Oh, damn. You're not on board with selling the house?"

"No, frankly. I live here. Selling the house is my dad's brilliant idea."

"I'm sorry. I didn't realize..."

"It's not your fault."

"Come on—let's humor your mom. Come for a quick walk around the block. Maybe I can scout out an alternative house to buy."

Lauren hesitated. He was just being friendly. And dinner had been pleasant. A little distraction to get her out of her own head wasn't the worst thing in the world.

"Fine. A quick walk."

Neil stepped close to her, too close. She tensed, but he just reached for the doughnuts. He opened the wrapping, retrieved one, and handed it to her.

"Take it for the road."

She tried to smile, to get into the playful spirit of things. "My mother will kill me. She has this weird control-freak side to her when it comes to serving dessert."

"Live on the edge," he said.

She looked at him, at his long-lashed, light brown eyes. Auburn hair. There was a hint of freckles on the bridge of his nose, freckles that she remembered as being more pronounced when they were young. He was attractive, though he hadn't been her type even back when she had a type.

Maybe he was interested in her; maybe he was just being friendly. She didn't know, and she didn't care. It was never going to happen.

It was amazing that people were born with the capacity to fall in love, to be in love. *To love,* as a verb. It was like breathing; at least, that was how natural and undeniable it had felt when she met Rory. Fifteen years old, she knew nothing about life, but she was about to feel emotion of that magnitude. Her love for him had felt hardwired. But now that he was gone, it was like she had lost one of her senses.

Lauren had never slept with anyone but Rory. She'd become a sexual being in the context of that relationship. No Rory, no sexuality. She did not know how she would get past that feeling. She didn't know if she wanted to.

It had taken her a long time to sleep with him. At least, a long time by high-school standards.

By the beginning of his senior year, they had done "everything but." If asked, Lauren would have sworn that Rory didn't pressure her for anything more. But the truth was, his "Catholic" patience toward her virginity was being tested to its limit.

Why was she holding out? A part of it was that she felt so in love with him, so deeply attached, she was afraid that the ultimate physical act would make her more vulnerable to the intensity of their relationship. And then there was the fact that he was leaving for college the following year.

They would be apart; there was no way around it.

His first choice was Harvard—if he could get a hockey scholarship. The college's hockey coach had been to a Lower Merion game, and Rory spent a weekend at Harvard in December. Lauren felt sick with loss the entire forty-eight hours he was gone. She imagined him meeting some brilliant Harvard undergrad and cheating on her. Or, worse, he would see his potential new life laid in front of him in all of its glory, and he would come home and break up with her.

Instead, he returned eager to see her, bringing her a Crimson T-shirt in her size. Nothing had changed between them! And yet, something had. The ground had shifted; Lower Merion was now just a way station between the life he had and the new life he wanted. She was part of the former, and the realization filled her with a sinking dread.

She felt desperate to hold on to him.

That winter break, Lauren didn't go with her family to visit her grandparents in Florida. Her decision to stay home sparked the first real argument she ever had with her parents.

"Your grandmother will be so disappointed!" her mother said. Lauren knew this and felt guilty, but her pangs of conscience were nothing com-pared to her desperate need to cling to Rory.

Two nights before Christmas, her first of total freedom, Lauren and Rory went out for Chinese food in Ardmore, saw a movie, and then returned to her house.

When the place was empty, they typically hooked up on the couch. But that night, she suggested they go up to her room. Rory knew her well enough to understand what the change in scenery signaled. When the two of them were stretched out side by side on top of her lavender Pottery Barn comforter, he propped himself up on one elbow and gazed at her. "Are you sure?" he said, scooping one arm around her, pulling her close. She nodded. And in that moment, it felt right. In that moment, she could almost imagine they would never be apart.

Afterward, they stood barefoot in the kitchen eating leftover Chinese and ice cream. She felt giddy, high, on drugs. He couldn't stay over—his mother would know something was up. When she was alone, she huddled underneath her covers, the bed still smelling like him. All of her anxiety lifted. She had never felt more certain of them, or of their future together.

First thing in the morning, he called. She smiled at the sound of his voice, sitting up in bed, her room taking on new meaning as the place where she had become his in every way. Nothing would ever change that.

"Lauren, it happened," he said. He sounded so excited. *Yes,* she thought—*it happened.* They'd slept together. And then he said, "I got the hockey scholarship. I'm going to Harvard."

"Rory, I'm so happy for you," she said automatically.

It was the first time, but certainly not the last, she felt she'd lost him.

In the kitchen, Lauren looked at Neil. "I'm sorry," she said suddenly. "I'm tired. You'll have to excuse me."

Matt shouldn't have been at Robert's Place drinking, but he was so con-sumed with editing, so mired in the film, he knew he wouldn't sleep if he didn't find a way to bring himself down a few notches. And he was still freaked out from Craig's call about the other Rory Kincaid movie in the works. At least Lauren shared his concern; maybe it would be the nudge she needed to trust him. The lesser of two evils.

He nursed a beer, watching the Phillies game on the screen at the end of the bar closest to the door. If he wasn't consciously waiting for Stephanie to show up, he certainly wasn't surprised when she did.

"Howdy, stranger," she said, sliding onto the stool next to him.

"Where's your new boyfriend?" he asked.

She snorted. "Oh, he's probably busy setting a wedding date with my sister." She waved Desiree over and ordered a shot of tequila.

"I'm not sure I follow."

She downed her shot. "Let me set the scene for you: I spent the first half of this night banned from the house because Neil was invited over for dinner with Lauren."

Matt felt an inexplicable pang, a decidedly negative rush of emotion.

"Lauren is dating that guy?"

Stephanie called for more tequila, downed shot number two, and shook her head. "My parents *wish*. No, she's not dating him. She was probably miserable tonight. But it's always about her. Always, always. See, my parents think I'm not good enough for Neil, but the truth is, guys like me."

"I'm sure they do."

She glared at him. "They like me more than her. Even Rory liked me."

"What do you mean, he *liked* you?"

"Buy me a drink, and maybe I'll fill you in."

Matt, his storytelling nerve twitching, flagged Desiree. Stephanie ordered a Tito's on the rocks.

"Make it two," he said.

Chapter Thirty

Lauren could hear her mother in the kitchen doing dishes. Her father's and Neil's voices carried up from the living room. She locked her bedroom door.

She opened her closet. The pile of boxes took up all the floor space and obscured some of her clothes. Not sure what she was looking for, she pulled the top box down. It was unwieldy and she lost control of it, so it landed with a thud. She froze, hoping the noise wouldn't summon her mother. A few seconds passed, and she felt safe enough to start cutting through the tape of the box marked *Rory/LA/Press Clips*.

The first thing she found inside was a copy of the *LA Times* from May of 2011. The LA Kings had made the playoffs for the second consecutive year, this after a seven-year playoff drought. But by that point, Rory was in a drought of his own. He suffered a streak of games with no points. Lauren tried to help him put it in perspective: No one expected him to be the star of the team. The Kings were doing great— wasn't that the important thing? Everything she said seemed to make him feel worse.

It had been so tempting to look for outside help, for outside answers.

She called Emerson, a move that would prove to be a tragic mistake.

"I'm worried about him," she told Emerson. "Maybe you can talk to him?"

Emerson came to visit the first week in May. The second night he was there, something happened to take everyone's mind off hockey: the U.S. military killed Osama bin Laden.

This dominated the conversation for days. Lauren got tired of it.

The two brothers took long walks, and she made dinner plans with friends from work to give them bonding time.

The visit must have done the trick, because in the days immediately following it, Rory seemed noticeably calmer. She said as much to him one night, climbing into bed.

"Yeah. I am," he said. "I've been doing a lot of thinking."

"Oh?" she said, giving him a peck on the cheek. "Anything you care to share with your future wife?"

She was being playful, but when he turned, the look on his face was serious.

"Yes, actually. It's something we need to talk about."

Lauren wanted to rewind, to go back two minutes before she'd climbed into bed. As if by avoiding the conversation, she could change whatever it was going on in Rory's mind. Because it was bad—she knew it was bad. Was he having second thoughts about the wedding?

Rory reached for her hand, and she closed her eyes.

"You know my contract is up this summer. I go into free agency."

Wait—this was about his career? "Yes, I know. Are you worried?"

"Not worried. But I'm thinking I can do something more meaningful with my life than ride the bench on a hockey team. There's so much going on in the world."

She nodded, pretending to understand. "Okay. Like what?"

"I want to join the military."

Oh my God. "Where is this coming from?" As soon as the question was out of her mouth, she knew: Emerson.

And she remembered a conversation from many summers ago, at Boston Style Pizza: *I don't think I'd be happy if I wasn't good at something. Great at something.*

"You know, you can quit hockey without doing something this extreme."

"It's not about that."

"Are you even physically eligible for the military?"

"What's that supposed to mean? I'm an athlete."

"You've had concussions."

"That was over a year ago. A nonissue." The way he said it, she knew this was past the hypothetical stage.

"You've already talked to a recruiter."

He nodded. He'd gone with Emerson. Behind her back.

Her eyes filled with tears. "What if something happens to you?"

"Oh, Lauren. It's more likely that I'd get another head injury on the ice and be fucked up for life. There's risk involved, yes. But there's risk in everything."

Lauren put her head in her hands. This couldn't be happening.

"We'll be apart," she said, unable to look at him. "We'll be apart for long stretches of time." Blood pounded in her ears. She could barely hear his response, something affirmative and empathetic and infuriating. She looked up. "You asked me to move here, promising we were starting a life together. We're not going to have a life together!"

"I understand what you're saying. It's not what you signed on for. And if this changes how you feel about the wedding—"

She sobbed, pulling away from him when he tried to hold her.

There was no way out of it. If she called off the engagement, she would be heartbroken and miss him for the rest of her life. If she married him, she would be heartbroken and miss him and worry herself sick while he was gone. There was no path to happiness.

Lauren turned away from the box, remembering that feeling of hopelessness as if it were yesterday. He'd given her no choice back then, all those years ago. But she had choices now.

She thought about what Matt had said to her at the restaurant that afternoon. Yes, she knew the real story. And yes, he could help her "get it out there." The thing was, she didn't *want* it out there. But she didn't want someone else's version out there either.

Lauren reached for her phone.

Matt told himself not to push, not to rush. He let the vodka set the pace. When Stephanie was halfway done, he let himself drink some of his own. And when she was finished, he said, "So, how much, exactly, did Rory like you?"

"Well, I slept with him. You know that, right?"

Was she for real? "No. How would I know that? You didn't mention that in the interview."

She shrugged. "Water under the bridge, as they say."

"Did Lauren know about it?"

"It was before they hooked up, and yeah, she knew about it. And she didn't care. I mean, maybe she cared that I'd slept with him but she didn't care about my feelings."

"You mean she . . . it was like she stole him from you?"

"No. It was over before they got together. But still, there's a code, you know? That's what I told her when I found out. There's a sister code. And she just didn't get it."

He nodded. Okay, this was only high-school stuff. Sisterly competition. The significance was nil. He signaled Desiree that he wanted to settle the tab.

"That's why," she said, slurring just a little, "that's why, when I fucked him again years later, I didn't feel that bad about it. And no, Lauren does *not* know about that." She leaned closer to him. "It can be our little secret."

Matt felt like someone had pulled the stool out from under him. He gripped the edge of the bar. And then his phone buzzed with a text. Lauren. I do want to get the real story out there. How's tomorrow morning?

Chapter Thirty-One

Lauren crossed her legs and slid back in the chair, uncomfortable with Matt's nearness as he adjusted her mic.

She had chosen her clothes carefully for the interview and wore a navy-blue dress with cap sleeves and seed-pearl buttons running down the front. Her hair was loose. She was flushed with anxiety.

"Are you impatient with me already? We haven't even started yet," he said, smiling.

"No, it's fine."

Matt returned to his seat opposite her, Henny's living room configured the exact same way it had been the last time.

"Henny must really like you to let you do this to her furniture. We had a book-club meeting here once, and when Nora tried to move a plant, Henny threw a fit."

He stood up and adjusted an LED light and then sat back down in the chair across from her.

"Henny's a good sport. I'm lucky I found her. I've been lucky in a lot of ways lately." He smiled.

Lauren looked around the room, trying not to fidget with the mic wire.

"When you said, 'Give me one hour,' you never really meant just one hour, did you?" she said.

He leaned forward in his seat. "That's not enough for me to get everything I need, no. But I hoped that one hour of talking would be enough to convince you that there was a story worth telling here. That even an ugly truth is more valuable than a beautiful lie."

They locked eyes for a minute. She searched for something to say, but before she could speak, Matt shifted into interview mode.

"So let's get to work," Matt said. "Are you ready?"

"I'm ready." And she was.

"During Rory's second season with the Kings, you lived with him in LA, correct?"

She nodded. "Yes. I spent the summer after my senior year in DC making up some credits—I traveled a lot and had to basically do a ninth semester—and Rory came to see me in August. He asked me to move to LA with him. This was heading into his second season."

"Was there talk of getting married?"

"It was unspoken, but there was the sense that school was behind us, geographical separation was behind us. We felt like, Okay, we can finally do this thing."

"So it was a happy time," Matt said.

"It was a very happy time." Except she had walked away from her mentors and a possible job at the *Washington Post*.

There were few journalism jobs in Los Angeles. She got an interview at *Variety*. Excited, she felt confident going into the meeting. But she quickly realized, talking to a guy who spent half the twenty-minute interview checking his phone, that her solid understanding of the Electoral College and global economic and energy crises, as well as her encyclopedic knowledge of nearly every major politician's position on fracking, meant less than nothing in that town. She hadn't gone to a movie in years and didn't know Colin Firth from Colin Farrell.

By late fall, two months after she moved to LA, she was desperate enough to consider taking a job at an entertainment blog called *Cinema Chick* that paid so little, it would cost her more in gas to get to and from the office than she would earn.

"Why are you putting so much pressure on yourself?" Rory asked her.

"Because I want to be good at something," she said. "You can't be the only one who's good at something."

He hugged her. "Where is this coming from?"

She didn't know exactly. She was twenty-two years old. Most people her age were moving to new cities with friends, living six people to a divided-up one-bedroom, and landing assistant jobs. Or starting grad school. They were free and it was all about trial and error. For Lauren, she couldn't afford an error. She already had something to lose—Rory. And maybe herself, a little. She didn't want her entire identity to revolve around being Rory Kincaid's girlfriend.

She cried to him that night. Cried, because she didn't know what to do about her career.

"You're going to be a great journalist someday," he said, hugging her again. "Come on, Lauren. You know you have to walk before you can run, right?"

She nodded. "But that's easy for you to say. You're running."

"But think about it—my starting line was probably the day I first laced up skates fifteen years ago. In fifteen years, you'll be working at the *Washington Post*. Or the *New York Times*."

"You think we can move back east some day?"

"Sure. I won't be playing hockey forever. Or maybe I'll get traded to the Capitals."

She smiled. "I'll be old and gray."

"And I'll still be hot for you."

They made love. And she took the job at *Cinema Chick*.

"Did Rory enjoy living in LA?" Matt asked.

"He did. We both did. We fell in love with the house we bought.

It was this Spanish-style bungalow just a few blocks from the Beverly Center in West Hollywood. It was so different from the suburbs we'd grown up in."

The house was a modest one-story with a clay-tile roof, arched windows and doors, and a galley kitchen. It seemed exotic to both of them. Lauren loved the colorful ceramic tiles in the entrance hall, and Rory was sold as soon as he saw the orange tree out back.

For two weeks, they scoured flea markets and estate sales for bargains on good solid furniture. Rory hated anything mass-market like Pottery Barn and wanted to leave the rooms bare until they found the right things rather than fill them with "commercial junk," as he called it. That was fine with Lauren. She kept calling it his house, and he always corrected her. "*Our* house."

The plants in the front lawn amazed her, the spiny Shaw's agave, the waxy chalk liveforever, and the grasslike giant wild rye. There was a certain smell to the air that permeated the house, their clothes, her skin. The beauty of Southern California was alien and surprising, and she was certain that no matter how long they lived there, she would always feel like a visitor.

In the early evening, they opened a bottle of wine while they cooked dinner. She was amazed by how easy it was to find fresh fish and organic meat and vegetables. Everything tasted better. She didn't know if it was the California produce or simply that the food was served under her own roof, but she had never felt such lust for meals.

Sometimes, they didn't make it through cooking dinner. Lauren would be stirring pasta, and Rory would sneak up behind her, move the heavy curtain of her hair, and kiss the back of her neck. Always, she tried to keep going, but after a few seconds she would turn and find herself in his arms, and then—barely remembering to turn off the burner—they would head to the half-empty living room to have sex on the rug under the Spanish candelabra left by the previous owners.

"How did Rory feel, physically and mentally, heading into his second season?" Matt said.

"He was excited. Determined to start making his mark."

If Rory was a little more short-tempered than she remembered, if he failed in his effort to hide his frequent headaches, it was nothing she couldn't deal with. They were together, that was the important thing.

But once the season started and she began working, it was challenging for them not to take their frustrations out on each other. While it was clear the Kings were on fire, Rory was riding the bench a lot. And her job at an entertainment blog wasn't exactly high-level journalism.

"When I interviewed the coach, he said Rory struggled with insomnia that year."

"Well, he was so adrenalized after games, he just couldn't sleep." Still, Lauren had been shocked to find a bottle of Ambien in his bedside-table drawer. Rory was anti-drug—even over-the-counter stuff. He'd get on her case for popping Advil when she had her period. When she found the Ambien and asked him about it, he became uncharacteristically angry and defensive. They had a big shouting match, the first of many.

"Was he experiencing any lingering effects of the head injury? Headaches? Short temper?"

"No. Maybe. I don't know."

Matt glanced at his laptop.

"When did Rory start thinking about enlisting?"

"That's a tough question. It honestly took me by surprise."

"So there was no turning point you could identify?"

She shook her head. "I mean, Rory had a military family. So I guess the idea of it was more in the realm of his thinking than maybe your average person's. And then everything in the news pushed that nerve."

"Like what?"

"Well, the Fort Hood shooting had a big effect on him," she said carefully. The November 2009 attack at the army base in Texas by a radicalized Muslim U.S. Army major who'd killed thirteen soldiers and wounded thirty others. "Rory followed the story obsessively."

"He felt like he needed to do something in the wake of this?"

"No, not exactly. I think it just underscored the divide between what was going on in the world and maybe the insignificance of what he was doing with his life."

"He felt playing hockey was insignificant?"

"He started feeling his role was insignificant. He would have felt better if he were playing and scoring more. He was frustrated sometimes at not being the best for the first time in his life. But everyone told him this was a natural transition from college to pro sports. I mean, he was still an exceptional player. But he was hard on himself. So he would look at those guys fighting in the Middle East and think, *They're doing something great, and I'm not.* It was just classic Rory, always wanting to excel."

"You said his decision to enlist was a surprise to you?"

"His decision to enlist was a big surprise to me," she said.

By that time, it seemed so many other forces were at play in his life. Some days, she felt she barely knew him anymore. And it scared her.

Beth beat together creamy peanut butter, heavy cream, and confectioners' sugar with perhaps more aggression than the task warranted.

Of all the things Howard had said that infuriated her lately, the crack about her baking with Ethan was the worst. What was this, 1950?

"When does the jelly part happen?" Ethan asked.

She had, to his delight, come up with a recipe for peanut butter and jelly doughnuts.

"We're going to use raspberry jam, and that part comes later. We'll fill one of these pastry bags with the peanut butter mixture, one with the jelly, and then we use these plastic tips to squeeze them into the doughnut."

His eyes widened. "Cool."

"The best part of these doughnuts is that we should eat them right away or else the dough will get soggy. You okay with that?"

"You mean *before* lunch?"

"Before lunch."

"What's before lunch?" Stephanie asked, her voice hoarse. Dressed in leggings and a tank top, her hair loose and knotted, she headed straight for the coffeepot.

She reeked of alcohol.

"The doughnuts we're making! Peanut butter and jelly," Ethan said.

"Sounds awesome." Stephanie tousled his hair. "E., do me a favor and scoot outside onto the deck for a few minutes. I need to talk to Gran."

"But no pool," Beth said.

Ethan crossed his arms. "I know, Gran, no grown-up, no water," he said, repeating the number-one rule she'd set at the beginning of the summer. He trotted off, and as soon as he was out the door, Stephanie wilted into a chair at the breakfast table. It was as if it had taken every ounce of her strength just to stand upright and speak to him.

"I'm so hung over." She groaned. Before Beth could respond, Stephanie held up her hand as if warding off a physical blow. Then, to Beth's surprise, she started to cry.

"Sweetheart, what's wrong?" Beth pulled out the chair next to her and hugged her.

"You were right," Stephanie said, sobbing in her arms. "Everything you said yesterday."

Beth glanced outside, hoping Ethan was occupied, not witnessing his mother's breakdown. He was on the far side of the deck.

"It's going to be okay," Beth said.

"I'm drinking too much. My life is a mess..."

"I'm here," Beth said. "Let me help you."

Stephanie cried harder, pulling away from her and burying her face in her hands. Beth could barely hear the muffled words through her sobs: "You can't help. It's too late."

Chapter Thirty-Two

Nora's annual Fourth of July party was in full swing by the time Lauren corralled her mother, sister, and Ethan and got them into the car to drive over. The delay had been due to the problem of how to transport the absolutely insane amount of doughnuts her mother had baked.

"Mom, there's enough for two parties here," she said, surveying the trays of red, white, and blue–frosted doughnuts, the apple-pie doughnuts, and the pale glazed ones that her mother had identified as margarita doughnuts.

"What makes a margarita doughnut?" Lauren had asked.

"My little secret. But I'll give you a hint: lime zest and tequila."

"Okay, Mom, we don't need to bring all of these."

"Earlier in the week, you said two parties, so that's what I prepared for."

That's right; Henny, still hurt and angry with Nora, had planned to boycott Nora's party and have her own. But after much pressure from their shared group of friends—and the realization that Nora's party was such an institution that no one would show up at Henny's—she caved and agreed to go to Nora's after all.

"Are we taking one car or two?" Stephanie asked. She was dressed in a tank top and Daisy Dukes.

"We're taking two cars," Lauren said. "One for us, and one for Mom's doughnuts."

Stephanie laughed.

"Okay, very funny. And to answer your question, we can take one car."

"And Dad's not coming back today? I can't believe he's blowing off the Fourth," Stephanie said. It was true; their dad loved the holiday. When they were little, he had been the one to drive them to Narberth Park to see the fireworks if they weren't at the shore. And when they were at the beach, he would give them turns sitting on his shoulders to watch the display. "What's going on?"

"We're just taking a little time apart," Beth said. "A little space."

"Space?" Stephanie said, incredulous. As confused as if Beth had said *outer* space.

"Come on, girls, let's go. You know I hate being the last one to a party."

Nora's front lawn was festooned with American flags, her trees decorated with red, white, and blue streamers. The front porch welcomed guests with robust bundles of star-spangled balloons. A few people milled around, and the front door was open.

"Happy Fourth of July!" Nora, dressed in a red, white, and blue patch-work dress, hugged Lauren before bending down to greet Ethan.

"Thanks for having us," Beth said, handing Nora the first of five trays of doughnuts.

"These look fantastic," Nora said.

"You remember my sister, Stephanie," Lauren said.

"Hi, hon. Welcome!"

Stephanie, looking distracted, just nodded.

"I'll take these gorgeous confections to the kitchen so they aren't devoured before dessert. The hot dogs and hamburgers are grilling as we speak, April brought her vodka watermelon, and we have both red and white sangria."

Beth whispered something to Stephanie, and Lauren guessed it was a reminder not to drink too much. Music played, 1970s stuff.

Stephanie, with Ethan in tow, followed Lauren to the back deck.

"What's the deal with Mom and Dad?" Stephanie said.

"I don't know. I guess they're having problems."

"About what?"

"Stephanie, I just told you, I don't know."

"He hasn't said anything about it to me."

"Why would he?" Lauren said. Yes, Stephanie and their father had always been close, but that didn't mean he would confide in her about his marital problems.

"I really thought he'd be back by now. They're basically spending the summer apart."

"It's only the beginning of July."

"Do you think they're going to get *divorced?*"

Lauren was surprised to see Stephanie this worked up. She so rarely seemed to think of anyone except herself. But Lauren supposed it was true what people said: no one, no matter how old—or, in Stephanie's case, how self-absorbed—wants to see her parents split up.

This, at least, was something she and her sister had in common. But she didn't want to discuss it in the middle of a crowded party. Across the deck, Henny spotted her and waved.

"I'm going to say hi to a friend," Lauren said. She looked down at Ethan, touching his shoulder to get his attention. "Are you hungry?"

"Do you know a lot of people here?" Stephanie asked, staying close to Lauren as she weaved through the crowd.

"Some. Most of these people are regulars from the café."

"Who do you spend time with all winter long?" Stephanie asked, as if it had just dawned on her that Lauren actually lived in this town.

"My friends," she said defensively. Lauren had no interest in introducing Stephanie to Henny or April, knowing how odd her sister would find it that her friends were all thirty years her senior, divorced or widowed and living alone. Lauren's fate mapped out by association. "Come on, I need food."

They followed the crowd to a line forming at the barbecue that was manned by... Matt?

"What's *he* doing here?" Stephanie said, stopping in her tracks.

"He rented a room from one of Nora's friends. She must have invited him."

Lauren hadn't seen him since the day of the second interview, weeks ago. She'd gone into that conversation reluctantly, but once she'd started talking to Matt, it felt surprisingly painless. Matt hadn't pushed her to discuss Rory's head injuries. She'd been able to bring up some good times—stories about the Rory she wanted the world to remember. And when she got home that night, she felt lighter, unburdened. It was like free therapy.

She felt so positive about it, in fact, that she'd texted him the following morning to see if he had gotten everything he needed during the interview. He wrote back that she'd done great and that he was leaving for New York for a "family obligation." And then, nothing.

Since then, she'd tried to put the film out of her mind, but she found herself thinking about Matt a lot, wondering if he would contact her again.

Now, apparently, he was back.

Matt gave her a friendly wave.

"I'm really not in the mood for this. I'm going home," Stephanie said.

"What? No. We just got here. Go get something to eat. I'll keep an eye on Ethan."

Stephanie hesitated and then walked back inside the house. Lauren took Ethan by the hand. "What do you like better, hamburgers or hot dogs?"

The line for food moved quickly. When it was their turn, Lauren felt herself smiling shyly.

"Hey there! Happy Fourth," Matt said. His time away from the beach showed in his pale face.

"Happy Fourth. When did you get back?"

"Just yesterday. I didn't mean to surprise you."

"Oh, not a problem," she said.

Ethan stared at the hot dogs with longing. Matt, with his filmmaker's eye, didn't miss a thing. He quickly stuffed one in a bun. "Hey, buddy. Mustard and ketchup right in that corner." He handed it to Ethan.

"Gran says hot dogs are bad for you," Ethan said, looking up at Lauren.

"Just one won't hurt," Lauren said with a wink. She was an aunt—she was allowed to indulge him, right? Aunts were just a notch down from grandmothers in the kid-spoiling hierarchy.

Stephanie marched over, glaring. What, did she have a problem with hot dogs too?

"Ethan, come with me. Someone brought a puppy and it's out front," she said.

And then Lauren realized Stephanie's dagger eyes were aimed at Matt.

Beth, at Nora's invitation, joined her in the kitchen for a glass of sangria. The table was covered with Beth's trays of doughnuts. Nora had already tried one of each variety.

"I have to say, Beth, these doughnuts are truly outstanding," Nora said. "Do you bake professionally?"

Beth smiled. "I used to, years ago. Before I got married I worked for a catering company in Philadelphia."

"Why'd you stop? The long hours?"

"No, it wasn't the hours. My husband's family had their own business and he wanted me to work with him there. Retail. I just started baking again this summer as an activity with my grandson."

"Well, you must miss catering if you're baking this many doughnuts for a backyard barbecue," Nora said.

Beth laughed. "No, no—that was just miscommunication between Lauren and me. She said originally that we were going to two parties."

"Ah, yes. She told you about the falling-out with my friend Henny?"

"Not in detail."

Nora shook her head. "I made a business decision, and she took it personally. You and your husband are in sales—you understand. Sometimes you have to sell everything you've got. Even the four walls."

Beth nodded, although she wasn't sure exactly what Nora was talking about.

"Well, I really appreciate you giving Lauren a job. I know what a difference it made in her life back when she first moved here full-time."

"Are you kidding? I'm lucky to have her. She's a wonderful young woman. I have to say, I wish I could do more for her."

"More?"

"You know. Helping her get on with her life in other ways. I'm sure you feel the same. It just seems, I hate to say, your daughter is frozen." And then, seeing the stricken look on Beth's face, she said, "Oh, I'm sorry. Did I overstep?"

"No, no. Not at all," Beth said quickly. "It's just...I don't have anyone to really talk to about this. My husband thinks I need to push her more. My friends feel sorry for me, for her, and they tell me it just takes time. But I don't see time helping one bit."

Nora poured more sangria into both of their glasses. She'd served the drinks in cute little mason jars. "I have to agree with you on that one, Beth."

Beth gulped her drink, looking out the window at her beautiful daughter standing surrounded by people yet alone on the deck.

Matt took a break from the grill, a glass of sangria in hand. The sudden rush of socializing overwhelmed him after the quiet, intense few weeks back in New York. First, a quick visit home for his father's birthday. As his parents' only remaining son, he simply couldn't miss some things. Then a seemingly endless string of days and nights in the editing suite in Brooklyn.

The film's narrative had developed a life of its own, branching off in directions he hadn't expected. He'd first come to Longport to finish it, and now it was as if he were just beginning. He'd considered turning down Henny's invite to the party, but he'd reconsidered when he realized Lauren would probably be there. He'd been wondering how to pick up the conversation in a natural way, and the party was the perfect opening.

He leaned over the wooden ledge of the deck, looking out at the bay. A boat sped by, breaking the no-wake rule. But it was a holiday, and there was a feeling of—well, if not lawlessness, something slightly edgy in the air.

Someone slipped up next to him. Stephanie.

"Oh, hey there. Happy Fourth," he said.

"Save it," she snapped. "What are you even doing here?"

"I was invited," he said carefully, not sure where the hostility was coming from. "Did I do something to upset you?"

"You took advantage of me," she said, her voice low, glancing around. "I was drunk, and you pushed me and pushed me until I said something I shouldn't have said. And I want you to forget I said it."

"I didn't push you. We were having a conversation. And I can't just forget it."

She shifted on her feet, agitated. "Are you going to tell my sister?"

"I'm not here to get involved in your personal life, Stephanie. Not yours, not your sister's. I'm just trying to make a movie about Rory. The truth about his life is all I care about."

"Are you going to put what I said in the movie?"

"I can't put it in the movie unless you or someone else says it on camera." He almost wished Stephanie hadn't told him. When had it happened? Why had Rory done it? Guys cheated, of course. But to sleep with Lauren's sister? Was the transgression just another manifestation of his personality changes from the head injuries? That was the only thing he really wanted to know. "Can I ask you something? Was he married to her at the time?"

"No," Stephanie said quickly, eager to absolve herself of at least that level of betrayal. "And I warned her not to marry him."

"You did?"

"Yes. I mean, I didn't tell her *why* I was saying not to trust him—I couldn't."

"Let me interview you on camera one more time," he said.

"No fucking way."

Lauren spotted Stephanie and Matt in heated conversation. What on earth was that all about?

"Let's go find Gran," she said to Ethan. She led him to the picnic table on the front lawn where her mother and Nora were busy laying out a buffet spread of dessert, and then she quickly headed back alone to the perplexing tête-à-tête by the water.

Matt and Stephanie didn't notice her walking over, not even when she was close enough to touch Stephanie's shoulder.

"Am I interrupting something?" Lauren said, and from the look on Stephanie's face, she saw that she was. But what? There had been a time, not so long ago, when she would have freaked out. But she felt in a better place with her sister. She trusted her.

"No," Stephanie said. "I'm just getting ready to leave."

"Why? Everyone's going to head over to the fireworks soon."

"Where's Ethan?"

"Out front with Mom."

Stephanie brushed past her without another word.

Lauren looked at Matt. "What was that all about?"

"I'm busy enough trying to figure out your late husband. I can't begin to decode your sister," he said.

Lauren didn't know how to respond except to say, "Yeah. That makes two of us." And then, "So how's the film going?"

"It's going." He held up his empty mason jar. "I need a refill. Care to join me?"

As they weaved their way through the crowd to the kitchen, Lauren had a faint, shimmering memory of a house party years ago. She was following Rory, feeling like she would lose him, but then he had reached a hand behind his back and found hers without even looking.

A few people recognized her from the restaurant and greeted her with intoxicated smiles. She felt a sudden urge to be very drunk, an impulse she rarely gave in to. The temporary high was not worth the crash that always followed. But it was a holiday, and she felt an unusually strong desire to share in the feelings of revelry around her. She wanted, just for an hour, to be like everyone else.

In the kitchen, five-gallon glass dispensers were filled with red or white sangria.

"Restaurateurs really know how to throw parties," Matt said. "Pick your poison." She pointed to the red, and he filled two large plastic cups.

Someone behind her touched her arm.

"Hey there, stranger."

Neil Hanes smiled, standing a little too close to her for comfort. He looked at her with an intimacy that suggested much more than their innocent evening of dinner with her parents and conversation justified.

"Oh, hi. What are you doing here?" She hadn't meant for it to sound ungracious, but she really couldn't imagine how he ended up at Nora's house.

"Your mother invited me," he said.

Matt moved closer, passing her a cup. "Hey," Matt said, holding out a hand to Neil. "Matt Brio."

"Neil Hanes," he said with a flicker of recognition. "Have we met?"

"I saw you at Robert's."

"Right!" Neil said. Lauren looked between them, confused. "You a summer guy, Matt? Or year-round?"

"Neither," Matt said. "I'm just passing through."

"So, how do you two know each other?" Neil said.

"You ask a lot of questions," Matt said. Lauren looked at him gratefully.

"Blame it on the sangria." Neil smiled, raising his glass. He turned to Lauren, his back to Matt. "Are your parents here? I didn't see them. I want to say hi."

"Um, my mother is here. Somewhere." She looked around, not seeing her. "Somewhere," she repeated with a shrug. Neil touched her arm, and she recoiled.

Matt, not one to miss a thing, moved between the two of them. "Neil, when you find her mother, just let her know that Lauren headed over to the fireworks early. Nice seeing you again."

Lauren looked at him in surprise. He took her gently by the arm and led her through the kitchen and out the back door. They threaded their way through the people on the deck and down the flight of wooden stairs to the driveway.

"What was that about?" Lauren said, smiling.

"I don't like that guy."

"You don't even know him."

"I think you feel the same way I do."

"Oh, he's fine. He's a family friend."

"You can do better."

Lauren stopped walking. "There's nothing going on between us."

Matt shrugged. "I'm just saying."

"I should go back to the party," she said.

"Why?"

She realized she couldn't think of one good reason.

Chapter Thirty-Three

How many years had Beth walked to the boardwalk with the kids at dusk on the Fourth of July for the fireworks? A dozen? More? And when had Howard ever not been at her side? Never. Not until tonight.

Walking down the boardwalk, looking for a perfect spot to view the fireworks, she resolved to try to enjoy the time with her family. She held on to Ethan's hand, remembering when it had been his mother's hand so small in her own. Beth glanced back at Stephanie, lagging a few steps behind, deep in conversation with Neil Hanes.

Beth sighed. It wasn't the way she'd planned for the night to go. Where had Lauren run off to?

Last week's dinner had seemed so promising! Sure, Lauren had called it a night early and gone up to her room. But still, it had been a start.

Had Neil called her since then? Beth didn't know but suspected that even if he had called, Lauren would have made an excuse not to go out. So Beth had thought, *Why not give things a little nudge by inviting him to the party?* It was a group setting, no pressure.

Ethan tugged on her hand.

"Gran, is Aunt Lauren coming to the fireworks?"

"What? Oh, I'm not sure, hon."

"Doesn't she like them?"

"She does, but maybe she's tired."

The truth was that until age eight, Lauren had been terrified of fireworks. She would cover her ears and stare up at the sky with her big brown eyes, her lower lip trembling. It broke Beth's heart; she always wanted to run and take her home, but Howard said she would outgrow it if they helped her to stick it out. And sure enough, one year, the hands slowly lowered from her ears; her eyes were just as wide, but this time she had a big smile on her face.

Stephanie caught up to them.

"Mom, are you okay with Ethan? Neil and I are thinking about going for a walk by ourselves."

Beth narrowed her eyes, but there wasn't too much she could say with Ethan right there.

"I think you should stay with us. Especially since *Lauren* might want to take a walk with Neil at some point."

"Lauren has no interest in 'taking a walk' with anyone," Stephanie said, playing along with the code. "I won't be home too late." She bent down and kissed Ethan. "See you later, buddy. Stay close to Gran."

The tide of people all walked north. Every year, the crowd of teenagers, couples, and parents with young children made Lauren wistful for the things she didn't believe she'd ever experience. A widow in a crowd of families, she felt she would never stand next to a man with their child on his shoulders.

They reached the boardwalk. She wondered if she would find her mother and sister but realized quickly it was a needle-in-a-haystack scenario.

They reached the beach side of the boardwalk and she staked out a spot.

"We'll have a good view from here," she said.

He smiled at her. He seemed about to say something but then stopped himself.

"What?" she said.

"Nothing."

"Well, you were obviously about to tell me something."

He looked her in the eye, and she had an unfamiliar and uncomfortable feeling. It was like she had an urge to lean into him. Instead, she took a step back.

"I probably have no right to say this," he said. "But I just feel bad that you live out here all by yourself, so cut off from the world. I mean, you're an intelligent young woman with your whole life ahead of you."

"I'm not cut off from the world."

"Lauren, you're a ghost. I couldn't find you for years. You don't exist on social media. You don't keep in touch with anyone from high school or college."

Lauren leaned on the metal railing and looked out at the ocean. "So how *did* you find me?"

The question had been eating at her since the day he'd shown up at the restaurant, but she'd been afraid to ask—afraid that someone she knew had betrayed her.

"I was at a lecture where a bioengineer from the Cam Lab at Stanford spoke. He'd developed a special mouth guard that helped track the force of injury in football players. The Polaris Foundation was listed in the program."

She looked at him. "I purposefully didn't use Rory's name in the foundation to keep it under the radar. How did you make the connection?"

"It was a hunch. I'd just been watching interviews with his mother. She showed me photos of the dog."

Polaris. Rory had loved that dog. Her eyes filled with tears.

"Well, what can I say? You're good."

"Tell me about the foundation," he said.

"I knew he suffered after those hits to the head. I searched the Internet for answers that his team doctors weren't giving me. I joined forums on concussions and sports. But when he was alive, no one we knew was talking about it in a real way. He just wanted to play. He just wanted to be great." She sighed. "I give money to research, but I don't know. Sometimes it feels worse to do too little too late than to do nothing at all."

"It's not too little too late. It means something," Matt said.

She shrugged, unconvinced.

"You're lucky that you love what you do," she said. "I used to want to be a journalist. I remember how exciting it was to chase a story, to feel like you were about to put all the pieces together."

"Do you ever think of getting back into it?"

She shook her head. "Not really." The truth was, she missed it. But somehow, leaving behind her life with Rory had turned into leaving behind her life in general. And she had no idea how to find her way back to it.

"Well, documentary film is journalism," he said. "And you're helping me."

She nodded, and their eyes locked. He reached for her hand. The touch lasted just a few seconds before she pulled away. But it was enough to set her heart racing, so much so that when the first firework flared seconds later, she barely noticed it.

It had been an impulse to reach for her hand. As soon as Matt saw the surprised look on her face, felt the quickness of her pulling away, he regretted it. He considered saying he was sorry but thought that would make a big deal out of it. Better to just move on. Mercifully, the fireworks started as if on cue.

Lauren stared at the sky with childlike wonder. It surprised him how happy it made him to see her smiling, enjoying herself.

After the fireworks peaked, a dizzying climax of sparks and booms that made it impossible to talk or think beyond the sensory overload in the sky, Lauren said, "I used to hate the fireworks. Stephanie would always tease me."

"I'm surprised more kids don't get freaked out. It's loud. In New York, we're farther away from the action, so it's less intense. It's really immediate here."

The tide of people began walking back to the streets, streaming off the boardwalk in all directions. She looked at her phone. "I should get going."

"It's still early," Matt said. It wasn't that early, actually. He just wasn't ready to say good-bye; he gave himself a pass for having that feeling, rationalizing that it was for the film. The more she talked to him off camera, the more she would be comfortable talking to him on camera. Still, he couldn't think of one logical way to prolong the evening.

She leaned over the railing, staring at the ocean. He stood next to her quietly, wondering if there was a way to suggest they go for a drink without sounding like, well, like he was asking her out for a drink. There wasn't.

"I can walk you back to your house," he offered. After that, he would probably hit Robert's for a round or two. The place would be packed, and the energy would help him let off enough steam to get to sleep.

"Tell me something," she said suddenly. "What was it like over there? In Iraq?"

Surprised, he turned to face her, his back pressing on the rail. She didn't look at him, her eyes fixed on the distance, as if the answers to her questions were out there. "Probably exactly the way you imagine."

"I don't want to imagine. I spent enough time trying to imagine. Rory's letters made it sound like it was a lot of hours patrolling neighborhoods, not much happening. I always felt like he was sugarcoating it for me. He didn't want me to worry. I feel like I missed the last chapter of his life."

"Well, every person's experience over there is different."

"Did you talk to any of the guys who were over there with him?"

Matt nodded. "I interviewed a few guys from his battalion."

"Did you talk to Pete Downing?"

"I did."

"I need to see the interview," she said.

"We can do that at some point."

"Now," she said. "Tonight."

Chapter Thirty-Four

She stood next to Matt's desk while he booted up his laptop and she felt herself shaking. Pete Downing had been one of the last people to see Rory alive. Pete Downing's voice might have been one of the last Rory heard on earth.

Above the desk, dozens of index cards were taped in even rows. On the top left, the card read *Opening image*. A blue Post-it note covered the wording on the next card, but she saw one that read *Theme stated* and one with the name of the coach of the LA Kings.

"What's all of this?" she asked, pointing to a small binder filled with plastic sheets and small squares that looked like the games in Ethan's Nintendo DS player.

"Those are drives holding all my interviews. I save them to my laptop but I keep the originals just in case."

Matt dragged a rustic wooden bench from the window to the desk so they could sit side by side.

He hit Play. A face she hadn't seen in four years. At the bottom, the words *PFC Pete Downing, 2/75 Rangers*. She braced herself to hear his voice, the voice that had tried valiantly to comfort her in the days following Rory's death.

Off camera, Matt said, "Can you tell us, in general, the duties of a U.S. Ranger?"

"As a U.S. Ranger, we engage in combat search and rescue, airborne and air-assault operations, special reconnaissance, intelligence and counterintelligence, personnel recovery and hostage rescue, joint special operations, and counterterrorism."

"What was your first impression of Rory Kincaid?"

Pete Downing smiled.

"I expected Rory to be a typical arrogant jock. Full of himself. But he wasn't like that at all. He was confident but humble. He kept his head down. He came in as a private, which in civilian terms is basically a nobody. I don't think he found it easy to take orders. Far more than it was for most of us, this was a challenge for him but he did the job he came there to do."

"Did he display leadership qualities?"

"Rory had an inner drive and focus," he said, looking thoughtful. "It gave us all more confidence about what we were doing."

"Would you describe him as just one of the guys?"

"Yes and no," Downing said. "There's a locker-room atmosphere when you're over there. Rory was kind of above all that."

"Did that ever make guys resent him?"

"Just the opposite—we looked up to him. And let's put it this way: I went in for selfish reasons. I wanted money for college. I wanted to feel like I was somebody. But Rory already had money. He already was somebody. He was there because he wanted to be there, in service of something bigger than himself."

"Can you tell me what happened on December 28, 2012?"

Downing nodded. He sat back in his chair, adjusting his tie. He took a minute before saying, "It was an ordinary day. Routine patrol looking for IEDs. We delivered water to a neighborhood near Route Irish."

"And Route Irish is?"

"A twelve-kilometer stretch of highway connecting the Green Zone to Baghdad International Airport. It also connects other areas. So, like I said, it was a routine mission. There were two vehicles working in tandem. I was teamed up with Corporal Kincaid for the day, but toward the end, one of our guys in the other group got sick. I was sent to join that group to make sure they had enough hands on deck."

Lauren knew this part of the story. Pete had said that he hadn't wanted to leave Rory, that being around Rory always made him feel safe. She wished he hadn't told her. The irony was painful.

"After ten hours, we had instructions to head back. Corporal Kincaid's vehicle was a few meters ahead of ours. The light wasn't great—we rolled out a little later than we should have. We hadn't been driving more than ten minutes when the IED went off. I don't remember the moments directly after the explosion. But at some point we got out of our vehicle to help, ah...to see what happened up ahead. I saw right away...Corporal Kincaid on the ground. There was a lot of blood. It was clear that, uh, he had been killed."

Lauren stood up. Matt paused the footage.

"I'm sorry," he said. "You wanted to hear—"

"I know, I know," she said. "It's fine. This is not news to me. Pete was with me a lot in the days following Rory's death. I asked him a million questions. I kept thinking that if I heard every detail, it would somehow make sense. I guess I'm still waiting for it to make sense. It never will."

"Lauren, there aren't any answers from his time in the military. If you're looking to make sense of it all, you have to go back."

She looked at him. "Back to what?"

Matt closed the Pete Downing interview and pulled up a new file. Lauren sat down.

A skating rink filled Matt's computer screen. In the foreground, a blue-eyed, thirty-something-year-old man.

Matt turned to her. "This is John Tramm, former assistant coach to the Flyers. Current coach of the Villanova men's ice hockey team."

Matt pressed Play.

"There was no hard-and-fast protocol for players who took a hit to the head. So they'd sit on the bench and the team trainer would evaluate them. And there is the expectation for the player to just shake it off. Nothing overt, of course. But hockey culture demands resilience. Guys feel pressure to prove their toughness, and, frankly, they know they can be replaced. Especially the rookies."

Lauren closed her eyes, suddenly back in Rory's first apartment in LA, his rookie season. *"Are you sure you don't have a concussion?"*

"Jesus, Lauren. Now you're a doctor?"

Matt, on audio, said something, snapping her attention back to the screen. "I understand there's a class-action lawsuit by about a hundred retired players."

The coach answered, "Yes. The lawsuit is in light of the new research about CTE. One of the first to be studied was one of our guys, Larry Zeidel. He was a Flyer. Nickname was Rock. A great guy—everyone loved him. Then he retires and suffers from debilitating headaches. Starts having a bad temper, gets violent, makes crazy financial decisions. Impulsive decisions. His entire life fell apart."

Lauren nodded, tears sliding down her face.

Matt closed the file and clicked on the next interview.

"I want to show you my conversation with a neurologist."

A doctor's office, plaques on the wall, a neat desk. The neurologist had white hair and a very direct gaze. Again, off camera, Matt led the subject of the interview through questions. This time, there were visuals, slides of the brain, normal and diseased side by side. Lauren leaned forward, barely breathing.

The sound of Matt's voice off camera: "And can you explain exactly what CTE does to the brain?"

"In CTE, a protein called tau builds up around the blood vessels of the brain, interrupting normal function and eventually killing nerve cells. The disease evolves in stages. In stage one, tau is present near the frontal lobe but there are no symptoms. In stage two, as the protein becomes more widespread, you start to see the patient exhibit rage, impulsivity. He most likely will suffer depression."

Lauren stood up and started pacing.

Matt closed the file. "Does any of this sound familiar to you, Lauren?"

She didn't bother answering. He knew it did.

"This isn't the film I was looking for, Lauren. I'd love to hear that Rory was just a gifted athlete turned selfless hero. But he was damaged. He was making irrational decisions by the end, wasn't he? As if his mind weren't his own?"

She turned to him, breathing so hard and fast she couldn't speak.

"I'm not trying to diminish his accomplishments," said Matt. "His talent. His bravery. I'm not saying that he failed. I'm saying the system failed *him*."

She nodded. "Maybe."

"Not maybe. Definitely. And I need to get this film finished, for other guys like Rory out there. And other women like you."

She didn't say anything, just moved her head in a slow, hesitant nod. It was all he needed to start staging the room.

Chapter Thirty-Five

Matt clipped the mic to her top and tucked the sound pack behind her, out of view. She wanted to rest her head on his shoulder, to have him hold her. Her emotional scale was really out of whack.

Matt sat in the chair facing her.

"Are you ready?"

She took a deep breath. "I'm ready."

"Let's jump ahead, to the summer of 2011. How did Rory react to the news that he didn't get an offer from the Kings?"

She'd known nothing about it until his agent mentioned it—*at their wedding.* Jason said something about how she shouldn't worry, that someone else would make an offer and he would land somewhere. "This is just a speed bump."

Lauren was furious that Rory hadn't told her.

"What's the point?" he'd said. "I'm done with hockey."

"No," she said to Matt. "I didn't know about the offer until his agent brought it up. He was just a month away from basic training."

After their honeymoon in Jamaica, they had only two weeks together before Rory left for boot camp at Camp Darby in Fort Benning, Georgia.

She crossed each passing day off her calendar, the deadline looming like a guillotine.

"Did he perceive that you were supportive of his decision to enlist?"

"I think so. I tried to give him that impression. I mean, I was scared, but who wouldn't be?"

She kept her negativity to herself. Rory was more excited and confident than she had seen him since she moved to Los Angeles. Maybe this is what he needs, she told herself. She had to trust him.

Lauren hated to admit it, but Emerson's words just before she walked down the aisle stuck with her. No, she didn't agree one bit that she could "barely handle" being a hockey girlfriend. She thought she'd done a good job, maybe even a great job, of keeping things working for the past five years. And if she had moments of worry or doubt, well, who wanted to see the man she loved get pounded bloody? Who wanted to know—not suspect but know deep in her heart—that head injuries were making her fiancé a different person? The chronic headaches. The insomnia. The recurring flashes of anger. She was afraid for his safety in the military, but the truth was, the NHL wasn't exactly safe. He'd admitted as much himself.

"I bet I get banged up less over there than I did right here at the Staples Center."

She tried to smile.

Basic training was nine weeks long. She didn't have any idea how often they'd be in contact, and so she prepared herself for the worst-case scenario.

"I'll be able to call," he assured her. "And look, we've been apart for nine weeks before."

Rory had urged her to join some of the military wives' groups. "It's an important support system," he'd said, sounding like he was reading out of the army handbook for How to Deal with Your Nervous Wife.

She'd lurked on some of the groups online, read through some of the chat threads. The basic training / boot camp chat rooms seemed to be frequented by parents of new recruits and maybe the occasional girlfriend. Lauren couldn't relate to any of the comments. Rory was older than most of the guys and she felt their circumstances were unique. She clicked around, desperate to find a thread that would help her feel connected. All the while, she told herself that this was temporary. In three years, they would move on with their lives. It was less time than college.

Just as she'd almost gotten used to him being away, he came home.

"He told me it was boring—frustrating sometimes. One day he spent eight hours mowing a lawn."

"Was this discouraging to him?"

"No. He said, 'I had to learn to skate before I could score.' But he did have to get through months of Ranger School, and that wasn't easy. I think people wanted to remind him that he might have been a star on the ice, but he was a nobody there. The thing they didn't realize was that by that point, Rory hadn't felt like a star in a long time. And he was deeply motivated to change that."

"And how did things go at Ranger School?"

"He graduated with the Darby Award. Top honors." Finally, he was the best at something again. "And his decision to do this was completely affirmed."

"And in your mind?"

Lauren took a deep breath.

"In my mind, I guess something was affirmed too. The understanding that my husband was an exceptional person and that everything that was happening was part of the deal. My life with him was going to be one of high highs and low lows, and it always had been."

The next six months apart would take it to another level. But they would get through it. There was no other choice.

The Rangers deployed for shorter tours than the general army—six months versus nine or twelve. But they also spent less time stateside between deployments.

"But you spent some time in Washington State, right?"

"Yes. We didn't know exactly when he would be deployed, so after Ranger School we rented an apartment near Fort Lewis."

"Rory didn't want to live on post?"

"He did. I didn't. It was one compromise he made for me, though he kept insisting it would be better for me to be in a place where I could meet other wives, not be so isolated."

"You didn't want to?"

"No. Not at all." Her stance on the issue, her "stubbornness," was one of the few things that almost pushed them into an argument during that time.

She had a bad attitude, she knew. And she could barely hide it. She hated Seattle. The change in climate from Southern California was a shock to her system. Yes, she had grown up on the East Coast where winters were cold. So it wasn't really the weather. It was that going from a sunny seventy-five degrees to damp, cold overcast days in the thirties seemed a representation of the dismal turn their life had taken.

As for the apartment itself, she couldn't really complain. It was a lot of space for very little money, with a view of the Tacoma Narrows Bridge. Under other circumstances, she might have found it charming.

Their last night before his deployment, she woke up an hour after she'd fallen asleep, rain landing like pennies outside on the metal air-conditioning unit. It was hard to imagine ever needing air-conditioning in that climate, and that's probably why the building wasn't equipped with central air, just the clunky window units.

It wasn't the first night she'd woken to the tinny clatter, but that night, she knew she wouldn't fall asleep again.

Next to her, Rory lay still, his back to her, inches from her own listless body. They'd had sex before going to sleep, but she had been too much in her own head to enjoy it. She spent every second trying to memorize him, the way the crook of his neck smelled, the thrill— still!—of his hands on her hips, the first few heart-racing seconds when his body pierced hers. But was there any true pleasure in it that night? For her, no.

Maybe it was different for him. When he shuddered inside of her, his cry muffled in the long tangle of her hair over her shoulder, she felt very, very alone.

Now, with that weighted, emotionally overburdened act punctuated by some sleep, she reached for him.

He pulled her close, and she could feel his heart pounding through his T-shirt.

"Are you okay?" she whispered.

"Yeah," he said. Then: "Laur, I'm sorry that this is hard on you."

"It's okay," she said, because in that moment, in his arms, it was.

"I've made some mistakes," he said. "I want you to know I'm sorry."

She kissed him. "You make fewer mistakes than anyone I know." Was this about the hockey stuff? Why was he so hard on himself? Or was the mistake he was referring to that very moment itself, the fact that they were awake in the middle of a rainy night, in Tacoma, Washington, getting ready to say good-bye for six months?

"Are you having second thoughts about this?" She didn't want the answer to be yes. Then it would all be for nothing, because there was no turning back now.

"No," he said, and the smooth directness of his voice told her he was being truthful.

"Okay, well, don't worry about me. I'll be fine."

"I love you, Lauren," he said.

She pulled back, ever so slightly, so he would not feel the sob catch in her chest.

"Are you okay?" Matt said.

Lauren looked at him, startled to be dragged back to the present.

"What? Yes, I'm fine." She unclenched her hands.

"Tell me about when he came home."

Chapter Thirty-Six

He came home to LA in August. I can't even fully describe the excitement of knowing he would be back. It was different than any other time we'd been apart, not just because of how long it had been, but because of my relief. For the first time in half a year, that constant worry in the back of my mind was turned off. He was safe."

"How much communication did you have while he was gone?" Matt said.

"We were in touch more than I'd thought we'd be. He e-mailed a lot—called when he was able. But I never knew exactly where he was or what he was doing."

"When he came home, did you notice any changes?"

"I did. And I was prepared for it. At the end of deployment, family members had reintegration meetings. They told us about some challenges we could face, and with Rory, well, it was textbook. The insomnia. His detachment. How irritated he seemed most of the time. Snapping at me. But then, that had started back with the head injuries, so it wasn't new."

"How long was he home before he had to return to post?"

"He had thirty days' leave."

By the second day, he was drinking during the afternoon as he sat on the couch watching the news. Sometimes she made dinner, but more often she wanted to get him out of the house, tried to get him to drive to Santa Monica to eat by the water or go to a new place in Venice. But big, open spaces made him jumpy.

Lauren looked at Matt, the camera all but forgotten. His eyes, colored green and gray and gold, were steady on her. She grasped the arm of the chair, her hand slick with sweat.

"We argued a lot more," she said. "We argued in a way that scared me."

"Scared you...how?" Matt asked.

She heard him, but she didn't. Her mind was completely locked in the summer of 2012. It was as if she were talking in her sleep. "I thought maybe we needed a change of scenery," she said slowly. "Maybe a trip east would be good for him."

Lauren would be packing up and moving to Washington State with him until his next deployment. But at the midway point of his time home, she thought maybe a trip to Philly might lift him out of his funk. Rory's mother hadn't been able to visit because of recent hip-replacement surgery, and she knew if Emerson could also arrange to fly to Philly, Rory would agree to the trip. She didn't particularly want to see the Kincaids— they hadn't spoken at all during Rory's deployment except for a few perfunctory check-ins. But she imagined taking a walk with Rory in Narberth Park, having pizza at Boston Style. Maybe they'd go for a run around the track at Arnold Field. Going home was a chance to remember who they had once been. Who *he* had been—still was.

She arranged for them to stay at her parents' house. There was plenty of space, and she was more likely to be able to see little Ethan if Stephanie could just bring him by the house rather than Lauren having to wait for an invitation to go over to Stephanie's. Her relationship with Stephanie had never recovered from whatever had derailed it years ago, and only her mother would be able to broker a temporary peace so Lauren could see the baby, who wasn't so much of a baby anymore.

She never made it to Philadelphia.

"I'm not staying at your parents'," Rory said.

"Why not? They're never home and there's so much space."

"We can stay at my mother's."

"There's no room, Rory. Emerson and Jane are coming with the kids."

"We can sleep on the couch."

"I'm not sleeping on your mother's couch."

"Why the hell not?"

"It's ridiculous. We can have our own room—"

"Goddamn it, Lauren. The second you have to deal with the slightest bit of discomfort, you turn into a two-year-old."

She couldn't believe it. "The second I have to deal with... are you kidding me?"

"We're staying with my family, and that's it. I haven't seen Emerson in eight months."

"Well, whose fault is that?" she muttered.

"What's that supposed to mean?"

"You wanted this—all of this. I'm living the life you picked for us, and you're mad at me for suggesting we have our own bedroom for our two-week stay in Philly?"

"No, I'm mad at you for acting so victimized by everything."

"Well, great. I'm sure you and your lovely brother will have lots to talk about, then."

"So now you have an issue with my brother?"

"He has never been anything but a total dick to me!"

As soon as she said it, she saw his face change. It was like looking at a stranger.

She hadn't realized how close he was to her, and the slap came quick and furious, a backhand to the jaw. It was hard enough to throw her off balance, and she stumbled and tripped over an end table. She fell backward and hit her head against the wooden leg of a wingback chair they'd found at an antique store in Silver Lake. Her phone slid out of her pocket, and she grabbed it, just that small motion dizzying to her.

"Jesus, Lauren—I'm sorry," he said, reaching for her, trying to help her up. "I don't even know—"

Lauren looked at Matt and took a deep breath.

"He hit me," she said. She waited a beat. It was the first time she'd said it aloud. Surely, something would happen. Something bad would happen.

But if Matt was surprised by her revelation, he didn't show it. "I was terrified. I knew that wives of soldiers were at greater risk of lethal domestic violence than any other demographic in the country. You know, Rory wanted me to be more involved, more informed as a military wife. The truth was, I knew more about what we were getting into than he thought. Maybe more than he knew."

"Was this ever addressed in a formal way by the military, that it was something you should be prepared for, look out for?"

She nodded. "I got lots of information. And to cap it all off, the day he got back from deployment, as I was walking to the bleachers to wait for him, military personnel handed me a little American flag along with literature on suicide and domestic violence."

"What did you think in that moment?"

"I mean, it put a damper on things. Let's put it that way."

"After he struck you, did you ask him to go to therapy?"

"Not at first. I was in shock, I think. And then he left for Philly without me. I don't know what he told his mother and Emerson, but they left me all sorts of crazy voice mails. They wanted me to come to Philly, to be, quote, supportive of him. I never answered my phone. I didn't want to tell them that he'd hit me if they didn't know, and if they did know and were still leaving me those messages? I mean, that actually wouldn't have surprised me."

"Did you tell anyone?"

She shook her head. "No. I just couldn't. It felt like I'd be betraying him. He was such a private person and had so much pride. And what would it have helped? I wasn't trying to punish him by keeping my distance; I really was trying to figure it out. And the only answer was therapy. It seemed obvious to me, but I knew it would be a tough sell to Rory."

"But you suggested it?"

She nodded. "Yes. He returned to LA three days before flying back to Washington. I said he couldn't come to the house, so he stayed with Dean Wade. I agreed to meet him for coffee and prepped my whole speech on why we needed therapy. I knew he would resist the idea, but I thought that ultimately he would come around. I truly believed that."

"So you were optimistic?"

"Yes. I was optimistic. And before he was due to fly back to Washington State, we met to talk."

Rory was already sitting at a table near the back when she arrived at the coffee shop. Their greeting was awkward. Her impulse was to hug him, but she held herself back and he kissed her on the cheek.

"How are Dean and Ashley?" she asked.

"Great. They say hi."

She nodded, remembering Ashley's words: "They all get nasty when they hit their heads."

She could feel other women in the café looking at them. Did they recognize him or were they just checking out a gorgeous guy?

"Lauren, I'm sorry. I fucked up. There's no excuse, but you have to know that's not who I am." He reached for her hand. She let him take it but she couldn't look him in the eye.

"I know that's not who you are. That's why we're having this conversation."

He smiled, and she knew he thought that it was going to be that easy, because in so many ways, it always had been with her. But that was over. She couldn't afford to be that person anymore.

"I need you," he said. "I need you to get on that plane with me to Washington."

She nodded, swallowing hard, resisting the urge to take the easy way out, to say, *Yes, yes, that's what I want to. I need you, I want you, I miss you!*

Instead, she said, "The only way that can happen is if you agree to counseling."

He pulled his hand away, sitting back in his seat. "Come on, Lauren. You know I don't go in for that crap."

"Well, I don't go in for domestic violence. So clearly we have a problem."

He looked at her like *Come on.* As if she were being dramatic. But she didn't waver, and he finally said, "That will never happen again."

"You don't know that."

"This is me you're talking to, Lauren. You've known me since I was sixteen years old."

She shook her head, her eyes filling with tears. "I'm afraid that person is gone."

"He's not."

"Well, that person, the man I fell in love with—the boy I fell in love with—would be saying therapy is not ideal, but okay. He would be saying he would never let me down again. Isn't that what you told me?"

He reached for her hand. "There's an adjustment period, Lauren. If you'd gone to any of the wife groups, if you weren't so intent on pushing this part of our life away, holding your breath until it's over—"

"Do you know that soldiers with PTSD are three times more likely to be violent toward their spouses?"

"Now you're a therapist, diagnosing me with PTSD?"

"I don't know what's going on, Rory! That's why we need a professional."

He stood up, dropping money on the table.

"Lauren, I love you. I want to be your husband. If you decide you still want that too, you know where to find me."

Was he kidding? After everything he'd asked of her the past few years, after every life decision she'd made had been based on his career, his injuries, his needs and impulses—he wouldn't even see a counselor after hitting her? She had friends in couples therapy because they didn't like doing the same things on weekends.

She followed him outside onto Melrose Avenue. He had no idea she was behind him until she was two steps away from him yelling, "I can't believe you! What, in the past ten years, have I ever asked of you? Ever?"

He said nothing and looked at her with something close to indifference. Without thinking, in a gesture of pure, impotent rage, she grabbed the heart necklace, tore it off, and threw it at him.

It bounced off his shoulder and landed on the ground with barely a sound.

She sobbed, unable to go further.

"What happened after that?" Matt prompted gently.

"There was nothing after that. He left for Washington; I refused to go with him." She'd forgotten about the camera. In some ways, she'd forgotten about Matt. She was talking to herself, going through the scenarios she had rehashed endlessly in her mind over the years.

"He called me a few times. Always insisting he loved me but never acknowledging that anything needed to change. After a while, I sent his calls straight to voice mail. I didn't know what to do."

She touched her necklace.

"A week or so after the argument, I got a package in the mail. It was this necklace. The chain was repaired." And Rory had included a note. *I still love you,* it read. "Then the calls stopped. I only found out he was redeployed from some routine paperwork that arrived at the house," she said. "I never saw him again."

Chapter Thirty-Seven

The weight of her words hung heavily. It seemed a long time passed before Matt asked, "How did you learn about his death?"

"I was at work. I was writing for an entertainment blog." The receptionist had appeared at her cubicle.

"Some men are here to see you," she'd said, wide-eyed. "I put them in the conference room."

Some men.

Her stomach had turned to stone. The walk from the cubicle to the conference room felt like it happened in slow motion.

The conference room was glass. Two officers stood inside.

"Mrs. Kincaid?"

One of the officers drew the opaque shades down for privacy.

It took Lauren seconds to process the fact that they were wearing Class A dress uniforms. She had learned about this scenario in a family-readiness meeting before Rory's deployment. Battle-dress uniform: injured. Class A dress uniform: killed.

Now, remembering it, Lauren broke down in sobs and looked around for tissues.

"Lauren," Matt said. "I'm so sorry."

"Can you get me a—"

"I'll be right back." He disappeared into the hallway and returned with a box of Kleenex. She wiped her nose, trying to calm herself from outright hysterics to a reasonable cry.

"I'm just surprised they came to talk to you at work. Why not wait until you were home? In private?"

She nodded. It was a good question. "They were afraid, because of Rory's fame, that the news would leak out before they could reach me. They couldn't risk waiting."

She sagged with exhaustion, her entire body weighted.

Matt moved close, unclipped her mic, and took the sound pack from her waist. She felt like collapsing against him. He steered her away from the camera and over to the bed.

"Just sit here for a minute. Let me get those off." He turned off the lights, clicking on only a bedside reading lamp. The room felt calmer, and her sobs quieted to hiccups.

Matt pulled up a chair so he sat facing her. He reached for her hands, damp from her soggy tissue.

"Lauren, I understand."

"No, you don't," she said. And then the words she'd been holding in for four years: "Because it's all my fault."

There. It was out. And maybe this was what she'd been afraid of revealing all along, not Rory's failings, but her own.

"Lauren, you know guilt is a common feeling in a situation like this. He died; you're still here. I felt it too with my brother."

"No, you don't understand. Rory volunteered for that second tour."

Matt said nothing for a minute, and she knew the storyteller in him could put the pieces together. She'd refused to see her husband and banned him from their home. And after two months of being shut out, he

240

turned back to the place where he felt useful, strong, in control; he sent himself back to Iraq. And he lost his life.

"I didn't even know it was possible for him to go back that soon," she said. "He had to have gotten special permission. He had to have wanted to get away that badly."

"He would have been sent back eventually. You know that," Matt said.

She shook her head, unable to speak. All she could hear was Emerson's words the day of Rory's memorial.

Hordes of photographers and news vans waited outside of her house. Two of Rory's former teammates went into the house first, returned with bedsheets, and used them to shield her from the cameras as they hustled her from the car and through the front door.

The doorbell kept ringing. The house was filled with military personnel, the guys from Rory's platoon and many more, plus the entire LA Kings team and guys from nearly every team he'd played on since middle school.

She noticed Rory's mother and Emerson heading toward the bedrooms. Lauren had offered to have Kay Kincaid stay with her, but she'd said she preferred the hotel where her son was staying. Lauren wondered if she was going to the guest bedroom to lie down, if she was feeling okay.

Lauren followed them into the hallway.

"Kay, are you doing all right?"

Rory's mother, tall for a woman and once spry and athletic, looked frail as she leaned on Emerson. She was in her late sixties; her hair was stark white and her olive complexion was uncharacteristically pale against her plain black dress. Her eyes were dark. They were Rory's eyes.

"Are you following us?" Kay said.

"What? No. I mean, yes. I wanted to check on you."

"She's fine," said Emerson. "Mother, go on ahead. I want to talk to Lauren for a minute."

This was it, Lauren thought. She and Emerson were finally united. But it was too late for it to matter.

"Rough day," she said.

"Save your crocodile tears for someone who buys it."

She looked at him, stunned.

"What's that supposed to mean?"

"If you hadn't thrown my brother out of this house, if you hadn't refused to join him on post, he'd probably still be here today."

She knew she shouldn't bite, but she couldn't help herself. She was already blaming herself for everything. Emerson's recriminations couldn't be worse.

"No one wishes more than I do that we'd fixed our marriage before...before..."

"He volunteered to go back, you know."

She hadn't.

"No. It was soon, but I thought—"

"He campaigned for redeployment. It was the only thing he could do to get over losing his marriage. I have all the letters to prove it."

She was shocked, but her instinct for self-preservation forced her to defend herself.

"He wouldn't have been there in the first place if it weren't for your influence!"

"You know, there's a reason they give guys dwell time, keep them stateside after a deployment. They need it. But a public figure like Rory jumping right back in? Permission granted. Still, you have to wonder how things would have played out if he'd waited to go back until he was more battle-ready. If he hadn't been running away from you."

"It's all my fault," she said to Matt.

"Lauren, listen to me: You know better than that. You think you should have stayed in a dangerous, abusive situation to keep your husband around so he wouldn't go back into a war zone? Think about this rationally. Just take a step back and look at it. I see things in terms of narrative, okay? My work is to understand cause and effect. You are not connecting the dots in a logical way."

She sobbed. "You really don't see it how I do?" she said. "It's so obvious to me."

"No, Lauren. No one would see it the way you do. Probably not even Emerson in a more rational frame of mind. And you have to stop blaming yourself. Or it's going to ruin your life. And you deserve to have a life, you know."

She cried and he moved his chair close enough that he could hug her. She sobbed against his shoulder, and he repeated, "You deserve to have a life." She heard it again and again, even after he was silent, even after her breathing returned to normal.

"I should go," she said, pulling back.

"Yeah, God, it's late. Um, okay. Let me find my car keys."

"Oh, it's fine—I can walk."

"Lauren, don't be ridiculous."

Outside, the air was thick with water and salt. Soon, the sun would be up. It was a magical hour, night just about to turn into day. Everything around her seemed to hum and vibrate with life.

She lowered the window on her side, letting the air whip through her hair. Matt turned on the radio and the car filled with a song she remembered from eighth grade, "Drops of Jupiter" by Train, *told a story about a man who is too afraid to fly so he never did land.*

Matt pulled up in front of the Green Gable and turned off the car. Through the open window, she heard the cicadas humming in the tall grass that framed the stairs to the beach.

"One summer, when we were in high school," she whispered, "I was driving us around in the rain. Rory opened the sunroof. Something about that moment... it was the most free I ever felt in my life."

Matt reached for her hand. "You'll feel like that again someday." She pulled her hand away.

"I never told anyone what happened between me and Rory."

"You mean about him hitting you?"

She nodded.

"Didn't you go talk to anyone after he died? A counselor? Anything?"

"I saw a psychiatrist. But all she did was give me a prescription for Zoloft."

"Fantastic," he said sarcastically. "Did you at least tell your mother? A friend?"

"No," she said. "No one. Until you."

Chapter Thirty-Eight

Beth sat up with a start in the early-morning darkness, her mind racing.

During her year in pastry school, she would start her day similarly, except she'd be thinking in French. It was just a few phrases without context or meaning, fragmented evidence that her mind had been churning overnight.

Now, the morning after Nora's party, it wasn't *mise en forme* or *le pétrissage,* but the words *four walls* rushing at her pre-coffee. *Sometimes you have to sell everything you've got. Even the four walls.*

She realized, pulling on her yoga pants, that Howard was dealing with the failure of the store all wrong. Or, rather, he was not dealing with it. And selling the Green Gable wasn't the answer.

It was still dark, but she padded down to the kitchen, expecting to find Lauren getting ready for her daily run. Surprisingly, her bedroom door was still closed. Stephanie's door, however, was open. And it was obvious her bed hadn't been slept in.

An hour later, nursing her second cup of coffee at the kitchen table and waiting until it was a decent time to call Howard, Beth heard the patio door slide open.

"Good morning," she said.

"Jesus! You scared the shit out of me," Stephanie said.

"Should I even bother asking where you've been all night?"

"I was with Neil, obviously. So you can officially stop pushing Lauren on him."

Beth sighed. "Well, I hope you're happy now."

"Do you?"

"What's that supposed to mean?"

"Do you really hope I'm happy? Because that would be a switch. I can't remember the last time you thought about anything other than Lauren."

"That's unfair, Stephanie. Lauren suffered a tragedy. If I've been more focused on her—"

"It's always been this way! Dad's the only one who gives a shit about me and now you've driven him away too!"

Beth was momentarily stunned into silence.

Stephanie headed upstairs. Beth followed her, saying in a loud whisper, "I'm going to Philly today. Overnight. I'm taking Ethan with me."

Stephanie turned around. "Why?"

"Why am I going to Philly?"

"No, why are you taking Ethan?"

"Because I can't in good conscience leave him here to be ignored for hours at a time."

"I resent that," Stephanie said.

"Well, if you don't start making some changes, one day your son is going to wake up and resent *you*."

It was the first time in four years that Lauren had overslept. She woke up thinking about the coach's interview as if it had been replaying in her mind all night long. *But hockey culture demands resilience. Guys feel pressure to prove their toughness, and, frankly, they know they can be replaced. Especially the rookies.*

She laced her sneakers, figuring she still had time to get in a quick run before work.

Outside, a mist settled around her. Lauren jogged in place on the boardwalk, taking deep breaths. *It's okay,* she told herself, launching into the run. Her legs found their familiar rhythm, her feet hitting the boards in steady repetition.

The disease evolves in stages... you start to see the patient exhibit rage, impulsivity. He most likely will suffer depression.

Lauren ran faster, willing herself not to think about the end. To think, instead, about the beginning.

Ojai, California. Christmas in the Southern California mountains.

"Laur, are you dressed? Come out here."

Rory on the hotel-room terrace watching the sun set. In the background, the Topatopa Mountains were bathed in pink light.

"Incredible, right?" he said, patting the chair next to him. She sat and he put his arm around her.

She nodded. It was breathtaking.

"The valley is lined up with an east–west mountain range so it gets this pink light at sunset. It's one of the few places in the world where you can see this." He kissed her, his hand grazing the silver heart around her neck. "I love that you still wear this."

"Of course I do. I never take it off."

He reached under his chair and presented her with a small white box.

"I hope you'll wear this—and never take it off."

"Oh!" Lauren said. "Are we doing gifts now? I have yours in the room—"

"Lauren, just open it."

Lauren ran faster, picking up her pace. Atlantic City was in view.

It was a solitaire diamond, set in an intricately carved, art deco platinum band.

"It's from the 1920s," Rory said. "One of a kind. Like you." And then he got down on one knee. "Lauren, will you marry me?"

Lauren couldn't breathe. She bent over, hands on her knees, telling herself it would be okay. The vise slowly loosened its grip around her chest.

There was no way she could run home. She didn't even want to try to walk. She didn't have her phone with her, no money. She never brought either, even though her mother told her that was a mistake. "What if something happens?" she always said.

She could ask someone to borrow a phone and call for a ride. She couldn't call her mother because she'd get too alarmed. She was always worrying about her; why give her more reason? She'd have to call Stephanie.

Matt found it difficult to watch the footage from last night, to see Lauren so upset. But the thesis of his film was confirmed. He had his movie, and yet his conversations with Stephanie at the bar nagged at him. His instincts as a filmmaker told him he was missing something.

Henny knocked on his door. "Sorry to disturb," she said.

"No problem. Everything okay?"

"Everything's fine. This is awkward and certainly not my favorite part of the job..." She nervously twisted the turquoise beads around her neck.

Money. He hadn't paid for the room since Craig pulled the plug. And his free nights were up. He was out of time.

Unless...

Matt composed an e-mail and attached last night's interview file. Without letting himself second-guess the idea, he e-mailed it to Craig.

"Thanks. Sorry to bother you," Lauren said, climbing into Stephanie's car. "Can you just drop me at work?"

Stephanie stared at her.

"You're a sweaty mess."

"There's a shower there."

Stephanie started the car. "I was half asleep. Why didn't you call Mom?"

"Because I don't want to worry her, okay? She already thinks I run too much."

"Yeah, well, that's because you do. It's pathological, Laur."

"A lot of people run."

"Not this much," Stephanie said, using one hand to fish around in her bag for a piece of gum. "You run down here and back every day? It's crazy. No wonder you feel faint. Maybe Mom *should* be worried."

Lauren barely heard her. She had a déjà vu, a flashback to another time Stephanie had picked her up. It had been a turning point in their relationship. The breaking point, actually.

Lauren and Rory planned their wedding for July 9, a date safely clear of the NHL playoffs. Beth pushed for their country club as the venue, and Rory's mother pushed just as hard for a Catholic church wedding. Neither option appealed to Lauren and Rory, so Lauren flew to Philly to find a spot that felt right for them.

Stephanie picked her up at the airport. It was strange to see her pregnant. Lauren hoped the baby was something they could bond over, hoped that impending motherhood would somehow soften her sister's attitude.

But before they'd even pulled out of short-term parking, Stephanie said, "I think you're making a mistake with this wedding."

"You've got to be kidding."

Where was this coming from?

"You can't trust him," Stephanie said. "Haven't you seen that over the years? You're signing on for a life of misery."

"I don't believe this!" Lauren said. "You're about to become a mother, and you're still jealous of my relationship with Rory."

"I'm not jealous, Lauren. I'm just being honest. You deserve better."

Lauren unlatched her seat belt and jumped out of the car.

"I really thought we were past all this," Lauren said, shaking. "I was going to ask you to be my maid of honor. But if this is your attitude, I'm not sure I even want you at the wedding."

And in the end, Stephanie didn't show up at the wedding. Looking at her now, after everything that happened, Lauren thought it all seemed so silly. If nothing else, she wanted to fix their relationship.

Stephanie drove up to the front of Nora's Café. Lauren opened the door, then turned around and said, "I'm glad you're here this summer. And not just for the ride."

Stephanie smiled.

Chapter Thirty-Nine

After sending the footage to Craig, Matt couldn't sit still. He considered a walk to the beach but found himself wanting to see Lauren instead. Being around her gave him the sense that he was making progress even if he wasn't technically working. At least, that's what he made of the impulse.

"Hey! Matt."

Matt, just outside of Nora's, looked around. He spotted Stephanie in a parked car.

"What are you doing? Staking out the joint?" he said.

"For your information, I just dropped off my sister. What are you doing here?"

Stephanie's hostility at the party the other night had surprised him, but he knew it shouldn't have. He'd seen it before: an interviewee said something he or she regretted, then felt "tricked" by the filmmaker. Matt had weathered more than one strongly worded legal letter. The thing was, Stephanie hadn't even made the incriminating statement on camera. What was he supposed to do with her drunken ramblings at a bar? Damned if he knew.

"Having breakfast," he said.

"Why are you bothering her?"

"I think that's your own guilt talking," he said.

"You're the one who should feel guilty, using my sister for your stupid movie."

"If she knew the truth, I doubt Lauren would agree that I am the one who should feel bad."

Stephanie's lower lip trembled.

"If you tell her, I'll deny it."

Matt barely heard her. His mind kept going over and over the same question: Why had Rory betrayed Lauren?

Matt had footage of all the coaches and teammates and military guys extolling his virtues. He had Lauren, acknowledging his injuries and the difficulties in their marriage toward the end. But there was a missing piece along the way, a breach between the man and the myth.

He needed Stephanie back on camera.

"I don't want to tell her, Stephanie. I have no interest in upsetting your sister or causing problems between the two of you. But if you're worried about her finding out—and someday she might, because the truth has a way of coming to the surface—then I suggest you take this opportunity to own it."

"How?"

"I'm offering you the chance to tell your side of the story. On the record." He waited, watching her mull it over. "I think you know I'm not the enemy here. And I don't think you're the bad guy either, Stephanie."

He could see her grappling with the idea of confessing. He'd witnessed it many times over the course of his career. People needed to talk. The need for absolution was a strong and universal impulse.

When Stephanie looked back at him, she had tears in her eyes.

"The guilt is killing me," she said. "And I have no idea what to do about it."

The house was empty when Lauren returned after work. Her mother's car was gone from the driveway. Lately, her mother had been spending a lot of time baking, but the kitchen showed no sign of activity even from earlier in the day. The deck was empty, the pool quiet. Would she have a rare night of the house all to herself? For once, she actually didn't want to be alone.

She dialed her mother's cell.

"How's it going there, sweetheart?" Beth said.

"Fine—I just got home from work. Are you here for dinner tonight?"

"Didn't your sister tell you? I went to Philly with Ethan for an overnight trip. I'll be back tomorrow."

When she hung up, she immediately tried Stephanie's phone, but it went straight to voice mail.

She walked upstairs, paced around her bedroom, then called Matt. Again, voice mail.

"Matt, it's Lauren," she said. "I've been thinking a lot about what I said last night, and I just don't want your portrayal of Rory to be so mired in the negative. I don't believe that's who he was. The end doesn't define the beginning. You know what I mean? Call me when you can."

The house was completely silent.

Lauren opened her closet.

The boxes from the attic were still taking up the entire bottom. She dragged them out, the one she'd already opened with her high-school keepsakes and another marked *2010–2011*. She remembered packing this one, basically dumping an entire dresser drawer into it: cards from her wedding, Ethan's blue birth announcement (*Stephanie Adelman is proud to announce the birth of her son, Ethan Jake Adelman, 7 lbs., 8 oz., April 6, 2011*), her wedding album (which she would not open under any circumstances), a few editions of the *Los Angeles Times* that mentioned Rory in the sports section, a scented candle from their honeymoon hotel in Negril, two shot glasses from Jamaica, and there, at the very bottom, a hotel-room key card that read OJAI VALLEY INN AND SPA.

She reached for it, clutched the small piece of plastic to her chest. *I held this on one of the happiest days of my life,* she thought.

Lauren placed the key card back in the box. And then she changed her mind about the wedding album—sort of. She wouldn't look through it, but she would hand it over to Matt. Maybe there was something in there he'd find useful. After all, Rory was more than a hockey player and then a soldier. For a time, a brief time, he had been a husband.

They'd married on the roof deck of the Franklin Institute, framed by a panoramic view of the Philadelphia skyline at sunset. The reception took place in the planetarium, under the stars.

Lauren walked down the aisle on her father's arm; she wore a simple A-line dress that she'd picked out with her mother at a bridal shop in Center City. Rory stood at the altar flanked by his groom's party: his brother, Dean Wade, and two friends from Harvard. Her bridal party consisted of friends from Lower Merion, her roommate from Georgetown, and Emerson's wife. She felt Stephanie's absence acutely and regretted their argument that day at the airport.

But all of that paled next to what truly marred that nearly perfect summer night: the secret she held deep and sharp in her gut. In six weeks, Rory would be leaving for basic training in Georgia. As he was a Ranger, his enlistment would be three years, and he could choose among a few places to be stationed. They'd decided on Fort Lewis, outside of Seattle.

And then, for a brief and shining moment, as she stood with Rory on the scenic roof deck, a warm summer breeze rustling her waterfall veil, the confrontation with Emerson didn't matter. Stephanie's absence didn't matter. Rory's enlistment did not matter. Hand in hand with Rory, both of them turned toward the nondenominational minister they had chosen, everything that had happened in the past nine years leading to that moment unfolded in her mind, a storybook montage. It was a miracle that they were standing there together, a beautiful miracle. Rory's dark eyes locked on hers as they exchanged their vows. She felt safe and sure, and everything else fell away.

Lauren rummaged through her desk for a pair of scissors. The next box, labeled *LM,* was wrapped in layers and layers of blue tape.

Underneath a thick layer of maroon and white clothing, she found the *Philadelphia Inquirer* article that Matt wanted to see. She stared at the grainy black-and-white photo of seventeen-year-old Rory standing in a face-off on the ice at the Havertown Skatium. She put it aside.

Next, a beat-up hockey puck saved from a game, the significance of which was long forgotten.

A midnight-blue velvet jewelry pouch. Inside, she'd tucked his dog tags, knowing she should keep them but not knowing when she would ever want to look at them again.

And then her fingers found a white sealed envelope scrunched in the corner. Lauren's hand covered her mouth.

Strange, how the mind worked. How it could obsess or obfuscate. How strange that it was possible to be the unreliable narrator of your own life. She shouldn't be surprised that she had forgotten about the letter. But she was.

She hadn't set eyes on it in four years.

In the days following Rory's death, she had been surrounded by friends and family, consumed with logistics and arrangements. The night of his memorial was the first time she'd been alone in the house, alone with his things. All she had left of him.

Two in the morning, and she was still wearing her black dress. She went to Rory's bureau and opened the middle drawer. It was filled with carefully folded T-shirts. She opened the top drawer, where his socks were all paired together. He'd always had a better organizational sense than she did. And he was neater than she was—the opposite of how it usually was between husbands and wives. She teased him about this.

In all of their months of separation, she'd never thought to move his belongings. Even in her darkest moments, she had not imagined that he would never return to the house.

She gathered a bunch of socks in her hands. They had to go—everything had to go. She couldn't live amid his clothes, his photographs, his furniture. But she couldn't part with them either. She would box it all up like she had the first half of their lives together, packed in the basement.

Next, his closet. She pressed her face to one of his sweatshirts, which somehow still smelled like him. She sat on the floor, trying to breathe.

So many sneakers, a pair of hiking boots. And then, a sliver of white caught her eye, peeking out from underneath a pair of Adidas pushed way in the back. On her knees, she reached for the envelope, saw her name written in Rory's familiar, precise lettering.

Lauren sank back on her heels. She knew what it was. She'd heard about them from other military wives. He'd left her a just-in-case letter.

She dropped it like it was on fire. It wafted to her feet.

When had he written it? Before his first tour? It had to have been then. There was no way he'd written it before the second. Either way, it didn't matter. The letter must not be read—not ever.

Once she read the letter, he would be gone forever.

Lauren took the envelope, ran back down to the basement, and shoved it into one of the many cardboard boxes they'd never unpacked. Then she taped it and taped it and taped it closed, as if the box were never to be opened again.

And now she'd opened it.

Lauren's phone rang. Matt.

"Hello?" she said, trying to sound normal.

"Hey, it's Matt. Sorry I missed your call but I was working. What's up?"

"Nothing. It was nothing."

"Are you crying?"

"No."

"Are you okay?"

She hesitated, trying to normalize her voice.

"Yes. I was just going through some old things."

"Where are you? Are you by yourself?"

"Yeah, I'm at home," she said, sobbing.

"I'll be right over."

Chapter Forty

Lauren climbed into the front seat of Matt's car. The night had cooled and she zipped her hoodie.

"Where do you want to go?" he asked.

"Just drive. Anywhere."

Atlantic Avenue was busy. At another time in her life, she would have appreciated the promise in the air, a beautiful night just waiting to unfold.

Stopped at a light, Matt said, "I'm sorry you got upset."

"It's not your fault. I wanted to find some things you could use for the film to counter all the negative stuff we talked about. I don't want him to be remembered as a tragic figure. I want people to understand why I loved him, to see what a happy life we had together, if just for a moment." She started to cry again. He pulled the car to the side of the street and found her a tissue from his glove compartment.

"Thanks." She sniffed. They were right in front of Lucy. "I used to love this elephant."

"What's that restaurant right next door? Want to get a drink?"

They waited a half an hour at Ventura's Greenhouse to get a table at the rooftop bar with a view of Lucy. The music was loud and commanding, courtesy of a live DJ.

"We're the oldest people here," she shouted.

"I know. I think we got reverse-carded—to see if we're under thirty, not over twenty-one."

She smiled. The waitress, sunburned and with a sheet of straight, white-blond hair, took their orders—a beer and an Italian hoagie for Matt, and for Lauren, a drink called a strawberry shortcake: ice cream, strawberry mix, and amaretto.

"Do you come here a lot?" he asked.

"I haven't been here in, like, ten years."

"Were you old enough to come here ten years ago?"

"No! That was the point."

"I didn't imagine you as a fake-ID type of teenager."

"Stephanie was a bad influence. She lured me here with promises of a bird's-eye view of Lucy."

"Such a crazy idea for a building," Matt said, looking at the six-story elephant. "Have you ever been inside?"

"My grandparents took me to the top every summer when I was little. We spent weekends at my grandparents' house—the house I live in now. The car ride from Philly seemed endless, but as soon as I saw Lucy, I knew we were here. I would get so excited. It's amazing how easy it is to be happy when you're a kid."

"This is a great town for kids. You're lucky."

"I know. I'm glad my sister is here this summer so my nephew can get to experience it."

"You're getting along with her?"

"I am." She smiled. "I feel like we're reconnecting a little."

A strange expression crossed Matt's face, a mix of surprise and puzzlement.

"What?" she said.

He hesitated, choosing his words carefully. "Well, you originally weren't happy about me interviewing her so I figured you two had some issues."

"Don't all siblings?"

He contemplated her question. "Not necessarily. I had more issues with my parents. I got along really well with my older brother."

"I'm sorry that you lost him. Do you mind if I ask what happened?" She had met only a few people over the years who had lost loved ones in the military. Each time, she felt a compulsive urge for details, to know when and where and how the person had died, as if somehow it would help her make sense of what had happened to Rory. This, maybe, was the appeal of war-widow support groups. But she was no more inclined to join a group now than she had been when she was an army wife.

"It was a blast. An IED near his convoy."

Her heart began to beat fast. "Like what happened to Rory?" she whispered.

"No," Matt said. "There is a parallel to what happened to Rory, but that's not it."

Their waitress arrived with Matt's beer and hoagie and Lauren's frothy pink drink. Lauren pushed it aside.

"What, then?"

"Do you know what the signature wound of Iraq and Afghanistan is?" he said.

"Traumatic brain injury."

He nodded. "My brother wasn't killed by the blast. He suffered what they call a primary blast injury and got a medical discharge. He had seizures. He was depressed, had memory loss. It was my junior year of college. I took some time off to be with him, but I barely recognized him. And then my senior year, I came home for winter break. We went to my aunt's on Christmas Eve, but Ben stayed behind. He got bad headaches.

My mother left the party early when he didn't answer his phone. She was the one who found him. He'd shot himself in the head."

Lauren covered her face with her hands. "I'm so sorry," she said.

"So I became really obsessed with traumatic brain injury. And the more I researched, the more I found how often athletes suffered the same thing."

"Okay, but it's different. I mean, you can't compare athletes and soldiers."

"In this context, you can. And Rory happened to be both."

"We don't know for a fact that he suffered from traumatic brain injury."

"I think it's textbook. You know it too."

She sipped her pink cocktail.

"Can I ask you a personal question?" he said.

"When have you asked me anything but personal questions?"

He made a waving gesture. "That was for work. I mean as a friend."

Were they friends? "Sure. Ask away."

"Why haven't you dated since Rory's death?"

The question felt like a slap. Her drink was suddenly too sweet, all sugar and no anesthetic effect.

"Because...because that part of my life is behind me."

He shook his head. "Lauren, you know that's not rational, right?"

"I don't expect you to understand."

"Lauren, your husband died. It's a tragedy. But it shouldn't define the rest of your life."

"Why shouldn't it?"

"Should I let Ben's death define me?"

"Aren't you? Isn't that what this whole thing is about? And besides, where's your wife? Or girlfriend?"

"Okay, I'll admit I've been a little consumed with work the past few years. My personal life has suffered. But I'm trying to do something positive."

"Well, maybe I am too."

"Or maybe you're afraid."

She pushed away her drink. "Maybe I don't *want* to be in love again. I had a chance, I tried, and I failed."

Matt shook his head. "Lauren, you didn't fail."

"Haven't you listened to a thing I've said these past few weeks?"

"I've listened to every word you've said. And I've watched the footage. I know what you've said better than you do."

"So then you know I left him when he needed me most."

"How do you figure?"

She bit her lip. "He wouldn't have been in Iraq that day if I had moved back to his post with him. He would never have asked to redeploy so soon."

"Lauren," he said slowly, "if anything, he failed you. Again and again. When did he ever put you first? You bought into this notion that he was special—hell, so did I. But guess what—he wasn't. He was just a man, a man who made mistakes, who hurt people, and who ultimately lost his life. He was gifted, but he was flawed. And the system is flawed, and for Rory—and for others, no doubt—the combination was lethal. But nowhere in this whole story do I see your culpability."

She covered her eyes with her hands, tears wetting her palms. "I could have made a difference in how things turned out if I hadn't been so damn passive. I let the NHL make the calls about his health, I let Emerson influence him, and I let him decide to join the military when really it should have been our decision as a couple. I let every external factor set the course. Because I wasn't strong enough to set it myself."

"I disagree. I don't think it had anything to do with lack of strength. I think it took a lot of strength to keep putting your own needs, your gut instincts, aside. Because you didn't want to get in the way of the great Rory Kincaid, because all you heard from his family was that you were a distraction, all you heard from coaches was that he was special and he was destined for greatness, and all you heard from him was that he needed to excel and dominate or he couldn't be happy. You two were living by different codes. They were impossible to reconcile. But your code was unconditional love, and you were true to that until it became dangerous. If you'd been with another type of person, you would have gotten back what you were giving. You would have been happy." He took her by the shoulders, turned her toward him. His face was emotional, the neutral listener gone. "And Lauren, I'm sorry to say, but you're fucking crazy for not giving yourself a chance to experience that."

"Experience what?" she said bitterly. "What, exactly, am I supposed to experience now?"

He stared at her for a beat, his hands moving from her shoulders to her face.

And he kissed her.

Beth tucked Ethan into bed, telling him that Aunt Lauren would read to him tomorrow night, for sure.

"Is she out with Mommy?" he asked.

No, Beth highly doubted that. "Maybe," she said. "I'm sure they'll be home soon. But it's bedtime for you. You'll see them in the morning."

She kissed him on the forehead and slipped out of the room. What an exhausting day. The last mile of driving on Black Horse Pike, she could barely keep her eyes open. But Ethan, overstimulated from a day running around Center City, Philadelphia, with her, had been a nonstop chatterbox. She probably should have stuck with her plan to stay overnight, but she felt compelled to drive back to the shore at the last minute.

A breeze blew into the kitchen through a window she'd left open. It was a beautiful night. She opened a bottle of white wine and poured a glass. She leaned against the counter and sipped slowly.

The day after Nora had mentioned selling everything, even the four walls, she realized she and Howard were looking at the business problem completely wrong. Their options weren't only to keep it going or sell it; they could sublease the space. With just one day in Philly exploring this option, she'd put out some feelers and had leads on potential tenants. Nothing concrete, but it was a start.

Howard had completely missed it. It wasn't like him. Howard thought he was being practical and strategic during the store crisis, but the truth was, the loss of the family business was more than just a financial blow. It was an emotional one, and that's why he made big mistakes in the end. Why he was still making a big mistake.

"Mom? Why are you standing here in the dark?"

Beth looked up, startled. Had Lauren been home after all?

"Did you just get home?"

"Yeah. I was...out. I thought you were staying in Philly overnight."

Beth explained it wasn't worth it; she wanted to wake up in her own bed. She didn't bother telling her about the store and the sublease. It was clear from the distracted look on Lauren's face that there were more important things to discuss.

"Are you okay?" Beth asked gently. There had been a time when Lauren was as transparent as a glass of water. But she had closed herself off after her marriage, and even more after Rory's death.

"I'm just confused," Lauren said, but in a way that was surprisingly light. In that moment, Beth noticed that there was a brightness about her, an energy that she hadn't seen in her in a long time.

"About what?"

Lauren opened the fridge, then closed it. She leaned against the counter facing Beth.

"My life. What it's supposed to be now. Who I'm supposed to be now."

Beth nodded. She'd been waiting for years for her daughter to come to her. She wondered if her sense of being pulled back to the shore that night had less to do with the need to sleep under her own roof and more with the universe making sure she was in the right place for this conversation.

She put down her wineglass. "Your relationship with Rory was a major part of your life. But your life is going to continue past that point. It already has, whether you realize it or not. You need to stop fighting so hard against it."

"I can't."

"Can't? Or won't? Lauren, I know you're trying to do the right thing, to be strong. But it's like that fable, the oak and the reed? Remember from when you were little?"

"I don't know. Vaguely."

"Okay, I might not be getting this exactly right. But the oak tree always seemed so strong because it never bent in the breeze, while the reeds swayed with the wind. But when the huge storm came and the oak tree couldn't bend, it broke."

"The reeds were fine, I take it?"

"Come on. I'm serious."

"So what are you saying? I'm being weak?"

"No," Beth said. "But I do think the storm has come. And I don't want you to break."

Chapter Forty-One

It was a mistake.

Matt woke up thinking about the kiss, and for a brief moment of self-delusion he told himself it was a dream, it was the alcohol, it was too much time in front of the computer screen—anything but reality.

A mistake, but not fatal. He would see her at some point during the day, act like nothing had happened. No, he would apologize—again. And then get back to business as usual. He wanted to see those newspaper articles and yearbooks.

But he couldn't stop remembering the way it felt. There was a strange relief to it, as if he'd been thinking about kissing her for weeks. He'd come to care for her—a complete mistake from a professional standpoint.

All in all, the transgression had lasted, what, twenty seconds? The shocking part—the reason it hadn't been even more brief—was the way she'd responded to him. As if it were the most natural thing in the world. Until it wasn't, and she freaked out.

"Oh my God, oh my God," she'd said, pulling back, her hand covering her mouth.

"Sorry!" he said. "My bad. And, hey—I guess that pink cocktail must be stronger than it looks." His attempt to lighten the mood failed. She became silent.

When he dropped her off at her house, he said, "Lauren, please don't be upset. It's as good as forgotten, okay?"

She shook her head, as if they had been debating something. "It's not your fault."

And then she got out of the car without another glance at him. He felt like a total jerk.

He'd spent too much time in that town. It was fucking up his head. The first red flag had been his mixed feelings about interviewing Stephanie last night and not letting Lauren know. It was absurd, of course; he didn't have to report everything to Lauren—*anything* to Lauren. But he was uncomfortable knowing the truth about Rory and her sister.

Then he realized that he hadn't saved Stephanie's interview from the drive to his laptop. Usually, he did the transfer immediately following the interview, but Lauren had left him a voice mail while Stephanie was there. As soon as she'd left, he listened and then ran right over to see her. The night unfolded from there. When he got back to his room after the kiss debacle, file management had been the last thing on his mind.

He downloaded the interview, labeled the chip *Stephanie #2,* and tucked it into the drive folder on his desk. He was meticulous about keeping two sets of every interview, one on his hard drive and the physical chip in the folder. Every filmmaker he knew had horror stories about corrupted drives and lost laptops.

His phone rang. Craig.

Matt waited a beat, steadying himself.

"Hello," he said, trying to keep his tone normal.

"Hey, man. Watched your updated reel last night."

"And?"

"I think maybe this conversation is worth continuing. When are you coming back to New York?"

Matt's heart raced. "I'm wrapping things up here."

"Tell you what—I'll come to you. I wouldn't mind a day at the beach."

Beth maneuvered her way past the line and into Nora's Café. She angled her body so the tray of doughnuts didn't get jostled or knocked out of her hands and finally spotted Nora in the back of the dining room near the specials board.

"Hi, Beth," Nora said cheerily. "Are you looking for Lauren? She's off today."

"I know. I came to see you, actually. I brought these." She handed her the tray. "I wanted to thank you for the party the other day. That little talk in the kitchen was just what I needed."

"Well, I appreciate the doughnuts—they were a huge hit and I wish I'd saved a few more for myself! But I'm afraid I don't remember a serious talk."

"It was what you said about business—about selling even the four walls. It gave me an idea. A financial lifeline, really."

"Lauren did mention at the beginning of the summer that you were thinking of selling the house." Her brow furrowed in concern.

"My husband wants to sell it. But I'm fighting every step of the way. And as I was saying, thanks to our conversation, I had a brainstorm and things are looking a little brighter. So enjoy the doughnuts."

Nora lifted the foil covering the French crullers, the chocolate glazed, and the peanut butter and jelly doughnuts.

"The peanut butter and jelly ones were my grandson's idea," Beth said. "I would eat them today. Just a suggestion."

"You don't have to twist my arm!" Nora said. "You certainly are talented."

Beth beamed. "Thank you. I realize how much I've missed it."

Nora walked to the counter and set down the tray. When she turned back to Beth, it was like she was seeing her for the first time.

"Would you be interested in catering the dessert for a party I'm throwing? It will be here, in the restaurant, so you could use my kitchen for anything you need."

Beth, mouth agape, took a moment before answering. "I don't know what to say! That's...I mean, I haven't catered an actual party since before Lauren was born."

"Nonsense! You basically catered dessert for my entire Fourth of July party. And of course, just tell me your fee."

Beth's smile faded at the mention of money, but before she could say anything Nora jumped in with "And don't you start thinking this offer is just because you mentioned financial troubles. I was thinking about placing an ad for a pastry chef before you walked in today. And here you are! It's meant to be."

"What's the party for?" Beth asked, stalling.

"I'm finally taking the leap and opening the restaurant for dinner service. I'm inviting about a hundred friends and loyal customers to celebrate and sample the new menu."

Beth swelled with hopefulness. It was just the sort of thing she'd fantasized about—baking again, working again, feeling in control of her own destiny.

"And if I cater dessert for the party and things go well..."

"Then we talk about making it an ongoing business relationship. What do you say?"

"I say...I'd better get home and start working on a menu."

It was her day off, but Lauren woke to the alarm she'd set for her run. And the previous night rushed back to her.

"Oh my God." She sank back against the pillows, covering her eyes with her arm. She could feel it all over again, Matt leaning close to her, the confusion as her body moved toward him while her mind blinked frantically like an emergency light. But her body won out, and she kissed him back.

It was the realization that it felt good, that it felt right, that made her pull away. The guilt was instant and almost physical, like nausea.

She could tell by the look on Matt's face that it had been an impulse, that the whole thing had taken him by surprise too. She'd wanted to just bolt, to walk home without another word to him. But she didn't want to make too big a deal out of it or, worse, make him feel bad. If she were a normal woman, if they were in a normal circumstance, she would have been flattered. In an alternative universe, without the anchor of her past, Matt would be the type of guy she would be interested in. He was good-looking, smart, curious about people and the world around him.

She'd felt his outrage, though he hadn't said a word, when she admitted that Rory had hit her. Maybe that was what freed Matt to see her as a woman, not just a widow. He probably lost a little respect for Rory. After it happened, she had as well. But then he died, and there was no room left for anger over an argument. No room left for resentment about the way their relationship had deteriorated. He was gone, and everything changed.

If he had lived, would they have gotten back together? Could their marriage have been saved? She hated to admit it, but the answer was probably no. All this time, she had been fighting that realization. But it was true.

Even though Lauren had set her alarm to go running, she felt oddly unmotivated. Instead of running clothes, she put on a bathing suit, then grabbed a towel from the hallway linen closet and walked to the kitchen. She'd barely reached the coffeemaker when she heard the splashing and laughter coming from the pool.

She looked out the sliding-glass doors and saw Stephanie standing in the shallow end with Ethan, Neil Hanes sitting close by on the pool ledge. *Well, good for her,* Lauren thought. At least she was paying attention to Ethan. And it probably didn't hurt for him to have a man around. Lauren spent as much time with him as she could, but it was clear the kid was lonely.

She watched him get out of the pool, take a running jump in, and splash

Stephanie, who squealed with delight. Ethan spotted Lauren watching through the door and waved. She waved back. He climbed out of the pool again and ran over; he had to use both hands and his body weight to pull open the door.

"Come swimming, Aunt Lauren!" he said, breathless.

"Um, maybe later. It looks like you've got enough company out there. Go on—have fun with your mom."

"I want *you*," he said, grabbing her arm with his little wet, water-pruned hand. She glanced outside and caught Stephanie's eye. Stephanie gestured impatiently, like *Just come out.*

It was pushing ninety degrees on the deck and it wasn't even ten in the morning. The water was enticing. The company? Not so much.

"Hey there, nice to see you, Lauren," Neil said, standing up to greet her. For a second it seemed he was going to try to kiss her cheek in greeting, but she stepped back. She realized in that moment that she didn't like Neil Hanes. There was no particular reason for it; he was nice enough, and she didn't hold it against him that he'd bounced from being interested in her to being interested in Stephanie. There was just something about the way he was always showing up that set her on edge.

"We're going to play Marco Polo," Neil said. "Now that you're here, we have an even number and can do teams."

"I'm just going to watch," she said.

"Aunt Lauren!" Ethan called, throwing her a beach ball. She caught it, and the feel of wet plastic pumped with air brought her back to the time when she and Stephanie had been children in that pool, when their grandmother used to sit on the steps in the shallow end, white-nosed with zinc oxide, and admonish them for swimming too soon after eating.

She tossed it back to him.

"Come on, Lauren. You seem game-ready to me," Neil said.

Lauren ignored him and arranged her towel on one of the chaise longues.

"With four people we could have a chicken fight," Stephanie said, already climbing onto Neil's shoulders. "Ethan, you get on Aunt Lauren's shoulders."

So typical of Stephanie. She was surprised Stephanie hadn't broken out the Woody's vodka coolers like she used to do in high school. Lauren, not wanting to be the most epic bad sport of all time, waded into the pool and lowered herself so Ethan could get onto her shoulders. She put her hands on his thighs, making sure he was secure.

"Hold on to me with your legs—just try not to strangle me," she said.

"Come and get me!" Stephanie said to him, holding a fluorescent green noodle and bopping him on the head with it. Ethan laughed.

"Aunt Lauren, can you get me the yellow one?"

Lauren reached for the wet, spongy plastic and handed it to Ethan. Armed, he and Stephanie jousted while Lauren and Neil stood facing each other, bolstering the dueling mother and son. Neil, maybe tiring of his purely functional role, launched Stephanie off of his shoulders into the deep end.

"I win!" Ethan said. Lauren eased him off her shoulders and swam with him to the shallowest spot. Then she felt, more than saw, someone watching them.

"Sorry to intrude," Matt said. He was wearing cargo shorts and an NYU T-shirt.

She started to say, *You're not intruding,* but he was. And besides, she was too unnerved by how happy she was to see him to bother with politesse.

"The door is open," she said, glancing toward the deep end at an oblivious Stephanie and Neil, frolicking like teenagers. "Go in the house and I'll be right there."

She climbed out of the pool, quickly wrapped herself in a towel, and told Ethan to sit on the steps. "Hey," she called out to Stephanie. "I have to run inside. Watch Ethan."

Matt leaned against the kitchen counter next to a pile of handwritten doughnut recipes her mother had left out. "Who's the chef?" he said.

"My mother. Remember the doughnuts on the Fourth of July?"

"That's right. I forgot. Look, I'm sorry to barge in on you. I just wanted to make sure you're okay with...last night."

"It's okay. I'm fine. It's...we're good," she said.

"That's a relief." He smiled at her and they fell into an awkward silence. "Well, I should get going."

"Do you want some coffee or anything to eat? I mean, you're here anyway. And we're in the kitchen," she said lamely.

"Thanks, but I have to do some editing. My producer is coming out to see me today."

His producer. The film wasn't just Matt's project; other people were involved. The world would see it. This was happening.

"I need your word that you're not going to make him look bad," she said.

"Lauren, Rory doesn't look bad. He looks human. And I know you want the world to remember the man you loved, not some myth. The real Rory—and what happened to him—is a more important story than some fake example of perfect valor that doesn't help anyone. You knew Rory's flaws but still loved him, right?"

"Yes," she said. "Of course."

"Then you have to trust that the world will too."

Chapter Forty-Two

Beth tried to juggle too many grocery bags and dropped the carton of heavy cream onto the driveway. She picked it up and inspected it to be sure that it hadn't split open. The last thing she needed was to have to go back to Casel's and stand in line again. All she wanted was to start baking, to experiment with the best possible doughnut varieties for Nora's party.

The opportunity felt overwhelming. For years, she barely baked. Now she'd just dipped her toe back in and made doughnuts for fun, and suddenly she had a party to cater. Humming with excitement, she rearranged her shopping bags. That's when she noticed Howard's car.

What on earth? Had she missed a call from him? A message that he was coming back?

She walked around to the back of the house.

Someone had left the pool area in disarray—wet towels were everywhere, noodles still floated in the deep end, and there were soda cans on the table. She hurried into the kitchen, closed the door behind her, and was greeted only by the silence of the house.

"Hello?" she called.

"Up here!" Lauren yelled from the second floor.

She climbed the stairs. Lauren's bedroom door was open, and she peeked in to find her looking through one of the big moving boxes she had brought down from the attic.

"Hon? Have you seen your father?"

Lauren looked up. "Yeah. He showed up like twenty minutes ago. Did you know he was coming back today?"

Beth, not wanting to admit how little they had communicated, said only "Where did he go?"

"To the beach. I think to see Stephanie."

Matt met Craig at Sack O' Subs. That had been Craig's request; a graduate of the Wharton School of Business, Craig was familiar with the Philly–Jersey Shore connection and the regional obsession with cheesesteaks.

They sat at a booth near the back and ate potato chips while they waited for their sandwiches.

"I have to say, the interviews are more than I'd hoped for," Craig said. "Lauren doesn't just confirm your thesis, she adds a depth of humanity to the whole thing. I feel the loss of Rory emotionally, not just intellectually."

Matt nodded. "I'm glad you feel that way."

The waitress arrived with their cheesesteaks on paper plates.

"These alone are worth the trip," Craig said. His steak was topped with provolone, onions, and sweet peppers. "It's the bread that makes it. And they can't duplicate this in New York because of the water."

"Didn't know that," Matt said, distracted.

He wrestled with the issue of whether to show Craig the footage of Stephanie. A part of him felt he should hold back. Maybe the Stephanie angle wasn't a place he wanted to go with the film. However, he wasn't in a position to play it safe.

"Craig, there's some footage I've been grappling with. I didn't use it in the cut I e-mailed you. It's relevant from a character perspective, showing Rory's personal weakness in contrast to his public accomplishment. But it sends the narrative of the film maybe too far in one direction."

Craig pushed his plate aside. "Well, now you've got me curious! Let's take these to go."

When they arrived at the house, Henny greeted them in the driveway.

"Matt, I've been calling you." Her smock and left cheek were smudged with turquoise paint. "Oh, a friend! Hello there," she said to Craig. "Henriette Boutine. I'd shake your hand but…"

"Nice to meet you, Ms. Boutine. This your place?"

"It is! Matt, sorry to interrupt, but I have a new renter coming at the end of the week if you're certain you're leaving."

"Yes," Matt said. "I'll be out tomorrow. Is that enough time for you?"

"Of course! I don't mean to shove you out the door."

"Not a problem, Henny."

Craig followed him up the stairs. "Do you need more time here?"

"You tell me," Matt said, letting him into his room.

Craig scanned Matt's index cards while Matt booted up the computer and opened the file of Stephanie's most recent interview.

"Just grab that bench over there…yeah, drag it over here and we can share it."

Side by side, they watched the footage of Stephanie, nervous and emotional, answering Matt's questions. When it was over, Matt turned to Craig.

"What do you think?"

Craig drummed his fingers on the desk. "There's no question you have to use it."

Matt had been afraid he'd say that.

You knew Rory's flaws but still loved him, right? Then you have to trust that the world will too.

Could he do this film right without hurting Lauren?

*   *   *

There was no dignified way to walk on hot sand. Beth sprinted from the house to the ocean, scanning the beach for her daughter and husband. She turned left at the water's edge, stepping around shell fragments and small marooned jellyfish the size of mini-pancakes.

A few yards away, near the lifeguard stand, she spotted Stephanie's long blond hair. Howard was dressed in shorts, a polo shirt, and a baseball hat.

Seeing him from a distance was like looking back through time; he was twenty-five again. Maybe Howard actually looked younger after some freedom from the daily grind at the store. And maybe her weeks at the beach were having an effect on her too.

Howard noticed her and waved. Okay, that was a good sign. A friendly start.

"Mom!" Stephanie said, following her father's gaze. "Look who showed up!"

"So I see. This is a surprise," she said, accepting Howard's kiss on the cheek. She realized that she'd missed him the past few weeks, and not just in sentimental moments like the Fourth of July fireworks. As challenging as it was to be together, it felt wrong to be apart.

"Welcome home," she said, pointed in her use of the word *home*. "Can I talk to you for a minute?"

They walked a few feet away, out of Stephanie's earshot.

"I've left you messages," she said, trying not to sound too accusatory.

He turned toward the ocean. "I'm sorry. I wanted to use the time apart to think."

Swallowing her hurt, Beth said, "I used the time apart to think too. And I might have found a solution to our problem."

He looked at her, crossing his arms. She explained her idea for subleasing the store. He seemed incredulous at first, but as she spoke, he began nodding.

"I can't believe I didn't consider that," he said.

"You've just been too close to the whole thing. Come on," she said. "I have paperwork back at the house to show you. And some good leads on tenants. But we have to follow up."

They walked back to the house and Howard called out to Stephanie, "I'll see you and your sister at dinner."

"Dinner?" Beth said.

"I thought we'd go out to eat. I made a reservation at Tomatoes."

She smiled.

Howard adjusted his hat, and she wished she had one of her own. She tried to make it a habit to use sunblock every day but still forgot sometimes. She shielded her face with her hands cupped over her eyes until they reached the house.

"This sublease strategy...you did a good job, Beth. Thank you."

She beamed, thinking maybe the time apart had been a real blessing in disguise. He opened the sliding-glass door to the kitchen, and a rush of cool air greeted them. Beth walked to the refrigerator and pulled out a lemon and a pitcher of iced tea she'd brewed earlier that day. She was bending down to the lower cabinet for the cutting board when Howard said, "But we do need to come to an agreement about this house."

She stood up and turned to him. "If this sublease works out, we won't be on the hook for the monthly rent. And we can live here. There's no reason to sell this place."

"I'm not living here year-round. It's freezing and isolated in the winter."

She stared at him, incredulous.

"You've always loved this house."

"As a summer getaway! Not as our home."

"Why not?"

His face turned red. "Because it feels like failure, that's why not. I didn't want to lose the store, but I did. I didn't want to lose our house—I can barely live with the fact that I did. But I'll be damned if I'll spend our retirement in your parents' old place, freezing our asses off ten months out of the year in a desolate town because it's our only option."

"What about what I want?"

Howard sighed. "I just can't do it, Beth. And if that's really what you want, I have to admit, I don't see the compromise option here."

"Neither do I," Beth said, the words catching in her throat. He left the room.

Chapter Forty-Three

Howard had picked a restaurant that Lauren typically never set foot in during the summer. Tomatoes was one of the trendier establishments in town; it had brightly painted rooms and pop-art lithographs lining the walls.

The hostess led them to the back dining room, and Lauren spotted a lot of regulars from Nora's sitting at the octagonal bar. It was strange for her to wait on people by day and then be a customer alongside them at night.

The three of them sat at a table under prints of Marilyn Monroe and Superman. The empty fourth seat was glaring.

"Isn't this nice? A night out with my girls," Howard said as the hostess handed around menus.

"I still don't get why Mom didn't come tonight. If you two would just start acting normally, things would go back to the way they were," Stephanie said. It took all of Lauren's strength not to roll her eyes at this typically simplistic and self-serving comment.

"If it's that easy, why didn't you just 'act normal' with Brett?" Lauren said.

Stephanie snorted. "You're comparing Mom and Dad to me and Brett? They've been together, what, thirty-five years?"

"It's complicated, sweetheart," Howard said, looking at the wine list, then closing it abruptly.

"Are we getting a bottle?" Stephanie asked.

"I don't think we need to drink tonight," he said, glancing at Lauren. She gave a subtle nod of agreement.

Stephanie slumped in her chair.

"So tell me what's been going on the past few weeks? A good summer so far?" Howard said.

"Are you serious?" Stephanie said. "We're going to sit here and pretend this isn't totally fucked up?"

Lauren was shocked to see tears in her sister's eyes.

A waitress came by to take their drink orders. Howard asked her to give them a minute. "Sweetheart," he said to Stephanie. "I don't want you to take this so hard. Whatever happens between your mother and me, we're still your parents. I'm here for you, always."

Stephanie started bawling. What the hell?

"The one thing I could count on was you and Mom. No matter how messed up things got, I knew I could always come home."

Lauren felt bad for being cynical, but really, what had Stephanie lost? A crap husband of a year and a half? And of course she had to make the whole dinner about her.

Their father got up from his seat and embraced her.

Is something wrong with me? Lauren thought. From her perspective, okay, her parents were having problems, but it wasn't the end of the world. She didn't want either one of them to be unhappy, so if this was what they needed—ultimately, it was their lives, not hers. And, yes, Stephanie always tended to make things about herself. But this was an unusual degree of drama even for her.

"We're still a family," Howard said, finally sitting back down. Nearby, the waitress hovered like a moth. "Right, Lauren?" He looked at her, and she recognized her cue.

"Um, yeah. He's right, Steph. It's going to be okay."

In a summer filled with craziness, this was maybe the most absurd moment yet: she was reassuring Stephanie—who had been pushing her away for years, who'd boycotted her wedding, who hadn't shown up when her husband died—that they were a family no matter what.

Maybe she'd been too quick to say no to the bottle of wine.

Beth tucked Ethan into bed, closed the door, and stood alone in the dark hallway. All night, she'd fought a persistent creeping sense of unease. Maybe staying home instead of joining them for dinner hadn't been the right thing to do. She was just so angry with Howard!

As a young wife, she'd sacrificed her dream of catering to join his family business. Her mother-in-law had seemed eager to pass the torch to the new Mrs. Adelman, hoping to attract a younger clientele. And she'd told Beth that, contrary to conventional wisdom, it wasn't children that kept a marriage intact, it was the common interest of working together. "Someday you'll thank me," Deborah Adelman had said.

Restless, feeling like the house was too quiet, Beth sat on the couch in the living room that had been decorated by her mother's own hand. She missed her terribly in that moment. She opened the latest Michael Chabon novel, but she doubted she would have the concentration to read a word.

She should go to bed, but she wanted to talk to Lauren. A conversation had been brewing in her mind for days now, and the reappearance of Howard and his push about the house gave it a sense of urgency.

But exhaustion won out, and she realized she had dozed off when the sound of the back door startled her. She moved the book from her lap, left it on the couch, and padded to the kitchen. Lauren was sitting at the table and drinking a glass of water in the dark.

"Hi, sweetheart," Beth said.

"Hey," Lauren said. "You doing okay?"

"Of course. Why wouldn't I be?"

"Well, because of your problems with Dad."

Sweet Lauren. Beth turned on a light and sat down.

"I'm fine, hon. Where's Stephanie?"

"She went to Neil's."

Of course she did—without so much as a text asking about Ethan, never mind a call to say good night to him. All the more reason to have the conversation with Lauren.

Lauren stood with a yawn, pushed in her chair, and bent to kiss Beth on the cheek. "Good night, Mom. See you in the morning."

"Wait, I want to talk to you about something." Tonight, while Ethan was asleep and Stephanie was out.

Lauren sat back down, wearily. "What is it?"

"I want to live here, at this house. Year-round. And I want to ask Stephanie to stay too. To raise Ethan here."

Lauren's face turned red. "Wait—back up. I thought you were selling this house?"

"That's your father's idea. I don't want to."

"So you plan to live here with Ethan and Stephanie? What about me?"

"This is your home too. For as long as you want to live here. But I want to give Ethan a sense of family. He needs us now."

Lauren nodded. "I get it. Does Stephanie know about this?"

Beth shook her head. "No. I wanted to talk to you first."

Lauren bit her lip. "I'm really used to being here alone in the winter."

"Hon, if you want privacy, maybe it's time to get your own place."

Lauren's eyes widened. "Wow. Okay, um, I guess I've been selfish trying to keep this house all to myself the past few years."

"No, sweetheart. It's understandable."

"I just love it here. Surrounded by all of Gran's things, memories from when I was a kid. It's like, when I'm here, I'm safe. I can't explain it."

Beth nodded. At some point, Lauren needed to move on with her life. Beth was afraid it would never happen as long as she was wrapped in the safety net of the Green Gable. But if she still wasn't ready, Beth didn't have the heart to shove her out the door.

"You don't have to explain it, hon. I understand."

And she did. The Green Gable was her safety net too. That's why she would never sell it. No matter what.

Chapter Forty-Four

A knock on her bedroom door woke her. Lauren checked her phone. Usually around this time, she was just getting back to the house after a run. She'd forgotten to set her alarm.

"Yeah?" she called out, sitting up and rubbing her eyes.

Stephanie walked in, still dressed in her jeans and blouse from the night before. She had raccoon eyes, yesterday's mascara and eyeliner having made an unfortunate migration south.

"You're still in bed? Are you sick?" Stephanie said.

"No. I'm fine." Had her mother already spoken to her sister about the house? Stephanie probably wanted to make sure Lauren was okay with it. And the truth was, Lauren didn't really know how she felt yet. She'd woken up a lot during the night with her mind racing. Living with her family would be an adjustment, but maybe that was not a bad thing.

"You have to see this." Stephanie handed her a bunch of typewritten pages.

Bewildered, Lauren looked down. The top page read *The Rory Kincaid Story, an original screenplay by Neil Hanes.* In the corner, the name and address of his agent.

Lauren's hands shook. She looked at her sister. "I don't understand."

"I think you do," Stephanie said.

"Where did you get this?"

"I found it in Neil's room this morning."

"He's writing a movie about Rory?"

Stephanie nodded.

"You knew about this?"

"Just since last night. He was asking me so many questions that I finally was like, What's your deal? And he told me. But he told me not to tell you—or anyone."

Lauren sat on the edge of her bed. So that's why he'd been sniffing around all summer. "Oh my God."

"I didn't want to upset you but I thought you'd want to know."

Lauren nodded, a wave of panic making it hard to speak. She thought frantically of her conversations with Neil over the past few weeks, wondering if she'd said anything about Rory.

Stephanie sat next to her.

"Thanks," Lauren said. "I do want to know. Of course I want to know."

"Laur, this stuff with Mom and Dad makes me realize how I've taken so much for granted. I see it all falling apart and I'm scared."

It was probably the most real, honest thing Stephanie had said to her since they were teenagers. Unfortunately, it was coming at a moment when Lauren could not think straight.

Lauren flipped through the screenplay, then jumped to her feet. "I have to go."

Matt woke to knocking on the door.

He was exhausted. The visit with Craig had been invigorating and daunting at the same time, reminding him that good footage was just the starting point, not even close to the finish line of a successful film. He had tossed and turned most of the night, wrestling with how best to use Stephanie's material.

The knocking continued.

"Coming, coming," he said. He got up and answered the door bare-chested and in his boxers, the comforter wrapped around his waist.

"I have to talk to you," Lauren said, walking past him into the room.

"Come on in," he said, squinting against the sunlight. He closed the door and surveyed the room's disarray: his unmade bed, the Sack O' Subs takeout bag on the floor, the empty soda cans lining his desk next to a bag of ranch Doritos. "Sorry, the place is kind of a wreck. I've been going twenty-four/seven the past few days."

"I'm freaking out," she said.

"I mean, it's not that messy," he said.

She didn't crack a smile. "Look at this." She handed him a manuscript, or, on closer look, a screenplay.

The screenplay. The Rory Kincaid feature film.

"Son of a bitch," he muttered. "Where on earth did you get this?"

"What difference does it make? I just want to know how we can stop this from happening."

Matt pulled out his desk chair and sat, thumbing through the pages. "We can't."

Lauren sat on the edge of his bed and put her face in her hands. "I was afraid you'd say that. Can you believe this?"

He wanted to jump in and start reading the thing. But Lauren had clearly come to him for some kind of reassurance, and the least he could do was try to give it to her.

"This doesn't mean anything," he said, tossing it onto his desk. "He doesn't have shit. We have the real story. By the time this thing sees the light of day, it will be old news because this documentary will be everywhere."

"How can you be sure?"

"This is just a draft of a script. It's only seventy pages. I doubt it's finished. It sure as hell isn't a shooting script."

She looked unconvinced. "I'm really upset about this," she said.

He sat next to her. "I know. It's understandable. But there's nothing you can do about it except know that (a) most feature-film scripts don't even get made, and (b) you helped bring the true story to the screen. You have your own say, which people will care about and listen to infinitely more than this guy's crap."

She looked at him. "I never thought I'd say this, but I'm glad you're doing this movie."

"Really?"

She nodded. And then, in his exhaustion and stress and relief and simple raw attraction, he kissed her. Again. She kissed him back, her arms moving around his neck. He pulled her on top of him as he fell back on the bed. The absolute force of his desire was shocking to him. It was as if the hours of intense conversation had been leading to this moment.

"Lauren," he said, gently moving her off him and onto her back. Her hair was coming loose from her ponytail. He found the purple elastic band and gently tugged it off. He kissed her just under her jaw, then lower, feeling the pulse at the base of her neck. He tried to slow it all down, to give her a chance to stop him. Hoping against hope that she wouldn't.

Lauren didn't want to speak, afraid the intense feelings she had for Matt, the overwhelming drive to have him touch her, would burst like a bubble if she said a word. In that moment, she felt like she was coming up for air after nearly drowning, and all she knew was that she could still slip back under. She took his hand and moved it to her breast, kissing him. He slipped his hand under her tank top, touched her, and then pulled it off. He unhooked her bra and drew her in close so they were chest to chest. The sensation brought tears to her eyes.

When his hand moved lower, to the top of her shorts, she helped with the button and zipper.

"Do you have anything here?" she asked.

"God, no…this was the absolute last thing on my mind."

It didn't matter, not really. She hadn't had her period in a while. Maybe it was the running. Or maybe her body had just given up, the way she had.

It was reckless, but she didn't care. Where had being careful, being safe and good, gotten her?

She pulled him on top of her, and all that had been weighing on her, strangling her, finally released its hold.

Afterward, her eyes filled with tears. For the first time in as long as she could remember, they were tears of happiness instead of grief.

Chapter Forty-Five

I'm too old for contact sports," Beth said, balancing on a raft across from Ethan, who whacked her in the shoulder with a noodle.

"Oh, come on, Mom," Stephanie said from the chaise longue. "It's fun. A good way to get out your aggression."

"That's what baking is for."

But she was just playing the part of the curmudgeon. She was thrilled to see Stephanie spending time with her son. And she had heard Stephanie knocking on Lauren's door first thing in the morning. Her instinct about this summer had been right. Things were getting better, at least where the girls were concerned. As for Howard? He was gone for the day, back in Philly working on sublease prospects. They'd barely spoken since the argument about moving. And now she was about to double-down on the house.

When Ethan climbed out of the pool for a snack, Beth swam to the shallow end and called for Stephanie to join her.

"I want to talk to you about something," Beth said.

"Wait, Mom. I have to say something first. You were right. I need to spend some time by myself. Be alone for a while. Focus on what's important."

"Really? And what about Neil?"

"I'm over it. Not happening," she said.

"Okay, well. I'm proud of you, sweetheart. And I want you to know you have my support. That actually brings me to what I wanted to talk to you about." Beth hesitated, wondering if the suggestion would seem too pushy, controlling. "I'm not planning on leaving here at the end of the summer. And I would like you to stay too."

"For how long? Ethan has to get back to school."

"He can go to school here. They have a wonderful elementary school."

"You want us to . . . live here?"

Beth nodded.

"What about Lauren?"

"Gran left the house to us as a family."

Stephanie's eyes filled with tears. "You mean it?"

"Is that a yes?"

Stephanie hugged her. Beth exhaled.

Lauren inched away from Matt under the sheet so he could slip from the bed to turn up the air conditioner. It was a window unit, and it wheezed loudly and seemed to rattle the entire room.

"How do you sleep with that thing?" She smiled, sitting up against the headboard, pulling the sheet high over her breasts and tucking it under her arms like a tube top.

"I usually don't," he said, sliding back onto the bed, next to her but over the sheet. He'd put his boxers back on. "So . . . *that* happened."

She smiled. He kissed the top of her head. "You okay?" he asked, and she nodded.

She braced herself for the guilt; so far, it hadn't come. Instead, she felt an odd relief, a sense that somehow a former version of herself had been restored. But since there had never been a sexual version of herself that didn't involve Rory, it couldn't be a return to anything. It was something new.

She reached for her top and shorts and put them on under the sheet.

"Don't go," Matt said.

"Just need the bathroom."

She didn't plan on staying, but still, it was nice to hear him ask her to. On the way to the bathroom, she passed his desk and the map of index cards taped above it. She told herself not to look, not to think about Rory and the film. She wanted Matt and Rory to be separate, not only in that moment, but forever in her mind. But one card caught her eye: *Stephanie reveal.*

She turned to Matt.

"What's this mean?"

Matt jumped up, looking at the board as if wondering how it got there. Or maybe wondering how he had left it there.

"It's nothing," he said, moving next to her, taking a few sheets of printer paper, and tacking them over the index cards.

Was he serious? "You're not letting me look at the storyboard?"

"Lauren, I don't want to talk about the film right now. I don't want to think about the film right now. I just want to be you and me—a man and a woman. I think we both deserve that for just an hour. I know you sure as hell do."

He put his arms around her, and she forced herself to look into his green eyes, not at the words hanging on the wall. He kissed her.

"I'm going to make a run down to the kitchen for coffee. How do you take yours?"

"Um, milk and sugar."

He hesitated.

"What is it?" she said.

"I'm hoping you'll come see me in New York."

She looked at him blankly, the words not quite registering. "You want me to...come to New York?"

"Well, yeah. Don't look so surprised. Some people find it an interesting place to visit."

She smiled. "So I've heard. But seriously. This is...I have to process this."

He kissed her cheek. "Okay, process. I'll be back with coffee."

When he was gone, Lauren used the bathroom, then looked at her reflection in the mirror. Her cheeks were flushed; her face appeared different to her own eyes. For the first time in a very long while, she felt pretty.

She ran her hands under the water and stared at her wedding band. A sob rose in her chest, but she held it back. *It's okay,* she told herself.

The ring should come off. But she couldn't bring herself to do it.

In the bedroom, the maze of index cards called to her. *Stephanie reveal.* What did it mean? Was Matt hiding something from her?

Lauren walked to the desk. She didn't know exactly what she was looking for, but the flip book was still there—the place where he kept hard copies of his interviews. All the discs were in chronological order, and she quickly found the one labeled with Stephanie's name and a date. But she'd seen it already. There was no "reveal," nothing much of interest at all. She kept looking, not sure what she expected to find. And then she saw it: *Stephanie #2.*

Heart pounding, she slipped both files in her pocket. And she left.

Beth placed the hot-dog buns facedown on the grill for just a few seconds before dropping them onto the serving tray. Stephanie had set up her iPhone on a dock to play a monotonous female pop album—Lady Gaga or Katy Perry or some such. But it was the sound of happiness, because it had been the backdrop to telling Ethan the news that he would be living at the beach from now on, and his little face had lit up in a way that Beth would remember for the rest of her life. She only wished Howard had been there to see it. A shared smile between them over Ethan's joy might have been a bridge back to each other.

"Aunt Lauren!"

Beth turned around. Ethan ran up to Lauren and jumped into her arms.

"Hey, kiddo. Easy there," Lauren said.

"I thought you were working today," Beth said.

"Yeah, long story."

"Aunt Lauren, I'm going to live here! With you! Forever!" Ethan said.

Lauren eyed Beth. "Forever, huh? Well, I don't know about that. We might have to ship you off to Hogwarts at some point."

"Sit and have lunch with us," Beth said.

"I can't, Mom. I have stuff to do. I need to be alone."

Okay.

Chapter Forty-Six

Lauren emptied every drawer in her bedroom hunting for her computer charger, mentally combing over the past week in her mind. When had Matt interviewed Stephanie a second time? Was there any way he'd just forgotten to mention it to her? Had she seen him the day it happened?

She finally found the charger under her bed. She didn't even bother moving to a chair. She plugged in her laptop and slipped the HD card into the port.

The clips filled her screen, and before she pressed Play, she could see that Stephanie was in Matt's room. This bothered her in ways she couldn't fully deal with in the moment.

Stephanie wore jeans and a T-shirt with a black and pink floral design. Her face was tight with tension.

Lauren watched impatiently, waiting for whatever it was she'd thought she'd find. Five minutes in, she paused, backed up a few seconds, and hit Play again.

"I'm not talking to you today to help you make a movie," Stephanie said. "I'm talking to you because you *shouldn't* make this movie."

"Why not?" Matt asked off camera.

"Because Rory Kincaid wasn't a hero."

"You're the only person out of the dozens I've spoken with who has a negative opinion of Rory Kincaid."

"Well, maybe that's because I'm the only one who really knew him."

"I doubt your sister would agree with that."

"She would if she'd ever, for one minute, trusted me when I tried to tell her that he wasn't worth her time. I tried to warn her."

"She might have thought you were jealous. Maybe you still are," Matt said.

Stephanie snorted. "So that's how you want to play this? I'll be the jealous-sister villain of your movie? Come on. You can do better than that."

"I can't—not if you don't give me something better."

"Nice try," she said.

"Where were you in the summer of 2010?"

"I was here. At the shore."

"Where was Rory in the summer of 2010?"

"He was also here."

"Where was Lauren that summer?"

"She was taking classes at Georgetown."

"Is there anything you want to tell me about that summer?" he asked.

"It was uneventful," Stephanie said. But her face told a different story.

"Was Rory faithful to your sister?"

Stephanie glared at him indignantly. And said nothing.

Lauren, heart pounding, paused the video. What the hell was Matt getting at?

The summer, a low point in her relationship with Rory, was a time she'd avoided going into detail about with Matt. It had been confusing and painful, and in the end she liked to think of it as an insignificant rough patch.

It was the summer after Rory's rookie season, the summer she should have just graduated from Georgetown. They had planned to spend July at the Green Gable, but she was two credits short of graduating, thanks to all the time she'd missed traveling to LA. She'd asked him to spend the summer in DC with her instead. Obviously, the steaming-hot city wasn't the ideal place to spend July and August, but she hadn't expected him to actually refuse. He gave her a litany of reasons he couldn't change his plans and go to DC instead of the shore.

"So what if we already told our friends?" she'd said. "So what if Emerson is visiting you for the Fourth of July? This is about us."

Rory was unmoved. Had he just been looking for an excuse to get away from her? Hurt, she'd said, "Fine. I can get more work done without you around."

They didn't speak for a few days.

When he finally called, the conversation felt perfunctory. Lauren was afraid to say what she was really thinking, which was *Is this over? If it is, let's just end it.* She wasn't ready for the answer.

Her one consolation was that a professor had helped her get an internship at the *Washington Post*—the newspaper once run by her idol Katharine Graham. Four days a week after her classes, she went downtown to K Street, where she experienced the energy of the real DC—not the academic bubble of Georgetown, but the bustle of the town. Every day, she would pick up her lunch at one of the cafés filled with people running to and from Capitol Hill, all of them wearing ID tags around their necks, signifying their importance and access.

She realized she had spent too much of her time in DC lamenting her distance from Rory. But that summer, she felt the magic she had experienced that first visit during junior year of high school. And if her love affair with Rory Kincaid was fading, the one she had with Washington, DC, was going strong.

Still, every morning between classes, she called Stephanie at the shore and asked if she'd seen Rory out the night before. The answer was always no, until late July.

"Yeah, I've been seeing him and his friends at Robert's Place."

"Did you talk to him?"

"Not really."

Completely unsatisfying. But what did she expect? Answers about what was going on in Rory's mind from a drunken bar conversation he'd had with Stephanie? She stopped asking.

Two more weeks passed without a word from Rory. She weakened enough to ask Stephanie, once again, if she'd seen him. Was he still at the shore?

"Forget about him already, will you?" Stephanie snapped.

"Why should I?" Lauren said. "We've been together six years!"

"Well, clearly it's over."

Lauren slammed down the phone. All sorts of clichés ran through her mind, like *Don't shoot the messenger* and *The truth hurts.* But none of them made her any less furious at Stephanie. How could she be so callous?

And then, the most surprising phone call of the summer. It came on a Saturday afternoon.

"Where are you?" Rory asked.

"In DC. Obviously," Lauren said. Where did he think she was?

"No. I mean where in DC?"

"Politics and Prose."

"I'll be there in ten minutes," he said.

What?

For fifteen, twenty minutes, she sat in the bookstore café, fighting the urge to look around the room. Instead, she stared at the same page she had been reading when he called, trying to figure out what was going on.

"Hey."

He pulled out the seat across from her and sat down. If this were a movie, or if he were a different person, he would have maybe used a cheesy line like "Is this seat taken?" But it was Rory, and Rory just focused his intense eyes on her. He was tan. He looked beautiful.

Before she could say anything, his big hands enveloped her small ones. "I've missed you."

She started to speak, but nothing came out. What was there to say? *He'd come back for her.*

A month later, they were looking for houses together in Los Angeles.

Lauren hit the Play arrow on Stephanie's interview, then skipped back a few minutes.

"Was Rory faithful to your sister?"

Suddenly, Lauren felt sick. The summer came back to her in sharp cuts. Stephanie had pulled away from her so completely.

And Rory had committed to her so absolutely.

No.

Hands shaking, Lauren removed the disc and inserted the first interview. She didn't realize what she was looking for, didn't understand that her subconscious was already piecing together what her conscious mind couldn't handle.

The thumbnail files lined up, still images of Stephanie but also of Ethan. She clicked on Ethan on the beach, running with a soccer ball. He dropped it to the sand and dribbled it with considerable deftness before kicking it to the edge of the water.

"Score!" he said, raising his arms in victory and then pulling his right elbow sharply in toward his rib cage, a gesture so familiar, so precise, she gasped.

The video kept going, but she was watching a different scene, a scene in her mind's eye. An argument, long ago, interrupted by a phone call.

It was two months into her life in LA with Rory. The stress of the new season was already bearing down on them, and she'd just found a bottle of Ambien in his nightstand.

* * *

"Since when are you taking Ambien?" she asked Rory.

"Since when do you go snooping through my drawers?"

"I wasn't snooping. I was trying to find a phone charger. Why didn't you tell me about this?"

"Probably because I knew you'd overreact."

His phone rang. He checked the incoming number. "It's your mother. Why is she calling my phone?"

"Probably because mine is dead—because I can't find my charger!"

He tossed her the phone.

"Mom, this isn't a good time."

"You don't have time for family news?" her mother said. Lauren sighed. Okay, she'd take the bait.

"What's the news?"

"Your sister is pregnant."

"Pregnant? Who's the father?"

"Well, Lauren, that's not something she's talking about. I get the feeling it was a one-night stand. But let's focus on the positive. You're going to be an aunt!"

Only after Lauren hung up did she think to wonder why Stephanie hadn't called to tell her herself.

Of course she hadn't told her.

Because she was carrying Rory's baby.

Lauren screamed, then pulled off her wedding band and threw it against the wall. She ejected the disc, tossed it onto the floor, and—driven by a rage so pure it showed there was, in fact, an emotion stronger than grief—she grabbed the picture frame holding the image of herself with Stephanie and used it to pound the plastic disc into pieces.

Beth waded into the pool up to her waist, then found a nice sunny spot and leaned against the wall. She adjusted her wide-brimmed hat, knowing it was a losing battle because of the reflection off the water. *Don't worry about your skin,* she told herself, *enjoy the moment.* She exhaled deeply.

Across the deck, Stephanie flipped through magazines on a lounge chair, temporarily relieved of mothering duty. Ethan, worn out from all the eating and swimming, was inside napping.

Beth closed her eyes. She could use a nap herself, but in a good way. She felt relaxed instead of exhausted.

"You're a monster!" Lauren screamed.

Beth pushed up the brim of her hat and saw Lauren looming over Stephanie's chair. She stood up straight, shocked by the sudden rancor between the two.

"What did Matt say to you?" Stephanie said.

"Tell me I'm wrong. Tell me I'm wrong, Stephanie."

Stephanie sat up, hugging her knees to her chest.

"It was a huge, huge mistake. But it was that summer the two of you weren't together—"

"That's just geography! Of course we were together!"

"That's not what he told me."

"Well, that's convenient. He's not exactly around to defend himself."

Stephanie looked stricken. "I don't mean that as an excuse; I'm just trying to explain my thinking at the time. I was just—I rationalized that you had done the same thing to me."

"In what universe? Do you even *hear* yourself?"

"I know it doesn't make sense now. But back then...I was young. I was drunk. And I was jealous of you. It just...happened. A onetime thing."

"And Ethan?"

What about Ethan? Beth waited for Stephanie to respond, but she didn't.

"I hate you," Lauren said, sobbing.

Stephanie covered her face with her hands, and Beth rushed out of the pool, almost tripping over the flip-flops she'd left at the edge.

"Girls, what is going on?"

Lauren didn't take her eyes off Stephanie. "Are you going to tell her? Or should I?"

"Lauren, don't—"

"I want you out of the house by the end of the day," Lauren said to Stephanie, then turned to Beth. "I need you to get her out of this house. I never want to see her again."

"Just...everyone calm down. Lauren, whatever the issue is between the two of you, you have to work it out. Stephanie isn't leaving."

Lauren walked back into the house. Beth, feeling the crisis temporarily on hold, sat on the edge of Stephanie's seat.

"Sweetheart, tell me what happened."

Stephanie cried, and Beth tried not to panic. She hugged her, wishing for magic words that would unlock whatever wasn't being said.

"Oh my God," Stephanie said, sobbing.

"Hon, it's going to be okay."

"No, it's not," she said in a voice filled with resignation, not her typical drama.

A tornado of clothes flew at them.

Lauren, back on the deck, scattered Stephanie's belongings all over the ground.

"Lauren, stop that this minute! What's gotten into you?" Beth said.

"Tell her!" Lauren said to Stephanie. "Tell her, you coward."

Stephanie picked up a pair of her jeans and a pair of shoes but said nothing. Beth ran over to Lauren and grabbed her by the arms.

"Stop this, right this minute. Ethan is going to come down here and be scared to death!"

"Funny you should mention Ethan," Lauren said, looking at Stephanie. Beth turned to her older daughter, who looked...well, she looked terrified.

"I don't want to upset Mom," Stephanie said.

"Yeah, right. As always, you want to cover your own ass. You don't want Mom to know what a horrible person you are."

"Lauren, what is it?" Beth tugged on her arm, forcing her daughter to face her. Lauren gulped.

"I can't say it," she whispered.

"Hon, I need you to talk to me."

"It's about Ethan."

Beth glanced at the house, her mind racing. "I want to help."

"You can't. No one can. It's done," Lauren said, sobbing. "Ethan is Rory's son."

Chapter Forty-Seven

Lauren knew where Nora kept her extra house key, under a loose board on the back deck. But she had one stop to make first.

Her phone had pinged all morning with texts and voice mails from Matt. She'd finally checked them just to see if he'd figured out that she'd taken some of his interviews. Apparently, he had not.

Whatever happiness she'd felt after her intimacy with him was destroyed. All she could think about was the fact that he'd known about her sister's betrayal and kept it from her. She wanted to give him just the tiniest benefit of the doubt that he hadn't figured out the truth about Ethan, but why else would he have filmed him?

She knocked on the door, and he opened it wearing headphones.

"Hey! Where did you run off to? I've been calling you all day." He hugged her and she recoiled. Had it really only been a few hours since she'd left that room? She looked to the corner where Stephanie had sat for her interview and wondered if her sister had hesitated, even for a moment, before making her confession.

Lauren just didn't understand it. Stephanie had seemed so upset, so shocked, when Lauren confronted her. What did she *think* was going to happen? Maybe she hadn't meant to spill it. Stephanie had always been bad with impulse control.

Lauren glanced at the wall. The index cards were gone.

"What happened to all your work up there?"

"I'm packing." He moved closer to her. "Are you okay?"

"Why didn't you tell me about Stephanie?"

To his credit, he didn't pretend not to know what she was talking about.

"Aw, shit," he said. "Come here—sit down." She hesitated but then let him steer her to his desk chair. He sat opposite her on the edge of his bed. "Lauren, I'm just supposed to be an observer. I'm not in the business of getting involved in other people's lives."

"Well, that's convenient," she said.

"Did Stephanie talk to you? What happened?"

"I took your files, that's what happened. I watched the second interview."

He shook his head. "I wish you hadn't done that."

"I bet."

"Lauren, the last thing I wanted was to see you hurt any more than you've already been hurt."

"And you think letting me live with this in my face every day, oblivious, was doing me a favor?"

She looked up at him. He reached out and put his hands on her shoulders. "I'm sorry I didn't tell you about what Stephanie said in the interview. But on a professional level, it's not something I would do. And on a personal level, it's not something I *wanted* to do. Rory is gone. There's no point in you feeling betrayed because there's no way to litigate this, no resolution. It's over."

"Over? How is it over with Ethan in my life?"

"I don't follow."

"For God's sake, Matt. Stop playing games with me!"

"Lauren, I truly don't know what you're talking about. I am not playing games with you."

"What would you call it? Pretending to be my friend, sleeping with me, all the while knowing that Rory had a son with my sister?"

"What took you so long?" Beth said, ushering Howard into their bedroom and closing the door.

"Beth, it's the middle of the summer. The turnpike was a parking lot. Why were you so vague on the phone?"

"I wasn't vague. The word *crisis* isn't vague. *We have a crisis,*" she said, deliberate in her use of the *we.* If there was ever a time they needed to be a unit, it was now.

"What's the problem?" he asked impatiently, his hands on his hips.

She sat on the bed and picked up a framed photo from her nightstand: her mother with Stephanie and Lauren when they were little girls. She started to cry.

"Beth, for God's sake, what is it? You said the girls are okay?" Alarmed now, he moved closer to her.

"Yes, yes." She sniffed. "Physically, I mean. But the rest...I don't know how to tell you this."

"Just out with it," he said.

"They had a terrible argument earlier, and I tried to intervene and then Lauren said...she said..."

Howard sat next to her and put his arm around her shoulders. "Beth, you can't force those two to be best friends. Maybe not even friends. Haven't I been trying to tell you this?"

She shook her head, pressing her fingers to her temple. "Lauren said that Rory is Ethan's father."

Howard shrank away from her.

Beth hated to tell him, hated for him to know what a terrible, unforgivable sin Stephanie had committed. She wished that *she* didn't know. But when she looked at his face, she didn't see shock or dismay...not even a little surprise.

"Did you...know about this?" she said.

Howard walked to the patio doors and looked out at the ocean. "Why do you think I was so against your plan to force the two of them—and Ethan—here under the same roof all summer?"

Beth jumped up. "You knew about this and you kept it from me? How? How did you know?"

He turned around. "Stephanie confessed to me after Lauren and Rory got engaged. She panicked."

"Why didn't she talk to me? Why didn't *you* talk to me?"

"She thought you would side with Lauren and that you would hate her. And she was terrified of Lauren finding out the truth. I gave her my word that I wouldn't tell a soul, including you."

Beth covered her mouth with her hands and began to pace. So many things that hadn't made sense over the years started to come together. Stephanie's refusal to talk about Ethan's biological father. Her boycott of Lauren's wedding.

"You should have told me." Beth marched over to him, forcing him to look at her. "You didn't tell me about the second mortgage on the house. You didn't tell me about this. We clearly haven't been partners in a very long time."

He shook his head sadly. "Let's not make this about us."

Beth fought back tears. "Isn't it, though?"

"No," he said. "I think our problems are our problems and this is something else entirely."

"Fine. So what do we do now?"

"The only thing we can do," he said. "We have to put our issues aside and be parents."

Chapter Forty-Eight

Lauren huddled on Nora's couch, surrounded by cats. She'd already texted Nora half a dozen times during the day, first saying she'd be late for work, then that she wasn't coming to work, and finally that she needed to stay at her house.

A few hours into her self-imposed exile, Lauren was cried out and couldn't stand to be alone. If she didn't find some way to distract herself, she was going to lose her mind. She laced up her sneakers and ran over to the café.

Long past the three o'clock closing time, the front door was locked. Through the window, she saw Nora standing on a short ladder hanging something on the wall.

Henny opened the door for her. Lauren, surprised to see her, wondered if their feud had blown over. Maybe the laws of the universe healed one wound while another split wide open.

"Hey there, Lauren. I thought I saw you leaving my house earlier today. Oh—is that indiscreet of me? I'm probably breaking some sort of land-lady rule."

"Yeah, it's not what you think," Lauren said miserably.

Henny hoisted a box onto the counter. It was filled with signs painted pastel colors, each one separated by bubble wrap.

"What a blessing this summer, having Matt as a tenant. This online-sales thing has just changed my whole approach. You know I'm selling by category now? I'm doing beach signs, family signs...love signs."

"I'm happy for you, Hen. But I really don't want to talk about Matt," Lauren said, thinking, *One woman's blessing is another woman's curse.* "And they're going back on the walls here?"

"She's got the beach signs going up right now. I have to head out, hon. Nora," she called. "I'm leaving the extras here if you have space for them. If not, I'll pick them up tomorrow." She gave Lauren a quick hug before breezing happily out the door.

Lauren made her way into the dining room just as Nora was climbing down the ladder. On the wall, a fresh new sign: THE BEACH FIXES EVERY-THING.

Well, not quite.

"I'm sorry I was a no-show today," she said. Nora unloaded her hammer and nails on a table and sat down.

"What's going on?"

Lauren sat in the chair opposite her and tried to speak but found she couldn't bring herself to admit what she'd learned. "I can't talk about it. Would it be okay if I stay at your place for a night or two?"

Nora glanced at her in concern. "Whatever you need, hon. I won't be home for a while tonight. Doing a little redecorating around here."

"What happened with the photographs?"

"It was a mistake. I shouldn't have worried about making an extra buck or two at the expense of Henny's feelings. You know, I was trying to avoid dealing with what I knew deep down I should be doing but was afraid to, and that's start dinner service. I'm so excited, by the way, that your mother is baking for the party."

Her mother. Lauren didn't want to think about the look on her mother's face when she'd told her what was going on. She couldn't imagine the conversation her mother and sister had after she left, and wondered how her mother would break the news to her father. But most of all, she wondered how they would explain to Ethan that Aunt Lauren never wanted to see him again.

She bent over the table and rested her head on her arms.

Nora put her hand on her shoulder.

"Remember when you first started working here? You told me how much it helped to be busy every day."

"It did," Lauren murmured.

"It's our instinct when things go bad to just stop, to curl up into a ball. But it's a bad impulse. I've found the answer to most things is motion."

Lauren looked up. "Motion."

Nora slid the hammer across the table. "I could use some help with these signs."

Beth sat across the kitchen table from her older daughter, barely able to look at her. Behind them, Howard paced in front of the counter. She'd never realized how loudly the kitchen wall clock ticked, but in the quiet of that moment, it was deafening.

"I'm just not sure what to do now," Stephanie said.

Maybe you should have thought of that before you slept with your sister's boyfriend, Beth thought. "I'm in a difficult position here," Beth said. "I have Lauren to think about, you to think about, and also Ethan to think about."

It was painful even to say Ethan's name, as if her adoration of her grandson made her complicit in Stephanie's betrayal.

After the blowup by the pool, when Beth had shut herself in her bedroom waiting for Howard to arrive, someone had knocked gently on her door.

"Hi, Gran," Ethan said, his cheeks still flushed with sleep, one side imprinted with crease marks from his sheets. His dark eyes, bright with rest, were so utterly his father's. How could she not have noticed?

How *could* she have?

"I'll leave," Stephanie said. "Of course I will. I'm just not sure where to go. I don't have the job thing figured out—"

"Because you haven't been looking!"

The doorbell sounded.

"I'll get that," Howard said. She'd almost forgotten he was in the room.

Beth pushed back from the table and walked without purpose to the sink. She ran the water for a minute, taking deep breaths and splashing her face, willing herself to stay calm. *We have to put our issues aside and be parents,* Howard had said. And he was right. They had to lead during a time of crisis. She could fall apart later, on her own time.

"I'm really sorry, Mom," Stephanie said. Beth turned around to look at her daughter who had committed a betrayal beyond Beth's wildest imagination. Even when the evidence had been right in front of her all along.

She realized, gripped with a terrible rage, that she had never been truly angry with Stephanie before. Not when she had trashed the Green Gable as a teenager on prom weekend. Not when she became pregnant by accident without so much as a boyfriend or a job. Not even when she cruelly cut off her sister for no apparent reason.

But now? She was angry enough for all the bad behavior of Stephanie's life, and then some.

"I don't want your apology!" Beth screamed, feeling out of control in a way she'd never experienced. "I'll tell you what you're going to do: You're going to stay sober, get a job, and spend time with your son. You're going to be a goddamn mother." Stephanie looked as if Beth had slapped her in the face, then burst into tears just as Howard walked back into the kitchen.

"Who was at the door?" Beth asked.

"The real estate agent," he said. "I asked her to come back tomorrow."

Beth didn't bother telling him to call off the agent. She didn't have the energy to fight it any longer. She thought of a line she'd read somewhere: *Only an idiot tries to fight a war on two fronts, and only a madman tries to fight on three.* Maybe it was no longer worth fighting with Howard about the house. Her dream of unifying the family was over.

Chapter Forty-Nine

Matt woke up facedown on his computer keyboard. He lifted his head, blinking at the screen, the same image of Ethan Adelman he'd been scrutinizing before finally passing out after editing for twelve hours straight.

He checked his phone, trying to orient himself to the day and time. Twenty-four hours since Lauren had dropped the bombshell, and it hit him fresh.

He turned back to his computer, clicked through the reel to just about eighty minutes into the film. It was footage he'd shown in the opening, Rory scoring a hat-trick goal in high school, then pulling his left arm sharply in, bent at the elbow, his fist tight: *score.* The first time the footage occurred in the film, it was accompanied by a voice-over from a former high-school teammate: "Rory was selfless on the ice. He was ruthless against the opponent but generous to his teammates. He was the definition of *team player.*" Now, the second time the footage ran, it was with Stephanie's voice-over. The audience had already seen Stephanie's interview, already knew her in the context of Lauren's sister. She was blond, she was beautiful. Her words, over the action of Rory's goal: "Rory wasn't a hero." Next, a clip of

Ethan running to his mother, kicking the ball into the ocean, then making the arm gesture that exactly mirrored Rory's just a few frames earlier.

Score.

It was a game-changing version of the story he had been trying to tell for the past four years, a piece of the puzzle he'd never imagined. The man who was arguably the most famous casualty of the war in Iraq had left behind a son.

He considered a new name for the film: *American Son.*

Pushing away thoughts of Lauren, he told himself it was the nature of the work. *This is real, this is true, and the truth has a way of coming to the surface.* He was just the vehicle.

Of course, Lauren wouldn't see it like that. Oh, what a massive, unprofessional mistake, sleeping with an interviewee. But in his defense, he'd thought the film was all but finished and that she was comfortable with how Rory would be represented—valiant but flawed, betrayed by the system. But the betrayed became the betrayer.

He logged off the computer, took a quick shower, and packed up the last of his equipment. Whenever he stayed someplace for an extended period, he felt a pang at leaving, almost like he needed to say good-bye to the room. He felt it especially in that moment, knowing that after the movie came out, he would not exactly be welcomed back.

Or maybe, if he was lucky, by the time the movie came out, Lauren would have come to terms with everything. The worst part was that she thought he'd been playing games with her—using her. It couldn't have been farther from the truth.

Someone knocked on the door.

"I was hoping you wouldn't sneak off without saying good-bye!" Henny said, surprising him with a hug.

"Oh, hey there, Henny. Yeah, well, it's early. I didn't want to wake you."

"I brought you something. A little parting gift."

She handed him a sea-blue sign that read I LEFT MY ♥ AT THE SHORE, with the ♥ made out of seashells.

"I thought you might like a reminder of the beach when you're back in New York," she said.

"Oh, Henny. You shouldn't have." *Really, you shouldn't have.* He didn't need a reminder.

"Are you kidding? The fact that you were my first tenant would be reason enough. But you launched Hen House Designs, and let me tell you—that, my friend, is the gift that keeps on giving."

She looked around the room, toying with the rope of turquoise around her neck. "All packed up, eh. Well, I'm sorry to see you go."

Sadly, she was the only one who felt that way.

Lauren jogged in place waiting to cross Atlantic Avenue. A breeze blew off the ocean, raising goose bumps on her sweat-soaked arms and legs. Every muscle throbbed, and her breath came fast but even and strong. She wished she didn't have physical limitations, that she could keep running and running to the end of the island. To the end of the earth. She couldn't stand the stillness of Nora's house. Her body at rest was at the mercy of her merciless mind.

And as she returned to Nora's house, she was sure it was her mind playing tricks on her when she saw Matt sitting on the front porch. She'd been trying so hard not to think about him.

He stood and walked toward her.

"I should have guessed you were out running. Though it's a little later than usual, right?"

"Go away," she said, suddenly light-headed. She leaned over, hands on her thighs.

"Just hear me out for a minute. I had no idea about Ethan. I've gone over all of my interviews, everything, in the past twenty-four hours, and frankly, there's no way that I could have known. I simply didn't have enough information to piece it all together. Maybe if I'd been looking for it. But I wasn't."

"Why do you have footage of him?"

"Lauren, I'm a filmmaker. I have footage of the inside of Sack O' Subs. I saw a cute kid, I thought maybe it could be used for juxtaposition...there was nothing more to it."

She stared at him, and he met her gaze, unblinking. It made sense. Maybe, just maybe, he was telling the truth.

He glanced back at the porch. "Can we sit?"

"Why?"

"Because I'm leaving town and I just want a few more minutes with you."

Lord help her—she wanted that too.

She sat on the wicker bench, remembering the night he'd first appeared, when she'd been swinging on this same bench, never imagining what the summer had in store for her. And now here they were.

"So...now what?" she said.

"Lauren, I meant what I said the other night. Come visit me in New York."

She looked at him, incredulous. "I'm not talking about us. I'm talking about the film."

"What about it?"

"You can't make this movie," she said. She spoke the words before the thought had fully formed in her mind, but as soon as she said them, she knew they were true, and they were absolute.

"Lauren," he said, touching her shoulder. "Come on. You know that's not realistic."

She jumped up. "You said you weren't out to make Rory look bad." And then it hit her: Why was she still protecting Rory? She was murderously angry with her sister. Why not at him?

"I'm not trying to make him look bad. He was a flawed person. We're all flawed. But Rory Kincaid's highs were higher than most people's, and his lows might have been lower than most. That's what makes him an interesting subject. It's not about him being a terrible person."

"What about the rest of us? I'm not just thinking about myself, though that's part of it. God knows I don't want this humiliation made public. But I'm thinking of…my nephew. He doesn't know, and if you open this up…*you have to leave Ethan out of the movie!*"

He shook his head sadly. "Lauren, I can't do that. It's my job to tell the whole story—the truth about Rory's decisions and their consequences."

Furious, all she could say was "I never want to see you again."

A car pulled up in front of the house. Her father?

She watched, dumbstruck, while he parked and calmly headed up the walkway. He spotted her, and she saw the surprise on his face when he noticed Matt.

"Dad, how did you know I was here?"

"Your mother is a good guesser," he said. He turned to Matt and shook his hand. "Howard Adelman."

"Matt Brio. Nice to meet you."

Um, no. This is not happening.

"You need to leave," she said to Matt. Maybe if her father weren't there, he would have refused. Maybe he would have said something to give her hope that he still might choose her feelings over the film. But as it was, he just nodded. When he said, "Good-bye, Lauren," she felt her entire body run cold.

And then he was gone, and her father said, "I'm here to take you home." And she didn't have the strength left to argue.

Chapter Fifty

Beth had to hand it to Howard: when he said he was going to do something, he did it.

"Do you want some French toast?" she asked Lauren by way of greeting.

Lauren mumbled something, brushed past Howard, and dragged her bag upstairs.

"Well, at least she's here," Howard said.

"What did you say to her?"

"Not a hell of a lot, to be honest. She doesn't want to talk."

"But you told her that Stephanie was still here, right? That the answer isn't to run away? The things we discussed?"

He poured himself the last of the coffee. Beth retrieved the bag of coffee beans from the freezer to make a fresh pot.

"There was a man with her," Howard said. "Matt somebody. Do you know about this guy? Is she finally dating after all this time?"

The filmmaker. Howard still didn't know anything about the documentary. "It's a long story," Beth said.

"You've been holding out on me?"

She turned sharply but then realized he was teasing her.

"I'm glad you're here," she said. "I couldn't deal with this alone."

"Of course I'm here."

"Mom!" Lauren yelled from the second floor. Beth, with a quick, alarmed look at Howard, bolted up the stairs. She found Lauren standing in the doorway of Stephanie's bedroom. "What is all of her stuff still doing here? When is she moving out?"

Across the hall, Ethan's door clicked open. When he spotted Lauren, he dashed over, threw his arms around her legs, and gazed up at her with adoration.

Lauren looked down at him and burst into tears.

It's just a house, Lauren told herself, throwing her clothes into a suitcase and then emptying her drawers; she'd pack the rest in garbage bags or whatever she could find. *It's just a house and it was never truly yours and it's time to move on. That's all.*

Lauren would have to find her own apartment. Maybe it was something she should have done a long time ago. Every summer, year after year, she'd felt encroached upon, but instead of staking out her own private space and doing the hard work of moving on, she'd just told herself it was temporary. Now the day was here, and she would not cry about it. She was just thankful that she'd been working hard, had saved her money, and was in a position to take care of herself and rent an apartment. As for tonight, for the next few weeks, a hotel would have to do.

But the boxes. She could not lug all the boxes with her, and yet she could not leave the artifacts of her life with Rory behind in enemy territory.

Or were the boxes themselves enemy territory?

She would not, could not, think about Rory. But when she let down her guard, the thoughts slipped through, like water seeping through cracks in plaster walls. All she could do to battle them back was tell herself this: It was not possible that he had known about Ethan. Yes, it was possible that he had betrayed her during that summer apart. But it was unthinkable that he would have fathered a child with her sister, known about it, and still asked her to marry him.

And yet, she was stuck in this hell of wondering and never being able to confront him about it, because she would never hear from Rory again.

It had been one of the hardest things to wrap her mind around in the beginning, the permanence of it. The notion of never hearing his voice, never being able to seek his counsel, never making another plan or sharing another hope with him, was as vast and incomprehensible as thinking about Earth as just one planet orbiting one star out of millions of stars in the galaxy. Once, Rory had played her a video that showed Earth's size in relation to the other planets' in the solar system, then the solar system in relation to the Milky Way galaxy, and then the galaxy in relation to all the other known galaxies in the universe. It mapped out the travel distances between the stars in light-years, and the vastness of it all felt like something her mind was not built to contemplate. But this was exactly what Rory loved about astronomy. Maybe, if she had been the one to die first, to die young, he would have known how to reckon with infinity. With permanence. More than four years out, she couldn't. That was why she had left the letter unopened. It was her safeguard against good-bye forever.

She stared at the boxes taking up most of the space inside her closet.

The boxes were all still open from the night she'd looked through them, poking around for things to share with Matt, hoping to make Rory more balanced, more human in the film. How arrogant, how naive she'd been to think she was the custodian of the truth.

How could you do this?

She couldn't remember what box she'd stuffed the letter in, and by the time she found it, the floor around her was littered with yearbooks, photos, and clothes. Sitting among the relics of her former life, she pressed her back against the closet door, staring at her name rendered in Rory's tightly looped handwriting.

If she wanted answers, if there was hope for any kind of response to the question that would haunt her for the rest of her life, she had to open it. It was time to face forever.

She peeled open the envelope carefully, thinking that it had been his hands that had sealed it. He had planned for this moment, just her and his words.

The letter was handwritten on yellow legal paper. He'd taken a page from one of the pads she left on the kitchen counter for her grocery and to-do lists. The routine had not carried over to her life in Longport, and the memory of such a mundane, day-to-day habit took her breath away.

January 15, 2012

Dear Lauren:

If you are reading this, it's because I'm gone. I'm so sorry, because I promised you it would be okay and I was wrong. Please forgive me for this mistake.

I wish I could say it was my only one.

I tried and failed with so much, but my biggest failures were in this relationship—the one thing I cared about the most. I know it didn't seem like it at times, but I wrote this because I want you to know that it's true. I love you and loved you even in my worst moments.

It's hard for me to imagine you reading this, being the cause of your hurt and at the same time not being there to help you through it. But I know you are a strong person. Don't let whatever you are feeling today ruin your tomorrow. You deserve to be happy.

To me, you will always be the girl I saw running around the track on Arnold Field. I have no right to ask anything of you, but I will: Be that happy girl who loved running, writing, and her big sister. Please know that the worst mistakes were mine alone. And Lauren, if you're out at night and you look up at the stars, remember that once upon a time, there was a boy who loved you and always will.

Rory

Lauren reread it and reread it. The date told her he'd written it before his first deployment but long after he'd betrayed her with her sister. The sentence that jumped out at her, that defined the entire letter, was the entreaty that she go back to being the girl who loved her big sister. *The worst mistakes were mine alone.* Well, technically that was not true. And maybe that event wasn't even what he was referring to. But she felt that it was, that he wanted to take the blame.

The one thing she couldn't find, even with the most creative interpretation of the letter, was any sense of whether or not he knew about Ethan.

She had to know. Unfortunately, the only living person who might have had the answer was the one person she'd sworn never to speak to again.

The house was quiet and empty. How many times had she wanted solitude but was instead surrounded by her family? And now she needed to talk to Stephanie and everyone was gone. Figured.

Late afternoon, close to four, was optimal beach time. The sun had peaked and ebbed; it was the perfect hour to doze off under an umbrella, read, or just comfortably watch the waves until dinner. She remembered when she was a kid, her grandmother had always been the last one off the beach, reluctantly dragging her chair back to the house only after her husband had showered, dressed for dinner, made a cocktail, and sent Lauren out to fetch her.

Out on the deck, Lauren cupped her hand over her eyes against the sunlight and looked toward the ocean. Sure enough, four beach chairs were lined up at the water's edge. She didn't bother walking around to use the gate; she just pulled off her sneakers and climbed over the wall separating her property from the beach.

As she trod through the sand, the idea of turning back crossed her mind half a dozen times. She didn't.

I have to know.

Ethan's delighted squeal caught her attention, and when she looked at the ocean, she saw him with her father, bobbing in the rolling waves.

"Be careful!" her mother called out to them, hidden from Lauren's view by the umbrella.

Lauren stood behind the wall of chairs, unnoticed.

"It's fine, Mom," Stephanie said from the chair next to her mother.

"Oh, for heaven's sake." Beth put her paperback down on the beach towel, stood up, and marched to the water, calling out, "Not so deep, Howard!"

Lauren slipped into her mother's chair, and Stephanie nearly jumped out of hers.

"Jesus! You scared me," Stephanie said.

"Let's walk. I need to talk to you."

Stephanie didn't say a word, but she left her chair with a quick glance at their parents and Ethan before following her.

They walked north along the water, just past the first lifeguard stand. It was so miserably uncomfortable to be near Stephanie, Lauren gave up on finding a quiet spot just so she could get the conversation over with more quickly.

"You have to tell me: Did Rory know about Ethan?" Lauren blurted out.

Stephanie looked at her in surprise. "No! Absolutely not. I thought you understood that."

"Understood that? Clearly, I didn't understand anything, thanks to you!"

"I tried to warn you not to marry him."

Lauren felt stricken. She'd thought about so much in the past twenty-four hours, yet she hadn't considered their argument in the car that day in the airport. She had been certain Stephanie was just jealous of her engagement. How could she have imagined the truth?

"Why didn't you tell me what happened?"

"If I told you that I... that we slept together, would that have stopped you from marrying him? Or would you have forgiven him and hated me?"

"If you'd told me about Ethan, I can guarantee I wouldn't have married him."

Stephanie shook her head. "You say that now."

They stood in silence. Stephanie broke it first.

"I never intended for this to come out. And I still hope that Ethan never knows the truth. How could I explain this to him?"

Lauren looked at her, incredulous. "You don't plan on telling Ethan? Ever?"

"What good would it do? Rory is gone. It's not like telling him the truth gets him a father. And the poor kid—his very existence isn't just a mistake; it's the biggest shame of this family."

Oh God. What had she done? By accusing Matt of knowing about Ethan and keeping it from her, she'd inadvertently given him the information. And now he had it, and he would use it.

"Stephanie, you're not going to like this, but... you have to tell Ethan about Rory."

"Lauren, please spare me a morality lecture here, okay? No matter how much I deserve it."

Lauren nervously toyed with the end of her ponytail. "It's not that. I... told Matt Brio. I thought I could convince him not to go ahead with the film. But he didn't listen to me."

Stephanie reached for her arm.

"You didn't."

"I'm sorry. I wasn't thinking straight."

"He's going to put this in the film?"

"I don't know."

"What about Ethan? He's innocent in all of this, and he's going to be the one who suffers!" Stephanie's eyes filled with tears. Before Lauren could think of a response, Stephanie ran back to the house.

Chapter Fifty-One

Brooklyn felt smaller and darker than Matt remembered it. And the editing suite was hot as hell.

"Do you mind if I turn these fans up higher?" he asked the one person left in the office. The guy, plugged into his computer and surrounded by empty coffee cups, gave a faint go-ahead wave.

Matt didn't need coffee. The return to the city had energized him, made the Sundance application deadline feel real, made the creative pressure of finalizing the cut he would send to the sales agent crushing. No matter how many times he went through this process, it would never be easy. And there was an added level of stress to this project.

He'd hoped that once he was back in New York, he would get some emotional distance from Lauren. If he could just stop worrying about her feelings, he would be free to make the best creative decisions for the project. But as it was, his thinking was muddled; instead of exposing the truth about Rory, cutting ruthlessly to bring his decline into sharp, dramatic view, he was pulling punches and trying to see what he could get away with *not* showing.

Matt paused the footage on an image of Lauren from the Fourth of July. She was wearing a sundress; her long hair was loose and her eyes especially dark against her sun-kissed cheeks. From an artistic standpoint, her loveliness made the story all the more poignant. From a personal standpoint, it made his job nearly unbearable.

He hit the Play button.

"He told me it was boring—frustrating sometimes," she said. "One day he spent eight hours mowing a lawn."

"Was this discouraging to him?" Matt asked off camera.

"No. He said, 'I had to learn to skate before I could score.' But he did have to get through months of Ranger School, and that wasn't easy. I think people wanted to remind him that he might have been a star on the ice, but he was a nobody there. The thing they didn't realize was that by that point, Rory hadn't felt like a star in a long time. And he was deeply motivated to change that."

"And how did things go at Ranger School?"

"He graduated with the Darby Award. Top honors. And his decision to do this was completely affirmed."

"And in your mind?"

Lauren took a deep breath.

"In my mind, I guess something was affirmed too. The understanding that my husband was an exceptional person and that everything that was happening was part of the deal. My life with him was going to be one of high highs and low lows, and it always had been."

High highs and low lows. Matt paused the video. Had it really been only two days since he'd seen her? He couldn't stop thinking about the look of anger and disgust on her face. *It's my job to tell the whole story,* he'd said.

But how far did he have to go to tell it?

The restaurant bustled with an early-evening run-through in prep of the dinner service starting next week. Nora had put together an inspired menu that was even closer to her super-foods cooking edict than her breakfast and lunch menu: a pomegranate-glazed portobello steak, three different varieties of stir-fries, a Mediterranean vegetable pizza, her specialty garden lasagna, a mesclun and Asian pear salad.

The one area where her menu veered toward the decadent was dessert. That was where Beth came in; it was strange for Lauren to have her mother baking in the restaurant kitchen, but at the same time, there was something wonderful about it. She felt the seams of her life knitting together, and she realized that the distance from her mother was a real downside to the way she'd lived for the past few years.

Beth pulled her aside, her face shiny with the exertion of baking in the heat of the kitchen, and steered her to the back of the dining room.

"Don't you just love this?" she said, stopping in front of one of Henny's new signs. A CHILD WILL MAKE LOVE STRONGER, DAYS SHORTER, HOME HAPPIER, CLOTHES SHABBIER, THE PAST FORGOTTEN, AND THE FUTURE WORTH LIVING FOR.

"Wow, Mom. That's subtle."

Lauren did not, in fact, love the sign. Nora was the one who loved it, but since Lauren had been helping her hang things, she'd been able to bury it in the back. She hadn't looked at it since the day she'd nailed it to the wall.

"I'm not trying to be subtle," Beth replied.

"You know what? We're all living under one roof and no one's killed anyone yet. I think that should be enough to satisfy you for now."

The truth was she spent every day avoiding Ethan.

He's innocent in all of this, Stephanie had said the other day on the beach. She was right, of course. That didn't make it any easier. Every time Lauren looked at Ethan, she saw so clearly what she had failed to see for six years: He looked like Rory. But it was worse than that; she didn't look at Ethan and see Rory's son—she looked at him and saw *Rory*.

It was seven p.m. by the time she got back to the Green Gable. She closed herself in her room, sat on her bed, and eyed her wedding band on the floor. She had not touched it since throwing it against the wall days earlier. Now she picked it up and placed it on her nightstand.

She thought of the vows they'd made to each other. Rory had broken his, not by betraying her with Stephanie—that had happened before their marriage—and not even by hitting her, because he had been suffering. The betrayal had been his refusal to try to fix himself so they could be together.

In the years since his death, she'd been carrying the burden of believing she'd failed him by turning him away. Now, all the pieces added up differently. He'd known he had slept with Stephanie. And if the doctor in Matt's film was right, Rory would have to have known he wasn't himself after those hits to his head. And he knew he was anxious and angry after his deployment. He ran away from it all, and, ultimately, he ran away from her.

Beth knocked on her door.

"I just wanted to check on you," she said.

They sat together on the edge of her bed. Lauren looked at her hands, fighting tears.

"I tried so hard not to let him down. To be worthy of him. And in the end, he was the one who let me down. And that scares me so much. Out of everything that happened, that's the one thing I can't get past."

"Sweetheart," her mother said, putting an arm around her. "He was just a man. He was your husband, but that's all a husband is. Just a man. Flawed. Infinitely fallible. The only way marriage works is to forgive and move on. And you can't do that for the sake of your marriage, obviously. But you have to at least do it for yourself."

"I don't know how," Lauren said.

"I think you do."

Lauren hesitated outside of Ethan's bedroom. The idea that seemed to make so much sense moments ago in the safety of her own room was now terrifying. She knocked once then turned the doorknob.

He was in bed, playing with his robot action figures.

"Hey there," she said.

He looked up with a big smile. "Are you better?" he asked.

"Better?"

"My mom said you were sick so we needed to give you some time alone for a while."

"Oh! Well, yeah. I'm feeling better. But, um, we've kind of fallen behind on *Harry Potter.* How about some reading?"

The look on his face was her answer. She walked over to his shelf to pull out the book; her breath caught at the sight of the astronomy book.

"Ethan? Are you interested in the stars and planets?"

"I love the planets. I'm going to be an astronaut," he said.

She took a deep breath, then asked, "Have you ever gone to the planetarium at the Franklin Institute?"

He shook his head no.

"I'll take you," she said.

"Cool," he said. Then: "Aunt Lauren?"

"Yes?"

"Why are you crying?"

Chapter Fifty-Two

There was something calming, almost hypnotic, about watching the rings of dough bubble and bob in the fryer. And it smelled heavenly.

Beth struggled to narrow down the doughnut options for Nora's party. Nora had asked for three varieties, and Beth was torn between traditional with a twist—German chocolate, apple-pie, and a vanilla glazed—or summer experimental, like salty margarita, spicy chai, or s'mores.

"Have you heard any news on the sublease?" Howard asked, startling her.

"Don't sneak up on me like that. And no, I haven't. Maybe you can call to follow up this week?"

He nodded. "I'll take care of it. By the way, I was just in Lauren's room. What's with all the boxes? Is she moving out?"

"Those boxes are from the attic. She's putting them in storage."

"Great. Are you finished with the attic?"

"No. Because I'm not going anywhere."

Howard ran his hand through his hair, his ultimate expression of impatience.

"That's the game plan? Living here for the rest of our lives with our adult daughter, raising her son?"

"Would that be the worst thing in the world?"

Howard sighed. "And what, Beth? You're going to bake doughnuts for a living?"

"Why not?"

"And I should just...what?"

"I don't know, Howard. And, frankly, that's not my concern. I gave up doing what I loved professionally to help you with the store for thirty years. Now it's my turn."

Lauren piled the boxes by the front door for the storage company to pick up later in the afternoon. She headed to the kitchen for coffee but hearing her parents in a heated conversation, she turned around.

She sat on her bed and her phone pinged with a text. Matt—again.

He'd started texting days ago, telling her that he was thinking of her, that he was sorry she was upset but that he believed he was doing the right thing. I hope someday you can forgive me.

Lauren had deleted them all. She wasn't the one whose forgiveness he would have to reckon with someday. Rory had a son who was about to have his life changed forever. She could only hope the press showed some mercy. If not, Stephanie would have to prepare herself. At the very least, she had to find a way to tell Ethan the truth before the media learned it.

She opened the top drawer of her nightstand, where a shallow glass bowl held her heart necklace, wedding band, engagement ring, and Rory's dog tags. Storage wasn't an option for these things, but neither was keeping them. Well, maybe the engagement ring. She couldn't stand to part with it. It was too special. God, it was all so confusing. So much!

"Lauren?" Stephanie knocked on the door.

She closed the drawer. Maybe the storage people had shown up early.

"Come in." She looked around for her wallet so she could tip the movers. "Are the guys out front?"

"What? No. I don't think so," Stephanie said, closing the door behind her.

"Oh. I thought...never mind."

"I just wanted to thank you. I know you've been reading to Ethan again and...it means a lot to him. It can't be easy for you and I want you to know that I understand that."

Lauren nodded. "Have you decided when you're going to tell him the truth?"

"No. I mean, before the film comes out, obviously."

"I hate to say this," Lauren said, "but I think there's someone else you need to tell. Rory's brother."

"Emerson? Why?" She looked appalled.

"He's Ethan's family as much as I am. And Emerson has kids—Ethan's first cousins." Lauren had thought about all of this during the many hours she'd lain in bed at night grappling with everything.

Stephanie shook her head. "It's too much. I can't."

"I've been going through all of my old boxes because of the move. Stuff I didn't want to deal with four years ago. A lot of it's Rory's and I've found some family photos Emerson should have. I'm going to get in touch with him anyway, so I can tell him if you want me to."

"Really? You would do that?"

She hadn't thought about the offer before the words were out of her mouth, but as she spoke them, she knew they weren't coming from a place of altruism; she wanted to say to Emerson, *See? I told you I wasn't the bad guy.*

No, she wasn't proud of this. But at least she recognized it.

She did, however, have one impulse that was pure, that came from a good place in her heart. She opened her nightstand drawer and pulled out Rory's dog tags.

"I was thinking that when the time is right, you might want Ethan to have these," she said, handing them to Stephanie.

Stephanie looked down at them in disbelief.

"Lauren," she said. "I can't take this from you."

"I don't feel like he's my husband anymore. But he will always be Ethan's father."

Stephanie burst into tears. "Can you ever forgive me?"

"I don't know," Lauren said. "But you'll always be my sister."

Chapter Fifty-Three

The Williamsburg bar, with its wall-mounted bicycle, exposed brick, and painted tin ceilings, was too cute for Matt's tastes. The craft-beer list was so rarefied Matt didn't recognize a single brand. Basically, it was as far from Robert's Place as you could get. He missed the shore. No, he missed Lauren.

It was still early—day-drinking early—so he and Craig got a seat at the bar. Craig ordered the beer for them both, something from the Netherlands. Matt checked his phone, a chronic and worsening compulsion as his texts to Lauren continued to go unanswered. He knew the definition of insanity was doing the same thing over and over and expecting a different result, but he was too far gone. It was impossible to forget about someone when you saw her face on the screen every day, when you listened to audio of her voice dozens and dozens of times, until you heard her words in your dreams. Until her words and your own thoughts were intertwined.

"You ready for the meeting tomorrow?" Craig asked.

They were having breakfast with their sales agent. A major step toward distribution.

"I'm ready," Matt said.

"To *American Son,*" Craig said. "Sure to be the most-talked-about doc of next year."

Matt halfheartedly raised his bottle.

"Aren't you happy with the cut?"

Matt nodded. "Of course I am."

"So, then, relax. All the years you put into this are going to pay off."

"Let me ask you something," Matt said, sipping the beer and finding it bitter. "Would you feel this way about the film if it was just the footage I showed you a few weeks ago?"

"The CTE angle is strong—important. But the reveal about the kid takes this thing to another level. It makes it more dramatic and personal. I'm sure you don't need me to tell you that."

"No," Matt said. "I don't."

"So what are you worried about? Sundance?"

"No. We'll get into Sundance."

"Distribution?"

Matt shook his head. How could he admit that in getting the one thing he'd always dreamed of, he would lose something he now wanted more?

For the first time in four years, Lauren walked into Nora's Café as a guest. She'd offered to work the night of the opening party, but Nora insisted that the regular waitstaff experience and enjoy the new menu along with the other guests—the restaurant regulars, local press, and a posse of shoobies Lauren didn't recognize but who somehow had the connections to wrangle invites.

Nighttime had a way of transforming a space, and the restaurant felt larger but at the same time more intimate. Nora had rearranged the tables to create more room for people to mingle and for the hors d'oeuvres to be passed. She'd hired waiters from a local catering company to serve samples of the appetizer menu, and the dinner menu would be set out as a buffet. Her mother was in the kitchen prepping fresh doughnuts for dessert. The one speed bump was Nora's lack of a liquor license; guests had been invited to bring their own wine.

Nora had a '70s satellite-radio station playing over the sound system, and it filled the room with an eclectic mix of singers ranging from Carly Simon to Donna Summer. Lauren made sure her father and Ethan got pieces of the white pizza before it disappeared and then poured herself a glass of wine from Henny's bottle of Oyster Bay sauvignon blanc.

"She shouldn't even bother applying for the liquor license," Henny said. "I'd rather bring my own than get fleeced for twelve dollars a glass."

"I agree," Lauren said, accepting a goat-cheese slider from a server. She hummed along to "You're So Vain." And then she saw Emerson walk in.

She had invited him during her phone call to tell him that he had a nephew. It wasn't something she'd planned.

"I need to see him," Emerson had said, the break in his voice moving her.

"Of course. At some point," she said. "My sister hasn't told him yet about his father. This is going to take some time."

"Lauren, I know I don't have a right to ask you for anything. But I can't wait. He's all I have left of my brother. I need to come now."

She couldn't invite him to the house. It would be too much for all of them: herself, Stephanie, and Ethan. But she couldn't refuse him outright. As tempting as it was to hold on to her anger and resentment toward him, now they shared a nephew. And so she thought of a compromise.

"We're all going to a party next Saturday night at the restaurant where I work," she told him. "It will be crowded and maybe not your ideal place to meet Rory's son, but it's best for him that way. He'll be around so many new people that night, you won't raise any red flags."

Emerson didn't like the idea, but she stood firm and said it was either that or wait until Stephanie decided to tell her son the truth. Until he actually walked into Nora's, Lauren hadn't known what option he would choose.

Across the room, Stephanie stood near the kitchen talking to their father. Lauren walked over to let her know Emerson was there.

"I thought your mother would be done by now," her father said. "Do you think Nora would mind if I took a peek in the kitchen?"

"As long as those doughnuts get on the buffet table for dessert, you can jump in and bake for all Nora would care," Lauren said. She had suggested that her mother prepare a few batches ahead of time, but Beth was intent on them being as fresh as possible. "You'd be surprised how many people have never eaten a warm doughnut," her mother said.

Howard left for the kitchen, and Stephanie grabbed Lauren's arm.

"Guess who's here?"

Lauren, surprised, said, "You saw him?"

"Saw him? He had the nerve to come over and say hi to me."

"Wait—I don't think we're talking about the same person."

"Neil Hanes. He came with his parents."

Lauren glanced around as Stephanie said, "Don't look!"

She spotted him. "Okay, that's unfortunate," Lauren said. "But it's the least of our concerns; Emerson's here."

Now it was Stephanie's turn to indiscreetly look around the room. She mouthed, *Shit.* "I'm really having second thoughts about this."

Lauren knew her sister had to be wishing for a glass of wine right about then, but she'd been sober for two weeks. It was for her own health, but also a gesture to her parents that she was intent on changing—as a person and as a mother.

"It will be fine. I'll bring Ethan over. You don't even have to talk to him."

"Too late for that."

Emerson was threading his way through the crowd, heading straight for them. He was taller and broader than any other man in the place, as well as less tan and more casually dressed.

"Where's Ethan?" Lauren said.

"I'm not sure. The last I saw, he was sitting at a table with a few other kids. Near the front window."

"Can you find him? The sooner we get this over with, the better."

"I don't know why I let you talk me into this."

Lauren was thinking the same thing. Stephanie slipped away before Emerson reached them, leaving Lauren alone with her former brother-in-law. After four years of not speaking to him at all, she had now dealt with him twice in one summer. How ironic that the last time he'd shown up, he'd warned her not to make Rory look bad. Now he was there to meet the son Rory'd had with her sister.

"I wish I could say it's nice to see you," she said.

"I guess that's fair," he replied. Then, glancing at her hand: "I see the ring is gone."

"Yes, well, nothing like finding out your husband had a son with your sister to make a ring feel like empty symbolism."

"That's the most cynical thing I've ever heard come out of your mouth, Lauren."

"It's just the truth."

"Look, I have no idea what happened. But I do know that my brother never meant to hurt you. He did love you."

"Wow. That's the most generous thing I've ever heard come out of *your* mouth."

"Like you said—just the truth. Now, where's my nephew?"

Beth zested a lime, humming along with Carly Simon.

In the end, she'd decided to go full-on summer-experimental with her doughnuts. The one hundred and twenty guests would be treated to spicy chai, salty margarita, and campfire s'mores doughnuts. She would have to fry the s'mores doughnuts just minutes before dessert was served, since they had to be eaten immediately, while the chocolate and marshmallow were still gooey. The only thing she could prep ahead of time was the crushed graham crackers, butter, and sugar mixture she would use as a topping.

"You're still busy in here? I thought maybe you'd have time to come out and enjoy yourself for a minute or two," Howard said from the doorway, where he stood holding two glasses of prosecco.

"I *am* enjoying myself," she said.

He smiled. "I brought you a drink."

She waved him away. "I'm on the clock."

He put the wineglasses down on a countertop. "So, is it like riding a bike? Do you feel like you never stopped catering?"

No, I just feel like I wish I'd never stopped. "In some ways. But it feels different because I appreciate it more now," she said, putting down the grater.

"Well," he said, looking around the industrial kitchen. "I'm proud of you."

"You are?"

Howard moved closer and she saw he had a manila envelope tucked under his arm. He handed it to her, and while she opened it, he said, "It's the signed paperwork for the sublease. It came to the house today. You really saw things clearly when I was too mired in panic. I owe you an apology for not coming to you sooner."

They were the words she'd needed to hear all summer.

She looked into his eyes, gray and steady; but for the crow's-feet, the same eyes she'd been staring into for half her life. He leaned forward and kissed her, and she forgot everything around them: the heat of the kitchen, the clamor of the restaurant guests, even the problems with their daughters.

That's all a husband is. Just a man. Flawed. Infinitely fallible. The only way marriage works is to forgive and move on.

"I wasn't angry at you for losing the house," she said. "I was hurt to be shut out of the decision-making."

"I know." He nodded. "Believe it or not, I was trying to spare you the worry."

"Why didn't you just say that in the first place?"

He shrugged. "Pride?"

"Oh, Howard."

He kissed her again, and she threw her arms around his neck. He pulled away just long enough to get the wine and hand her a glass.

"A quick toast. To you, Beth. You were right about this summer. I'm lucky to have you as my partner. I'm lucky to have you as my wife."

She put down the wine and kissed him again. A timer pinged.

Howard glanced at the dozens of doughnuts cooling on the counter. "Can I help you plate those?" he asked.

She looked pointedly at his sports jacket.

"What?" he said. "You think I'm afraid of rolling up my sleeves?" He pulled off his jacket and set it on a wall hook. Beth, eyebrows raised, pointed to the sink. She stood beside him as he washed his hands.

"What's with your sudden interest in the kitchen?" she asked, passing him a clean towel.

"Beth, you weren't right about just the summer," he said. "You were right about something else: it *is* your turn."

Chapter Fifty-Four

Lauren held on to Ethan's hand and felt her own shaking as she led him to Emerson. She glanced back over her shoulder at Stephanie, who was watching like a protective mama bear.

When they reached Emerson, she found her tough, stoic former brother-in-law staring at Ethan with tears in his eyes.

"Ethan," Lauren said. "This is a…family friend. Mr. Kincaid."

Emerson glanced at her, and she nodded. He pulled out a chair and sat so he could talk to Ethan eye to eye. He asked Ethan about school and about what sports he liked to play. Ethan told him soccer.

"We should kick the ball around sometime," Emerson said, looking to Lauren for the go-ahead.

"That sounds great, doesn't it, Ethan?"

Ethan nodded, and Emerson held out his hand for a high five, which Ethan delivered before darting off.

"I remember when Rory was that age," Emerson said. He turned to her with tears in his eyes. "Thank you, Lauren."

"No problem. I mean, we're family now, right?"

He nodded, clearly unable to speak. When he collected himself, he said, "What's going on with that film?"

"The documentary? I don't know. It's...the truth will come out, Emerson. As we've seen."

Stephanie made her way to them. Lauren wondered when they'd last seen each other. Not at her wedding, since Stephanie hadn't been there. It might have been sometime during the summer when Lauren was at Georgetown instead of at the shore. The summer when their fates changed forever.

"Hey," Stephanie said.

"You have a great boy there," Emerson said.

"Thanks." She looked at Lauren and shifted uncomfortably on her feet.

"I'd really like to see him now and then. Have a relationship."

Stephanie nodded. "I appreciate that. And it will be good for him to have a man in his life. But I need some time. I'm going to tell him about his father. I'm just not sure exactly when. Before the film comes out, obviously."

"You're worried about the documentary?" Emerson said.

"That, and the other one."

"What other one?" Emerson said.

Stephanie told him about Neil Hanes and finding the script in his house.

"I'd like to give that guy a piece of my mind," Emerson said. "And my fist."

"Well, it's your lucky night—he's here."

Stephanie pointed to Neil, who was sitting at a corner table refilling a young blonde's wineglass.

"Ladies, excuse me for a minute."

They watched Emerson cut across the crowded room.

"I almost feel bad for Neil," Lauren said.

"I don't," said Stephanie. And then: "Lauren, I know I just said I would tell Ethan the truth. I just don't know how I'm going to find the words. Maybe I'm weak, but it's just…I don't know. I can't do it."

"You have to."

"I wish it could just…happen."

"It's going to be okay," Lauren said.

Stephanie reached out and hugged her, and the feeling of being in her big sister's arms, alien and so familiar at the same time, brought fresh tears to Lauren's eyes.

"I love you," Stephanie said.

"I love you too."

The sign on the door read PRIVATE PARTY. NORA'S CAFÉ OPENS TOMORROW AT 7 A.M. FOR BREAKFAST. THANK YOU. Matt could see from the street that the dining room was packed with people.

He had been halfway through his shitty craft beer in Williamsburg when he remembered the party. It came to him because a group of hipsters piled in with bags of doughnuts from Dough in Bed-Stuy. They made a big show of offering some to the bartender, who set them out on the bar. And Matt thought of Beth Adelman.

It was Henny who had originally invited him to the party, but Lauren had mentioned it in passing with a casual "You should come if you're still in town." That had been before it all went to hell, of course.

Driving for two and a half hours after an abrupt good-bye to a confused Craig, Matt tried to figure out what he was going to say when he was face to face with her. He wasn't entirely sure; all he knew was that he needed to see her.

Inside the restaurant, he made his way through a throng near the front counter. Lauren was difficult to miss in a pale orange sundress, her dark hair long and loose. How had he not noticed how beautiful she was that very first day when he'd met her in this place? He could see it like it was yesterday, the wariness when he tried to chat her up, her disgust when he'd handed her his card. By some miracle, he'd been able to break through all that and not only get what he needed for the film, but also get close to her as a person.

And then he'd wrecked it.

Lauren needed air. She couldn't walk around making small talk with the party guests after the intense conversations with Emerson and her sister.

She pushed open the door, and it had barely closed behind her when someone said her name. At first she thought she'd imagined it.

"Lauren," Matt repeated.

"What are you doing here?" She turned around, her face stony while some deep, primitive, and inconvenient part of her fluttered with joy.

"You didn't respond to any of my texts."

"Why should I? We're not *friends,* Matt. You got what you wanted. Now leave me alone."

He moved closer, and she felt the pull of her attraction to him.

"I miss you," he said, and he kissed her. She gave in for a second, then pulled away sharply. They stared at each other, both breathing heavily. *I can run twelve miles a day but one kiss from him and I feel like I'm going to pass out.*

"Listen to me," he said. "I know you want me to scrap the film, but that's not how it works. Sometimes the truth is upsetting. But that doesn't diminish its value. At the same time, I don't want to hurt you."

"You can't have it both ways."

"I think I can."

"What are you saying?"

"I won't use footage of your nephew in the film. I won't use Stephanie's interviews. And I'll still have the film I came to this island to make."

Lauren stared at him. "Are you sure?"

"Yes," he said. "I'm certain."

"That would make a huge difference. To all of us. But you could have told me that over the phone."

"I had to see you. Because you're wrong—I didn't get what I want."

He reached for her, and she let him hold her, everything else falling away. Her entire being seemed to say yes. The feeling was new and familiar at the same time, and it scared her.

In the past she had run too quickly into her love for another person. She had given up too much to sustain it. And for what? In the end, it had failed. Now a second chance was there, right in front of her. But she knew that if she didn't fully heal before rushing headlong into it, this, too, would disappear.

"I'm sorry," she said. "I'm not ready."

Matt nodded in reluctant acceptance. "Okay," he said. "I understand. I just hope someday you will be. And when you are…"

"You'll be the first to know," she said, fighting back tears, rocked by competing feelings of happiness, sadness, fear, and hope.

The front door of the restaurant opened. Stephanie appeared; if she was surprised to see Matt, she didn't show it. It was just one of those nights.

"Mom's bringing out dessert," Stephanie said.

Lauren turned to Matt. "Have you ever tried a s'mores doughnut?"

"As a matter of fact, I haven't," he said, taking her hand. "But I'd love one right about now."

Chapter Fifty-Five

Beth hovered near the dessert buffet. The guests lined up to fill their plates, as excited and expectant as children waiting for slices of birthday cake. She swelled with pride.

"It's so good, Gran," Ethan said, his mouth smeared with chocolate and melted marshmallow.

"*You're* so good," she said, bending down to kiss his head. The music seemed to grow louder, a song that always reminded her of her wedding party, Kool and the Gang's "Celebration."

Howard appeared beside her, holding a full plate, and slipped his arm around her.

"Your new career is going to wreak havoc on my waistline," he said.

"You've never looked better," she said, and it was true. She thought of the day she'd spotted him down the beach, how it was like looking at him thirty years earlier. With the success of the evening, she herself felt decades younger. And she'd never wanted him more.

As if sensing what she was thinking, he leaned over, kissed her, and whispered, "I can't wait to celebrate later, just the two of us."

Ethan tugged on her hand. "Can we go sit with Mom?"

"Yes," Howard said. "Good idea. Beth, you've been on your feet all day. Everyone's over there waiting."

Everyone?

Sure enough, at a table tucked away in the corner, she found Stephanie and Lauren sitting side by side. And the filmmaker. And Nora and her friend Henny. And was that...Rory's brother? Incredulous, she looked at Howard. He shrugged.

"Life happens when you're making doughnuts."

When only close friends and family were left, Nora pushed all the tables aside and the dining room became a dance floor. Lauren's parents hadn't sat down in half a dozen songs and showed no signs of stopping.

Matt said he had to drive back to New York, and Lauren walked him to the door.

"Don't come outside. I won't be able to leave," he said.

"So don't," she said, surprising herself. "Stay."

"I have a meeting first thing in the morning."

She nodded. Maybe it was for the best. She didn't want him to go but she wasn't ready for him to stay.

He hugged her and she clung to him. "Good-bye," she whispered.

"For now," he said. "Only good-bye for now."

But when the door closed behind him, she wasn't so sure. The warm, crowded room suddenly felt empty.

Stephanie appeared, handbag over her shoulder, trailed by Ethan.

"Are you leaving?" Lauren asked.

"He's tired."

"I'm not!" Ethan said, stifling a yawn.

"I'll take him home," Lauren offered.

"No, stay. It's fine."

"Matt left and I was about to get going anyway. Really. I'd be happy for the company."

Outside, the air was heavy with moisture. Lauren inhaled, taking Ethan's hand, then led him to the boardwalk. The feel of the wood planks under her feet reminded her she hadn't gone running in the past few days. She looked out at the ocean, glowing silver-black under the bright moon and stars. A clear night, a transparent sky.

Ethan hummed quietly to himself.

"Did you have fun at the party?" she asked.

"It was a *great* party!" he pronounced.

"What was your favorite doughnut?" she asked.

"S'mores," he said.

"Somehow I knew you were going to say that." She squeezed his hand.

The Miley Cyrus song "Party in the U.S.A." played in one of the nearby houses lining the boardwalk. A teenage couple with sun-bleached hair walked by holding hands. They looked like such babies, and yet they were no younger than she had been when she fell in love with Rory.

"Aunt Lauren, who was that man at the party?" Ethan asked.

She stopped walking. "Um, my friend? Matt?"

"No," Ethan said. "The big, big tall one."

Okay, Lauren thought. This was it. Sooner than expected. But it was here.

"That man," Lauren said, "was your father's older brother."

His eyes widened. "Did you know my father?"

Lauren nodded. "I did. His name was Rory. He was . . . he was very special."

Ethan seemed to consider this. "Did he like soccer?"

"Soccer? Yeah, he did. But his favorite sport was ice hockey. And he was one of the best players I've ever seen."

Ethan just stared at her. She wasn't sure if she should say more or if she was overwhelming him. She'd thought it would be difficult to start the conversation, but the reality was that it was hard to stop. It felt good to talk to him about Rory. It felt right. "You know what else he loved?" She looked up and pointed. "The stars."

Ethan smiled. "Like me!"

"Yes," she said. "Just like you."

Then she gasped as she noticed three particularly bright stars that had been pointed out to her by a boy on a night just like this, only a lifetime ago.

She bent down next to Ethan. "Ethan, look. Those three lights are Vega, Deneb, and Altair. The Summer Triangle. Do you see?"

"Yeah," he said. "A constellation!"

"Actually, it's not a constellation. It's a star pattern called an asterism. Your father taught me that."

Ethan grabbed her hand and they continued on toward the Green Gable. When the house came into view, Lauren said, "We're home."

Chapter Fifty-Six

The invitation arrived at the Green Gable on a windy day in March.

It had a New York City return address.

Lauren knew what it was before she opened it. She left the rest of the mail, most of which was for her parents along with a few clothing-store-sale postcards for Stephanie, on the counter. She sat alone at the kitchen table with the envelope, looking out at the pool covered with its winter tarp and fighting her mixed feelings.

Matt had called her a few months earlier when the film was accepted in the Tribeca Film Festival. It was a big deal, because he'd missed the application for Sundance recutting the film to omit Stephanie and Ethan. He was upset about not making Sundance, but it was the first moment Lauren fully let herself believe that he had kept his word.

She still hadn't left the island, not even to visit Matt, whom she thought about every day. Not even to visit Rory's grave on the five-year anniversary of his death.

Instead, on that day, she had walked to the edge of the ocean, the sky as gray as slate, the air misty and freezing. She'd held Ethan's hand, and together they tossed a few flowers into the sea.

"The waves are bringing them back," he said.

"That's okay," she told him. "Let them rest here for a while." Standing by the freezing water, she had thought that five years was a long time and yet, in the big picture of life, it was no time at all.

Lauren carefully tore open the envelope and pulled out a stiff white card.

You are cordially invited to the Tribeca Film Festival's world-premiere screening of the documentary film *American Hero: The Rory Kincaid Story*. Please join director Matt Brio and producer Craig Mason at the City Cinema Paris Theatre in New York City on April 17 at 7 p.m. A panel discussion will follow.

"Can't you just send me a digital copy of the film?" she had asked when he called. "I mean, even as just a professional courtesy."

She had donated funds, through the Polaris Foundation, toward finishing the film.

"I want to see it with you. No—scratch that," he said. "I want to see *you*."

"You could come here," she'd said. But he hadn't, and she knew that he was right not to. At some point, she had to decide what he meant to her, what she was willing to mean to him. Eight months after he'd left the island, she still didn't know.

But she did know that she had to see the movie—if not before the public saw it, then at least along with it on opening night.

She booked a hotel room and left Longport at ten in the morning on the day of the screening. By the time she was in the standstill traffic queue to get through the Holland Tunnel, she felt sweaty and her heart was beating fast. She texted Matt in a panic. He responded: That's how everyone feels on approach to the Holland.

She wrote back, Very funny.

I have to do press now for a few hours. Do you want me to pick you up later for the screening?

She told him no, that she would meet him at the theater. A pause before the dots appeared to show him texting back, then disappeared. He still didn't believe she would actually show up.

Finally: Okay. Your name will be at the box office. Text me when you get there.

The traffic inched forward.

Lauren stood on the corner of Fifty-Eighth Street and Fifth Avenue, next to Bergdorf Goodman and half a block from the Plaza Hotel. Surrounded by the grand buildings and bustling pedestrians, she felt her trepidation give way to excitement.

She wore new clothes she'd bought for the occasion: tapered black pants, a crisp white blouse, and a pale blue spring cardigan. The only thing that wasn't new was the heart necklace she had on. She'd come to realize she didn't have to throw everything away. And she didn't want to.

Lauren expected to feel exposed and vulnerable walking into the theater, but the crowds of people helped her feel perfectly anonymous. Then she saw the theater marquee with the movie poster, the title *American Hero: The Rory Kincaid Story* in red, white, and blue with a close-up image of Rory in his U.S. Rangers uniform and beret in front of the American flag. It made the film seem more real, but at the same time, looking at Rory's face, she felt like she was seeing a stranger. His time in the military had taken on a distant, dreamlike quality in her mind, while memories of high school were still so sharp, she could be walking in the supermarket, hear a song from 2004, and it was like he was right there next to her.

"Here we go," she whispered to herself.

The line to get into the theater stretched all the way to Sixth Avenue. Adjusting her sunglasses and pulling her hair around her face, she followed Matt's direction to check in with a festival rep at the box office.

The rep seemed very young. When Lauren gave her name, the woman startled as if she'd been confronted with a celebrity.

"Mrs. Kincaid, we are so honored you could be with us tonight," she said. "I'll take you to your seat."

The theater was empty except for a group of people standing in the front, under the curtained screen and before a narrow stage. She spotted Matt immediately but he was engrossed in conversation with a guy setting up a microphone stand. Lauren followed the festival rep down the aisle to the front row.

"Thanks," Lauren said to her. She didn't want to sit there—wasn't sure she should be in the very front row. But then Matt noticed her, and the expression on his face told her she was exactly where she was supposed to be. With him. She realized it was maybe the height of stupidity to have planned their reunion in such a public and stressful situation.

He came over and hugged her, holding her just a beat longer than a friendly greeting.

"I'm so glad you're here," he said. "Come meet some people."

Before she could hesitate, she was shaking hands with the woman who had cofounded the festival with Robert De Niro. Matt introduced her to his producer, Craig Mason.

"Great to finally meet you," Craig said. "Matt was saying you should come aboard for our next film."

"Oh, I don't think so," she said. "This film fit into the mission of the Polaris Foundation but I'm not making a habit of funding films."

"Actually, I thought you'd be great as a researcher on the next one," Matt said.

She looked at him. "Research? Really? What's the next project?"

"I was hoping we could talk about it over dinner tomorrow night."

People began filing in.

"I need to borrow you for a minute," a tall African American man in a charcoal suit who was wearing an earpiece said to Matt. The two of them walked to the mic, leaving Lauren to find her way back to her seat.

She resisted the urge to turn around and watch the seats fill, but the buzz of conversation grew around her until it felt deafening. The energy in the room was electric. Matt's producer and a few other people filled out her row, leaving room for Matt in the aisle seat next to her, which he used for just a second before jumping up again to greet someone.

A photographer wearing a press pass took photographs of the room before focusing her camera on Lauren and the front row. She asked the producer for his name, then turned to Lauren.

"Can I please have your name? This is for the *New York Times*."

Lauren hesitated for a second, causing the woman to look at her more closely.

"Lauren Kincaid," she said.

"You're Rory Kincaid's widow?"

Lauren nodded.

"Can I speak to you after the film?"

Again, Lauren hesitated. Five years, and she'd never spoken one word to the press. The lights dimmed, signaling the audience to get settled in their seats. It was happening. The time for truth had come.

"Yes," Lauren said. "We can talk after the film."

The man in the charcoal suit took the microphone and welcomed everyone to the festival and the premiere of "this important film."

Matt slid into his seat.

"We are delighted to host the world premiere of *American Hero: The Rory Kincaid Story*. Five years after the death of hockey star turned soldier Rory Kincaid, *American Hero* takes on an emotional and challenging topic—head trauma in our athletes and soldiers. The people behind this film are dedicated to helping foster an informed and rational dialogue on the issue while honoring a man who inspired a nation. I am thrilled to share this film with you tonight and honored to introduce director Matt Brio."

The room erupted in applause. Matt jumped up and returned to the stage and took the mic. Lauren's stomach did a tiny flip, a combination of nerves and pride—for Rory, and for Matt.

"Thanks to all of you for being here today. And a special thanks to my producer, Craig Mason, and to the Polaris Foundation." More applause. When it quieted down, Matt said, "When I began this film, I found a motto engraved above the entrance to Rory Kincaid's high school: Enter to Learn, Go Forth to Serve. It was an amazing benediction to me, because I went into this project haunted by this question: Why do some men and women answer their nation's call when so many others are deaf to it? I wanted to illustrate what it means to be a hero. And what I found was that even our greatest heroes are vulnerable and flawed, just like the rest of us. So while they bravely go forth to serve, we need to do a better job of serving them. I hope that after watching this film, you'll agree. Thank you, and enjoy the film."

The crowd erupted in vigorous applause. Lauren watched the curtain rise on the giant screen in front of her. Matt returned to his seat.

She smiled at him.

"You ready?" he asked, leaning closer. He started to put his arm around her but then hesitated.

Lauren reached for his hand.

"Yes," she said, her eyes locked on his. "I'm finally ready."

Acknowledgments

This novel was a tough one. Thank you to my agent, Adam Chromy, for being a tireless sounding board and reader of the dreaded first drafts. (I'm sorry if I sometimes shoot the messenger.) I want to thank my extraordinary editor, Judy Clain, for asking all the right questions to help me dig deeper into this story and get it to the finish line. Alexandra Hoopes, thank you for your valuable input. To my rock-star publicist Maggie Southard Gladstone, I appreciate everything you do. Ashley Marudas and Lauren Passell, thank you for your energy and creativity in getting these books out there. Reagan Arthur and Craig Young, I am so fortunate to be working with you and the entire team at Little, Brown.

A special thank-you to Tanya Biank, author of *Army Wives: The Unwritten Code of Military Marriage,* for generously taking the time to read an early draft of this novel and answering my questions about military life. Any errors are entirely my own.

Thanks also to Donna McCarthy, owner of Hannah-G's restaurant in Ventnor, New Jersey (the inspiration for Nora's Café), Ellen Rosenberg of the Lower Merion Ice Hockey Club, and the Jewish Book Council.

Acknowledgments

I am grateful for the incredible support of the Great Thoughts' Great Readers community and its creator, Andrea Peskind Katz. Andrea, you are one of a kind and I look forward to many more book adventures with you. A shout-out to Robin Kall Homonoff and her fabulous Point Street Reading Series! Brenda Janowitz, I cherish our friendship.

Research for this book brought me back to my beloved Jersey Shore, where I spent the best summers of my life with my family. Thanks to Aunt Harriet and Uncle Paul Robinson, my cousin Alison Anmuth, and my father, Michael Weisman, for joining me on a spontaneous day trip to Longport in the summer of August 2016. I wish we could do it more often!

Finally, thank you to my husband, who saw me through my own dark hour. I love you.

About the Author

Jamie Brenner is the author of the national bestseller *The Forever Summer,* also chosen as one of PopSugar's must-read books of spring 2017. Her previous novels include *The Wedding Sisters* and *The Gin Lovers.* She lives in New York City with her husband and two teenage daughters.